MW00977866

The Unearthing of Mr. Diggins

A novel by

Dave Lauby

BookLocker
Trenton, Georgia

Print ISBN: 978-1-958889-04-6
Ebook ISBN: 979-8-88531-453-4

Published by BookLocker.com, Inc., Trenton, Georgia.

Printed on acid-free paper.

BookLocker.com, Inc.
2023

First Edition

Library of Congress Cataloguing in Publication Data
Lauby, Dave
The Unearthing of Mr. Diggins by Dave Lauby
Library of Congress Control Number: 2023901630

For Carolina,
who I really dig

1

When her mother first noticed that the little girl was no longer playing with her sisters, she wasn't worried about her well-being or her whereabouts in the least. After all, what was there to worry about? If she had skipped off in search of her father to check on what interesting things he might be up to he would bring her back dirtier but happier soon enough; if she'd wandered off to visit the neighbors, well, every neighbor took care of every child like their very own (and if that meant the occasional swat on the bottom there was never any objection, except of course from the swatted bottom). The little girl had been her mother's most curious child all her seven years, and so, for her to tire with her toys and scamper off to check on the big spider web or to harass the covey of quail which frequented the hedgerow was just what her mother expected of her. Hungry tummies always brought all her children back to her skirts soon enough.

But when suppertime came and went without the return of the little girl, her parents' trusting assurance was replaced by anxiety. Where could their daughter's curiosity have taken her? Visits to the neighbors turned up nothing, and no one remembered seeing her all afternoon. With night drawing near the situation became an emergency. A search was launched, focusing on the surrounding woods, the creek where the little girl loved to wade and catch frogs, and the nearby hillside where more than once, having worn herself out from running up and down, she'd been found sleeping it off in the long grass as peacefully as if she were at home in her own bed. But no indication was found that the little girl's adventures had brought her to any of her favorite spots. Then a shout went up- a small sandal had been found, confirmed by her father that it was his daughter's; and then, as the evening's first hoot owl announced the fade of dusk, the searchers' efforts earned them the saddest of rewards: here was the little girl's lifeless body, in a treeless field not far from her home, her throat cut, left abandoned but not hidden, almost laid out in display as if whoever had done the thing had been eager for his handiwork to be discovered while some daylight still remained. It had required three large men to pull the frantic mother off the girl; and with everyone filled with equal parts anger, grief and shock, the little girl was carried home as the first stars of the evening began to twinkle above the forlorn procession.

No sooner had the girl been found than the task of solving the murder was undertaken. Although her family was neither well to-do nor prominent, the strong sense of community was such that, for everyone involved in the investigation, their efforts could not have been more vigorous had the common-born child been a princess. Theirs was a small community, even isolated, making it no difficult thing to question everyone and leave no stone unturned. One and all, even the smallest children, were interviewed and made an account of their whereabouts and activities that fateful afternoon. Without exception every story was corroborated and every alibi checked out; and so, despite the concerted effort, no progress was made toward solving the crime, resulting in the investigators to conclude that a vagabond, some rogue predator of no provenance and not belonging to the community, had either lured the little girl away from her quail and spider webs or had seized her when she wandered onto her hill, and from a motive too barbaric and primitive for anyone to comprehend had taken the girl's life and then disappeared just as invisibly as he'd arrived.

On the morning when the little girl was to be buried, the same procession which had carried her away from the lonely hilltop bore her once again, making the solemn journey to what would be her final resting place. A neighbor had stitched the little girl's burial dress (the girl's grieving mother had not been emotionally capable of sewing it herself). At the gravesite, the little girl's friends from the neighborhood had each given the mother one of their own toys to be buried along with their dead playmate (whose hands had been folded to hold her favorite doll), and each adult expressed condolences to the parents, with not a few of the men among the neighbors whispering their dark assurances to the father that they would never rest until they found the perpetrator and delivered justice. Then, once the final words of comfort which spoke of the promise of the afterlife had been delivered, the little girl was laid in the ground and covered over with earth, with her new toys beside her and wearing her new dress which she would wear only once but forever; and as the midsummer sun, respectfully low during the morning ceremony but now upstanding once again to its midday height, led the way down the solitary hilltop, the solemn line of neighbors, families and friends left the little girl to her perpetual rest, at which point the aforementioned afterlife commenced. Or, at the very least, the life-after commenced, for all those left living, the lives of those who dwelt on the land surrounding her hilltop grave, the families and friends and neighbors and child killers who continued on, day after day, year after year, all passing away themselves eventually but the little hill still remaining, its red-clay earth receiving more and more eternal residents over the years, over the decades, over the centuries, in the land which thirteen thousand years after the little girl's burial would come to be known as Georgia, where new tribes, permanent tribes, not nomadic like the little girl's but recent arrivals nevertheless, if three hundred years can be thought of as recent when compared to thirteen thousand, would cut the hill's land into squares and surround those squares with fences, inside of which they would build houses for only themselves, communities unto themselves, insular and isolated, locking their gates and forsaking community, suspicious and afraid of community, for in the community dwelt child killers, or worse, neighbors like Travis Riggin's neighbors, the kind of neighbors who did not mow their lawns.

It was one such low-quality neighbor upon whom Travis gazed Saturday morning from the seat of his John Deere E100 42-inch lawn tractor, having taken a break from mowing the golf course carpet surrounding his three-bedroom two-and-a-half-bath raised ranch at 1418 Crested Boulder Drive in Smyrna Georgia, the address which had been the object of his unconditional love for the past five years.

It was his second home, by that meaning his second homeowning experience, his first a little two-bedroom cottage which he'd purchased back when he was still single, the kind of house others refer to as their "starter home" but which he called his "practice home," for it was there he honed his skillset as a homeowner, a comprehensively demanding undertaking which Travis had come to appreciate as the mortal combat it was. Homeowning, as he viewed it, was no passive state-of-being, where merely "keeping it up" was all that was demanded; it was full-contact sport, requiring proactive vigilance, always anticipating the shitstorm which was sure to come and preparing for its arrival, knowing that forces intent on the annihilation of both home and homeowner arrayed themselves for attack continually, be those forces natural, municipal, criminal or even neighborial. Indeed, the very laws of thermodynamics (the Second Law in particular, which provides the comforting assurance that all systems tend toward chaos and disintegration) join in on the assault, moving Travis to assume the most fatalistic of attitudes, that being, to view everything and everyone as the enemy out to fuck his shit up. He had made his mistakes on House #1, some from simple ignorance (painting his deck instead of staining it, resulting in the paint peeling off in a year; planting rhododendrons in full sun and watching them shrivel into tumbleweeds), but more often, his mistakes had been of the trusting kind, from assuming the best of his fellow humans, believing naively that when they promised to do a thing that they'd actually do it, or deliver it, or return it, or repair it, or not steal it. His misadventures with House #1 had taught young homeowner Travis that only Travis was looking out for Travis' best interests and only Travis could be trusted; now, on House #2, he was older (though not yet forty) and wiser, and had elevated his castle-keeping skills to Master level, so that House #2 could well be described as much a fortress as a living space. For security, he had installed redundant alarm systems, snip-resistant fencing, six livestream security cameras (as well as four "dummy" cameras which appeared functional to the bad guys), multiple motion lights and iron window bars; to support the physical plant, Travis invested in surge protection, sump pumps, a humidifier for upstairs, a dehumidifier for downstairs, solar panels, leaf-guard gutters, rain barrels and a 3500-watt generator in case of power outages. From the pedestal-mounted locking mailbox in front to the faux-wood double-wide barn roof storage shed out back, Fort Riggins featured aspects from every home improvement show ever aired; for the visitor, passing through the wrought-iron gates and turning onto Travis' interlocking paving stone driveway was not so much an approach to a home but an entry onto a compound.

But structural integrity and airtight security did not tell the whole story of 1418 Crested Boulder Drive. To fully appreciate the depth of loathing Travis was feeling as he stared at the property across the street, a foot tour of the Edenic paradise upon which his tractor sat was in order. One might first admire the trees, not only the compositional balance of their spacing but their variety of species. Most were young; one of Travis' first moves was to remove the underachieving trees from the property (their failure was not their growth, for the trees he uprooted were perfectly fit- their underachievement was purely esthetic) and replace them with saplings of Chickasaw plum, pink and white dogwood, wax myrtle, weeping cherry and river birch, and with his hovering attention, all thrived. Then there was that lawn; Travis' alchemy with soil treatments and seed hybrids (and his own secret fertilizer recipe which Guantanamo-level torture methods could not make him reveal) had resulted in a lushness of emerald which disproved the old cliché that the grass could possibly be greener on the other side. Threading this exquisite turf was a winding path of flagstone, where shrubs, benches, arbors, sham-ruin walls, a koi pond with a fountain and art nouveau-replica statuary dotted the way like so many eye-pleasing islands. Painstaking research provided guidance for his choices of flora; he took care to plant only those trees native to north Georgia, hating carpetbaggers as he did, even the leafy variety. Wreathing vines luxuriated across trellised archways; a food court of bird feeders commanded the view from the French doors, where winged visitors added flashes of color to the spinners and pinwheels he'd strategically staked about like so many kinetic sentries. Birdbaths and houses, flower boxes and wagon wheels, a scarecrow made of burlap, pine log deer, a hammock swing (never napped in for there was work to do), a fire pit, even a grotto whose canopy was edged by dozens of tiny ornamental skulls through whose hollow eyes twinkled white cafe lights- Travis Riggins had designed an Arcadia of earthly delights, transforming a mere half-acre city lot into a verdant world, meticulously woven into a scattered, smothered and covered suburban jungle, but a jungle of the highest evolutionary order, civilized and sophisticated yet retaining its primitive roots. He was God the Creator at 1418 Crested Boulder Drive, and Travis Riggins took his godhead seriously.

And what the Lord Most High's offended eyes viewed at the moment reminded him of the reason he'd been able to invest so much capital toward the improvement of his property. He was by no means a wealthy man by middle-class Smyrna standards, and had been limited accordingly as to how much house he could afford. But having whetted his teeth on his practice house, Travis knew he would not be happy unless he could implement all he'd learned on a bigger one, and so, in order to double the size of his domestic playground from his practice home's quarter-acre to a half acre and still keep enough cash to fund his landscaping dreams, Travis had opted for one of Smyrna's more run-down neighborhoods which the listing had euphemistically described as "emerging," realtor jargon for a shithole. Thanks to the home's depressed setting, the asking price was too tempting to ignore; and when Travis crunched the numbers and realized that buying the same house in a better neighborhood would leave him barely enough to buy a wire rake, he rolled the dice on the neighborhood's future prospects, gambling that it was in fact emerging from its dolor and would improve. With fingers crossed and the first load of flagstone already ordered, Travis made the plunge. And five years later, the neighborhood had in fact improved, quite

Great.

dramatically- but only at 1418 Crested Boulder Drive. The rest of the block and the surrounding blocks remained a shithole, and thanks to reassessments which reflected the increase in value from all his improvements, Travis now paid a greatly increased property tax for the privilege of dodging the occasional drive-by bullet and picking up from the end of his driveway the latest deposit of hypodermic needles.

But without question, the fecal centerpiece of the shithole diadem was the notorious 1413 Crested Boulder Drive, the address which currently (and daily) elicited Travis Riggins' antipathy. To call it notorious was to undersell its reputation. For nearly thirty years, 1413's dilapidated wreckage had served as Smyrna's one-stop shopping location for domestic disturbance, narcotic transaction, rodent husbandry, random gunplay, animal abuse, unexplained odors, and of course police activity, rivalling the finest crack houses of the southeast region. Its single occupant was someone called Sheila- surely she had a last name, for, as Travis told himself, how else were her welfare checks mailed to her- but to the surrounding neighbors she was simply Sheila, and like Oprah, Donald, LeBron and Sadaam, the single appellation was all that was needed for instant recognition. For the first fifteen years or so a revolving coterie of inseminating men had lived at the house and then moved on, leaving behind what inseminating men are wont to leave for Sheila to care for alone, with one final man taking things a step further and actually marrying her; for the last ten years that husband had lived at the penitentiary, not expected to be released in Sheila's lifetime. Six children in total (five sired by the coterie, one by the husband), none of them stepping onto a high school campus other than to sell Chinese molly, and all save the last temporarily reunited now and then with their stepfather(s) during their own respective stays in jail, were raised in the house, despite the fact that, for more than twenty of those thirty years, the house enjoyed the benefit of no utilities- no running water, no gas, no electricity- which attracted to the home the attention of every county agency, particularly Child Welfare, who over the years labored tirelessly to provide assistance for Sheila's children while simultaneously working toward removing them from the premises, failed endeavors each. Somehow the kids remained despite the conditions (remained, that is, until the age of fifteen, when the inevitable streets subsumed them one by one); Sheila remained in perpetuity, but her empty nest left her by no means alone, for the off-the-grid nature of her property made itself attractive to all manner of hangers-on, where those who sought to hide off-the-grid might disappear in plain sight. With the children gone, 1413 became the ideal staging center for all manner of illicit enterprise, and when this drug dealer was arrested off her front stoop and that abandoned stolen car was towed away to impound, others immediately took their places. But as far as could be told, Sheila was not an active party to any of the bigger crimes, merely her existential ones, an oblivious Mrs. Surratt enabling but not abetting the nefarious undertakings occurring under her rotted roof. Those neighbors who cared (or dared) to involve themselves in seeking remedy for the situation made repeated calls to everyone they could think of, to the Code Enforcement office, Animal Control, the city council, the mayor's office, but after years of unenforced warnings and bureaucratic entanglements, Sheila emerged unphased and unremoved in her four-walled litter box, burning scavenged wood in the winter to keep it a toasty 50°F, burning wood in the summer to "smoke out the rats," pooping and peeing who knew where, subsisting on a diet of who knew what. What's more, Sheila's husband's mother had made her other children promise on her deathbed that they'd never sell the house out from under Sheila and her incarcerated son so long as least one of them lived in it, thus securing the property for themselves *ad infinitum*. What Travis and his frustrated neighbors came to learn from their futile efforts was how difficult it was to have a property condemned and its occupants removed, which in a society constitutionally founded on the individual's unalienable right to life, liberty and the pursuit of happiness is a very good thing. Unless you happened to live downwind of that happiness at 1418.

From the observation point of his lawnmower seat, Travis shook his head with disgust and widened his gaze beyond 1413 to take in the 180° panorama, but was not greatly encouraged by the expanded view. To the right of Sheila's squalor heading north up Crested Boulder stood two ordinary-looking homes, and beyond them could be seen the ugly gray cinder-block convenient store called iffy Grocery (the "J" had fallen off years before) where robbers had pulled the ATM machine clean out of the place with a truck and chain only a week earlier. Next door left of Sheila's and directly across the street from Travis was a three-bed two-bath bungalow which had been rental property all the time Travis had lived in the neighborhood but which its owner had recently put on the market; Travis could not imagine the house selling even at its below-market asking price due to its next-door proximity to the gaping maw of Sheila's open landfill. A look south down the street revealed a string of dreary residences which had languished unmaintained and unloved for decades, occupied by a revolving door of apathetic renters. But then came a structure not only loved but worshipped, where worshipping was its chief activity: the prepositionally-redundant Church of God of Prophecy of Smyrna Georgia, a drab edifice as churches go (a perfect fit with the neighborhood's esthetic profile) but a center of bustling activity despite the modest size of both the building and the congregation. Travis could take or leave the church; he could take or leave all churches, for he was an atheist, a belief in non-believing which he kept to himself. On balance, the Church of God of Prophecy represented to him a minor pain in the ass, with its loud carryings-on every Sunday (especially the shouting and singing in the afternoon after services, taking place outdoors on the church grounds with gospel music blaring from loudspeakers you could hear half a mile away, why they couldn't keep it inside the church Travis didn't understand) and the annoying way that the church helped out Sheila from time to time by bringing her baskets of food and driving her around in the church van to who the hell knew where after she'd spent all her cash on lottery tickets and malt liquor and had no coin left to take the bus. But at least the church kept its grass mowed, which few on the block but Travis seemed able to do. Yes, these people did take care of their churches, if not much of anything else. These people all so unlike him, the shouting singers at the church, the lawn-neglectors encircling him, made Travis feel acutely that he was the minority, a lonely island in a sea of Bible-thumping and decay. They clearly looked out for one another, something which Travis had no experience with but which he assumed must be an admirable thing, and their sense of community only added to his feelings of isolation. Of course there was the racial component, which Travis had dealt with as honestly as he could, and he was convinced in his heart-of-hearts that his problem with Sheila (as well as the church and his low-quality neighbors) had nothing to do with her race but with her behavior as a human being and the blight she brought his neighborhood. No, Travis was not a racist, of that he was sure. But he did have to remind himself of it now and then.

As Travis restarted the lawn tractor, a flash of movement caught the corner of his eye. It had come from the "For Sale" bungalow across the street, where a smallish young man and a woman who looked like a realtor came out of the house through the front door. He hadn't noticed until now the car parked up the home's driveway, and he realized that this young prospective buyer was being shown the house. This kid, Travis mused, has no idea what he's getting himself into. Hadn't he noticed Sheila's shithole next door when they'd first pulled up? Surely the kid had dismissed the idea of buying it after one glance at the half dozen thugs currently throwing dice against Sheila's front porch and had only gone ahead with the house tour with the realtor out of politeness. But what if he was seriously considering it? In a surge of impulse, Travis knew he had to warn him. But why? Someone was going to live there eventually after all. Besides, nothing could help the moribund neighborhood more than for responsible homeowners (hopefully with values like his) to move into it. So why discourage him? Did he want to warn him about Sheila because he gave a fat rat's ass about the welfare of the young man? Travis knew he'd be lying if he said that he did. Hell, let him make his rookie homeowner mistakes like he had done and learn from 'em. There was only one reason why Travis found himself hopping off the mower and hurrying across the street: he wanted to feel the power of influencing someone's decision-making with his superior understanding of things. That feeling was its own justification.

"Hi, sorry to interrupt you guys." The young man and the realtor turned to greet him. The realtor was smiling benignly. "So are you thinkin' of buyin' it?"

"Actually I'm- "

"He's closing on Friday!"

The young man nodded. Travis was too late; the main thrust of his mission was defused. But he was still carrying ordnance and was determined to fire it. "Oh. Wow. Are ya buyin' next door too?"

The realtor pretended she hadn't heard him. The young man bit however. "What do you mean?"

Travis stepped up a little closer. "Well, so that you can bulldoze it. Because you obviously can't live next door to- "he gestured toward the dice game. "- *that.*"

The young man smiled weakly. "Um... yeah..."

Travis reached his hand down to the shorter man. "Well, looks like we're neighbors come Friday. I'm Travis Riggins."

"Corey Chapin." As they shook hands, Corey peered over Travis' shoulder at the Versailles gardens across the street. "Wow. Your yard. It's amazing."

"Thanks for noticing. Next tour begins at ten forty-five." Corey laughed while the realtor only smiled nervously; it was clear to Travis that she knew he was here to cause trouble and couldn't wait for him to leave. She was in the frying pan, so he turned up the flame. "So I know your realtor didn't tell you anything about 1413 over there."

Corey looked with dismay to the realtor, whose response was the sound of innocence itself. "What do you mean?"

"Oh you know." Did she know? Travis looked into her eyes. Yep. She knew alright. "The code violations, the 24/7 traffic in-and-out, the noise, the police activity?"

The realtor could feel Corey's eyes upon her. "I checked the history of the property and there really wasn't anything out of the ordinary."

"Well it's kinda funny" Travis said, enjoying the way she was lying, "that your realtor research tools didn't pull anything up- "

"No, there really wasn't anyth- "

"- because I'm a realtor too." He let it run down her face for a moment, and then poured on some more. "...so I know what info is out there at your disposal. And how easy it is for you to retrieve it."

"Like what info?" Corey asked, his attention now fully on Travis.

He answered Corey but directed it toward the realtor. "Well, like in the five years I've lived here two-hundred sixty-one weeks to be exact, there have been ninety-four visits by the police at 1413, and if you're stuck on the arithmetic that's an episode of COPS every 2.78 weeks. Ninety-four is probably also the number of spent bullet casings you'll find, I'm sure if you asked those dice-throwing gentlemen they'd be happy to let you come over and hunt for them."

Corey stared next door as if just finally seeing it. "Ninety-four police visits?"

"And your realtor knew nothing about it. Is that right?"

"Now you yourself as a realtor know that I'm not allowed to give out that kind of information because of the Fair Housing Act. I can't even make general comments about crime in a neighborhood."

Corey gazed up to Travis for confirmation. "Is she right?"

"She's right Corey. By law your realtor here wasn't allowed to tell you about the full-on shootout less than a year ago which blasted out the side window of this very house you're closing on." Corey was starting to look a little dizzy. Travis had him where he wanted him. "But remember Corey, when I asked her just now if her research had turned up anything, *before* she knew I was a realtor, she lied and said 'No, I didn't find anything.' It wasn't 'til *after* she knew that I *knew* she knew that she revised it to 'I'm not allowed to give that info because of the Fair Housing Act.' As long as she thought I was as dumb as you pardon the expression she was happy to lie and say she didn't find anything bad. Because if she would have said right up front 'I can't tell you about it because the Fair Housing Act' then it would have- "

"It doesn't change the fact that the law- "

"- then it would have tipped you off that there was something she was hiding and you'd have backed out instead of closing this Friday." Travis knew he was one remark away from getting spit at. At least he hoped so. "So wasn't it convenient for your realtor that she was able to hide behind the Fair Housing Act and not be up front with you in order to unload a property next to a crack house to a gullible young first-time home buyer and get her sale at your expense?"

The realtor was finally angry enough to fight back. "Oh, so you're saying that if you showed the house you would have broken the law and told him everything?"

Like a street magician, Travis presdigitated a business card from thin air and handed it to Corey. "I'm too late for you this time, but if you know anyone looking to buy, have them call me."

Corey looked at the card and shook his head. "It just doesn't seem right."

The lady realtor breathed again, hoping the worst was past. "That's why we encourage people to do their own research. An informed buyer is his own best agent."

"Meanwhile his second-best agent is still gonna collect her commission.'"

Without a word, the lady realtor strode off toward her car and waited impatiently for Corey to follow. Travis smiled down at his new neighbor. "A real snake in the grass that one. Lots of snakes unfortunately in my line of work. 'Course she did make one good point. You really should have done better research. But that's a pretty common first-time buyer mistake. You'll learn from it. Believe me, I made my share of first-time buyer mistakes. After a while you- "

"Ninety-six."

"Ninety-six what?"

"Ninety-six police calls. There's been ninety-six at 1413, not ninety-four." All traces of the naivete and confusion Corey had manifested earlier in his realtor's presence had miraculously disappeared from his face entirely. "That's why the price for this house was so low. That and the fact I'm buying a piece of shit."

"I see."

"But it won't be shit for long. Start with the plumbing, it's all degraded copper prob'ly been on the house since the 70's, rip that out and go with PEX tubing which you prob'ly know is like a third of the cost of copper and it doesn't leak near as much. Then this winter do the roof, cheaper to get a roof installed in winter of course, get rid of this shitty 3-tab shingling and go with a Tuscan tile or maybe like a textural slate. Then hand-scraped hickory flooring which I'll be putting down myself, god can you imagine what rotten crap I'm gonna find on that subfloor, prob'ly have to replace the joists and the underlayment both. Once I finish the renovation I'll be able to flip it in five years and double my money. I can live next door to any fucking thing for five years. Hell, Sheila might even do us a favor and die by then."

Travis scrambled to keep up. "You know Sh- "

"Sheila Gavins, fifty-one years old, has lived at 1413 since 1987, back when there was running water and electricity. No felony record but twenty pages of everything else. Research, Mr.- " Corey paused to read from Travis' card. "- Riggins. An informed buyer is his own best agent." Handing the card back to a speechless Travis, Corey looked past him, across the street. "I see you planted the little dogwood in your front yard right next to your neighbor's big oak. That's why it doesn't bloom for you in the spring. Too much shade. Guess we learn from our mistakes. Well, better rejoin my realtor and go back to pretending I'm stupid. It helps her self-esteem to see herself as the know-it-all. You know the type. Nice meeting you." And before Travis had a chance to lie about the dogwood already being there when he moved in, Corey and his second-best agent had driven off.

Travis' wife Alicia was waiting for him at the mailbox. "So who was that?"

"Bob Villa." Alicia was holding out a set of keys. "I take it it's not opening?"

"Not opening. Not even going in." Taking the keys, Travis found the one for the mailbox and jimmyed it about in the lock as Alicia watched. She was dressed for a run but couldn't head out yet because she had a funny habit of not being able to do anything as long as she knew the mail had been delivered and she hadn't looked at it. She had kept her last name of Donald rather than Riggins because she'd built a client base as a personal fitness trainer as Alicia Donald and knew how important word-of-mouth referrals were in her business. She was a fit and attractive thirty-five in a curvaceous sort of way; high-energy to the point of overcaffeination everywhere but at home, her explanation being that her job required her to be a perky cheerleader all day so she wasn't about to be bubbly in her own kitchen; and if you asked her she would tell you she hated the squawky sound of her own voice but her clients told her that when they hear her counting out reps and shouting at them to "give her one more" her voice is a real motivator and motivation was key to fitness training. After almost a minute of trying, Travis had gotten no farther than Alicia had with the mailbox lock.

"I think I know what the problem is. It's dry."

"How do you mean 'dry'?"

Travis handed back the keys. "Dry inside. No lubrication. It won't go in because it isn't lubricated."

"How does it get dry?"

"Just neglect. Left alone it dries out."

Alicia checked the time on her smart-watch. "Do you know how to lubricate it?"

"You don't think I know how?"

Finally there was the suggestion of a smile from her, which was all he was waiting for. "I have a client in an hour and a half."

"A little WD-40. Take me less than a minute." Glancing back across the street, Alicia now noticed that "Sold" had been added to the top of the "For Sale" sign of the vacant house. "So the Bob Villa guy bought the house?"

"Closing day after tomorrow." Remembering their conversation, Travis stared critically at his unflowering dogwood.

A victory shout from the dice throwers caught Alicia's ear. "Who could buy a house next to that?"

"There's a sucker born every minute." That little Corey son-of-a-bitch was right. Travis had in fact planted the dogwood under the nearly unbroken shade of the next-door neighbor's oak tree. How had he not taken that into consideration?

"So, you finally noticed." Alicia had meanwhile slipped up next to him and was looking at the oak tree as well.

"Don't tell me *you* noticed it."

"How could I not? How could you not?"

It was out of character for Alicia to take note of Travis' improvements on the property or to acknowledge the labor he expended and the choices he made. When they'd first bought the house he had excitedly dragged her outside again and again to show her the symmetry of his hostas, his placement of the new birdbath, the cedar enclosure he'd built for storing the trash cans, but her reaction had always been unenthusiastic at best or, not infrequently, critical ("yeah but don't hostas die back every winter?"), and so Travis came to learn that his garden world was to be his own private playground and the pleasures therein would be his alone. For Alicia therefore to have made this observation of her own, without Travis having to manually turn her eyeballs onto it for her, was a first. "I don't know how I could have missed it."

"Well it's not like there was anything you could have done about it."

Travis' exasperation began to build. "Whaddya mean 'wasn't anything?' I could have planted it somewhere else!"

Alicia was incredulous. "Huh? Plant the neighbor's tree somewhere else?"

"Are we talking about the same thing?"

Alicia pointed to the giant oak. "Keith's tree. The way it's leaning?" Travis studied the giant oak, then turned quizzically back to Alicia. "Right over our house?"

Moving back a dozen steps or so to expand his view, Travis took full measure of the oak in his neighbor Keith's yard. Yes, if one looked very closely there was the slightest suggestion of a lean toward his house, but not even remotely severe enough to cause the least bit of alarm. "I mean, it bends a little this way I guess, but it's nothing."

Alicia snorted. "Nothing?" She leaned her head and body severely to one side, as if mimicking the very steep tilt of an imminent disaster. "I don't think *that's* nothing."

"Oh stop bending like that you're exaggerating!" Shaking her head, Alicia jogged back toward the house. Travis shouted after her. "You finally notice something in the yard and it's a hallucination!"

"I'm getting the WD-40."

As Travis stared at the oak tree *which was not leaning goddammit* a shapeless smudge appeared in the distance, a small mass of indeterminate form, which seemed to ooze itself over the sidewalk rather than walk upon it; unnoticed by Travis, the shapeless figure flapped and shambled ever nearer, inexorable yet aimless, as if kept in motion by inertia alone. The braying of a banshee spun Travis around to face the sound.

"Hey mistah Diggins!"

Over the years of living on the block, Travis had developed a third eye which had only one job: to always watch out for Sheila (no evolution of his hearing apparatus had been required however, for Sheila always managed to be heard above everything no matter the distance or the competition of other sounds). To catch a glimpse of Sheila in the distance was Travis' cue to drop down behind the hydrangeas and hide until the scourge passed. But this time the non-leaning tree had distracted him; he had foolishly exposed himself and Sheila, omnipresent and hovering as a buzzard, had found him. And to be found by Sheila was to be trapped and held by Sheila until Sheila had run her exhausting and maddening course.

"Hey Sheila." She was standing at the end of his driveway, wobbling in place from one foot to the other.

"Whatchoo lookin' a' dat big-ass tree fo' Mistah Diggins?"

When Travis and Alicia first moved into the house, Sheila had somehow mis-heard "Riggins" as "Diggins," and had called Travis "Mistah Diggins" ever since. For his own part, Travis felt no need to correct her; the idea that his never-ceasing planting of trees and shrubs might have sub-consciously prompted her to think of her digging neighbor as Diggins was amusing to him, and what's more, for one such as Sheila to not know his real name was no bad thing. "My wife thinks it's leaning over our house."

Sheila's listless eyes wandered everywhere but at the tree, which did not prevent her from pronouncing her diagnosis of it. "Oh yeah dat tree gon' hit yo' house enny day now I need fo' dollahs fo' cig'rettes Mistah Diggins."

On that fateful first day, Sheila had welcomed Travis to the neighborhood by asking if he had fo' dollahs fo' cig'rettes. At that time Travis had laid down the law that he might have to endure panhandlers in Midtown or Little Five Points but he wasn't having it from his own neighbors in his own driveway. Sheila vowed to never do it again, and honored her vow by asking for cash twice per week every week for the next five years. He'd caved on rare occasions; once when he had found her at the end of his driveway sobbing incoherently about a son in jail and he couldn't call her 'cause she had run out of Tracfone minutes an' if I had fo' dollahs I could git me some mo Tracfone minnits , another time when through the swelling of her beaten face she had simply mumbled the word "Advil," another time at dusk when she had reported that "they" had stole her candles from her unelectrified house and if she had fo' dollahs she could get more candles and light them and then she would have enough light to find wheh huh matches was an' light huh candles. Travis knew it was the only sort of illumination he could help her to attain in this life. "No cash Sheila. You know not to ask."

"Ah know Mistah Diggins you don' need dat agg'avation." Which was what Sheila always said every time she came around to agg'avate him. Now she seemed to stare into a murky place which only her eyes could see. "Tha' dog he tied up when dey somebody call dem peoples o'er by they othuh time when dey."

Another shout went up from the dice game on her front stoop. "Whatcha got goin' on at your house today Sheila?"

Sheila made a disparaging waving gesture, presumably referring to the dice-throwers but delivered in the opposite direction of them. "Yeah dat's dem boys dey's always you know." No, Travis didn't know. But yeah, he knew.

"Well I got work to do Sheila."

"Yo flowahs lookin' good Mistah Diggins you don' got fo' dollahs?"

"No Sheila. And I won't the next time either."

Sheila violently shook her head like she was shaking out a dustmop. "Dey ain't gon' *be* no nex' time Mistah Diggins ah jus' need dis *one* time!"

It was the same scene as always and its script never changed. "I'm going back to mowing my yard Sheila."

"I come back wi' my cup you gimme ice fo 'ice wattah?"

"I'll give you ice for ice water, yes." It was a concession to the enemy he could not refuse, just as on cold nights he could not help but carry leftover lumber from his building projects to her for firewood. The Geneva Convention mandated such gestures.

Sheila shuffled herself around until her starboard bow was pointed in the general direction of her house. "Go git mah cup git me some ice dat tree gon' fall right own dat house Mistah Di- ."

The sound of a gunshot dropped Travis flat onto the grass. It had come from the dice game. From the ground, Travis could see the dice-throwers scurrying about and could hear a voice saying "damn I told you not to play wittit!" It appeared to have been an accidental discharge without anyone being hit instead of an actual shootout. Sheila was wobbling and wringing her hands as she hollered. "Gott damn no, take that shit away damn po-leece come now ah tole you 'bout dat shit!" With arms waving and mouth hollering, Sheila rolled off across the street like a runaway shopping cart and back to her house where the dice throwers were jumping into cars and speeding away.

Alicia had returned with a can of WD-40. "What was that I heard?"

"Exactly what you thought you heard."

Instinctively, Alicia looked up the street toward Sheila's. "Again?" Another neighbor had obviously heard the shot and called it in, for now the sound of a distant police siren grew in volume. "Have they got it all out of their systems? 'Cause I gotta go running and I don't need to get shot." Remembering the mailbox, Travis turned his attention to it, where Alicia was already spraying the WD-40.

"I see you lubricated your box all by yourself." But like the errant shot his joke had missed, for she'd already removed the mail and was flipping through it on her way back to the house. Across the way the police had arrived, two bored officers performing for the ninety-seventh time the obligatory motions of a futile ritual as Sheila screamed her unfocused outrage in their bored faces. And as she thrashed and howled, Travis finally saw that, yes, the oak tree was leaning, not only over 1418 but away from 1413.

2

"These bay windows are fantastic!"

Travis stepped back to allow the couple to check out the view. The husband was already sold, had been from the moment Travis had driven them up the driveway. The wife? Not so much. She was careful and critical, not allowing herself to let emotion sway her judgement. It was often this way when he showed a house, one party head over heels with a property, love at first sight, the other riding the brakes and steering. For Travis, real estate wasn't so much about selling a house but standing back and letting people buy one, for his efforts at "salesmanship" were typically met with skepticism and distrust by the steering half of the couple, resulting in an off-putting effect, the very opposite of selling. No, the less he said the more homes he sold. And once again, he now stood invisibly behind them in the empty front room as they gazed out the bay windows and talked themselves into and out of things.

"So this part of town is what they call Smynings, right? Cool." *The husband's biting on the 'Smynings' bait! Yeah he's all in. Too bad she controls the money.*

"Gerald I told you they call everything in south Smyrna "Smynings" that's their way to make you think you're just thiiiiiis close to living in Vinings with the beautiful people, it's just real estate trickery. Am I right Travis?"

"Tina, be nice, don't put Travis on the spot like that!" *Thanks Gerald. By the way, your bitch wife is right.*

The couple moved on down the hall, with Gerald casting a sympathetic "Well I for one love the house, sorry about my wife!" glance over his shoulder. Tina continued on with her expose' of the Smynings deception. "And Travis you also know as well as me that this house is priced like forty grand higher than the same house half a mile north just 'cause they're calling it Smynings am I right?"

For Travis, the non-answer tended to be the best answer of all. "It's funny about real estate sometimes, about what adds value and what detracts. A lot of what we call value is really subjective." *There. Dodged it by saying absolutely nothing. Didn't admit that we're trying to hook suckerfish like Gerald with it, but not denying it outright to the fish's shark wife.* Value. That word, the commodity he traded in, the very spine of his chosen profession, had always been a curious one to Travis. How ludicrous were the factors which determined the value of a thing! The nature of value- what enhanced or diminished it- appeared to him as random and arbitrary, defined by capricious whim and tempered with fear and self-delusion. A house costs 200K in Smyrna; the same house in Smynings (still Smyrna but with an ornamental "ings" tail added) costs double. The homes in neighborhood X are more "valuable" because the subjective perception is that the neighborhood is "hot." And from there things take a darker turn, in more ways than one. If better house Y is surrounded by predominantly brown faces its "value" will be less than the value of shitty house Z surrounded by whiter faces. Then if shitty but more "valuable" house Z is refurbished so that it becomes a better house in every way than house Y, but then the brown faces surrounding Y move and end up surrounding refurbished house Z, house Z's value will begin to dip below Y's once again even though its renovation has made it a better structure than Y. Travis understood the absurd XYZ's of value intimately, and the better he came to understand them the uglier they looked. And while more objective factors also existed of course which affected a property's value (the quality of the home itself, schools, proximity to loud highways, etc.), these factors were observably obvious and measurable, thus interesting Travis very little. It was the murky and intangible, those insidious and subjective factors such as race, ever-present but not openly spoken of, which Travis found fascinating and, due to his professional involvement with them, not just fascinating but troubling.

Tina's tour of the house (by this point the menfolk had been reduced to accessories) took them back to the kitchen where they'd started. The showing had really been over and done three rooms earlier, Travis knew it full well; he took pride in his ability to determine if a showing was pointless, and he was seldom proved wrong. But Tina wasn't ready to put him out of his misery.

"There really isn't all that much storage space."

"But it's an easy attic to get into, and it's clean." *Thanks Gerald. Give up son.*

Tina was at the front window. "That big tree. It's really leaning over the house."

Gerald joined her and looked out as well. "Wow. Didn't notice that before."

Against his will, Travis played along and looked at the tree. To his dismay, the

tree which was worrying Tina was leaning less than Keith's tree was leaning over his own house. "It doesn't look like a problem to me."

Tina glared at him contemptuously. "Definitely a realtor's answer. That lean is baaad." *How come everybody else sees shit leaning except me? Am I leaning???*

As Tina stepped away from the window, Travis hoped against hope she'd head for the door. Instead, she took center-stage in the kitchen to perpetuate the pretense of being interested. "So what's the crime like in this neighborhood?"

Travis saw his chance to end the madness. "Well I'm not allowed to comment on crime in the area because of the Fair Housing Act."

Gerald's face dropped. "Even I know what that means. Well, thanks for showing it anyway."

When Travis left the office at the end of the day his mind returned to the Tina and Gerald showing. They had not made an offer, just as he'd predicted. It was just as well, Travis considered; they were a black couple after all, which for him presented a red flag that financing might be a problem. It was one of the stereotypical assumptions which he didn't enjoy making but which he made nonetheless (he rationalized by explaining to his conscience that It wasn't as if he would act upon his assumption in any way; Tina and Gerald would be put through the financing process just as fairly and equally as everyone else and, if they were approved, well, then Travis would be the first to admit to his conscience that his assumption had been wrong and enjoy the pleasant surprise). Turning off South Cobb Drive, he passed through the neighborhoods leading up to his own, neighborhoods which steadily deteriorated with each passing block, and drove by a house for sale which could have been the identical sister of the one Travis had shown Tina and Gerald. He was familiar with the listing, and Tina would have been vindicated to know that it was, indeed, priced 40K lower than its Smynings twin. What Tina would not have been thrilled to hear but which she knew as well as Travis was that a critical feature which made Smynings Smynings had to do with how few of its inhabitants shared Tina's and Gerald's skin tone, the horrible irony being that if savvy brown-skinned buyers like Tina refuse to pay the over-inflated Smynings prices and instead buy a more reasonably-priced home in a browner neighborhood then her financially-prudent decision to not buy in Smynings would only help to accomplish Smyning's goal of keeping the Geralds and Tinas out of it. That he earned his living as a player in that same distasteful game was an unsettling realization. At least it wasn't a game that he'd created.

Once home, Travis stepped out of his truck and averted his eyes from glimpsing the oak tree. He knew his behavior was ridiculous; if the tree was a problem then it was a problem whether he chose to look or not, and not looking did nothing to help straighten its posture. Embarrassed by his childishness, Travis finally looked full-on at the tree, and regretted it instantly. It was leaning more now than it had been over the weekend. That was impossible. But it was. Attributing his skewed vision to temporary insanity as he removed the mail from the lubed-up mailbox, Travis heard the tailgate of a truck opening across the street. It was Corey, loading hardwood flooring into what was now his house, having closed that very morning. Noticing Travis he waved, and Travis recalled with a twinge his first encounter with the young man who had so handily beaten him at the game of Know-It-All Asshole. Still, Travis reciprocated Corey's wave with the sportsmanlike response of walking over to congratulate him on his new membership in the Homeowner Club.

"So, are you officially in it to win it?" Corey was wearing a carpenter's tool belt. It was clear that he wasn't merely loading the flooring in but was ready to get to work on it, even as the ink was still drying on his closing paperwork.

"Hell yeah. Gotta get this floor knocked out before I move in. Big pain in the ass to do a floor with a house full of furniture." Now Travis noticed that Corey wasn't alone; in the front seat of his truck was a friendly-looking blue tick hound, his paws up on the open window and his mouth hanging open, begging to say hello to his owner's new friend. "That's Ralph. He's been with me since high school."

"Hey Ralph." Walking over to scratch his happy head, Travis noticed half a dozen DIY home improvement books on the seat of Corey's truck. "You ain't foolin' around. Gettin' at it on Day One."

"Well, I don't guess you created that spread of yours by putting things off, right?" Corey was at the window too, and the double attention that the irresistible Ralph was receiving sent him into rapturous slobbering. Anybody with such a cool dog couldn't be all bad, Travis reasoned. From the day they were married Alicia had wanted to start the baby factory, but Travis had pushed back; when he then suggested they get a dog, Alicia had said she was too allergic to have one in the house. He'd never really believed her claim about the dog allergy, suspecting that it was just her way of getting even, ie, if she couldn't have a human baby then Travis couldn't have a canine one. "I'll bet you started diggin' in the dirt the minute that dirt was yours."

Diggin'. Which reminded him. "So have you met Sheila yet?"

Corey's face became steel. "Oh yeah. Had the nerve to come up to me about an hour ago and ask for four dollars for cigarettes. You believe that? Right out of the box."

As if hearing her cue, Sheila's incoherent yelp from somewhere down the street now mingled with the birdsong. "Yeah, well, Sheila definitely lives out of the b- "

"I told her to get the fuck off my property and stay the fuck off. Corey's right hand rested on his tool belt as if a six-gun was holstered there. "I also told her that my dog only looks friendly. So I don't think I'll be having any more trouble from her."

A flicker of admiration mixed with envy welled up within Travis. *Why hadn't I been that tough on Sheila from the start*? Oh sure, he'd told her that first day that he wouldn't have any of her panhandling, but he'd said it reasonably, firmly but politely, naively believing that she would respond in the right way. But she'd repeatedly taken advantage of his civility and as a result Travis had endured five years of bullshit from her and from the human overspill of her clogged toilet of a dwelling, all because he'd made the nice guy/dumb guy mistake of treating her like a human being. Had her behavior merited such treatment? No. But Corey had done his research. Corey was doing things right, from the start. Just as Travis wished he had done with his unflowering dogwood...

"So Corey, let me ask your opinion about something. The big oak which you correctly pointed out is drowning my little dogwood with shade. How's that oak look to you, just in general?" Not wanting to put ideas in Corey's head, Travis was careful not to ask him straight out if he thought it was leaning. But he had quite obviously put something in his head, because right away Corey's face took on a shade of queasiness.

"Well, um... if you're asking me then I guess... you want the truth..." He stalled, kicking an imaginary piece of gravel. "It's, um... it's kinda leaning over your house."

"Have you been talking to my wife?" It came out much weirder than Travis intended it.

"Um, no. I noticed it the day the realtor showed me this house."

Now Travis was the queasy one. "Okay, but it's not like the tree's going anywhere, right? It's been there prob'ly two hundred years."

"Which means maybe it's overdue." All Travis could do was stare at him, a magnet which pulled out still more. "Especially when you consider the sick branches."

"Okay just stop."

"No, seriously, look at 'em." Travis did, and didn't need to look very closely to see the truth for himself. The branches were only thinly leafed out, sparser than the other oaks on the block, which was a sign that a tree was in decline. Travis felt himself declining as well. "When the branches are only thinly leafed out that m- "

"Yeah I know!" All Travis could do was shake his head and stare at it. "So how long you think I got?"

The queasy look returned to Corey's face. "They're calling for thunderstorms this week. Some severe." Even Ralph's face took on a look of round-eyed sympathy for Travis' plight. "Could you talk your neighbor into trimming it back?"

Travis winced at the mention of his neighbor. Keith Walters had lived with his wife and son at his ramshackle dwelling since before Travis and Alicia had moved next door, more than ten years in all. It was anyone's guess what Keith's hovel might have looked like before he infested it; probably a fit and trim little home, clever enough in its layout and design, but ten years of abject neglect (the kind of neglect that requires real effort to attain such a level of it) that his once probably-fine home had fallen into the kind of condition which proved just what the earlier-mentioned Second Law of Thermodynamics can do if allowed to proceed unchecked. The house had no guttering, so that years of rain pouring off the roof had created deep moats in the grassless dirt along the front and back, providing year-round mosquito larvae habitat; the fall-down front stoop was covered with scrap plywood, a broken tricycle (his son was now fifteen years old, giving some indication of how long the trike had been interred there) and other broke-to-shit miscellany; the hard-scrabbled yard was a Potter's Field of snarled weeds and potholes where a lawnmower, if one risked the journey across the perilous terrain, would fall into one of the numerous abysses and become permanently mired like a La Brea mastodon. The wooden boards of Keith's fence (which the two properties grudgingly shared) could no longer be seen, for the Walters side of it was completely covered by weedy vines, requiring Travis to continually fight back the aggressive overgrowth which attempted to scale the fence and overrun the ramparts, the weeds having long ago subdued Keith's domain and therefore sought out new kingdoms to conquer. Cracked cement blocks and random chunks of plastic strewn like debris deposited by a retreating glacier, a broken-down Corolla that no longer drove, a car seat from a car that no longer existed, a wheelbarrow without wheels, a dog crate without dog, a screen door without screen and a swing set without swings all contributed to form a cheerless no-man's land which spanned a lachrymose quarter-acre, where at night there were no lights and by day there were no songbirds. Travis had long ago abandoned hope of Keith finding the initiative to make improvements, for Travis had come to understand that his neighbor was nothing but a slug, a no-good lazy insensate soulless slug, one who saw no beauty in the world and therefore felt no need to create any, nor suffered from its absence. Litter from the street would blow onto and collect in Keith's front yard and remain for weeks, until, when he would fire up his mower for one of his bi-annual bush-hoggings, he'd mow over the scattered trash and broadcast it skyward in a million pieces where it would settle like filthy snowflakes onto, of course, Travis' unspoiled preserve. If Keith was at all chagrined by the condition of his wasteland and the strikingly miserable contrast it struck with the loveliness across his fence he did not show it; in fact, in five years of knowing him, Travis could not remember one time when he had seen Keith actually look in the direction of the Riggins property, let alone make mention of anything Travis had done with it in any of their rare conversations (work performed by him which had raised the property value of the

Walters dump, *you're welcome Keith*). For Travis to entertain the notion therefore that such a schlub would do anything so proactive as trim a tree which wasn't even leaning toward his own house but toward someone else's, a house which Keith had failed to acknowledge as even existing these past five years, was to him beyond ridiculous. Keith lived his life like so many do, in passive, inert disarray, always reacting to life after life happens rather than acting first and thereby making life his bitch. Another assessment Travis had made was that Keith was broke-to-shit, and so the expense of cutting back the tree was out of the question on that plane as well (not that he found Keith's financial condition any excuse for his property's condition however; the deficiency was one of resolve, not of money, for as per the old Tom Waits lyric which Travis always thought of whenever he looked across the fence, "there's nothin' wrong with her a hundred dollars wouldn't fix"). No, there could be no help from Keith, of this he was certain. And now, looking over Keith's yard as he had done so many times before, Travis made an ominous first-time observation: there, so overgrown by weeds as to have remained camouflage these five years, were two giant tree stumps, proof that other huge trees had lived there and, under unknown circumstances and with unknown consequences, had come down. It seemed even more sure now to him that little Corey was right. Tree #3 was overdue.

"...is what an arborist would probably tell you."

Corey had been talking to him the whole time. "I'll let you get back to your floor. See ya Ralph." With a final scratch of Ralph's happy dopey head, Travis trudged back home and imagined, as he gazed upon it, how a two-hundred year-old oak tree might look sticking out of its roof. Alicia was going through the mail in the kitchen.

"More good news, not." She was reading an official-looking letter of some kind.

"Don't fucking tell me. The tax assessor?"

"Yep. Went up another $1800."

Travis took the letter from her, but felt too ill to read it and put it down. "It's okay. We'll be able to dispute it. After the oak tree goes through the house that is. Property value will really take a hit. Get it?"

Alicia's laugh which would have relieved his spirits was not forthcoming. Instead she said "You think maybe we could talk Keith into cutting it back?"

"Come on dear. You know that guy by now. Remember what he did when the drunk driver knocked over his mailbox? He just went without a mailbox for a year and a half and picked up his mail at the post office because he was too lazy to turn a screwdriver. He's not gonna be any help."

Alicia dropped the mail on the counter. "We sure are surrounded by losers."

Her indirect reference to Keith and Sheila as being losers was the closest he could remember of her saying that he, by comparison, wasn't one. "Well this Bob Villa Corey kid seems okay after all. Fixing up his place at least. Has a great dog."

"Does it bite?"

Travis rolled his eyes. "Every dog bites dear. That's how they eat." It always drove him a little crazy, Alicia's Defcon-One fear of dogs. He knew it wasn't all her fault; as her entire family was afraid of dogs it followed that her fear resulted from the culture she was raised in. To refer to Alicia's culture implied that Travis was raised in another, which was true: Travis and Alicia were a racially mixed couple. He'd always wondered, given the nearly-equal balance of black and white in the Atlanta area, why black/white relationships were not more common than it was. But no- despite the level of diversity surrounding them compared to so much of America, Travis observed that white folk and black folk in Smyrna still found ways to not have much to do with one another except when work or other unavoidable interactions required it. And as of late, the white folk and the black folk who lived under Travis' own roof weren't having much to do with one another either besides what was required. He saw it as a valley through which they were passing, not one of critical depth but a valley nonetheless. Right now for example, Alicia was tying her shoes to go running, alone (Travis was also a runner, but running with a partner only worked for Alicia if both ran the same pace and she'd made it clear she wasn't about to slow down for him), and he was about to change into shit clothes and work in the yard, alone. It was totally normal he realized, even healthy, a little distance, a little separation. But he felt that he already enjoyed about as much distance and separation from the human race as a functional person should, and so he considered it overkill to maintain a similar arms-length relationship with his own wife. "Oh well," he told himself, "maybe when the tree destroys our house we'll be brought closer by shared tragedy. I'm saying 'when' now. Fantastic."

Stepping outdoors to refill his bird feeders, Travis looked over the fence and saw

Keith out in his yard, which in and of itself was newsworthy. Keith was never in his yard; he fostered no relationship with his land whatsoever to the point of denying its existence. Bent over at the waist and creeping stiff-legged like a beer-bellied flamingo, Keith must be searching for something on the ground, Travis reasoned. Recalling his conversation with Alicia, he saw the perfect opportunity to broach the subject of tree trimming, and while he knew in advance it would amount to a gesture in futility, he would at least be able to report back to her without lying to say he tried. With his expectation bar set at the lowest notch, Travis walked around the fence and stepped gingerly onto Keith's minefield.

"Looking for something?" Keith was kicking about the weeds near one of the cautionary tree stumps.

"My kid. Lost his cell phone." Travis found this odd. Both Mrs. Keith and Keith's Kid (who knew what their names were) were shrouded in Boo Radley reclusivity, observed even less frequently than the hermit-like Keith, darting furtively from door to car when leaving the house and from car to door when they returned, without detour. So when and why had Boo Jr. ventured out into the wilderness? Travis sidestepped the obvious question of "Why isn't your kid the one out looking for it?" and fought his way closer to Keith through the brambles. "Hey I wanted to ask you about somethi- "

"He's at that age when he can't stand his parents so he gets away from us out here with his phone." *Maybe he can't stand his parents because when he asks them a question they interrupt him mid-sentence.* "Said he saw a snake when he was out here so he won't come look for it himself." *Well there's my answer. Snakes. Chowin' on all the rats no doubt.* "How do ya even get rid of snakes?" *A) if you knew of a way to get rid of snakes you wouldn't do it anyway Keith so why ask? B) for ten years you've created the ultimate DIY snake habitat. Enjoy then the fruits of your labor.* "Oh well. Prob'ly nothing you can do about it anyway." *Perfect. Talked yourself out of that job in record time. That's my Keith.*

Travis stepped over a mysterious puddle (it hadn't rained in two weeks) and pointed at the oak. "So Keith, have you ever noticed the way your oak has grown?"

"You mean besides up?" *Priceless. Unintentionally so of course, but priceless.*

"Besides 'up.' Over, toward us next door."

Keith stared somewhat upwards in the approximate direction of the oak. "It is?"

"Yeah. I only noticed it myself recently."

Keith squinted despite the cloudy skies, which Travis attributed to the unfamiliar strain of focused vision, then offered his assessment. "Huh." After a few moments, Keith looked down from the tree and simply stood, silent and puzzled in general. Clearly Keith had no idea what might be the point of Travis' visit. Travis was wondering himself.

"Yeah, if it were to come down it would fall right on our house." More silence.

For Alicia's sake he soldiered on. "We were wondering, is there any chance you'd maybe consider having that one big limb trimmed back? Just enough so we'd only have like a minor calamity instead of a major disaster?"

"I don't see that it's leaning." Which in that moment Travis knew to be a true statement, for Keith had already gone back to staring at the ground and searching for the phone. Travis had only recently passed through his own period of denial about the tree's leaning; apparently Keith was now in his.

"Alicia noticed it first, even our new neighbor Corey across the street noticed it."

"We got a neighbor?" Keith remained bent over, and it was obvious to Travis that he would remain that way for the rest of his days.

"Okay then. I'll leave you to your search. Give the tree a thought though. It really is leaning."

"I don't have to by law." Travis had begun to walk away, but now turned back; Keith was still bent over and not looking up. "By law. I don't have to trim it."

"Which means you *have* realized it's leaning then?"

Still bent over like a slovenly jackknife, Keith continued to speak to the mud. "It doesn't matter anyway because none of the branches extend over the property line into your property. If they did then you could by law trim the branches yourself but only up to and not past the property line but they don't cross the line so you can't touch them. If it falls over in a storm it's considered an act of god and so if it hits your house then the owner of the tree isn't liable you are. By law the owner of a tree has no responsibility to trim his tree branches so by law I don't have to do anything so I'm not." He'd spoken it all without looking up, which was fine with Travis since it had enabled him to give Keith the finger during most of it. It was quintessential Keith Walters; having clearly known that the tree was seriously leaning and, fearing nothing about the damage it might do to Travis' house or its inhabitants but fearing instead that he might actually be required to do something to prevent it, Keith had researched the law exhaustively to determine just how much effort expense and responsibility he could weasel out of, and to his delight had found he was "by law" 100% weasel-free. As Travis turned to go, his one regret was that he hadn't recorded Keith's weaseliloquy on his phone for Alicia.

"You prob'ly shoulda noticed it before you bought your house." Turning back at this parting shot, Travis couldn't help but notice, as he regarded the man he so wanted to bury alive in one of his own potholes, exactly which portion of Keith's bent-over anatomy was pointing at him.

When Travis returned to his side of the fence, Sheila's expectant side-to-side wobble awaited him at the end of his driveway.

"Mistah Diggins you cain't be walkin' them peoples' yahd over theah snakes ovuh theah." Sheila carried a paper bag in one hand and her stained plastic cup in the other.

"Whatcha need Sheila?" Although it was a foregone conclusion by now that, if Sheila appeared at his driveway, it was only because she needed something, it was still a matter of some shamefulness to him that he greeted her in such manner, "Whatcha need?", the sort of unwelcoming rudeness with which he would never greet anyone else who might approach him (unless perhaps they were carrying Bibles). "You got a bottle there Sheila? What's the occasion?" It was still several days until her government check would arrive and so her celebratory paper bag was premature.

"No I don' got a bottle my son he git me a cell phone gotta chawge it up." From the bag Sheila removed an old flip phone. "They" had stolen her TracFone over a year ago, this was a new acquisition. "Now I kin talk to mah fam'ly."

"That's good Sheila." She was still wobbling. He knew there was more to come. "So whatcha need?"

"You got a 'dapter fit this phone Mistah Diggins?"

"No Sheila." *That's how you do it Travis. Per the Corey template. Quick and firm. Don't equivocate, punctuate.*

And just like that she was weeping, collapsing like a sand castle in the rain, shaking and sinking. "Dat man he punch me in mah face, who know why bud I got me a cell phone mah son's plan I gots to call my fam'ly you din' see mah eye wheah he hid me Mistah Diggins I need ta call mah fam'ly."

"What man hit y- ?"

"You see mah eye Mistah Diggins why all diss bad shit always happen ta me!?"

"Hold on hold on- "

And like that he was rifling through his desk drawers, looking for 'dapters, yanked into her urgency yet again, never able to predict or prepare for it, resolved that the next time Sheila wouldn't pull him in but now he found the 'dapter and now he was back on the driveway. "Okay here, here's the adapter. But where you gonna charge it at?"

And now he was plugging her phone into the outlet on his own front porch, to use his electricity since she had none, and Sheila was mumbling everything except thank you. "I jus' come back when it chawge up." Then she was gone, the jump-track freight train careening away, back on the sidewalk and blowing its horn at no one and everyone. As Travis recovered at the end of his driveway, there was Corey across the street, watching it all in silent wonder.

Finally settling in to his work, Travis was grateful that the physical exertion of the task would put this latest episode of Sheila ridiculum and how she'd tsunamied him yet again out of his mind. Or at least that was what Travis hoped would happen; what actually happened was that Travis could think of nothing else but Sheila as he gathered his tools and began digging (he'd found online a fantastic 8' tall kinetic windmill spinner, and as luck would have it the perfect place for it to live was on the last remaining undeveloped square of earth in his front yard, the crest of the small hill which marked its very center). As he had done countless times before, Travis reviewed the events leading up to his home being turned into Sheila's personal charging station to see where he'd gone wrong. But he hadn't gone wrong; Sheila had simply happened, and Travis happened to be powerless. He had begun with No but Sheila turned it into Now. His weakness of resolve troubled him, his spineless surrender and shows of compassion. For it was indeed just a show; he was not

...mpassionate, not generally nor specifically toward Sheila. Sheila was to blame for Sheila's life, not Travis. Travis had not been placed in this neighborhood for the purpose of taking care of Sheila. But he did, over and over again. Resentment, Travis realized as he began to dig into the clay, was at the bottom of his sour feelings, resenting how Sheila, with no abilities, intelligence, resources or design, got what she wanted, while he, the High and Mighty Mr. Diggins, superior to Sheila in every way, could only stand by helplessly until a giant tree crushed his home. Hers was a miserable life, yet in her scratch-along way Sheila succeeded in it. And Travis resented the hell out of her success, yet here he was, helping her time after time to achieve it! For five years his happiest dream was to one day wake up and find she was gone, but by providing adapters for her phone and ice for her water and scrap lumber for firewood and fo' dollahs fo' candles Travis only facilitated her remaining. Looking up from his shoveling he noticed Corey's truck drive off with Ralph's head bobbing and ears flopping in the passenger window; well, good for that little sonofabitch at least, he's nipped Sheila in the bud. But with the dust now settled from the 'dapter nonsense, Travis was able to consider it all more reasonably and proportionately. Sheila's phone was plugged into his wall. So what? How did that hurt him? In no way whatsoever. It cost him nothing, and was he using that prehistoric phone adapter anyway? You did a good thing, Travis told himself. His mood was improving with each shovel-full.

As he was imagining just how pretty his spinner was going to look in the hole he was happily digging, something flashed across his peripheral vision, rushing up his driveway so fast that he almost thought he'd imagined it. Turning toward the house to track the apparition, he saw Sheila up on his porch, bending over her still-charging phone and mumbling to herself.

"I don't know Sheila if it's fully cha- "

"Out his gott dam mine he thank I put up wit mufuckin'..." Sheila was now fumbling about with the phone and the adapter, pushing buttons with manic fury, the adapter no longer plugged into the wall but its cable still attached to the phone and dangling about. "See whud I got fo'him he thank he gone do he gott damm Mistah Diggins why I git dis heah on mah phone whud it say?"

Trudging reluctantly onto the porch, Travis was greeted by the screen of Sheila's phone pushed into his face, but because of her delirium tremens he could see nothing but a quavering blur. She was getting more agitated by the moment. "Your son can probably help you wi- "

"Who dat man thank he is Mistah Diggins he know mah son he know mah son'll fuck 'im up." Now Sheila began pacing back and forth across the porch, the adapter cable whipping her into a frenzy, as Travis stood by in helpless attendance. An all-too familiar sensation of foreboding welled up inside him, the sense of doom he imagined people at the bottom of a mountain slope feel upon seeing an avalanche high above them and knowing that it was only a matter of time before they would be buried. "I ain't skehd he lookin fo'me let'im fine me mah son fuck 'im up."

"Somebody's looking for you?"

Sheila stared at Travis as if he were an idiot. "Dat man! Who fuck up my eye!"

"And you say that now he's- "

Suddenly Sheila's remaining good eye widened into a bloodshot saucer as she looked past him toward the street; turning to find what might be the object of her alarm, Travis saw a dark car cruise by, slowly and suspiciously. Sheila's agitation exploded into full-throated single-breath unpunctuated hollering. "YOU JUS' DRIVE OWN MUFUCKAH HIT MAH EYE YOU OUT YO GOTT DAM MINE I PUT UP WIT YO SHIT I CALL MAH SON WHUP YO ASS MUFUCKAH!" The car was well past them, a full block away, but nowhere near out of hearing range of Sheila's bellowing, for now the car screeched to a stop and sped full-speed in reverse, tires burning, backing recklessly toward Travis' driveway. Sheila bobbed and danced like a flame. "Oh it own now Mistah Diggins, it OWN!"

"No it ain't 'on' Sheila! Don't- " But as Travis stepped off the porch toward the threatening car in hopes of defusing a confrontation, the cable from Sheila's 'dapter wrapped his ankle and, like a roped rodeo calf, Travis tumbled face-first down all four steps in a single belly-flopping dive and landed on the cement. Meanwhile, Sheila and Dat Man shouted back and forth, with the former hurling her salvos from the porch and the latter from the gates of Travis' driveway. Both instinct and inability to move his lower limbs prevailed upon Travis to play dead, a role requiring no acting ability, and as the shit-show continued, Travis simply awaited the inevitable sound of gunfire and the mixed blessing of Sheila's murder. But the sound which followed instead was that of a car door slamming, and with squealing tires and the smell of rubber the car sped away, leaving Travis in lassoed paralysis and Sheila hurling victory taunts in its wake.

"Out his gott dam *mine* he think I put up wit 'is shit why you on da groun' Mistah Diggins?"

Travis had finally rolled himself up into a sitting posture on the cement. "Go home Sheila."

"I need some ice fo' my ice wattah aftah all dat Mis- "

"NO ICE SHEILA!" Scrambling wildly onto his feet and unwinding himself from the cable with a furious spin, Travis squared off with his uninvited guest. "Take the phone and the adapter and go! You hear me? Go! I can't have this bullshit in my own front yard! Take your shit and go. Just go. *Go*!"

"Now you don' gotta-"

"GODDAMMIT Sheila!" He was literally pulling at his hair. "I don't need your shit DO YOU HEAR ME?"

Only moments before it had been Sheila who was screaming and thrashing; now it was Travis who spluttered and shouted. For her part, she had magically transformed into the picture of tranquility, her sad doleful eyes gazing up at him with confusion and hurt, her voice a soft, warm turd. "Wha you talk ta me like dat Mistah Diggins?"

He threw the adapter to the end of the driveway. "You don't know when to stop Sheila! You ask for one thing and then another and another and it grows and grows until you're starting fights on my fucking front porch! You're out of control Sheila!" Travis was full-on hopping up and down, his screaming voice breaking from the strain. "You're out of control! GET OUT!"

Shuffling her way slowly down the driveway, Sheila sniffed back a tear as she picked the adapter up off the cement. "Don' know wah you talk ta me like dat Mistah Diggins. We frens. You don' need talk ta me like dat." She was back on the sidewalk now; Travis watched her wild-eyed as his heart hammered kicked against his ribcage. "You git back to yo' right self, ah be back wit my cup fo' ice. Don' need talk ta me like dat Mistah Diggins. Gon' git mah cup. Ah be back." Turning back toward the house, Travis caught a glimpse of Alicia inside at the front window, now turning away from the window while shaking her head.

With Sheila's storm clouds blown over (but the threat of bad weather's return imminent), Travis' pulse rate gradually returned to normal; forcing himself to breathe slowly and deeply after drinking his entire bottle of water, he shook off the ordeal as best he could and returned to his digging project. Picking up the shovel, he replayed the film in his mind, and cringed at having lost his cool so utterly (yet again, for he had blown his lid with her many times before), the way that Sheila had once again reduced him to the very behavior which in her he found so primitive. It was all drama with her, unrelenting drama, uncontainable drama, an always-shaken soda can popped and overflowing and spraying anyone standing in her spew zone. Travis despised drama, denying it access to his evenly-planted existence... except with Sheila. Sheila always found her way in, and once under his skin, managed to light the fuses of all his explosive flashpoints, his barbaric impulses which he not only strove assiduously to suppress but pretended did not exist. To be rendered as primitive as she, for him to undo so many millennia of his species' hard-won evolutionary progress by hopping and hollering in the street like a mad ape, worked hell on Travis' peace of mind like nothing had ever before. But he was digging his hole once again, and feeling a little better now, for into it he'd be planting his brand-new multi-colored kinetic spinner, a kaleidoscopic *objet d'art,* a pleasing delight to the eye which would bring yet more beauty to his already beautiful domain. This then was the real dividend to be gleaned from his toil and investment, he realized, that his efforts to create beauty, the simple fact that he cared enough about beauty to want to create it, was the surest proof that he was of the highest order of primates, proof that the real Travis Riggins was not primitive at all, but civilized, sophisticated, refined. This pursuit of beauty was why it was all worthwhile, why he himself was worthwhile. This was the true measure of Travis Riggins' value. And as his shovel plunged deeper, a scrape against a rock opposed his progress; another scrape, and another, until it was necessary for him to kneel down with his garden trowel and pry out the impeding stone. But when he touched the stone it was not rough, but smooth; removing the soil surrounding it, the stone emerged as almost round. Some dirt still obscured the stone's surface, and when he removed it, deep sockets which once held eyes returned his gaze; the jaw with teeth told Travis that it was no stone at all. And as his shaking trowel revealed the ribs, the tiny ribs which could only be a child's, Travis knew his metallic thing of beauty would have to wait its turn. A beauty of a more somber sort was demanding its discoverer's full attention.

3

When Travis looked up from his phone he realized his people had left the room without him. It was just as well. Let them have their "talk it over" space. Let them make whispered comments to each other about the house without the realtor overhearing them. Still, it was unprofessional of him, to be staring at his phone during a showing. But he was justifiably distracted. The forecast was thunderstorms, 60% chance, and an angry-looking troublemaker had been developing on his weather app for several hours, so Travis had been checking its path on the radar every few minutes. Winds were predicted to gust at 50 mph. Keith's sick oak tree was doomed.

Catching up to the couple in the back upstairs bedroom, the husband (or were they both husbands, or did they just call each other "partner"?) spoke first. "Why the hell did they ever paint this room green? In a bedroom?"

A distant rumble of thunder twisted Travis' face toward the window as the husband/partner responded. "Yeah but who cares, paint it something brighter and this room is fantastic!"

"Do you think they'd come down on the asking price? Travis?"

"Do what? Oh, yes. I mean, yes, I think so. They've come down once already but I don't think they're at bottom." Risking a glance out the window, Travis saw the treetops beginning to rustle under the darkening sky. "So have I missed showing you anything? I don't think s- "

"Let's look at that fabulous foyer again!"

"Yes!"

Heading obediently back downstairs, Travis stood by in a pretense of patience as the couple oohed and aahed and pointed about. Another growl of thunder, this one closer, accelerated the rate of Travis' speech. "So do you have any other questions?" *Of course,* Travis thought to himself ruefully. *I get somebody who's totally into the house and I'm in a hurry to rush them out of it.*

The partner/husband smiled at Travis, his hands on his hips. "There aren't any skeletons in the closet you haven't told us about are there Travis?"

He had acted quickly and efficiently upon finding the child's bones that evening two days earlier. Covering the grave with a waterproof tarp was obvious, but the hole also required a solid cover which, if walked upon, wouldn't give way, and so underneath the tarp he had placed a half sheet of ¾ inch plywood to serve as both roof and floor. As for the dirt he'd dug out, Travis piled it all on top of the tarp and plywood, in that way ensuring that the hole would not be inadvertently walked over or otherwise disturbed. It looked like hell of course, a big ugly pile of dirt over a plastic tarp in the center of his meticulous front lawn, but Travis had seen no alternative. As for calling someone such as the police, well, that was out of the question for the moment, for reasons which were his business. But the hurryup coverup was only a temporary solution. Something had to be done. He had an open grave in his front yard. It was kindof a big deal.

Another clap of thunder jumped him back to the room. "So guys, are we thinking about making an offer?"

Their answer was in harmony. "Yes!" It was exactly what Travis was afraid they would say. This meant paperwork, disclosure forms, etc., which meant more delay in getting home, and already he could see the first big drops of rain hitting the pavement outside. As quickly as he could without being obvious, Travis hurried them through it all (disguising his haste as the by-product of his eagerness to get the offer to the seller as quickly as possible), and after dropping them off back at the office without putting his car in park, sped through the increasing wind and rain toward home. Hitting the brakes and skidding to a stop at a red light and praying for it to change, Travis' brain hit the brakes as well- what the hell was the big hurry? Was he planning to stop the tree from falling? Push the hundred-foot monster in the direction of Keith's house perhaps? He was halfway home when the storm finally lived up to its billing, as a nauseated Travis watched trees healthier than Keith's bending like blades of grass and lightning popping everywhere. Slipping and sliding around the final corner, he was finally home, and his eyes beheld what remained of his house- which was all of it, since barely a twig of the oak had fallen. As the dangerous part of the storm moved out and a steady but windless rain replaced it, Travis' relief was equaled by his feelings of foolishness. Well of course the tree hadn't fallen. How many hundreds of thunderstorms had it survived before this one in its life? Was it now impelled to fall just because Travis had finally gotten around to noticing it leaning the same way it had been leaning for decades? Yes, he'd definitely been a fool about the tree, but a little embarrassment was all it had cost him- his garden was still Eden, and the tree had taken no bites out of his lovely apple. All was in perfect order. Except of course the open grave in his front yard.

Getting out of the car with his umbrella, Travis saw Alicia dressed head to toe in plastic, standing in the rain at the side of the house. When he approached her, Alicia's eyes were ready for the obvious question. "So, why are we standing out in th- "

"Wind is gone now, I suppose we can go back in."

"You mean to say you were- "

"I ain't gonna be in the house when that tree comes down."

As Alicia led them up onto the porch, she paused before opening the front door and directed her gaze down at the electrical receptacle, clearly intending for Travis to look as well. There he saw Sheila's flip phone, plugged in and charging. "Looks like we had two storm fronts pass through today."

After an unamused roll of her eyes, Alicia went indoors and began removing her rain gear. "I promise you Alicia, I never told her to come back here with that phone."

She assumed her best "you've got to be kidding" face. "But you didn't tell her *not* to come back here with that phone didjoo? No."

Under the plastic Alicia was dressed for a run. "She always catches me off guard."

"All I know is" she said, retying the knots of her running shoes, "that for somebody who says he hates her so much you sure show it in a funny way."

It was Travis' sincerest wish- had been for years, nearly as long as they had lived at 1418- that one day, without pain, without trauma, without conscious sensation or awareness on her part, Sheila would simply fail to awaken one morning, and by so doing his long residential nightmare would end. For Sheila to simply not wake up would be the answer to his prayer, were there a god to pray to. With Sheila's presence no longer an obstacle, the house would finally be condemned. With only her husband remaining and him perpetually incarcerated, his surviving siblings would no longer be bound to honor their mother's request and could finally sell the property. The shitbox would be bulldozed. An actual house would be built. New neighbors would move in. The sun would shine and the birds would sing. Of course it went unspoken, his wish for Sheila's endless sleep. Nice people weren't supposed to wish such a thing. But try as he may, Travis could not come up with any worthwhile reason for her to remain living, either for herself or for others. She'd never behaved as a functional parent, even before all her children had left, and her dealings with them now were combative at best. Sheila performed no useful service, contributed nothing of any worth to the community. She was nothing but a liability, a thing to be suffered, a bringer of chaos, a disturber of the peace, a detractor, a polluter, a drain. She was entirely a negative; there was nothing positive which she offered in counterbalance. Only womanish sentiment argued for her continued survival, the maudlin sort of sympathy which was either ignorant of or in denial of the facts. Alicia had used the word "hate," but Travis didn't believe that it was hate he felt. No. If he truly hated Sheila then her peaceful death wouldn't be enough. He would need to know that she felt it; she would not only need to pay for what she was, but to know that she was receiving her just desserts, would need to know that Travis was getting even. Hate was a very personal thing, but for Travis it was not personal with Sheila. She was simply a problem that needed removing. There is no *mano a mano* hate for the cockroach, just the determination for the thing to go away and stay away. He desired a purely dispassionate sort of extermination.

By now Alicia had left for her run; himself now changed into his yard clothes, Travis set out on his every-day routine of pruning, clipping, weeding and hovering-over his precious half-acre. Before getting to those routine tasks however, the decidedly non-routine "new thing" demanded his attention; when referring to an obvious but unspoken preoccupying issue, people sometimes use the idiom "the elephant in the room," but Travis had that one beat with "the open grave in the yard." Yes, he could lay claim to being the only kid on the block to have one, that was for sure. Today he was over the initial shock of the discovery; now he was relaxed enough to think reasonably and logically about just what it was he had and how it might have gotten there. And while those questions might have been foremost in anyone else's mind, there was another which ranked ahead in Travis' thinking: what on earth literally would happen to his pristine landscaping if he were to report his find to the authorities? Yes. This was the terrifying concern which was preventing Travis from making the call. Five years of horticultural design, delicately executed and intricately balanced, surrounded the 4 X 4 tarp-covered pimple, and were a CSI team to come do their work that pimple would be popped- flagstone would be torn out, periwinkle trampled, azaleas crushed and camellias uprooted. The hole which he dug did not fully expose the skeleton, so the police would certainly need to enlarge it, doubling or even tripling its size, which meant there'd be no preventing his in-ground koi pond from being destroyed in the process. Then there were the dozens of back-and-forth trips through the yard to and from the grave; there'd be no question that so much heavy-booted traffic would take its decimating toll as well. For a moment- for more than a moment, truth be told- Travis considered simply re-covering the bones with the dirt and going on as if he'd never found anything (perhaps planting a bed of lilies atop it as a secret memorial, the child deserved at least that much); after all, he no sentimentality about the bones, for people die and are buried all the time, so in a purely objective way there was nothing remarkable about finding a former human in the condition that all humans eventually end up in. Why not then just throw the dirt back in and let it go at that? Why destroy everything he'd created for a someone who was no longer anyone? Such were Travis' thoughts as he stood over the pile of dirt and contemplated his next move; or rather, his ultimate move, for his next move wasn't in question. It was time to uncover the hole and study more closely the coolest thing he'd ever found.

Once he'd moved the dirt aside and satisfied himself that no wives or Sheilas were near, Travis knelt beside his macabre treasure. As it was an archaeological site of sorts, he had determined it would be useful to bring to his dig appropriate tools, and so he brought along his 4-piece stainless steel barbecue kit, complete with basting brush, spatula, fork and tongs. By the size of the skeleton, Travis guessed the child to have been no older than seven or eight, and seemed to have been laid out carefully with its hands folded across its stomach. As he carefully dislodged clumps of clay with the tongs and then whisked them away with the basting brush (and feeling very Indiana Jones in the process), questions as to the child's story began to enter his mind. Was it a boy or a girl? How long ago had the bones been placed here? Had the child died from illness, or perhaps met with violence? After removing as much of the dirt from the bones as he dared without doing damage with his hardware store implements, Travis noticed a curious shape to the hands; all the fingers were bent, with the fingertips touching, giving the appearance that when buried, those fingers and hands had been holding an object which must have deteriorated and disappeared over the years. Had the child been buried holding a favorite toy? A doll perhaps?

"Whatcha got down there, a body?" It was Corey, crossing the street and heading straight toward Travis and the hole.

"Yes. It's the best fertilizer ever!" In a mad rush Travis slid the plywood over the top and was resetting the tarp just as Corey walked up to the dirt pile. Travis could literally feel Corey's disappointment that the hole was no longer open for him to look into. Travis had observed from his many years of being a guy an annoying trait among guys, an article of the Guy Code if you will, that all guys are to be nosy about all projects other guys are into, and all guys working on those projects are to show other guys what they're doing so that those guys can tell guys how they're doing it all wrong and the way the guy should be doing it instead. Covering the hole was in flagrant violation of the Guy Code. "I dug this hole for the base of my new yard spinner, wouldn'tcha know it's right over the water line. Just checking to make sure I didn't nick it with the shovel."

"Are those barbecue tongs?"

"They are indeed."

Corey looked out at the curb in front of Travis' house. "But the water service is over there. Why would the water line run all the way over here, and uphill at that?"

By now Travis had finished returning the dirt to the tarp, and in record time. "Go figure, that's Cobb County for you, so, where's Ralph?"

"Oh he's back at the house." Glancing across the street, Travis could see Ralph inside Corey's screen door, eager to come out and join the party. Corey was looking at the oak tree. "Looks like you dodged a bullet with that storm today."

Travis pushed the spatula out of sight with his foot. "Nah, not really. We were all probably a little hysterical about the tree. It ain't going anywhere."

"Walters won't trim it huh? Well, I'll have my chainsaw ready when you need to borrow it." In a slow 360° turn, Corey took in the surrounding splendor. "Gotta say, it's all even more fantastic up close in detail. Is that a sundial next to your pond?"

"You bet it is." *And two feet below it are two feet, below it.*

Corey's 360 stopped at Travis' front porch. "I notice you're a charging station now."

"Don't remind me." It was an embarrassing topic, Sheila's phone plugged into his house, but it did at least pull Corey's focus up out of the hole. "I've learned you have to pick your battles with Sheila. What about you, still managing to keep her at a distance?"

Corey nodded gravely and smiled with narrowed eyes. "Oh I set her straight from the beginning. Shut that shit down. Haven't heard a word from her since." Just then, a dog began to bark somewhere across the street. It was Ralph behind his screen door, and the objects of his arousal were two young people walking up the sidewalk in the direction of Corey's house. "That's Sergeant Ralph for you, on the job, won't let anybody walk by without letting them know he's there." The approaching storm was a young woman (carrying a baby and a baby's bottle) and a young man (also carrying a bottle but not for a baby), with the young man loping ahead with long strides, as if trying to distance himself from the girl who was clearly following him, speaking indiscernibly to his back in imploring tones as the baby squawled accompaniment. Travis recognized them; he had seen them at Sheila's often, and from what he could guess either the girl was her daughter or the young man was her son. Both the girl and the baby were getting louder and more strident, and the young man grunted monosyllabic responses in between chugs from the bottle without turning to face them and without slowing down. Corey watched as they passed in front of his house, muttering under his breath "That's right, keep going, take it on down the street." But then the girl said something which must have been the dreaded magic word, for the young man stopped as if he'd been hit in the back with a rock and spun to face her, screaming high-decibel incoherencies. Meanwhile, Ralph was making known his outrage, as was Corey, but unlike Ralph in a voice only Travis could hear. "No, keep going! Dammitt now they got my dog all stirred up." But if Ralph had been stirred, he was about to be shaken, for a fourth voice, more piercing and shrill than the other three, now screeched above them all; it was Sheila, barreling down the sidewalk and joining the fray with her own special style of incendiary gibberish.

"DON' YOU MAY DAGGAH MYNO LEHMAH WI MAH GRANBABY GOTT DAM NO!"

By this point, the young man and woman had squared off face-to-face, forgetting themselves enough to have moved from the sidewalk onto Corey's front yard as they howled and spit their vulgarities, close enough to make physical contact but for the moment holding off from it, the young man waving his bottle and the young woman waving the bawling child. Sheila was between them, screaming into the face of each by equal turns and lunging with clumsy desperation for the howling infant. Behind his screen door, Ralph was losing his shit; across the street, Corey was helpless.

"I'm calling 911. Should I call 911?"

As Travis murmured "ninety-eight" under his breath, the inevitable first blow was struck, by the girl no less, who while holding the infant in one hand began pounding on the young man with the baby bottle which she held in the other. Sheila, seizing her opportunity, snatched the terrified child and ran away with it under her arm like an all-American halfback, but then spun back around and inexplicably charged once more into the breach, pausing only for a split-second to first deposit the infant onto the grass where it began crawling toward the street. While the three grown-ups bitch-slapped and brawled and the howling baby dragged itself closer and closer toward traffic, Ralph finally reached the limit of his endurance, and on his hind legs clawed furiously at the door's screen, shredding it to bits. Corey was spluttering on his phone. "Yes I need to report a fight in my front ya- *oh fuck my screen door!* RALPH!" As the liberated Ralph came bounding through the obliterated screen and out onto the yard, Travis was already flying across the street, dodging the traffic and taking up the baby just as it was reaching the curb. Upon finding a giant dog yapping and bouncing at her feet (with no intention of attacking but only to join in on the humans' game), Sheila howled in mortal terror, scampering up onto the tailgate of Corey's nearby truck and climbing into the safety of its bed where she taunted the baying animal from high ground. Now aware of some man presuming to hold her baby, the girl turned the blowtorch of her wrath fully upon Travis, clubbing him about the head and shoulders with the baby bottle while jerking the child from his grasp, an assault which the young man was more than happy to assist her with by himself employing the baby bottle which until that point had been bouncing off his own head. While Sheila shouted obscenities, Ralph thrilled at the new game of jumping up at the hollering madwoman berating him from the truck, and in the process his huge and untrimmed claws left deep scraping gouges up and down the pearlescent paint of the truck's side panels. At the very apogee of the madness, Alicia rounded the corner, headed homeward on the final leg of her run, and seeing the melee ahead, made the business decision that her workout needed to turn right back around and continue in the opposite direction. Now a distant police siren was heard, and in a twinkling, the yard was empty; all but Travis, who remained sitting in the grass and holding a shattered baby bottle as Ralph licked dripping formula off his face.

That evening, the two men determined it was just as well the police never arrived (the siren they had heard was for some other call, thereby leaving the Sheila total at ninety-seven but with an asterisk), since the facts of the case amounted to Corey's own dog who had destroyed the screen and paint job and Travis' own ass being whupped by a girl with a baby bottle. But as they sat drinking a beer on Travis' front porch at sunset while staring at Sheila's fully-charged phone glowing in the twilight, Corey defiantly reminded Travis and himself that he could live next door to anything for five years. And now Corey only had four years and three-hundred sixty-one days to go.

The next morning was Saturday, but for the Riggins' it was not a day off. Alicia was already working with clients at the gym, and Travis was heading out soon to show three homes. It was a mild annoyance, going in to work on a Saturday, especially during the growing season, tearing himself away from his botanical children at their neediest time of the year. Gardening had always struck him as an equivalent to what he imagined the job of human parenting to be. Both roles required unwavering nurturing, feeding and watering while striving to optimize growing conditions; for both plant and child, protection from the elements and fending off strangling weeds required constant vigilance, not to mention the many destructive organisms which would seek to eat their leaves; neither the horticultural nor the human parent could settle simply for growth, but demanded from its sprouts the best kind of growth, which meant pruning back undesirable shoots and trimming away flowerless branches which bore no fruit. But despite their similarities, Travis knew that gardening was preferable over parenting for one significant reason: while there was no guarantee for either the human or the botanical caregiver that one's efforts would produce a desirable crop, at least with gardening you could do your work without getting, back talk, ingratitude, defiance and resentment in return. Yes- when his workday was over and he could rush home to his planted family, he would at least know that they'd be waiting there for him, yielded and compliant, and would never ask to borrow the car on Saturday night.

Stepping out of the house, Travis' eyes performed their daily visual inspection of the property; recent events had re-prioritized the sequence of his scan, for now the first thing he checked was the tarp-covered hole. Nothing had been disturbed. Thing To Be Checked #2 was the oak tree, and when Travis viewed it this morning, he was sure its lean had disappeared overnight. How strange the brain is, Travis thought. Now that his panic over an imminent collapse of the tree had passed, its appearance to him had been restored to its pre-panic condition. What else might he be viewing in exaggeration due to excessive worrying over them he wondered? Was he also exaggerating the trauma he imagined would be done to his landscaping were he to report the grave? But no- the flora really would be trampled and the pond would be destroyed and the flagstone would be ripped out. Yet how long could he maintain a secret morgue?

Glancing across the street, Travis saw the shredded screen door, and recalled the previous day's debacle. Corey wasn't home, and Travis knew why- by no means beaten, Corey had assured Travis that he'd be at Home Depot first thing in the morning to buy a new roll of screen. Now the drone of a lawnmower could be heard somewhere, and at first, Travis was sure that some illusory echoing phenomena was in effect, for it sounded like it was coming from Keith's yard, a near-impossibility. But when shredded bits of a Wendy's wrapper fluttered down at his feet, Travis knew he wasn't imagining things. Glancing over the fence, there was Keith, wearing flip-flops and grappling with his push mower up and down the pock-marked terrain. With shredded litter in hand, Travis swallowed back his temper and crossed the property line Rubicon.

Just as Keith's spluttering mower lumbered over a giant mound of fire ants, Travis arrived on the scene, and was greeted by ant-filled red dirt sandblasting his face. After frantically brushing the biters out of his clothes and hair, Keith finally looked up to notice he had a visitor and hollered his greeting over the mower's roar.

"WHY'S YOUR FACE SO DIRTY?"

A heat-seeking ant made its presence known under Travis' collar. "Shit!" As he dug into his shirt to kill the man-eating mite, Keith went back to mowing, oblivious to everything. Travis walked in front of the dust-spraying mower to gain Keith's undivided attention.

"Keith!" The dull man now paused his mowing, but not cutting off the engine. Travis shouted over it. "COULD YOU MAYBE TURN OFF THE M- "

"I CAN'T TURN OFF THE MOWER 'CAUSE IT WON'T START AGAIN!" Through his stinging tears, Travis saw two creepy round eyes looking out through the curtains of the Walters' kitchen window; in a flash the curtains were pulled shut tight.

"I THOUGHT WE TALKED ABOUT THIS!" Travis was holding out the mowed-up bits of burger wrapper. "MOWING THE TRASH!"

Keith squinted and stared; looking past Keith at the house, Travis saw the eyes reappear, this time in a bedroom window. "DO WHAT NOW?"

"THESE! MOWING THESE!" The curtains in a bedroom window now shut as well.

Two perfect areolas of sweat had soaked through the t-shirt covering the nipples of Keith's ponderous man-boobs. "YOU WERE MOWING THOSE?"

"NO!" His exasperation mounting, Travis saw a discarded lottery ticket laying in the path of Keith's mower and picked it up. "YOU! WHY ARE YOU MOWING THESE?"

"THAT LOTTERY TICKET IS NO GOOD. IT'S JUST TRASH!"

The eyes had returned to the kitchen window. Now there were four. Losing his shit, Travis picked up a styrofoam cup, then a ketchup-covered napkin. "THESE!

STOP MOWING OVER THESE!"

Keith pointed toward a muddy bog near his driveway. "THERE'S ONE OVER THERE TOO!"

"NO!" He flung the trash back to the ground. "IT'S ALL FLYING INTO MY YARD!"

As the four cryptic eyes kept watch through the curtains, Keith resumed his grinding rumble across the taiga. "GOTTA KEEP GOING, GOT NO MORE GAS IN MY CAN IF I RUN OUT!" Seeing two more towering fire ant mounds looming directly in Keith's path, Travis rinsed the ketchup off his hand in a stagnant puddle and trudged back home in defeat. Awaiting him on his driveway were a woman and a man dressed for Sunday church, each carrying Bibles and a stack of flyers. Travis knew them all too well; they were members of the Church of God of Prophecy up the road, and they had come for his soul. They came for his soul on a monthly basis, and rather than growing discouraged over the years at his soul's unavailability, the sidewalk evangelists seemed positively energized by Travis' increasingly rude resistance to their message. The woman wore a hat for which a flock of endangered birds had given their lives; the man's oversized suit was a pinstriped tent. They stood between Travis and his truck, having been directed by the Holy Spirit to do so since Travis needed to get into his truck to drive to work.

"Brother Travis!" The plumed woman smiled sweetly, tottering slightly on her wedge pumps.

"Well look who's here, it's... um..." Each time they visited they introduced themselves; each time Travis made sure to forget their names.

The woman chided him with a waving finger. "Now Brother Travis, you know I'm Sister Beulah, and this is Pastor Kenneth."

"Brother Travis."

Inwardly, Travis debated which route to his truck would be the least treacherous, around the giant ostrich or the circus big top. "No time this morning, sorry, off to work."

"The world always provides a reason to put off the word of God." After a mumbled "Amen" from the pastor, Sister Beulah continued. "We're still praying that we'll see your face at service on Sunday mornings."

Not unless you serve mimosas. "No need for me to be there. I can hear ya'll carryin' on every Sunday all the way from here."

Pastor Kenneth raised his Bible toward heaven. "Brother Travis, that's us makin' a joyful noise unto the Lord." Down the street, a less than joyful noise now rose above Ralph's yapping and Keith's mower; it was Sheila, flailing her way up the street, the howitzer of her voice aimed at the trio, quickening her pace while waving wildly.

"Oh praise Jesus, what devils are plaguin' poor Sister Sheila now?" It was Sheila's way, due to her deficiencies in breeding and restraint, to begin every "conversation" instantly, upon first sight of her interlocutor, no matter how many blocks away that person might be; every stimuli in her world required an instant response with no regard for anything other than the satisfaction of her impulse. Her most private and personal matters therefore were shouted up and down the street. Adding to the unpleasantness was the fact that sometime over the years her volume knob had broken off, so that Sheila's decibel level from 100 yards remained unchanged at 100 millimeters. She was turnt up to 11 as she stood before Travis and the believers.

"Oooh Pastah dat man he back ta fuck me up bless God!"

Sister Beulah began praying in tongues as the Pastor commenced to pastoring.

"Who is 'that man,' Sister Sheila? Your husband, is he out of jail?"

Sheila's arms flapped like wings. "Ah hell no he ain't nevah gettin' out I mean dat man who think he all dat think he can do as he like you see mah eye Pastah?" Now Sheila thrust her head Pastor-ward for him to inspect the damage, but the default state of her facial discoloration rendered any new trauma to her eye undetectable.

"Sister you don't need to be trespassin' with that man or any other man but your husband."

"I ain't trespassin' he trespassin' on *me* at *my* gott damm house!"

"Well, gotta get to work, sorry to- "

"Mistah Diggins I got call mah son I needs chawge up my phone agin yo poach."

At this Sister Beulah interrupted her heavenly mumbling. "Brother Travis charges your phone?"

"I've told you, I'm not 'brother' Tra- "

"Oh hell yeah Sister!" Sheila raised one hand heavenward while affectionately pulling on Travis' shirtsleeve with the other. "Dis man heah praise God he hep me evah day Sistah. Chawge mah phone gimmee ice light mah candle gimmee wood tah burn, he done fell out dah sky from heaven dis man heah did."

Pastor Kenneth considered Travis with admiration. "I had no idea Brother Travis that you were so full of Christian charity."

Travis retracted his arm from Sheila's clutches. "I'm not, Pastor. You don't have to be a Christian to be charitable. And I'm *not* charitable, either." *I'm a fool is what I am. And you don't have to be a Christian to be a fool, even though it really helps.*

Sister Beulah shook her head with a smile as Sheila *avec* adapter helped herself up onto Travis' porch. "I don't know Brother Travis. You may be tryin' to cover your light with a bushel basket, but the

Lord means to unearth it. We'll be seein' you this Sunday, praise Jesus."

"I really gotta be- "

Suddenly the growl of a throaty V8 on Crested Boulder closed in from the direction of Sheila's, and Travis recognized it at once as Dat Man's black muscle car.

Sheila recognized it as well and came flying down from the porch, hiding behind Travis and watching the street from behind his shoulder. "Oh gott dam its dat man Pastah pray fo me I don' stab 'is ass!"

"In the black car?"

"Yeah dat black car an' now it's OWN again'!"

"Oh *hell* no!" With a firm snatch, Travis grabbed the distraught woman by the arm and dragged her down the driveway, as Dat Man's car drew nearer.

Sister Beulah raised both hands in praise. "Oh Hallelujah, see how Brother Travis is walkin' right beside Sister Sheila to go face up to that violent man himself!"

Pastor Kenneth's eyes were closed in prayer. "Protect him Lord! Make Brother Travis like David before the giant Goliath!"

"Wrong!" Determined that the sequel "The Return Of Dat Man" would not be filmed on his property, Travis released Sheila's arm and left her derelict at the curb as he marched back up the driveway. "Take it on home this time Sheila. TAKE IT ON HOME!"

"Mistah Diggins!" In a desperate lunge, Sheila grabbed Travis' hand and spun him around. "You gotta hep me!" Now it was a stumble-bum square dance on the driveway as one dancer fought to escape while the other held on for dear life.

Meanwhile, Dat Man's car screeched to a stop at the end of the drive.

Sister Beulah fired the first shot. "You just drive on away, Man-In-The-Car, we here are the Lord's people!"

Pastor Kenneth bravely echoed the woman of God's bold sentiment from a position three steps behind her. "That's right, her husband is the head of her house!"

The passenger-side window now began to open, as did Sheila's mouth, her arms still entwined around Travis' leg. "NOW YOU FIND OUT WHAT HAPPEN FOOL, MISTAH DIGGINS HEAH GONNA WHUP YO' ASS WUSS'N MY SON DID!"

"SHEILA SHUT UP!!!" Having heard Sheila's challenge, Dat Man turned off the engine, and the ominous silence inspired the Pastor to an even deeper retreat while reigniting Sister Beulah's glossolalia. As Dat Man's car door opened, a piercing needle was jabbed straight through Travis' scrotum, followed instantly by a half dozen hot zaps to his adjacent Little Travis. "FUCK FUCK FUCKING FUCK!" A contingency of fire ants, at least a platoon in number, had completed their subterranean march to the embedded outpost of Travis' balls and were feasting on the spoils. Travis writhed on the cement in agony, hands plunged into his pants and pawing at his junk furiously.

"Wut got inta you Mistah Diggins?" Having released her grip on the frantic man, Sheila stood over him in wonder, as the believers stepped nearer to inspect.

"Damn, Mistah Diggins be DIGGIN!"

Sister Beulah's diagnosis was metaphysical. "Is something attacking his spirit Pastor?"

"I believe something's attackin' his nuts Sister."

"FUUUUUCK!" His situation desperate and finding no relief, Travis tore at his belt and buttons, finally pulling his jeans down to his ankles; now only impeded by his boxers, Travis redoubled his mad digging with his feet kicking the air.

"You go at it witch yo' fine ass Mistah Diggins! GIT SOME!!!"

As Sheila cheered on the tormented man and the believers shouted encouragements in the tongues of men and angels, Dat Man seemed to reconsider the prudence of having anything to do with the ensuing spectacle, for after shutting tight both car door and window, the engine fired up once again and, with a squeal of tires, the car lurched forward, spinning a 360° donut in the middle of the street and tearing off in the direction from whence it had come. By so doing the car cut off another driver whose bad luck it was to have happened along at that moment; it was Corey and Ralph, returning from the hardware store, and when Dat Man's fishtailing car made the full circle from the opposite lane into his own, Corey had no option but to careen onto the curb to avoid the collision, and when he did, the side of his truck (the passenger door, the one panel not damaged by Ralph's clawing) completely wiped out his very own mailbox, post and all. Speeding off down Crested Boulder, Dat Man made his getaway; all that could be heard now was the spluttering drone of Keith's mower. And as Corey angrily threw the new roll of screen at the mailbox's remains and the evangelists escorted Sheila away from ground zero, Travis was left pantsless on the pavement with a smoldering groin and a final mowed-up bit of lottery ticket fluttering down at his feet. Leaving the neighborhood to go in to work no longer sounded like such a bad idea.

Showing his three homes that afternoon was just the uneventful event Travis' mind needed to recover from his turbulent morning. But on the drive home he thought once again on what had been the scene, the most vivid image being the carnage at Corey's he'd gazed upon as he left the house for work. The kid was getting the full 1413 Welcome Wagon treatment, that was for sure. And while he was confident Corey would follow up with law enforcement and try to track down Dat Man, Travis knew the real perpetrator, the Manson behind The Family, would again get off blameless. None of it- no bad which ever happened on Crested Boulder- happened without Sheila. Yet again, it was her existence, the mere fact of her being alive, which had precipitated the breaking loose of all hell. But: was it Sheila who crashed into the mailbox? No. Was it Sheila who ruined the truck's paintjob and shredded Corey's screen? No. Did Sheila take the charger cord into her hands and tangle Travis' feet with it, did Sheila shoot the weapons which made him dive being shrubbery, did Sheila's hand wield the implements of disaster which wreaked so much havoc on the block? No as always. But her guilt, though associative in nature, remained inescapable. Yes, Keith's mower had played a cameo in this morning's horror show, but he was not the star by any means. Sheila was the fountainhead, the common denominator, indeed the commonest, and were the diseased Sheilanoma tumor scalpeled out, the symptoms of the disease would go away too. But as long as there were those with "christian charitability" giving her succor (and one not-so christian who was simply a sucker), Sheila would continue to endure and to metastasized. But it was nauseated Travis who felt like he'd been put through chemo.

His mind's next stop was the problem of the bones. Something had to be done, and he had pretty much decided what. Dat Man v2.0 helped make his decision; after a morning like today's, Travis didn't need more disruption and certainly no more drama. What he needed was peace of mind and orderliness, and an open grave provided neither. He would therefore go with his first idea of re-burying the bones and be done with it. Travis hadn't researched his legal responsibilities concerning the discovery of human remains on one's property, and was set on keeping his ignorance intact. All he knew was that it wasn't his fault the bones were there and therefore he was unwilling to suffer the physical and emotional disruption to his world which their revelation would trigger. It simply wouldn't be fair to him. And so he decided, as he turned onto his driveway, he would fill in the grave just as soon as he could change into his Mr. Diggins clothes. Peace and order would be restored within the hour.

When his eyes fell upon Keith's fallen oak tree protruding from what was left of Travis's crushed house, a strange peace came over him, the sort of peace which he imagined the soul experiences upon departing the body at death. There was a surreal and violent beauty about the sight, a beauty nearly equal to its horror, what with the enormous gnarled root ball fully disgorged from its centuries-old home, the giant trunk resting comfortably in 1418's second-floor, nestled in what used to be their bed; even the crushed fence and shattered windows created a strange longing in Travis that he could have been home to have seen the impact and enjoy the display of power. As his body stood outside his truck and his detached soul floated a few feet above, Travis felt himself gobsmacked by the absurdity- and had Paul Bunyan walked up Crested Boulder at that moment and plucked the entire tree up out of the collapsed roof, tucked it under his arm and marched away, Travis wouldn't have been surprised in the least. For in this moment Travis had been rendered unsurprisable. Keith's tree had fallen on his house.

Now Corey was standing beside him. "Fuck."

Travis looked down at the sympathetic man. "How the hell did it fall?"

Corey's brows raised in puzzlement. "Well you know. The storm."

People tend to use the phrase "I thought I was dreaming" when they relate how they weren't able to comprehend something told to them, but it's always hyperbole. They know full well they're not dreaming. But Travis thought he was dreaming. "No. There wasn't a storm."

"Yeah. We had a kick-ass storm here. For about twenty minutes."

"Twenty minutes." Now he risked a glance about. By god, it had rained after all; puddles and leafy twigs were everywhere. Travis had shown three homes in three areas of Cobb County. It hadn't rained at any of them. He had seen dark clouds on the horizons, but there were dark clouds on the horizon every afternoon in Georgia in the summer. Just twenty minutes. And obliteration.

"I got like six numbers of tree services for you. Was gonna call one myself but then I thought you probably already had somebody picked out in advance for... when it happened." Something wet began to happen at Travis' left- it was Ralph, licking his hand. The good dog was consoling him. There was no doubt about it.

It had taken this long for Travis to notice the flashing blue light. Two Smyrna cops (who must have been shocked to find themselves in the neighborhood for a reason not Sheila-based) were blocking a fallen power line. Another flash of blue caught Travis' eye- on his gouged-out roof, a blue tarp covered a portion of the impact crater. "Who did that?"

"I did. It was still raining so I got up there with a tarp and tried to cover what little I could. To keep down your water damage inside."

Travis was resuscitated enough to appreciate what it meant: Corey had taken a ladder and crawled up on Travis' house while it was still storming to do what he could. That was a neighbor. "Thanks man."

"Nothing you wouldn't have done." People were stopping on the sidewalk now, looking at the wreckage. Some were looking over at Corey's house as well, wondering how the tree could have also taken out a mailbox across the street. "Well I got some repairs of my own to do. Lemme know if you need anything Travis." Corey turned to go but then turned back. "I've got tarps in the basement if you need any."

"No thanks. I've got some." Once again, Corey and Ralph turned toward home. Then something flipped in Travis' stomach. "Corey-where did you get the other tarp?"

"Your wife gave it to me."

Left alone on his driveway, Travis felt the piece of paper in his hand on which Corey had written the tree service numbers. He would call them soon enough. But there was a larger elephant in the room to deal with, larger even than a fallen oak tree. There was an open grave in his yard. And forcing his body to turn so that his eyes would be required to look upon what they dreaded to see, Travis saw the pile of dirt, no longer in a pile but pushed off to the side. The tarp was gone. Alicia stood next to the grave and stared back at him, holding the barbecue tongs.

4

It was nearly dusk when the last branches of the fallen colossus were fed into the wood chipper and the tree removal crew was finishing up with nailing down the tarps over the gaping wound of 1418 Crested Boulder. As disaster recoveries go, Travis' and Alicia's was off to a pretty good start; the very first tree service Travis called was able to come out right away since there were no other calls from anywhere in the county about storm damage (the answering service had even asked Travis "how did it fall on a sunny day?"), and the insurance adjuster was scheduled to visit on Tuesday. During his initial walk-around inspection after calling the tree service, Travis had glanced toward Keith's house (easier to do with so much of the fence no longer blocking the view) and had seen, moving from window to window like a mobile haunting, the return of the eyes, three pairs of them now, faceless and unblinking, choosing to rubber-neck their neighbor's calamity rather than offer any gesture of condolence or assistance. As for the house itself, Travis was sanguine despite the carnage; this is what insurance was for, he told himself, and homes are hit with trees and get repaired all the time. There would be some weeks of inconvenience, but it would pass. As he picked up pieces of broken shutters and shingling, Travis was struck by a pleasant sort of surprise that his predominant emotion in the immediate aftermath of the event was relief more than anything else, for now that the worst had happened, the sleepless nights worrying and waiting in fear for the worst were a thing of the past. Keith's fucking tree could never hit his house again, ever. It was a lesson in life, how worrying over the possibility of trouble could be debilitating, but with the arrival of that trouble one was jump-started into taking action to remedy it, the very antithesis of debilitation. All that would be required ahead was a lot of work, and work was Travis' beauty pageant talent.

But were it not for a true miracle which accompanied the fall of the tree, his outlook on his situation might not have been so

Panglossian. Remarkably, the crown jewel of the property, his landscaping, had escaped with only a minimal hit. A crushed hydrangea, some gouges to the sod, one broken hummingbird feeder, a window box of flowers, but hardly anything more. The trajectory of the huge trunk had even missed the little dogwood which grew beneath its shade, at which he observed wryly that perhaps now the little tree would finally bloom. The loveliness of his home's environs had been left virtually intact, and with chaos reigning in and on the home itself, Travis' yard now stood out by contrast as even more of an oasis of beauty and order than before. The ensuing weeks would bring roofers and carpenters, plumbers and painters, scaffolding, trucks and dumpsters, but beyond the twisted wreckage, far from that madding crowd, Travis' outdoor world would be his safe harbor from the storm, his escape to sanity. And with that sanity depending more than ever before on preserving his bucolic paradise, it was all the more important that the troublesome grave not be reported to the authorities. For something more miraculous than even the giant tree not destroying Travis' wonderland had occurred, or rather, had not occurred- Alicia had not discovered the grave after all. She had indeed moved the soil and taken up the tarp for the roof but, in perfect keeping with her disinterested character, had not taken the next logical step of peeking under the plywood. Her only question had been why the barbecue tools were out by the koi pond, and his joke about a fish fry was just stupid enough for her to drop it. It appeared that his secret was still safe. He would carry through with his plan to rebury the bones and then focus single-mindedly on his home's repair. One crisis at a time was quite enough.

Alicia stood beside a garbage can in the kitchen which was catching the last few drips of rain water leaking through a crack in the ceiling. "I guess we're living downstairs for a while."

Travis was resetting the clocks that were blinking from the earlier power outage. "Won't be so bad. Gotta share one bathroom is all." Looking out the kitchen window, Travis' gaze (no longer blocked by the fence) fell upon the kitchen window of Keith's house next door, where two round eyes stared back. Travis shut the curtains. "I don't suppose our concerned next-door neighbors came over when it happened."

"Oh hell no." A drip of water plinked into the can. "Only one to come over was Corey. Of course Your Sheila was hanging about out on the sidewalk the whole time." When speaking to Travis, Alicia had come to refer to his nemesis as "Your Sheila," her sarcastic dig for the many times he'd been unable to deny her over the years. And over those years his ear detected that Alicia's digs were getting deeper. "Oh, and also that pain-in-the-ass pastor and the church lady who's always with him came by."

"They're gonna lift us up in prayer I suppose."

"Well, that..." Alicia was gingerly poking at the ceiling with a broom handle.

"...and they were asking about the chunk of plywood you've got out in the yard."

He felt his throat tighten but stayed in character. "Plywood? Plywood... oh, you mean that bit under the pile of dirt that the tarp was covering?"

Alicia continued prodding the ceiling with the broom handle. "Yeah. Seems that Your Sheila has a broke front door, and that she saw from the sidewalk that chunk of plywood and the church people were asking on her behalf if we'd be willing to give it to her to fix it. I told him I was pretty sure Her Mr. Diggins would let her have it, seeing's how you already give her firewood all winter."

Travis turned to face her with all the indifference he could fake. "Ah. But you told me you didn't... move the plywood or anything, was that right?"

"Well when I first went to get the tarp for Corey to put on the roof I had started to lift it but then I figured there'd be snakes under it. So I set it back down." He felt his heart resume beating. "I told them to come back and ask you about it when you were home. You believe that shit? Here we got a tree stickin' out of our house and they're worrying about Your Sheila's broke door, as if every damn thing of hers isn't already broke."

It now felt to him like a blinking neon arrow was pointing at the suddenly-popular plywood. The sun was setting so he'd have to hurry. "Well, gonna go out and make a final walk-around before it gets dark."

"And I'll drag down whatever I can salvage from upstairs. Haven't been up there yet. Gonna make me sick to look at it."

Snatching his shovel out of his shed, Travis trotted toward the front yard and headed for the plywood. It had been an even closer call than he realized. The thing had to be done right now, before dark. Knowing by the sight of her flashlight in one of the remaining upstairs windows that Alicia was otherwise occupied, Travis got down on his knees and slid the plywood away from the hole; and just as the opening of a music box triggers the playing of its sound, the opening of the hole triggered Sheila, whose rasping cackle now rattled at the end of his driveway.

"Why you fuckin' roun' witchyo' yawd wouk dis time o' day Mistah Diggins?"

"Oh you know me Sheila, work work work." Quickly pulling the plywood back over the hole, he decided in a moment what had to be done. "Alicia tells me you need this piece of plywood."

Sheila wobbled side-to-side, wringing her hands. "Dat Man Mistah Diggins, he done knock a ho' through mah doh so now ah needjor piece a wood t' covah it up ."

"No problem." With that, Sheila came charging toward him up the driveway; Travis scrambled to his feet with the plywood and met her halfway. "Here you go, here you go, okay, I gotta get back to work."

Sheila's motor idled in neutral. "No but ah got mah cup Mistah Diggins, I needs me some ice too you got some ice Mistah Diggins?"

Here then was a dilemma- to get rid of Sheila meant getting her the ice, but getting her the ice meant leaving her alone, which meant her snooping curiosity would surely impel her to look into the uncovered hole. Travis took the plywood back from her. “Fine. Lemme cover the hole and go get your ice.”

“Nah nah Mistah Diggins ah’ll watch yo’ ho’ fo’ you.”

“No!” Replacing the plywood over the hole, Travis ran a forty-yard dash to his freezer, got the ice, and ran back, to find Sheila just about to lift the plywood. “Stop I’ll get that here’s your ice I GOT THAT!”

She popped up in alarm. “Damn you edgy Mistah Diggins wha’s wrong witchoo?”

He laughed involuntarily as he handed her the cup of ice, stepping in between the troublesome woman and the covered grave. "Sheila, did you fail to notice that we got a giant hole in the roof of our house?"

Sheila nodded somberly. "Yeah, that hole gon' need fixin'. Just like mah front doh need fixin'."

Despite the pressing urgency of the problem directly behind him, Travis could not help but pause and marvel at Sheila's amazing comment. She had just declared matter-of-factedly that her broken front door was "just like" the Riggins' caved-in second floor, assessing each situation as equally serious. For Sheila, one problem was just like like any other, one hole was just like any other hole. Size didn’t matter. Problems and holes were simply matters of course, expected and unsurprising. Had the tree crashed through her house, he was convinced that Sheila would simply be asking him for a larger piece of plywood, her equilibrium otherwise untipped. Was it that dismissive attitude, so anathema to Travis’ approach to life, which enabled Sheila to live out her terrible existence with no apparent sensation of its terribleness?

He lifted up the plywood once again, using it to block Sheila’s view of the grave. “Okay. Here you go.”

Once again she was stalled. “Ah cain’t carry the cup an’ wood bose same time.”

“You’re killin’ me Sheila.” After a quick glance to make sure Alicia’s flashlight was still upstairs, Travis lifted the plywood over his head and headed to Sheila’s, running the entire way. Dropping it off in her yard, Travis ran back, passing Sheila who had only made it halfway across the street. "There you go Sheila, good luck with it."

"HOW THE HELL AM AH S'POSED TA WUT THE HELL AM AH S'POSED TA..." As the sound of her heartfelt gratitude trailed off behind him, Travis scampered up the driveway and stood again beside the grave. Catching his breath and taking up his shovel, he scooped up some dirt, but paused before dumping it in. Now that he was reburying the bones he realized he would not be seeing them ever again. Struck by the event's finality, Travis set down the shovel and knelt, not for anything so maudlin as to say his goodbyes, but just for a final look at his strange secret which would remain so from this moment forward. There it was, the child's torso, the little hands folded across the ribs in their grasping position, the tiny skull staring up emptily into nothing. The skull was unattached; and so, as a final gesture, Travis lifted it out of the grave and studied it, Alas poor Yorick-style, at which point a small flicker of emotion, despite his resolve, could not be suppressed. "Goodbye little kid." Returning the skull gently to its proper place, he resumed his solemn task, and in short order the hole was no longer. The light of sundown had nearly disappeared, and as Travis returned his shovel to his shed and went indoors for the night, a pair of round eyes which had watched it all from a window next door disappeared as well behind the closing curtains.

\\\

The next seventy-two hours were busy ones for the Riggins'. Sunday was devoted to the salvaging of the upstairs which Alicia began the night before, then reconfiguring the downstairs to accommodate the living which had previously taken place above it; things would be cramped but they'd get by. Travis was of course in charge of the home's exterior, cleaning up twigs and leaves and acorns, broken fence boards and the like; at one point he "thought he was dreaming" when he heard the annoying speakers from the Church of God of Prophecy up the block which, to his horror, were blasting a voice bombastic enough to not require electronic amplification, that of Pastor Kenneth (*crap, I remembered his name*) leading the congregation in a hundred-decibel prayer for none other than the Riggins family, that Christ Jesus the Heavenly Carpenter would rebuild their home good as new, at the same time praying that the Holy Spirit would simultaneously make restoration projects of Travis' and Alicia's lost souls. Confident that the Heavenly Carpenter wouldn't be showing up any time soon with a circular saw, Travis had scheduled a merely human contractor to come by on Tuesday and assess the damage with the insurance adjuster present as well. Pastor Kenneth's heavenly appeals for assistance were unnecessary, thanks anyway- everything was under control and being dealt with, and Travis understood more and more just how relatively minor a disaster they'd really suffered. The house was still livable despite its squishing, which meant they weren't required to relocate during the repairs. The cars hadn't been hit. No one had been hurt (it was with no small amount of self-reproach that, when he thought about the tree landing on their bed, it hadn't crossed his mind that Alicia could have been lying on it at the time). As big and dramatic as the initial event had dropped, its aftermath was playing out to be a fairly mundane ordeal, just another annoying something to deal with; and when he remembered how Sheila had dismissed the Riggins' crushed roof as no more traumatic than her kicked-in door, Travis couldn't help but admit that her assessment had proven truer than he'd first realized. He only hoped that Corey's attitude concerning his own difficulties was just as sanguine.

Corey indeed. No, Travis was pretty sure that his stress level at the moment was lower than that of his equally unlucky new neighbor. Taking a break from his clean-up on Sunday afternoon, he had paid him and Ralph a visit, and found Corey sinking a new post in his yard for the mailbox (the truck's paint and the screen repair now relegated to the back-burner, "gotta get this done before the mailman comes on Monday.") Corey had in fact filed the police report about the side-swiping incident involving Dat Man, but when he told the cop that he hadn't gotten the car's tag number and wasn't certain if it was a Charger or a Challenger, Corey had seen the lights go out in the officer's eyes and knew that nothing was going to be done. As Travis wished him luck with his punch-list and turned to head home, Corey had asked him if he'd been able to "get Sheila taken care of last night." Apparently, Corey had watched as Travis lugged the plywood across the street for her, and Travis was embarrassed, even ashamed, to admit to Corey that he'd been helping once again the very person who was the primary cause for Corey's calamities. Had the plywood incident taken place during wartime he would have been court-martialed for providing comfort to the enemy. But in that moment Travis had dealt with an emergency the only way he could, and to explain to Corey the reasons for his treasonous act was simply not an option. What's more, the morning after had proven to Travis that his treason was fully justified, for upon walking onto his yard and seeing smooth, clean earth instead of the eye-catching pile of dirt covering the tell-tale plywood, his anxiety about the bones had smoothed as well. His home might be a wreck, but order had been restored to the plot beside the pond. His new yard spinner would have its home after all.

On Tuesday afternoon the contractor and the insurance adjuster arrived within minutes of each other, and along with Travis and Alicia made the tour of the Riggins' injured property. The contractor confirmed that Corey's quick action with the tarp had helped significantly with limiting the water damage; the floor of the second floor was in good shape and so only minor repairs to the first floor ceiling underneath it would be necessary. The contractor and the adjuster were in agreement that the rebuilding/re-roofing of the exterior and the restoration of the interior could be finished in less than a month, and once the insurance check was cut (perhaps by the end of the week) the work could begin. It was the good news the Riggins' were hoping to hear.

Having said their goodbyes to the contractor, Travis and Alicia walked out into the yard with Steve the adjuster, who told them his inspection required one last step. "You guys are gonna love this thing." Opening the trunk of his car, Steve removed a device which resembled a small 4-bladed helicopter, approximately two feet across, with leg-like appendages bearing cameras extending from a center module which gave it the appearance of a robotic insect. "Ever see a drone in action?"

"Oh I know what it's for I know what it's for!" Alicia was always more bubbly around other people than just her husband. "You fly it over the house and it takes aerial photos to help you write up your claim paperwork! I saw it on HGTV!"

"Way more accurate and safer than me tryin' to crawl around on your roof." After explaining the basics of its functionality and making some adjustments, Steve sent the drone skyward, guiding it with the remote here and there over the damage zone. "Take a look at the monitor. See how rock-steady it holds its hover for filming? The resolution is fantastic." Clearly this was Steve's favorite part of his job.

Travis was more interested in getting back to his yardwork. "So how soon do you think we'll get a check?"

"No later than Tuesday okay let's fly it over to the root ball, get some shots over the hole to show the distance it fell." As Steve guided the drone across the property line into Walters Family airspace, the monitor showed the abrupt change in terrain from Travis' verdant fescue to Keith's pock-marked barrens. Now the uprooted tree stump came into view on the screen. "All righty, we're at Ground Zero."

"Less than zero." Even Alicia had to fist-bump Travis for that one.

"Wait, what?" Steve was staring at the monitor as he hovered the drone directly over the enormous hole. "What the hell is- sorry, what's that?"

"What's what?" All Travis could pick out on the monitor were chunks of clay and broken roots.

"Lemme zoom in." Using the remote, Steve zoomed in to make it appear that the drone was only a few feet from the ground. "There, that! No way..."

Alicia's hand flew up to her mouth. "Oh fuck!"

As the drone tightly held its position, all three stared at the screen, and saw that what had first appeared as clay and roots, when zoomed in closer, were instead unmistakably a human skull and ribcage, now exposed by the tree's uprooting. No one spoke. Finally Steve broke the silence. "Well this is a first for me."

"Ohmygod" said Alicia, unable to look away from the monitor. "It's just been under the tree, right there, and nobody knew." An absurd impulse made Travis glance quickly at his own plot of earth to make sure it hadn't been disturbed.

"I've heard about this at construction sites. Earth moving equipment discovering like old cemeteries and such."

Now Alicia stared wide-eyed at Steve. "So maybe there's more down there?"

"Maybe."

"Oh god!" A visible chill ran through her despite the summer heat. "So now what?"

"Well Mr. Riggins" Steve said, as he flew the drone back home and landed it on Travis' driveway, "we go inform your neighbor. Except that... well, I would think he'd have already seen it by now."

"You don't know my neighbor." Almost on cue, Travis saw a pair of eyes appear in a side window.

Alicia was shaking her head furiously. "Well you guys go. I'm not goin' near that." After shutting down the drone and returning it to the trunk of Steve's car, the two men made the walk across the breached fence line and into Keith's yard, where they paused a moment by the side of the uprooted stump. There were the bones, approximately two feet below the surface.

Steve took a photo with his phone. "Actually sortof cool isn't it?"

Why didn't I take a pic of my bones before I reburied them? "Let's tell Keith."

Travis noticed the eyes disappear from the window as he and Steve stepped up onto the shambled front porch. Travis knocked and waited. A minute later there was still no answer. Another series of raps; still no one came.

"Are they home?"

"Oh he's home." Once again Travis knocked, as hard as he thought he could do without loosening the decrepit door from its hinges. Still no one answered.

"Well we gotta let him know somehow."

"I guarantee you he's standing right on the other side of the door."

"Maybe we can leave him a note or- "

"Alright stand clear." Travis pressed his face up to the door and trumpeted. "YOU GOT HUMAN BONES IN YOUR HOLE!" The force of Travis' blast sent Steve reeling to the edge of the porch. Travis hollered again, even louder. "YOU GOT BONES IN YOUR HOLE! HUMAN BOOONES! IN YOUR HOOOLE!!! There that oughtta do it. Let's go." The two men retreated quickly to Travis' driveway, where Travis hunkered them down out of sight behind the bed of his truck. "Now watch." After a couple of minutes Keith's front door cracked open, and then Keith's head, eyes darting side to side, emerged like a wary prairie dog. Having determined the coast was clear, he scuttled across the debris field and up to the gaping maw, where, after observing its lifeless occupant, scurried back into his house and shut the door behind him.

Steve shook his head in wonderment. "That... was awesome."

"Well, now he knows at least."

"Right. Which means now he has to do the next thing."

"Which is...?"

"To report it to the police. Georgia law." Steve stood up from his hiding place. "Anyone who discovers human remains on his property must notify law enforcement." Having finished up his business, Steve shook Travis' hand and walked with him back to his car. "You'll be hearing from me soon. Don't worry, we'll getchoo guys all taken care of." As Steve drove away, Travis couldn't help but look back at the Keith window one more time, where he now saw all six eyes peering out toward the big news of the day.

A second skeleton. What the hell was going on? As he sat on the tailgate of his truck to process this new discovery, Travis kicked clay from his shoes which he'd picked up from Keith's burial site. A burial site- is that what it was? Travis' child had clearly been buried with some care, and the idea that the two skeletons were coincidental and had nothing to do with each other was absurd. Had both homes been built over an old cemetery then? Surely that was it. And if there were two, then weren't the chances high that there were more? Many more? It was clear there was about to be a lot of activity at the Walters residence, more than had ever been seen perhaps. Apparently, the only thing which could make Keith's yard come alive was finding a dead person in it.

Back inside, Travis walked into the kitchen where Alicia was pulling the curtains closed on the kitchen window which overlooked Keith's yard. "I ain't lookin' out at that. Damn Stephen King film happening right next door."

He recalled Alicia standing by the plywood with the barbecue tongs and thought of how close she'd come to starring in that film. "I don't see why it bothers you. It was layin' there all these years the same as it's layin' there now. How's it different now that you know about it? Not like it's gonna stand up and walk over here."

"Great, thanks for setting up my next nightmare."

"You're ridiculous dear." Heading upstairs to change into his Diggins clothes (though the upstairs was unlivable, his clothes closet had been spared any damage and was still accessible), Travis snapped on the clip-on work light which he had plugged in from downstairs, and his eyes took in the yawning expanse of roof which was roof no longer, covered over by the tarps. He could tell a light breeze was blowing outdoors, for the tarps fluttered and billowed up and down slightly, creating a gentle popping sound reminding him of tent camping when he was a boy. This then is all that's separating us from the elements, he considered, some fluttering plastic, a makeshift tent. It was a sense of exposure that Travis couldn't remember ever feeling before. No longer did even that most basic cliche which expressed the concept of home, "having a roof over your head," apply to 1418 Crested Boulder. Even Sheila could boast that her shithole was at least covered by a solid-ish roof. He'd often wondered at her vulnerable way of life, tried to imagine its many susceptibilities, its unprotectedness, compared to the insulated security of his own. But where was that security now? What good had the superior construction of Travis' home done him when Nature decided to render its condition sub-Sheilanesque? Before the tree, he couldn't consider his secure world and her precarious one any farther apart. But now, Travis' world was roofless. Yes, he enjoyed the advantage of being able to remedy his disaster with insurance, but enjoyed no greater ability than Sheila in preventing disaster from occurring. He'd made so many preparations toward defending his home from invasion, preparations the likes of which Sheila had not made in the least, yet it was his home which had been invaded. To be no less vulnerable than Sheila therefore to the forces of destruction was a common ground they shared, and it troubled him deeply to share it.

But there was an even commoner ground which Travis unhappily shared with a neighbor, ground which was by no means figurative. It was not just the destruction of the fence which had removed the barrier separating Travis' and Keith's properties and joined them as a continuous terrain, however different the two might appear on the surface. Travis' land held mysterious bones, and Keith's land did too. They had shared this unusual distinction always, or at least shared it before either had lived there, and while two unrelated homes sheltering two very unrelated families had been built above those bones, it was that unmarked and forgotten shared history under the surface which told the truth of the two properties' unification. As with Sheila, Travis chose to view Keith as dwelling on some other planet for all intents and purposes, separated from him by light years in every way but geographical. But taking such an attitude was not so easy to do now, what with the discovery of their hidden subterranean bond which was so very undeniable. And in Travis' imagination, it was as if the buried souls had grown tired of keeping their secret and now demanded to be known to the surface dwellers, for just when he had reburied the bones in his hole, Keith's bones had popped up in his, like some macabre Whack-A-Mole game, an uncontainable buildup of ghoulish pressure demanding release. Alicia imagined herself living next door to a horror story- well, she had no idea that she had only read the preface.

When Travis turned onto Crested Boulder after work Wednesday afternoon there were blue lights flashing ahead, somewhere on his block; five years of Sheila had conditioned him to wonder what her crew had gotten into this time. But then he realized- Keith must have reported his bones. Sure enough, two squad cars were parked on Keith's chunked-out driveway, as well as a white van marked "Coroner;" two officers stood around the disgorged root ball while the coroner was down in the hole. Corey and Ralph met Travis on his driveway.

"Travis, you know what's goin' on over there?"

"Homicide detectives. They found the body of Keith's dead lawn." Ralph was licking his hand hello. "Nah. Better actually- he's got bones in his hole. Human ones."

"Whoooah!" Even Ralph's ears picked up at the news.

"Yeah." The cop who'd been in the hole was out of it now and removing his gloves and booties. "Wonder what they're gonna do with 'em?"

Corey and Ralph were already walking toward the old fence line to find out. "Let's get a little closer." While the police talked among themselves, Keith noticed the two curious men and dog, and ran directly up to them onto Travis' property with his arms high and waving, shouting at the top of his lungs.

"HALT! DO NOT LET THAT DOG APPROACH THIS HOLE! WE HAVE EXPOSED HUMAN REMAINS! EXPOSED HUMAN REMAINS!"

"Yeah I know Keith, I was the person who- "

Keith continued shouting at point-blank range through his invisible megaphone. "TITLE 31 OF THE GEORGIA CODE CHAPTER 21 DEAD BODIES GENERAL PROVISIONS: ANY PERSON WHO

ACCIDENTALLY OR INADVERTENTLY DISCOVERS OR EXPOSES HUMAN REMAINS SHALL IMMEDIATELY NOTIFY THE LOCAL LAW ENFORCEMENT AGENCY WITH JURISDICTION IN THE AREA WHERE THE HUMAN REMAINS ARE LOCATED!" Ralph sat and whimpered, clearly disappointed to learn that Georgia law prohibited dog noses.

Nosy Corey however was undeterred. "Any idea whose they are?"

Keith pushed his palms at Corey like a traffic cop. "Sir! Sir! Law enforcement is determining that right now sir, in the meantime I'm gonna need you to maintain a perimeter sir, maintain a perimeter."

Travis stepped up into the officious man's personal space. "You wanna maybe maintain the perimeter of your own yard there Keith?"

Looking down at his own feet and discovering with amazement that he had in fact breached the demilitarized zone, Keith did not risk turning his back on the potential grave robbers, but instead performed three backward hops in retreat.

Travis whispered in a stage-whisper to Corey intentionally loud enough for Keith to overhear. "He seems pretty nervous about them bones. Come to think of it, I haven't seen that wife of his in months..."

Quick as a snap, Keith was back in Travis' face. "Hey funny smart guy. Just keep it up. Keep it up. 'Cause if you keep it up then I got somethin' I know about *you* I could tell those cops over there right now." Keith's eyes widened with delight at seeing Travis' eyebrows raise. "Ooh-HOO! The funny smart guy didn't know I knew did he? Well I do. So yeah. Keep it up. Juust keep it up."

"Uh, sir?" It was the coroner, beckoning to speak to Keith.

Keith's leering stare into Travis' eyes remained unbroken. "I'll be right there!" Risking one step still closer to his neighbor, Keith spit out a final whispered warning. "Like I said. Just keep it up." With a lingering smile, Keith turned and joined the officers and coroner beside the hole.

Corey looked up at the taller man. "What was all that?"

"Got me."

"Whut the gott dam hell evahbody lookin' at ovah theah?" It had come from behind them, and turning to face the sound was not required for determining its source.

Corey bristled. "Just keep that bitch away from me and my dog." A low growl from Ralph expressed a shared sentiment.

"Don't worry. I know how to send her off." Travis turned toward Sheila and addressed her gaily. "Oh it's nothing Sheila. Just a human skeleton down in that hole."

"Aw hail no! HAIL no!" Like a scalded rat, Sheila scurried off across the street toward her house, all the while invoking the names of Jesus and the Devil in equal bewailing measure.

Corey watched as Sheila scampered onto her yard, past the chunk of plywood (still unmoved from the spot where Travis had dropped it) and in through her broken door. By now the police and the coroner were heading back to their cars, leaving Keith to turn once again and provide his neighbors the courtesy of an update.

"Hey smart guy! Guess what? The coroner says it ain't a crime scene so they're contacting Natural Resources. Yeah! Bringin' back a arch'ologist. That's right! A real arch'ologist! These bones are special!" As the squad cars drove away, Keith trudged triumphantly toward his porch, where four eyes watched his approach from a bedroom window. Before heading into the house, Keith shouted a final imperative. "Just keep that dog away!" He slammed the door behind him as he disappeared inside.

"What a strange dude."

Travis led the threesome back toward his driveway. "Gotta get that fence fixed first thing."

Corey looked over the landscape. "Yeah, but if the fence is back up won't that get in the way of fixing your house?"

Not even a glance was required for Travis to realize it was true; if the fence were back up, the only other route for the scaffolding and what-not required by the construction crew to get over to the impact zone would be right through, over and atop Travis' articulated wonderland, resulting in an outcome most devastating. "Dammit you're right. Great. Guess I gotta 'maintain a perimeter' until my house gets fixed." Up the street, the Church of God of Prophecy's van was turning onto Sheila's driveway; Corey and Travis watched as Sister Beulah stepped up to the broken door and knocked, and then Sheila followed her into the van which pulled back out onto Crested Boulder and drove away. Meanwhile, Alicia jogged up the street from the opposite direction, finishing up her afternoon run.

Corey watched the church van drive away. "A funny time for church isn't it?"

On the grass, Travis' belly-rubbing hand was making Ralph's wildest dreams come true. "Any time's a funny time for church. Hey dear."

"Hey. Hey Corey." After a pejorative frown at Ralph, Alicia's eyes followed where Corey's had been aimed." So who you say's going to church?"

"Well either my next-door neighbor is going to church or church is going to her, not sure."

Alicia was sitting on the driveway now, stretching her hamstrings. "Oh, the church van! Nah, she ain't goin' to church. Didn't Travis tell you? It's part of their outreach ministry to the poor and less fortunate."

Corey closed his eyes. "Am I gonna wanna hear this?"

"No you won't and so I'll continue." Knowing what was coming, Travis focused his attentions on the happier topic of Ralph's abdomen. "Our neighborhood church people see Miss Sheila as an opportunity for them to practice doing their good works on. So they like drive her to the store and to the clinic and to her court dates and to some place with running water for her monthly hosing-down, they drive her all over Cobb County. Wherever she needs to go."

"Why, won't her boyfriend in the black car drive her?"

"Oh but wait Corey there's more. All the time they're also bringing her food. Sometimes clothes. Sometimes blankets in the winter and water in the summer. They even replaced the glass in her front window like three times when it got shot out."

"I wonder if they fix screen doors."

"After that third time I guess they figured it was God's will for that window to not have glass so they finally gave up. But yeah, the church is always lookin' after her, that your neighbor next door doesn't go without." Travis knew she was coming to her main point, and hid himself behind dog flesh. "And you know what's funniest about it Corey? My husband here bitches and moans all the time about how somebody like Sheila always gets bailed out by 'those gullible Christians' while people like you and him gotta take care of their own shit without help from God or nobody, but look who helps her more than anybody Corey. Who's her best friend of all Corey? It's Her Mister Diggins."

Corey stood by in obvious discomfort as Travis untangled himself from tongue and paws. "Sorry my love, were you saying something?"

Alicia was back up on her feet. "Every day, there's my husband in the kitchen, scoopin' a bucket of ice into that nasty-ass plastic cup of hers. What'd Your Sheila do for that ice? I just ran four miles. You should go in and bring me some ice."

"You want some ice? I'll go get you some ice."

"I don't want any ice."

"I will totally get you ice."

"I can get my own ice!" Alicia started up the driveway toward the house. "And wash your hands before coming in, they smell like dog. Bye Corey."

After saying his awkward goodbyes, Corey headed home; and while rinsing the Ralph off his hands under the garden hose, Travis ruminated on the matters at-hand, and was struck by one word which seemed to sum up his mood better than any other: unfair. Not the unfairness of the obvious inequities comprising the current situation- of course it was unfair that Keith's tree had hit Travis' house and not his own, and unfair as well that Corey and his property had already been repeat victims of Crested Boulder's special brand of domestic intranquility. Yes, he realized regretfully, it was unfair that the primary recipient of his many lovingkindnesses was his worst neighbor, the same one who contributed the most to the unhappiness of his best neighbor. He was also forced to admit that it was unfair for Alicia to be married to a husband who seemed more helpful to His Sheila than to his wife. No, it was not any of these readily apparent unfairnesses which bothered Travis at the moment, but a nagging irritation which he knew was small minded of him to harbor, but harbor it he did nonetheless. Here he was, the owner of a mystery skeleton, but forced to keep its grave a secret because of the destruction it would bring to his immaculate world were it revealed, and there was Keith, lazy, good-for-nothing Keith, with a skeleton of his own but on open display to the world and inviting further investigation, exposed on a property so unloved and uncared for that further digging could do only enhance its appearance! How unfair it was that Travis, because of his dedication to the cultivation and preservation of beauty, was tied and bound by it, forcing him to keep his treasure buried, while Keith, the ultimate slacker, aware of nothing and disregarding everything, was free to examine what might turn out to be a specimen of archaeological or even historical merit, and Travis could only stand in his yard and watch it all unfold. He knew it was petty jealousy on his part, to feel that this worthless trash-mowing clod owned him in such a way. But added now to that jealousy was a sneaking suspicion that the clod might own him in a deeper way altogether: when Keith had gotten in Travis' face and delivered the cryptic warning about "knowing something" about him, Travis was certain he had seen the sneering man's bloodshot eyes glance at the earth beside the koi pond. Did Keith somehow know what Travis had unearthed and reburied? To what else could his "something he knew" refer but that? And if Travis did not "maintain his perimeter," if he didn't kiss the ponderous ass of the fool next door, might he blab it to the police and thereby force the excavation which he dreaded so? For Travis, this was the unfairest cut of all, that Keith, having already dropped a tree on the Hiroshima of his house, now seemed poised to rain shovels down upon the Nagasaki of his nature park.

And as Travis opened the door and entered his tarp-covered impact crater, Keith's front door opened as well, where out stepped a teenage boy carrying a tarp of his own on orders from his indolent commander-in-chief, who marched sullenly out to the bedside of the Walters family's newest addition and, covering the hole over with the tarp, tucked the sleeping stranger in for the night.

5

The next several days saw Travis' prediction of an increase in activity next door come true. The state archaeologist was scheduled to arrive Monday morning; in the days preceding, Keith installed himself in his yard as a continual fixture, not so much as a guard to secure his treasure, but an ever-ready tour guide for any passer-by who might take up Keith's eager invitation to come take a gander at "my historical bones." Those who took the graveside tour were glimpsing two rare sights at once- the roadside attraction, yes, but also its owner, for few residents of the neighborhood could recall setting eyes on any member of the Walters clan, even after years of walking past the moribund home. But now the paranoid hermit of Crested Boulder had morphed into a hand-shaking, back-slapping man of the people, thanks to the celebrity status he was convinced his scenic overlook accorded him. Finally, Keith Walters had something special, and so, he was something special. Keith thought himself the only kid on the block who had a real-live dead skeleton. Only the kid next door knew better.

It was a slow day for real estate on Monday, which allowed Travis to stay home nearly the entire morning and thereby check out the subterranean proceedings. With Alicia at the gym, Travis was allowed to open the curtains of the kitchen window and observe the scene at the gravesite. As expected, a large white and green SUV from the Georgia Department of Natural Resources/Preservation Division was parked on Keith's gravel, and a man and a woman were working in the hole, with Keith (no doubt having called in sick from whatever job he had, Travis had never known what it was) leaning over their shoulders just above them. Travis noticed that Keith's attention was split between the activity in the hole and the traffic on the street, or rather the lack of it. For while the weekend had supplied a steady stream of walkers for Keith to strut before and pull in by the arm to view his side-show, the weekday morning found Crested Boulder nearly abandoned; Travis watched as the frustrated man gazed up and down the sidewalk, searching for signs of life, then trudge dejectedly back to the bones, only to rush back to the sidewalk and scan the unpeopled horizon once again, repeating his pitiful round trip over and over. Upon seeing Travis coming outdoors for a closer view, Keith puffed up like a peacock and scampered over to the fence line.

"The arch'ologists. That's them. From the state. They got the bones all cleaned off now. Looks even more awesome. Too bad it's in my yard and you can't see it. Which you can't."

Travis noticed the belligerent man gaze longingly toward the sidewalk once again. "Too bad nobody can see it."

Keith's eyes snapped back to his tormentor, then back to the street. "Yeah. Where is everybody?"

"At work I guess. Too bad. You got archaeologists and everything. And not one person to see how cool it is. Not even one."

A minute later, Travis was standing at the edge of the hole next to Keith, watching the archaeologists work. "Five minutes. That's all you get."

The woman archaeologist was making measurements while the man was carefully clearing away soil from each side of the skeleton. "I suppose it's too soon for you to be able to tell anything, right?"

"I didn't say you can talk to them!" With that, Keith grumbled under his breath and scuttled back to the sidewalk in search of better-behaved guests. The woman rolled her eyes, clearly for Travis' benefit. "Sorry. Yes, a little too soon."

"It doesn't look like there was ever a coffin, we're pretty sure of that much." The man was putting a soil sample in a plastic zip-lock bag. "Which in itself is unusual."

"Would that make them old?"

The woman reeled in her tape measure, clipping it to her belt. She was maybe thirty, Travis guessed, and her ball cap and rolled-up sleeves served to enhance rather than diminish her outdoorsy attractiveness. "Not necessarily, but one thing does date them a bit."

Crawling out of the hole, the woman stood on its edge and pointed down. "You see where the root ball was before it was pulled up, and how close the bones were to it? And how shallow?" Now Keith noticed the archaeologists speaking to Travis, and came running back toward the grave. "There's no way anyone buries a body right next to a big established oak tree. You'd strike roots right away when digging the grave."

"Exactly," said the man. "Which means the body must have been buried before the oak tree was here, and as it grew the root ball expanded toward those bones until they were pressing right up to them, and pushed them closer and closer toward the surface until they were only about two feet from the top. And from looking at the root ball that tree was nearly two hundred years old."

"What, what are you telling him, what?" Keith was sweating and panting hard, his cardio-pulmonary system straining under the unfamiliar shock of ambulation. "They're my bones so you need to tell me not him."

The woman made a point of speaking directly to Travis. "So depending on what we find from the soil samples, it's looking like this body was buried without a casket before that old tree was ever planted."

"Fucking A!" Keith was strutting like a corpulent rooster. "I got ancient bones. You heard her! I got ancient as all-hell bones! Where *is* everybody?!" Once again, Keith hurried out to the sidewalk as the DNR man shook his head in amusement and resumed brushing and digging at the soil.

"Well, I'll let you guys get back to it" Travis said, after taking a final look down at the main attraction. "Oh, one last thing. What do you think the chances are that there, might be, any others, you know, like a cemetery?"

The woman shook her head. "Not likely. If in fact there was no casket it would seem this was a one-off burial, perhaps done in a hurry for some unknown reason.

We wouldn't expect to see multiple burials without caskets. Unless they were- " she now assumed her best approximation of Keith-speak- *"ancient as all-hell bones."*

"Gotcha. Okay, thanks guys." Stepping away from the hole, Travis noticed across the street a plastic shopping bag with an empty 40-ounce which had been tossed onto Corey's yard. *Well, it's the least I can do* Travis thought, as he crossed Crested Boulder to pick it up. Keith was still out soliciting on the sidewalk, and Travis was glad for the opportunity to demonstrate for Keith the correct response when one encounters litter. In Corey's fenced-in back yard, Travis could see Ralph sleeping in front of his dog house, and when Ralph noticed the intruder he instinctively barked, but then ran happily up to the fence upon recognizing his master's friend and stood on his back paws against the gate where dog and man slobbered and scratched, respectively.

"Tha' dog bite yo' han don' say I din' tell you so." Sheila stood on the sidewalk in front of Corey's house, carrying a similar plastic shopping bag with a 40-ounce of her own. "Who ovah deh pokin' roun' in yo' neighbah's ho'?"

"Archaeologists from the Department of Natural Resources." Right away Travis understood that he had used far too many syllables and revised it accordingly. "State of Georgia, bone experts, here to learn about the skeleton."

Sheila pulled her arms in close as if feeling a chill. "All dey need know izz, dem bones is dead. Dey needs jus' bury dem back up an' leave go." Swaying slightly now from side to side, Sheila's voice shifted strangely into a hazy sing-song, her eyes gazing into an invisible cloud, no longer aware of Travis' presence. "Jus bury 'em. Leave em be. Don' poke aroun' at bones dead and gone. Jus' leave whass gone as dead 'n gone. Let it be an' nevah see no mo." Still floating in her other place, Sheila's hand produced the open bottle from the bag, from which she absent-mindedly took a slurp.

"Kinda early for that isn't it Sheila?"

"Sto' bin open since eight aclock." Shuffling away with a belch, Sheila shook her head as she headed toward her estate. "Hope you prayed up good Mistah Diggins, dey done dug up th' muhfuckin devil ovah deh." After ear-rubbing his goodbyes to Ralph, Travis returned home to dress for work. A few minutes later he was in his driveway, about to jump into his truck, when a hand waving for him at Keith's gravesite caught his eye. It was the lady archaeologist.

Travis was at the hole in an instant. "What is it?" She stood beside Keith, who was beaming like a new father. Down in the hole her colleague was brushing away soil.

"There." As Travis looked into the hole at the spot where she was pointing, the other archaeologist took a break from his dirt removal and, climbing up onto the edge of the hole with the others, began snapping photos with his phone. In a newly-cleared stretch of earth lying parallel to the skeleton was a second skeleton.

Keith's whisper in Travis' ear was a triumphant hiss. *"Ancient as all-hell bones!"*

\`\`

There had never been a day when Travis found leaving home for work so difficult. After finally tearing himself away from the unfolding drama at Keith's, Travis had nearly sprinted through his showings; if his clients had been interested in the properties he hadn't noticed, for his mind was only interested by the property next door. Hurrying back in the afternoon, he discovered that not only was the DNR truck still at Keith's, but a second DNR vehicle had joined them, bringing to four the number of investigators working the site. A total of three skeletons had been unearthed now, each one no more than two feet apart from the next and progressively deeper as they moved farther away from the oak, thereby confirming the archaeologists' theory that the bodies were planted before the tree and that over time the growing roots had pushed the bones toward the surface. Travis learned about the third skeleton directly from the lady archaeologist, who upon seeing him had taken a break from her work and given him the update. But this time, Keith had not resented or even noticed her attentions to his rival, for the proud new father of triplets had his audience now, what with the foot traffic returning to Crested Boulder in the late afternoon. His richly-embellished tour guide script was rehearsed and memorized by this point, and after each visitor had been regaled with the amazing account of how "ancient Walters Man had been discovered beneath the thousand-year oak tree," that person was asked to move along to allow the next curious party to enjoy his allotted three-to-five minutes of Keith's fame. His curiosity for the moment satisfied, Travis headed into the house, where Alicia was in the kitchen cooking. The kitchen window's curtains were once again pulled shut.

Travis kissed her as she lidded the rice. "So, been over to see the big show yet?"

Alicia's glare said it all. "Three. Three damn skeletons now."

"Oh, so you did stop by?"

"Oh hell no." Alicia reduced the flame to a simmer. "Went out to get the mail,

Mr. SuddenlyFriendly who never speaks now hollers 'Hey, we got three skeletons now, come look!' Come look, as if. Whole front yard's a mass grave."

Alicia turned to open a cabinet, and Travis took the opportunity to risk a furtive glance out the forbidden window. The archaeologists had stopped work and were talking among themselves near the hole. He shut the curtain just before Alicia returned to the stove. "The contractor called today- gonna start work next week."

But Alicia would not give up the ghost. "If I lived there I would move. I would. Knowing you got dead bodies under you, oh no no no." If only she knew the rest of the story, Travis thought to himself, that the unearthing of each new skeleton- and thus the expansion of the hole- was moving in the direction of the Riggins' property line.

"They're gonna take 'em away, right? Surely they're not gonna let 'em stay out there now."

Travis headed toward the stairs to change into his Mr. Diggins clothes. "Why not? Those bones are the best-behaved neighbors we have." Once changed, Travis returned to his front yard, where the archaeologists were calling it a day. Seeing Travis, the lady archaeologist waved and met him at the fence line.

"Well, we're at three and counting."

"And counting?" On the sidewalk in front of Corey's and across the street from Keith's, a new group of curious onlookers stared at the proceedings and chatted among themselves. "What does 'and counting' mean?"

The archaeologist lowered the bill of her cap to block the angle of the setting sun. "If we've found three, there's no reason we might not find four. Or more."

"So it was a cemetery then?"

"We still don't think so. It's too- "Catching herself, the woman shook her head and smiled. "I really shouldn't be conjecturizing at this point. We've got studying to do before we start sharing with the general public."

Travis matched her smile with a broader one. "But I'm not the general public. I'm specifically Travis. Travis Riggins."

The archaeologist laughed. "And I'm specifically Linda Myers." The two shook hands; meanwhile, Keith took notice of the dozen or so people watching from across the street who were clearly awaiting an invite which was strangely not forthcoming. "But really, it's too soon to give out any opinions. Professional protocol."

"You forget that your expanding dig is putting me in clear and present danger."

"How so?" With an arm sweep, Travis indicated his landscaping. "Oh. Oh, wow! I've been staring into that hole all day, I didn't even notice. Your place is fantastic."

"Thank you Linda."

"Is that a koi pond?" After an irritated glance at the group across the street, Keith waved to an unseen someone in his house with an impatient "Come on!" motion of his arm.

"It is indeed a koi pond."

"And the bare spot of dirt next to it, what do you have planned for that?"

Travis put a finger melodramatically to his lips. "Shhh. That's where *my* bones are buried!" As they laughed, Keith's front door opened, and his seldom-seen teenage son emerged with not one but two tarps.

"Linda, let's pick it up tomorrow!" With a final shake of Travis' hand and assurances of returning the next day, Linda rejoined her colleagues; as the DNR trucks drove off, Keith's son placed the tarps over the bones and trudged back up to the house.

Keith was following his son's path to the house when Travis noticed the assemblage of potential customers across the street. As Keith reached the door, one of the group shouted "Hey can we come see your bones?" But without a pause or an acknowledgement, Keith slipped quickly into his house, shutting the door behind him.

The man who had shouted now directed it toward Travis. "Yo Travis! What's the matter with your neighbor?"

A pair of eyes popped into Keith's kitchen window as Travis answered. "Y'all know what's the matter with him. Same thing as always."

"Yeah. We know what's the matter with him." Muttering to themselves, the group of black neighbors headed off down the sidewalk, revealing Sheila who'd been holding to the back and now commenced to chide them as she followed them away. "Don' know why y'all even wanted t' go see dem bones down in th' pit o' hell, thass lookin' inta th' devil's wookshop right theah." Just then Corey pulled into his driveway, and as he emerged from his truck, Travis watched him stride with annoyance onto his lawn and pick up the plastic bag with the empty 40oz which Sheila no longer carried.

By the end of Tuesday, the intrigue surrounding the discovery of "Walters Man" had taken yet another dramatic upswing. The body count for Linda and her fellows had grown to six, two adults, two smaller adults or teenagers, and two infants; the latest three, like the first three, were lain side-by-side, none showing evidence of having ever been casketed, and each spaced within two feet of the next, suggesting they'd all been buried at the same time (Travis' suggestion, not the archaeologists', who were sharing less and less as they uncovered more and more). Behind the scenes, Keith had been a busy boy as well, for when Travis returned home from work, the Channel 7 Action News van had joined the DNR trucks on the crowded driveway; no longer was Keith working the sidewalk like some cheap streetwalker out to solicit the occasional walk-by, for now he'd made it onto the airwaves, or was about to, and rather than beg visitors to come on to his property to see the skeletons, Keith was simply telling people to "watch me on the news tonight!", even shouting it into the windows of passing cars who slowed to check out the activity. Travis stood nearby as Linda was interviewed, close enough to learn she had a fancy title, the Deputy State Archaeologist, and to hear her repeat for the reporter that the skeletons were at least older than the tree but beyond that making no assumptions as to their specific age or provenance. Despite impressing the news team from the start that he shouldn't be allowed anywhere near a microphone, one eventually ended up being pointed at Keith, who'd waited for his moment in the sun so impatiently that another minute's delay would have meant peeing his pants; and as Travis watched his neighbor's performance, it was clear to him that little if any of the brief interview would be usable on-air, due to Keith's painfully Malapropian attempts to come off sounding more educated than he was ("the falling down of the tree exposed its bottom," "the bodies decayed away due to hundreds of rotten years," etc.) From the filming the cameraman did of the site it looked as though the Riggins' broken home would share top billing with the Walters', and sure enough, when Travis and Alicia sat for the eleven o'clock news to watch the segment, there was tarp-covered 1418 in all its damaged glory; in a twist of irony recalling Poe, one camera shot of the graves and the Riggins home in the background included the conspicuously barren square of tell-tale dirt covering Travis' secret grave, hiding in plain sight to be stared at by thousands of unaware viewers. One of those viewers was fully aware of one thing however.

"Travis! You seein' what I'm seein'?"

"How great my flagstone path looks from that angle?"

"The bones! They're getting closer to us!" Travis had in fact noticed it and had hoped his wife wouldn't. With each newly-unearthed skeleton, the edge of the open grave crept that much closer to the Riggins' property line, now no more than ten feet away. "What happens when they make it to us?"

"It's private property. I'm pretty sure they can't just come dig in our yard."

"Pretty sure?" Alicia was on her feet. "We need to *be* sure! Find out! God I can't watch." As she stomped off to the kitchen, Travis was left to ponder the situation. No, he was certain that the state was not allowed to dig without the property owner's permission; yes, he would make sure of it tomorrow. But his phone was in his lap- why wait? Typing "human remains Georgia private property," the top result was a link to the Georgia Council of Professional Archaeologists. Professional archaeologists in Georgia- well, that was Linda. Surely she would know the answer, so he'd ask her tomorrow. Setting his phone down and returning his attention to the news story, Travis considered how silly it was to be one click from the answer to Alicia's question but was waiting until the next day. To find out now would make his wife's night's sleep (and therefore his) that much sounder for the knowing. Why was he waiting to ask Linda? As he pondered his reticence, Alicia popped into the living room with her phone in hand.

"I found it out. They can't dig unless we let 'em. I'm going to bed."

"Okay. I'll be in soon." Back on the TV, the report had come to Linda's interview; as Travis studied her image on the screen, which included her ever-present ponytail and DNR ball cap, he pictured how she might look with the cap removed and her hair freed from the ponytail and falling loose about her shoulders. She was explaining the overall function of the DNR's Preservation Division and the role which archaeology plays when artifacts and remains are uncovered. Yes, Alicia's question would have been an easy one for her, it was obvious. And as he imagined the onscreen Linda's hand brushing back the flowing hair from her eyes, Travis decided that tomorrow he would go ahead and ask her Alicia's question anyway. Just to be sure.

\`\`\`

It's been observed by no less perspicacious a philosopher than Pete Townsend that all men are bored with other men's lives. For many, such a statement rings untrue; the human animal's voyeuristic appetite for news and gossip about their fellows is clearly bottomless, and *The Other People Show* never fails to entertain. But the truth in Townsend's remarks pivots on the word "lives." Yes, we are fascinated with the tribulations of others as long as we're detached observers watching from the audience and gobbling up the lurid details at a hands-off distance, but our interest wanes appreciably when closer involvement pulls us into the mundane concerns of their day-to-day lives and the prosaic truths of their existential predicaments. For when the show loses its entertainment value- when the performers are no longer engaging in YouTube-worthy hijinks but simply living their uncinematic, everyday lives- our interest turns back once more to the only show which always keeps us watching, despite the dreariness of so many of its episodes: the twenty-four hour circus which is ourselves.

That all men were bored with Keith Walters despite the high viewership of *The Keith Walters Show* was of no concern to Keith Walters. Keith Walters believed himself to be the star of that show, which was all that mattered. That it was the death found at the Walters home rather than Keith Walters' life which attracted his neighbors' interest did not diminish his enjoyment of his celebrity status a bit. The world was spinning around him, and his ego thrilled at the dizzying sensation. But Keith's big spin was nearing its end, or was at least about to slow considerably. All-day digging Wednesday and Thursday had produced several dozen new exploratory holes all about the yard but no new remains; Linda's DNR team dropped shovels in every direction, radiating out from the discovered six (an unearthing which took them all the way up to the Riggins/ Walters property line), and when they'd reached the consensus that the six skeletons amounted to all of them, the archaeologists were left with a host of questions. Why were there as many as six, yet no more? If the site had once been a cemetery a larger number would've been expected. What's more, they'd all been placed nearly elbow-to-elbow, with no individuality of treatment, suggesting that the burial had been a single event, and a hasty one at that. Had their deaths been the result of an individual event as well? What might explain the inglorious manner of their interment? And with the age of the remains almost certainly exceeding the one hundred-fifty year age of the oak tree, could any of these questions be answered after so much passage of time? After mulling over the situation with her colleagues in the Atlanta Office of the State Archaeologist, Linda and her fellows returned to the site on Friday to inform Keith of the state's desire to remove the remains for further study, citing the Preservation Division's opinion that the discovery held a very real potential for significant archaeological value. Upon hearing the words "significant" and "value," Keith was all in; convinced that the DNR's deeper study of "Walters Man" would only confirm that the remains were as ancient as he hoped and would make him not only famous but wealthy (assumptions fueled only by his own uninformed imagination), and with his worries (shared with the Preservation Division) mounting as to the site's security, Keith offered no resistance to the exhumations. And so, with an assist from the county coroner via the use of the Medical Examiner's van, Linda's team spent all of Friday carefully labelling, photographing and removing the remains, preparing them for transport to their temporary home in the State Archaeologist's Office in downtown Atlanta where, following painstaking study, a determination would be made as to their permanent resting place.

As the last of the bones were loaded into the van late Friday, Travis caught Linda's attention and waved her over. "Ready to take the show on the road are you?"

Linda removed her latex gloves and folded them into her back pocket. "Your poor neighbor. What's he gonna do for fun now?"

"Well he's run out of trees to drop on my house, so good question." Glancing down into the excavated area, Travis thought it more curious looking now that the bones were missing than when it had held them. "You were good on TV last night."

"Thanks. As you probably noticed I didn't say anything of much substance."

"Yes I did notice. If archaeology doesn't work out for you there's always politics. But you could make up for it now by passing a little substance my way."

Linda folded her arms and smiled. "Ah, wish I could. But I promise when we know some things for sure you'll be the first to know."

"But you suspect at least that they may be important, right?"

"You mean finally important, now that it's too late?"

"Umm... okay you got me there, what's that mean?"

"Sorry." Linda kicked mud off her boots. "Professional sarcasm. Or maybe irony. It's just the way we found those people, it didn't seem like they were very important when they were alive. Funny how we might come to think of them as important- "

"- now that it's too late. Got it."

"Leaving for the office!" It was Linda's partner archaeologist from the first day.

"Alright, I'll meet'cha there." Out of his peripheral vision, Travis saw a pair of eyes peering out from a window. But this time it was his own kitchen.

"Well before you go, can you at least give me some idea of a return date?"

"Oh we're nowhere near deciding if the bones would be returned, or if-"

"No, not the bones. When are *you* returning?"

The coroner's van pulled headed off down Crested Boulder as Linda grinned with embarrassment. "Sorry, I'm dense. Well... I'm pretty sure as we learn more about our important people we'll have more questions, and so I'll need to return to, you know, do more soil samples, dig around some more. So... soon."

"Good." Over at Keith's house the front door opened; out stepped Keith who held it open as his son followed, burdened by a large square of plywood which he half carried and half dragged. Attached to the plywood were two wooden legs, suggesting a sign of some sort. Once off the porch, the boy left the sign with Keith and trudged back up to the door, at which point Keith shouted for him to return, then handed the boy a hammer and pointed to a spot in his yard near the street. Silently protesting all the while, Keith's son dragged the sign down to the spot Keith had indicated. From the fence line, Travis and Linda watched the curious proceedings.

"What the hell is my neighbor up to now?"

As Keith supervised the installation, his son clumsily pounded the sign into the yard, then moped and grumbled his way back to the house. Keith meanwhile had stepped out onto the street to read his sign; smiling and nodding, he eagerly looked up and down Crested Boulder, as if offering an unvoiced invitation to one and all (well, not to *those* people of course) to come and see. With an exhalation of pride, Keith marched back up to his porch, and by the time he'd walked through his front door Travis had already hurried down to the street, followed by Linda.

"Oh what have we here!" It was in fact a sign which Keith's son had hammered into the earth, more than three feet square, painted beige-brown with handwritten lettering rendered in black marker and a black border drawn all around the sign's edges.

"Travis, it's a historical marker!"

It read as follows:

The Discovery of Ancient Walters Man

On the afternoon of June 27 2018 a sudden thunderstorm swept across the estate of Keith Walters, where is located the house you see behind this sign but where no longer is located a large tree. The fierce wind was blowing the enormous wood until it came, out of the ground, uprooting the now fallen old oak tree causing significant damage to an unrelated home which Keith Walters was not legally responsible for, and where the root ball was extracted there was discovered bones in Keith Walters hole, a skeleton of bones which was named Walters Man in honor of its discoverer who is the owner of the estate behind this sign. Fully complying with the law Mr. Walters reported his ancient find, and archeologists from the state of Georgia arrived and started to begin digging, and there, located on the spot at which the earth was removed and in its place a hole was installed, there they found five more skeletons also deceased. The skeletons were then pulled out of Keith's hole and taken to the State Archaologists Office where they are now being examined and where the archologists will begin dating them.

After taking photos of the amazing sign and assuring Travis that neither she nor her colleagues harbored romantic intentions for the bones, Linda said her goodbyes and drove off to rejoin the skeletons in the Atlanta office. When Travis walked into his kitchen, a beaming Alicia stood waiting with a glass of wine in each hand.

"Oh hell. What's today? Today is something. What did I forget?"

"It's No More Bones Day!" Taking his glass, Travis joined her in toasting the departure of Walters Man, at which point Alicia strode to the kitchen window and threw open the curtains. "I am FREE!"

Travis was already adding more content to his glass. "Wish it was that easy for me. I'm jealous."

"How do you mean?"

Travis dribbled a few more drops into Alicia's glass. "Just imagine: the van pulls up to Sheila's, they load *her* old bones in, and drive her away forever. Problem solved."

"Wouldn't work. Rats travel up to ten miles to find their way back to their nest."

"Mmm." From the same kitchen window, Travis saw two dog-walking neighbors who had stopped in front of Keith's "estate" and were reading his sign. "That's why I'm jealous. Dead bones can't find their way back."

Alicia nearly spit chardonnay on the counter. "Oh fuck. Wait. They can't can they? What if the DNR does their thing with 'em and then brings 'em back?"

Travis knew a lie was needed to sustain his wife's newly-restored sanity. "Not happening. The bones are definitely getting relocated. The archaeologist confirmed it."

"You mean the hot blonde?"

"Excuse me?"

"The one we saw on TV last night?"

If it was a trap, Travis was determined to sidestep it. "The archaeologist we saw on TV was the one who confirmed it."

"Thank god." As she baptized her relief with a swallow of wine, Alicia retraced her steps to the window. "I don't know and I don't care if those bones turn out to be famous people or cave-man people or what. All I know is that it's sooo good to look out this window and not see Oh goddamn now what?"

In a moment, Travis was beside her at the window. "Oh great..."

Across Crested Boulder, blue lights were flashing for the ninety-eighth time on the street directly in front of Sheila's house, where two Cobb County squad cars were parked. As the car doors opened, four crouching officers stepped out of the vehicles with weapons in hand and moved warily onto Sheila's property.

"I ain't ever seen the po-leece come visit Your Sheila with their guns drawn before. You might get your wish about her bones bein' carried out."

"I gotta get a better look."

"Don't go out there!"

Walking out to his porch, Travis watched the officers fan out across Sheila's yard and around the corners of the dark house, each with a revolver in readiness at his side. Then another blue light caught his eye, but on his own property- it was Sheila's phone, charging in its now familiar spot on the porch. And far down the street, coming from the Iffy Grocery nearly two blocks away, the phone's owner came into view and extended her greetings to Cobb County's finest. "WHY DA FUCK YOU AT MAH HOUSE WIN I'M NOT THEAH GIT OFF MAH GOTT DAMM YAHD!"

"Miss Sheila, we're lookin' for your son, where is he?"

As Miss Sheila hollered back with a string of unintelligible invectives, the charged-up phone at Travis' feet began to vibrate. Looking up from it, his eyes landed on a back corner of Sheila's backyard, and hiding behind a tree- in a spot which Travis could see from his porch's vantage point but which the officers could not- was Sheila's teenage son, the one who had administered Travis' baby bottle beating, his phone to his ear but not speaking. A surge of mischief rushed into Travis' hand as he picked up the phone and took the call without a second thought. "Boy wheah you at?" Not a bad Sheila impression, Travis assessed, but maybe not masculine enough.

"Tell them po-leece I ain' here!" From his hunkered-down hideout behind the tree, the boy couldn't see that his mother was not the one on the phone.

"HE AIN' HEAH!" Sheila screamed telepathically.

The young man whispered frantically into Travis' ear through the phone. *"Tell 'em you ain't seen me all day!"*

Sheila shouted at the cops right on cue. "AH AIN' SEE 'IM ALL WEEK!"

"Yeah all week, that's better!"

The officers paused their search and were approaching Sheila to question her. Behind the boy was tall unscalable fencing, which meant his only way out was through the front yard, right past the officers. To run, Travis realized, would mean the young man's certain capture, and toward this end Travis screamed his Sheila-best into the phone. "RUN boy! Run NOW!" Knowing his own mother would never steer him wrong, the boy pocketed his phone and, in a burst of energy only a teenage boy fleeing the law could muster, ran for all he was worth- but vertically, not horizontally, scaling the unscalable fence to Travis' slack jawed amazement and vaulting over it, a move which dropped him neatly into Corey's fenced-in back yard.

"Ah gotta go git mah phone!" In a moment Sheila was rambling across the street and heading straight for 1418, where Travis watched her approach in terror while still holding her phone to his ear. In a panic he replugged the phone into the charger, barely avoiding being busted by the agitated woman who came spluttering up the drive.

"Mistah Diggins I gotta call mah son tell him stay 'way poleece wanna take 'is ass back t' cownee jail."

"No kidding? Sorry to hear it." Presenting the very picture of innocence, Travis stepped aside to allow Sheila access to her phone. A hissing voice from the ether stopped her in her tracks.

"Where they at now? Where they at now?"

Sheila sniffed the air. "Whuzzat? Travis froze. In his hurry to replug the phone he had not ended the call from the boy, who was still speaking at her from Corey's yard. *"Where they at? I cain't stay here!"*

Without pausing to wonder at how her son could already be on the phone- thus offering a glimpse into her unexamined approach to the world, that being, to never consider why something was, but rather, like any wild animal, simply realizing *that* it was and react accordingly- Sheila took up the phone without skipping a beat and

…where Travis left off. "Well you need stay right wheaheveah …is cuz poleece swarmin' th' house like bugs."

As the officers talked amongst themselves at Sheila's front stoop, the young man whispered in urgent tones. *"Nah nah, you don' get it, I CAIN'T stay here, that muhfuckin' big-ass dog here, the one that- aw, SHIT he AWAKE!"*

The burglar alarm of Ralph's barking confirmed his discovery of the intruder. "Why dat mean-ass dog bahkin' ovuh deah?" The officers clearly wondered as well, and following the direction of the sound, all four crept into Sheila's back yard, once again drawing their weapons as they neared the spot by the fence where the young man had been hiding at the rear corner of the property. But at the front, the gate of Corey's fence rattled violently, and when it swung open, out flew Sheila's son, sprinting like his ass was on fire across Crested Boulder in the general direction of Travis' house. And Ralph was in hot pursuit. "Oh gott damm no dat dog comin' fo' me agin!" As Sheila hid behind Travis, the police officers ran to the front in the direction of the sound of the gate to find Ralph still barking like mad but having cut short his pursuit without crossing the street, the loyal sentry holding post while defending his territory. Upon seeing the officers, Ralph turned his barking toward the new threats, who instinctively responded by pointing their weapons at the dutiful hound. At the same moment, Corey's front door burst open, and out stepped a wild-eyed Corey, armed with a shotgun.

"Ralph! Corey! Noooo!" With arms waving, Travis ran toward the street just as Corey, who could only see his gate open and his dog barking at someone unseen just around his hedge, approached it with his shotgun aimed; what he did not realize was that those unseen someones who were about to find a shotgun pointed at them were gun-wielding Cobb County police officers. Meanwhile Sheila's son, having eluded detection thanks to the diversion of the dog, searched desperately for a new hiding place and found it; like a foot soldier diving into a foxhole, the boy slid down the earthen walls of the newly-vacated grave of Walters Man and took his refuge there.

"Boy git up outta that devil ho'!" As Sheila commanded her son over the phone to escape the jaws of Sheol, Travis made a final screaming attempt to prevent a massacre. "COREY STOP!" Momentarily distracted by the sound, Corey glanced toward Travis and lowered the barrel of his shotgun, just as the cops rounded the hedge.

"DROP THE WEAPON! DROP IT NOW!"

Seconds later, with Corey's shotgun safely retained by the police, a trembling Corey was frisked and questioned while Ralph licked the hand of his master's neighbor. Then the cops picked up the search for the fugitive once again; having been released by the officers, Corey staggered numbly to his front porch and sat in a daze as the four officers fanned out across the area. Hoping to secure Ralph in his gated yard, Travis realized it was a no-go, as one cop was still poking around the dog house; returning the dog to his owner was also not an option, with the latter clearly experiencing PTSD. "Corey, lemme take Ralph to my house until this is over and you're... okay." Corey only gazed up numbly; taking Ralph by the collar and seeing the shotgun on the ground, Travis added in a stage whisper, "It's damn lucky you were white!"

Sheila shouted into the phone, unaware that not only her son but the whole block could hear her perfectly well without it. "DEH'S DEMONS DOWN IN THA' HO' GET ON UP!" Upon seeing Travis approaching with friendly, tail-wagging Ralph, she was catapulted into a fresh new frenzy. "Oh no no no not the mufuckin' ass-eatin' dog!"

Travis held tight to Ralph's collar. "Where's your son, Sheila?" But before she could respond, Travis received his answer by glancing next door, where he saw two frightened eyes peering up over the rim of the skeletons' former home. Had his glance continued up to Keith's kitchen window, he'd have also observed six additional eyes staring out at the uninvited visitor.

Still on the phone, Sheila had come unglued. "You git a curse on you bein' down wheh dead bones lay, come on izz clear, now's yo' chance!" Emboldened with resolve, the boy leapt up bravely onto the rim of the grave; just then, two of the officers began to cross Crested Boulder toward Travis' side of the street.

"Oh heh dey come boy get back down in dat ho'!" In a blink the young man slid back in; as the two officers expanded their search, the number of eyes in Keith's window went down from six to four.

"Mistah Diggins you gotta hep mah son!"

Travis stared at the madwoman in disbelief. "Sheila, what I gotta do is tell the police where he is!"

She was rocking side-to-side with anxiety. "No you cain't do tha' Mistah Diggins my son only one p'tects me from Dat Man!"

"Sheila this is bullsh- "

"Please Mistah Diggins!"

"Sir!" It was one of the police officers, standing in Travis' driveway. "Did you see where he went? Did he come over here?"

Travis did not hesitate in his civic duty. "Yes he did." In a flash, Travis recounted to himself the young man's crimes. He had trespassed onto Corey's private property. He had opened Corey's gate and allowed his dog to escape. He had nearly caused both dog and owner to be shot. He had trespassed into his other neighbor's glory hole. He had been a major player in Corey's screen door/scratched truck disaster. Not to mention whatever crimes the boy had surely committed to warrant the police chase in the first place. Also, Travis saw his chance to reverse his troubling trend of aiding and abetting his best neighbor's nemesis and work *for* Corey rather than against him for a change. As he opened his mouth to speak, Travis' eye glimpsed a stream of greasy tears running down Sheila's face, at which point his hand pointed in the opposite direction of Keith's newly occupied grave. "He ran off down Crested Boulder, toward the church."

"Thanks!" The cop turned and jogged off down the street, away from the young man's hiding place.

A grateful Sheila expressed her thanks to Travis. "So how da fuck long he gotta stay down in that ho' now?"

"Look Sheila- "

"Hey, officer, hey!" Spinning to the sound of the shout, Travis saw Keith standing next to the grave and pointing into it. "He's right here!" At once all four policemen rushed up to the edge of the gaping pit, their weapons pointed at the crouching teenager. "Come up outta there. Now!"

As the unfortunate young man complied, the cop who Travis had misdirected approached him. "I thought you said he went that way, toward the church?"

Even Ralph looked at Travis to hear his answer. "It was like... I mean, the dog was barking, Sheila was screamin', the guns were pointin', all the runnin' around, I had a glass or two of wine..." But the cop had already joined one of his partners and was taking the boy back to a patrol car; Sheila followed close behind, snapping at their heels with every curse she could think of and inventing new ones.

Back at the hole, the remaining two officers crawled down into it and searched all around, to Keith's annoyance. "Why now do you two gotta go down in my hole?"

Still bent over and not looking up, one officer answered. "Just looking for evidence sir."

"Evidence my ass!"

At this, both officers straightened and peered soberly at their recalcitrant host. "Sir? You got a problem with us down here?"

A venomous response filled Keith's mouth- but in a rare moment of self-editing, he swallowed it back. "Fine. Whatever. Play in the dirt." Resuming their search, the officers determined the hole held nothing of evidentiary value and climbed out; and as the young man was placed in the back seat of a squad car, Keith turned and stomped back toward his house, muttering to himself but loudly. "Goddamn nigger cops crawlin' around in my historic site... fucking niggers!..."

Travis watched as the police cars drove off and Sheila disappeared into her house through the broken front door, then heard his own door open behind him. "Is she gone?" Alicia stepped warily onto the porch and watched the squad cars' departure. The bottle of chardonnay in her hand was mostly empty. "Why is Corey just sitting on his front- " Looking down the steps where Travis stood, she saw Ralph for the first time, the slobber dripping off his lolling tongue. Without a word, Alicia drank straight from the bottle and finished it off, then turned tipsily and went back inside.

After reuniting dog and owner (and convincing Corey to carry his returned shotgun back indoors), Travis headed home and, sitting on the stone bench next to the koi pond, recounted the events of this latest goat rodeo. It had been classic Sheila in every way; as always, Sheila herself had not scaled any fences nor opened any gates nor pointed any weapons, but had there been no Sheila trouble magnet, trouble would not have been pulled in. Her mere presence had once again been enough to disrupt and endanger everyone within the expansive range of her bellering voice. But a more troubling component to the mayhem, more so due to its increasing frequency, was Travis' tragi-comic role in it, a part he did not audition for but, when offered, seemed to play all-too willingly. Travis never asked Sheila to charge her phone on his porch, yet he allowed it; Travis never wanted her son to drop into Corey's yard and thus pull Ralph and Corey into the pandemonium, but his foolhardy stunt with her phone which Travis had played as a childish impulse had backfired/quite nearly frontfired, and no one could be blamed for that but himself. Travis never wanted the kid to hide in the stupid hole, but when he could have ended the bedlam he'd instead given in to Sheila's wet face and lied, actually lied to the cop, intentionally misleading him. All for a woman he wished dead! As he watched the large orange fish swim lazily in his pond, Travis considered the care it required to keep them healthy and happy, and for the first time marveled at just how many ways it could go wrong if he were not at all times vigilant. The proper balance between the number of fish per gallons of water, the constant maintenance of the filter, the recirculating fountain which added aeration, proper food levels carefully adjusted with the changing seasons, adjusting the pH levels, preventing ice in the winter from getting too thick, watching for sudden weight losses or odd swimming patterns which might indicate health issues... there was little doubt in his mind that human parents did not care, in the hands-on, practical, providing-for-care sense of the word, for their children any more than Travis cared for his koi. For stupid goldfish. Yet for Sheila, a human being, no less human than himself, with thoughts and emotions and desires and perhaps even dreams, he wished her to wake up dead. If one of his fish were to list slightly to its side he would fly into a panic; if Sheila leaned a little he'd wish for the wind to push her straight over. What's more absurd, Travis wondered, that he valued stinky fish more than stinky Sheila, or that, despite valuing her in no way, he could not bring himself to deny her? His answer wasn't long in forthcoming. The fish were absolutely deserving of the greater value, for the fish provided nothing but good; they were undemanding, unharmful and esthetically pleasing (and so good at controlling algae), while Sheila's "superior" humanity only served to make her the inferior creature. No, Travis' absurdity was the way he always looked out for her; it was weakness on his part, nothing else, and he must resolve to do better at treating her worse. Enough had finally become enough. Across the street, Corey's front door opened and out he came, a little shaky, and sat on his steps looking out at the last bits of the sunset, apparently deep in thought. He had left Ralph indoors. But his shotgun lay across his lap.

6

Monday was a highly anticipated day at the Riggins home, for that was the day its healing was to begin. The workers were due at eight AM; Alicia had already left for the gym, but Travis had managed to work out his schedule be at home when they arrived (when the contractor assured him no one needed to be home for them to begin the external repairs, Travis assured the contractor that he'd be there to watch their every move). Along with fixing the damage to the frame, a new roof would be installed, which meant of course the existing roof and the damaged boards underneath would first be completely removed. It was this phase of the operation which Travis feared the most, assuming that such a dismantling operation would create collateral damage to his landscaping. But when he realized that the dumpster for all the debris could be parked on his driveway instead of his yard he was greatly relieved. Right on time the truck with the dumpster arrived, followed by the crew; after parking the dumpster temporarily out on Crested Boulder, the foreman approached Travis to discuss strategy.

"Mornin'. Ready for us to get started?"

"Been ready. Moved my truck across the street so that you can park the dumpster on the driveway." Ralph had happily given the Riggins permission to share Corey's driveway for the duration of the project. Corey was okay with it too.

"Oh we can't park the dumpster on your driveway."

An alarm sounded in the pit of Travis' stomach. "Oh. Why not?"

The crew unloaded ladders and scaffolding frames, laying them on Travis' lawn. "The garage is the problem. The driveway comes up to the garage which is detached from the house. That would put the dumpster too far away to throw the shingles and what-not all the way, from the house. 'Cause the garage is detached." It was true. Parking the dumpster on the driveway would put it too far from the house. How had he not noticed that from the first?

Travis asked a question, afraid of the answer. "So what's your plan then?"

"Gotta put the dumpster in the yard on the end of the house where it's damaged, no choice. So to get it there we either gotta take it through your yard or around at the side through your neighbors' yard. Take your pick. "

As Travis knocked on Keith's door, the foreman looked about at the dozens of gaping wounds which dotted the Walters' front yard. "What happened out here?"

"There's a historical marker which explains it." The door cracked open, and one suspicious eye peered out at the uninvited guests.

"What?"

"Keith. Good morning. We're starting the repairs today and we need a favor."

Darting looks in every direction as if wary of an ambush, Keith opened the door just a little wider while remaining inside. "I gotta leave for work."

Who would employ you for anything? "You won't need to lift a finger. My roofing crew just needs to bring the dumpster through a little part of your yard in order to park it by my house."

"What's wrong with your yard?"

"Nothing yet. Which is how I'm trying to keep it."

Keith's narrow eyes narrowed even more. "So what do you want from me?"

"Um, your permission? To bring the dumpster through?"

A perverse smile now crawled across Keith's mouth as he stepped out onto the porch. "Uh-huh. Sooo! Looks like you need a favor from me."

"Yeah, that's what I- "

"Well, well!" Rocking back and forth on his heels, Keith stared down his nose at the two taller men. "Gotta come through my property or it'll mess up your little, whatever you call it with the vines on it there."

"My trellis. Also my arbor swing and my espaliered apple tree and my- "

"I don't know..." Walking to the edge of his stoop, Keith stared out at the area in question. "You'd have to go right by my arch'ologic site. Might leave tire tracks."

The foreman looked again at the open hole. "Archaeologic?"

"There's a historical marker."

Travis could feel his pulse quickening. "Keith, it was your tree that hit my house, the least you could do is- "

"I'm not legally responsible!" A moment later his perverse smile returned; skulking up to Travis until they were nose-to-snout, Keith lowered his voice into a rasping whisper. "Kinda funny that now you need a favor from the guy who knows somethin' about you that you don't want nobody else to know. Isn't it?"

"Keith why do you have to- "

"Mr. Everything Perfect, thinks he's better than everybody, not so much on top of the world now that you got a hole in your roof and I got something you want."

Travis' need to get the dumpster close to his house was exceeded only by his need to get far away from Keith. "What will it take for you to let us through your yard?"

Later that evening, as the roofers called it a day and the first lights appeared in windows up and down Crested Boulder, Travis threw the final shovelfuls of dirt into the last of the archaeologists' holes in Keith's yard which he'd agreed to refill to purchase the dumpster's safe passage. All that remained empty was the one hole not to be filled, the famous large one which had held the skeletons; the three hours of shoveling had kicked his ass, as much as any work he'd ever done in his own yard, and as he inspected the fresh crop of blisters on his hands which his self-imposed sentence of hard labor had earned him, a cold wet something startled the back of his neck. "Ah! Ralphie!"

On the sidewalk was Corey, holding his end of Ralph's retractable leash. "Why are you helping Walters?"

Travis pointed at the dumpster. "In order to get that filled I agreed to get these filled." As he scratched Ralph's head, Travis looked up to see that Corey's belt had been newly accessorized by a holstered 45-caliber Beretta. "Giving Ralph his walk?"

Corey nodded as Travis did his best to look anywhere but at the enormous handgun. "Could you do me a favor while I walk him?"

"Sure. What?"

Corey stared darkly toward Sheila's unlit house. "Watch my house?"

"Um, sure."

"Thanks. Come on Ralph." Leading the good dog away, Corey and companion headed off down the sidewalk. This was a new wrinkle, and an unsettling one. If Corey left for the weekend and asked Travis to be watchful it would have been one thing, but Corey's and Ralph's walks were never more than ten-minute affairs, hardly an absence which called for security monitoring. Clearly, the effects from Friday evening's unhappy hour had not waned for Corey in the seventy-two hours subsequent; rather, it appeared that those effects, like the progressively debilitating symptoms of an insidious disease, had worsened as a result of having become embedded, serving to deteriorate the host organism's psyche and corrode its peace of mind. A sidearm, just to walk around the block? As he patted down the dirt on the last of the former holes, Travis glanced just as Corey had toward the shadows of 1413. No, it was not an emotional holdover from the Cobb County firing squad which explained Corey's condition; though shocking in the moment, such moments pass, and the soreness of its shock is soothed by the balm of having escaped alive. What hadn't passed, what had strapped a handgun to his hip for brief strolls and prompted requests for vigilant surveillance during short walks, was Greater Sheila; not merely Sheila the single person but the whole feral network of miscreants which were born from and thus comprised it, the Greater Sheila which was that festering wound of an unlit house and every one and every thing which radiated out from that wound like streaks of infection. Corey had painfully learned how Greater Sheila could not be prepared for nor predicted and could strike from any direction at any time. And as if Travis' thoughts had been the cue for which it was waiting, the Church of God of Prophecy's van now pulled into Sheila's driveway, and from the van Sheila's lumpish form emerged and disappeared into the darkness of her dingy cave.

Having paid in full his hole-filling debt to Keith, Travis untwisted his legs into standing and returned the shovel to his storage shed; upon walking wearily back to his front yard, he was angered by the sight of the church van, no longer parked at Sheila's but on his own driveway. He was mad at himself mostly; on any other evening by that time, Travis would have shut his gates for the night and so prevented any 4-wheeled intrusions, but having been derailed from his normal routine by his work detail next door it had slipped his mind and so the church van, like an opportunistic mosquito searching for a hole in the tent through which it might enter and feed upon the sleeping campers, had darted in through the breach of his defenses and was poised to suck the blood out of the next few minutes of his life. A moment later, Pastor Kenneth and Sister Beulah stood before him, wielding as always the heavenly weapons of Bibles and salvation tracts and smiling their insipid smiles.

"Brother Travis!" As always, the good sister took the lead. "So we noticed today that the work's been started on your house. God is good!"

"God is good!" echoed Pastor Kenneth, rocking on his heels.

"Yes, well, so is our insurance." Travis' left shoulder now joined his aching knees and his blistered hands in a chorus of complaints. "Guys, you know how I'm usually not in the mood for this? Well tonight I'm really not in the m- "

"Remember what the word of God tells us brother Travis." Closing her eyes, Sister Beulah read the scripture from the page of her memory. "'He has torn us to pieces but He will heal us; He has injured us but He will bind up our wounds.'"

Not to be undone, the pastor dredged up the Book of Psalms. "'Lord, though you have made me see troubles, many and bitter, you will restore my life again; from the depths of the earth you will again raise me up.'"

"Well I've had my fill today of 'the depths of the earth' so-"

"We know you must be weary from your labors Brother Travis and so we won't keep you but a moment." At this, Sister B. produced a printed flyer of some sort. "At church we take up collections from time to time, above and beyond Sunday offering."

"For special causes and special needs" said Pastor Kenneth.

Travis mechanically took the flyer. "Now if I've never come to your church after all your invites what makes you think I'll give you money?"

The armor of Sister Beulah's spirituality insulated her from offense. "But it's not *for* us, Brother Travis. The cause we're collecting for is one you're very familiar with." Knowing his driveway would remain occupied as long as he put off looking at the flyer, he reluctantly did so, and regretted it instantly. At the top of the page was a photo, no, a mugshot, of Sheila.

"You know as well as anyone," Pastor Kenneth intoned compassionately, "the troubles that poor woman has endured."

Sister Beulah raised a hand heavenward. "Amen Pastor. The situation is critical."

Travis nodded as he read. "Critical, right." Looking again at the grainy photo, he could almost hear it asking for fo' dollahs. And now she had someone doing her asking for her. "And I thought I had good insurance. Hers is clearly the no-fault variety."

"Now now Brother Travis" scolded Sister Beulah. "This is not a joking matter."

"Who the f- who's joking?" Down the street, Greater Sheila's namesake lit her first candle of the evening as unlit shapes trudged toward it on the sidewalk as if drawn by the candle's dim light. "You really expect me to contribute to this 'cause'? This- " he shook the flyer disdainfully, "- *this* is the most worthy recipient that the Church of Whatever You Call Yourselves can find to offer your helping hand?"

An unusually honest and unaffected tone replaced the Pastor's normally pedantic pulpit-speak. "There are things about Sister Sheila's life, about her past, which you're not aware of, Brother Travis." Sister Beulah affirmed with an "Amen" which was mouthed too softly to be heard.

Travis held firm. "Well you know what? I don't care about her past. Because it's not her past I have to deal with. It's her present which is the every day pain in my ass."

"Yes but there's more to know about her life that-"

"No!" He crumpled the flyer and held it in a fist. "I don't want to know more about her. I want to know *less*! I want to think about her *less*! I want my mind to be *totally* Sheila-less. But of course that's not possible." Down the block, the flotilla of sidewalk drifters finally made landfall at 1413, where the lady of the house greeted them with a salvo of feral barkings. Travis pointed toward the unruly residence. "That! *That* is why I can't think about her less!" Unfolding the crumpled flyer, he made a show of flattening and smoothing it, then handed the wrinkled litter back to Sister Beulah. "So if you feel the need to do good works to earn your way into some sort of heaven, or to keep yourselves out of hell, then good luck with that. I'm going indoors."

Sister B. shook her head as he turned to leave. "Finding fault with those who show Christian charity to the less fortunate. That's a sad state of mind Brother Travis."

The comprehensive soreness of Travis' body did not prevent him from spinning back like a top. "Christian charity to the less fortunate? That's what you're about? Well then, I got somebody for you who's had some bad fortune lately, but you're probably not aware of him because he doesn't holler and shout all day and night up and down the street complainin' about it. Name's Corey. Lives right there." Sister Beulah and the pastor turned to where he was pointing. "You know, that house there with the new mailbox thanks to Sheila and the new screen door thanks to Sheila and the scratched truck thanks to Sheila. So by all means, go help out poor Sheila. Gotta keep her goin' strong so she can continue sending blessings Corey's way."

"His name is Corey?" But Travis had already marched up his driveway, successful in his efforts to not hear the good sister. Removing his boots at the back door, he was not so successful in not hearing Sheila, still cussing out creation, and when he looked up the block he could see her single candle hop and twitch with the frenzy of a seizure, a fierceness befitting the sound. He saw in it a metaphor of Sheila's very existence; how the candle flame, clinging tenuously to life at the tip of the wick, just one breeze away from extinguishment, was nevertheless surviving somehow the violent ups and downs to which it was being subjected. Travis found the flaw in his metaphor- the candle flame was the innocent and unwilling victim of its vicissitudes, but Sheila was to blame for hers. Okay, fine, she'd been dealt a bad hand, he got that, but it was clear she'd also done all she could to mishandle the cards. Remembering that Corey and Ralph would soon be back from their walk, Travis glanced across th street, and noticed two shadows passing through Corey's gate. The hair on his neck bristled like a guard dog; taking a few steps down his driveway for a better look, he was able to make out who the intruders were. It was none other than Sister Beulah and the pastor, who after giving up on Travis had walked up Corey's porch steps and were already knocking on his front door. Clearly, they'd taken Travis' sarcastic rant about Corey's "need" at face value, and had accordingly redirected their soul-saving/charity- dispensing energies to the opposite side of the street. And now here was Corey and Ralph walking in through his gate, unaware that it was by no means safe to do so; and as Corey blundered into the holy ambush, Travis could only watch as the intrepid evangelists turned from his front door to greet the surprised man on his return, and watched as well as Corey returned their friendly greeting with the unholstering of his handgun, the cocking click of the Beretta's hammer piercing through the white noise of crickets, Sheilas and tree frogs.

``````````````````````````````````````````````````````

"Here, let me have a shot."

Travis pulled the chain on the ceiling fan just as his client had. Nothing.

"Wait. There's a wall switch."

Walking across the empty room, the client (one Steve, an unremarkable middle-aged guy shopping for a condo to move his elderly mom into) flipped a wall switch, and the ceiling fan began to spin. "Magic."

"Embarrassing. They teach us that in realtor school on the first day."

As he had done in all the previous rooms, Steve walked out of it as quickly as he had entered. Travis followed dutifully. "So five, ten years. Probably what we're talkin."

It was all Travis could do to keep up, both with Steve's train of thought and pace of walking. "Ten years. For...?"

"How long we'd have it. Then I'll be selling." They were in the kitchen. If Steve was taking it in and inspecting it Travis couldn't tell. "So whaddya think?"

"I think your mom would appreciate this kitchen. Nothing hard to reach, the appliances are all- "

"No. I mean how much you think the value's gonna appreciate in five years? Sorry, my phone, hang on..."

Travis stood by in the empty kitchen as Steve walked off to take a call. His pocket vibrated; it was his own phone, a text from Alicia, sending him photos of bathroom tiles for the upstairs bathroom under repair. The workers were two weeks into the job now, two weeks since that first day with the roofers, that day which ended with Corey nearly adding two names to history's long list of martyred evangelists. It was Greater Sheila, ironically enough, which had saved Sister Beulah's and the good pastor's lives that night, when at that moment a car had turned up the decrepit property's gravel drive and its headlights illuminated the terrified visitors sufficiently for Corey to
``````````````````````````````````````````````````````

uncock his 45 and allow them to escape in the church van (but not without leaving Sheila's fundraising flyer wedged in his screen door). The event had left Corey edgier than ever (compelling him to install both a lock on the front gate and a motion light above the porch the very next day), to the point that even daytime chores out in his yard, even rolling his garbage can to the curb, were performed now with the accompaniment of his holstered sidearm. That Travis had caused the near miss with tragedy remained his shameful secret; once again, it had been his one good neighbor, the only neighbor of his who deserved nothing but good, to whom he'd delivered evil, and he watched guiltily as Corey's defenses, both external and internal, grew before his eyes on a daily basis. Adding to Travis' guilt was the positive upturn in his own affairs of late, specifically, the repair project, which was proceeding right on schedule- the roofers had finished the exterior a week earlier, the dumpster was gone, and quick progress was taking place on the interior. And coinciding with those repairs was another, wholly unexpected and quite welcomed by him- that of Alicia's attitude to their home in general. Rather than defeating or discouraging her, the tree-smashing seemed to have cracked open a new something within herself, and to give Alicia, who'd always been uninvolved in Travis' outdoor projects, a project indoors which she could call her very own. With the obliteration of the bedroom and bath so utterly comprehensive, Alicia had a clean slate to work from, for her to restore any way she liked (a carte blanche which, once he saw the light of interest come into his wife's eye, he was quick to proffer). Carpet, paint, window treatments, bathroom fixtures, floor tile and lighting, all were opportunities for the newly emerging Alicia to give, for the first time in the five years of living in the house, a damn (although the bed was undamaged Alicia announced that it "just wouldn't agree" with her new ideas and that a new bedroom suite was required, and while his blessing for the new furniture had been immediate, it was unnecessary, for her roll would not be slowed regardless). Their home seemed, for the first time, to be her home as well, and Travis watched in silent awe as a brighter and happier Alicia threw herself into the project and smiled more frequently than he'd ever remembered. And while some of her pricey improvements exceeded the insurance settlement and were therefore out-of-pocket, he was more than glad to write the check, if paying for a few upgrades was what it took to come out of the renovation with an upgraded wife.

"Sorry." Steve was back from his phone call. "Where were we?"

"I don't know if you noticed, all the storage. Does your mom- "

But Steve had already walked up to the living room's front window and was surveying the street below. "Lot of construction, sidewalks tore up, they're widening the street, right?"

Travis joined him at the window. "Yeah. Probably gonna be a little difficult to navigate for about a year. Think it'll be a problem for your mom?"

The question flew past Steve's ear and right out the window. "But after that year, the whole block will be upgraded as a result, Value's gonna go up, right?"

"That's usually the pattern."

"Nice. I can live with a few holes in the ground for the payoff in five/ten years. Lemme do some figuring." Strolling off again, Steve returned to crunching numbers on his phone, leaving Travis once again to look out on the street. He had not missed Steve's pronoun, *I* can live with holes in the ground instead of my *mom*. It was clear to Travis that her living or dying with the holes was of no consequence to him, provided the woman would be accommodating enough to survive the five but not so inconsiderate as to outlive the ten of Steve's five-to-ten year plan; upon her death (a day which her loving son had no doubt guesstimated and figured into his calculations) the property would be his, free and clear of the collateral parent, and he would sell it off and glean the property's appreciated value. Value. There it was again. How randomly and absurdly it could be accorded to things and people, and how haphazardly it could be weaponized. Steve saw the gaping holes in the sidewalk as one day being filled by profit and saw little else; Travis, on the other hand, was reminded by those holes of the gaping one next door to his home, and the bones which had been in the archaeologists' possession these two weeks (as always, whenever he thought of Keith's bones, he thought of his own, reburied now in his yard. What damage to Alicia's new-found happiness might be done if she were to learn the subterranean truth? Travis had hoped that by reburying the skeleton the event would be buried too, but every now and then Keith would find an opportunity to deliver some cryptic remark as to "knowing something," accompanied with leering smiles aimed toward the bare spot, making Travis feel his secret was just as exposed as ever. But did Keith *really* know about them?) As for his neighbor's bones, no report had come from the DNR as of yet; meanwhile Keith, boiling with anticipation of when he might receive confirmation of his treasure's ancientness (and thus their *value*, that word again) and unable to restrain his giddiness during the interminable wait, had channeled his energy into developing the site to better accommodate what was sure to be a steady stream of visitors once the proof of Walters Man's prehistoric provenance was officially announced. This most indolent of men, who before the discovery of the remains had been allergic to exertion, had somehow summoned the industry of an army ant and added quite the array of classy features, such as: a plywood-on-cinder block walkway from street to hole bridging over the yard's quaking mud bogs; a wood fence encircling the hole's edge (prompted by Sheila's son's impromptu visit while fleeing the cops) to which were tacked not one but three signs declaring the prolix message, "WARNING VIEWING AREA WARNING MAINTAIN PERIMETER WARNING"; and his proudest construct, a dubiously-nailed wooden step unit *with a hand rail* leading to the bottom of the hole (plunging to a depth of nearly three full feet), down which Tour Director Keith was prepared to lead the curious (for a fee of course) to see up close the very bed of clay out of which the bones had been sticking and would, not soon enough for Keith, be sticking out of once again. That it was unlikely the bones would be returned to The Lost Tomb Of Ancient Walters Man (as another of his signs proudly described the hole) was a buzz-kill which Keith's giddy mind was not about to entertain.

But Keith's brain was not the only giddy one on his block. No thought of the mystery bones being studied for their archaeological merit could pass Travis' mind without also thinking of the Deputy State Archaeologist. Two weeks of not seeing her had made it all too clear that Travis had himself a full-fledged crush on his hands. It was innocent enough, he reasoned, since he knew nothing would ever come of it, for the simple reason that he had no intention of making anything come of it. Linda was just one of those infrequent delights who flutter into one's life now and then, who linger and land just long enough to deposit a little wing dust and then fly away forever, as of course she would once the mystery of the bones was solved. But despite the innocence of his crush, it was nevertheless guilt-producing, for its timing coincided with the thaw of his previously chilly wife, who as previously mentioned had warmed appreciably thanks to travertine tile and a claw-foot tub; warmed, not just in a public way, but also in a most private one, creating for Travis the irony of being Linda-distracted at the very time when he had more reason than ever to remain Alicia-attracted. But irony and guilt notwithstanding, today found Travis just as eager as Keith for the delivery of the DNR report. But when that report might be deliv-

"I'll take it." Steve stood before Travis with his arms crossed, rocking back on his heels with decisive confidence.

"Well alrighty, let's make an offer." Steve was already striding toward the door; it was clear that Travis' usual "Did you want to take one last look at anything" would not be needed today. "I think your mom will be very happy here."

Steve stopped at the door and looked back at Travis as if it were the first time he had ever heard him speak. "Why's that?"

It was the strangest question Travis had ever been asked. "Well... I believe there's another elderly lady living next door to her actually."

Steve turned once again to leave; his final remark, tossed over his shoulder as he opened the door, sounded like another Travis had heard somewhere before. "Doesn't matter. It's only five years. She can live next door to anybody for five years."

Late that afternoon, when Travis' truck drove through his gates under the clouds of an imminent rain shower (no longer a threat since the only tree which a storm might bring down on his house had already made that dream come true), a curious sight awaited him next door at the absented home of Ancient Walters Man. Out in the front yard were Keith and his son; in their hands were shovels, and they were digging like hell. Too curious to mind the perimeter warning mind the perimeter, Travis walked up.

"Hey Keith. Whatcha up to?"

"What's it look like I'm up to?" Travis glanced over at his sullen teenage coworker, who as he shoveled shook his head in silent protest.

"You're digging holes." Keith mumbled something unintelligible; Travis made closer inspection, and saw that the holes they were digging had been preceded by nearly a dozen others. Travis saw something else as well.

"You're... you're re-digging all the holes that you had me fill in two weeks ago."

The boy was no longer shaking his head; now he was nodding "yes." Why are you re-digging all the holes, Keith?"

Leaning painfully on his shovel handle and wiping his forehead, Keith explained to his neighbor though refusing to look at him. "The holes you filled in were the holes the arch'ologists dug looking for more Walters Man and if they're filled in people won't know all the history of the excavation which was not just one hole but this whole yard of yard holes." Miles away, low thunder grumbled; Keith grimaced at the clouds and resumed his shoveling, and the boy resumed the shaking of his head.

"Ah. Too bad you didn't think of that two weeks ago."

Once again Keith paused his digging, but this time, stared back at Travis, the now-familiar leering smile curling his lipless mouth. *Oh fuck. Here it comes.* "Yeah. But maybe you shouldn't worry so much about my digging. Probably oughtta worry about your own instead." And after darting a glance toward the bare spot next to Travis' koi pond, Keith was digging once again, mumbling softly under his breath and chuckling in the weird private amusement which always followed Keith's remark and look. This time there was no mistaking it. "My digging." So Keith did know. And if Travis provoked him with one poke too many, everyone else would know too.

Leaving the disconcerting sphinx to his ridiculous labors, Travis passed Sheila's ubiquitous phone charging on his porch and went inside, where Alicia, as was her recently-adapted habit, awaited him with a kiss and a glass of wine. "So what did you think of those shower tiles I sent you? Fantastic, right?"

"Life changing." Sipping his wine, Travis checked for the mail on the kitchen island, which was covered by flip books of carpet squares, paint tiles and window moldings. "Have you gone running yet? Looks like it might- "

But Alicia was already dragging him upstairs. "No I wanted to wait 'til you got home so you could see what we did today." His wine sloshing as he was pulled along, Travis came to the top step; by now the workers had restored the electricity and finished the sheetrock and were working on the final details of the two rooms. "Look in the bathroom look in the bathroom!" Obeying, Travis entered the bathroom, where the new wife-arousing clawfoot tub sat on the new vagina-moistening travertine tiles.

"Okay... what?"

Alicia skipped into the bathroom and hopped in place. "You're not looking! You're not looking!"

"Well help me! Help me!" With the ecstatic glee of a little girl, Alicia pointed one finger straight up; and there, not noticed at first by Travis because of the darkness of the clouds, was a skylight- a lovely and in every way kick-ass skylight, vented and vaulted through the attic and following the angle of the roofline to provide a dramatic angle against the southern sky. "Holy crap! This thing is- it's so- "

"Fabulous?"

"I was thinking out-of-pocket." The little girl's glee fell into a big-girl pout. Travis repented instantly. "A joke! Yes! It's fabulous! How did you keep it a secret from me?"

Alicia embraced him and, with her chin on his shoulder, stared at the skylight as she explained. "Well, you're always neck-deep in yard work outside which used to piss me off *but it doesn't now* because I get it, I get how it feels from doing all this work on the inside (the psycho-emotional metaphor did not escape him), and so with you so busy pulling weeds and fixing birdhouses I've been plotting and sneaking up here and please tell me you're not mad tell me you're not mad."

Travis held her at arm's length and smiled. "My dear, if you're not concerned about fly-over drones with cameras at bath time then neither am I."

"Yay!" Alicia kissed him; a break in the clouds passed over, and the sunlight streamed in through the new upgrade. It was poetic actually, her big surprise; Alicia's skylight served as a memorial to that day when the tree had crashed through the bathroom roof and the sky rushed in like an invader, but now, with the glass installed in the exact location of that forced entry, the sky was no longer invading but invited, on their terms. Gazing at the skylight in the new bathroom, his wine glass in one hand and her hand in the other, Travis couldn't help but feel like they were newlyweds who had just moved into their first home, thrilled at the prospect of beginning their lives together. "Okay. Going running now wanna beat the rain." And just like that she was scampering down the steps; and after a quick inspection of the upstairs to check for any other out-of-pocket expressions of Alicia's domestic bliss which might have missed his notice, her husband followed.

Travis put his wine glass in the sink as Alicia tied her shoes. "Didja notice what our neighbors are up to out front?"

Alicia stood and side-stretched. "Now that the fence is fixed I'm glad to say I don't see shit over there anymore." But although the fence had returned the Walters' front yard could still be seen;

through the kitchen window Travis saw Keith's kid throw the shovel down in exasperation and march back into the house, with his father screaming curses while pursuing him indoors. "Okay. I'm hittin' the road." After another kiss, Alicia went out the front, but then came back in right away. "She's back."

"Ugh." Travis cringed. Of all the times when Sheila was not wanted, Travis was least in the mood for engagement the first thing after coming home from work. "She's probably just come to get her phone, or to get ice, or... ugh..."

"Not Your Sheila. Your archaeologist. Next door." Travis looked out the front- there was the DNR van, and there was Linda, picking her way between the newly-redug gopher holes on her way toward Keith's house and carrying a manilla folder. A happy feather flipped in Travis' stomach, which he was glad Alicia couldn't see into. "She better not be bringing back the you-know-whats to put back into the you-know-where."

"She's bringing news of some kind, that's for sure. "Travis looked again, and noticed Linda taking in Keith's most recent "developments," but also glancing now and then toward Travis' house between steps.

"You need to go find out from her." Alicia stood facing him, hands on her hips. "Go over there and talk to her. Now."

Travis swallowed back the flipping feather the best he could. "Oh, but I wouldn't want to butt in and- "

"Go talk to that woman!"

"If you say so dear." Having laid down the law, Alicia spun away and jogged down the driveway, disappearing down the street. Needing no further encouragement to obey his loving wife's mandate, Travis also jogged, but around the fence and onto Keith's property. "Hey stranger!"

Linda spun to face him as if hoping to hear him. "Travis!" She was prettier than he'd remembered her, and he wondered if he'd only imagined the increased brightness to her face which appeared at the precise moment of sighting him. She glanced about and shook her head. "Correct me if I'm wrong, but does it look like all these holes we dug a few weeks ago were just dug today?"

Travis pointed to one of the abandoned shovels. "I could answer, but I wouldn't deprive you of hearing it from the shoveler himself."

"I'm surprised there's no sign explaining it."

"Leave her alone, she's *my* arch'ologist!" Keith was on his porch in his stocking feet. "She's here to talk to me not you!" Behind him, two pairs of eyes in two different windows in two different rooms peeked out through the curtains.

Travis stepped closer to Linda as a very light sprinkle began to fall. He whispered to her urgently. "So quick! Tell me what you found out!"

The sagging wood of Keith's porch complained as he hopped up and down in anger. "Hey! You need to talk to me not him! Get off my yard Riggins!"

It was Linda's turn to stage-whisper. "He's right Travis, I should really tell the property owner first."

"Is there news?" It was Corey, out front on the sidewalk, his Beretta holstered as always. Across the street, Ralph watched the proceedings from behind his fence.

"We're about to, but the mean archaeologist says we gotta wait our turn." Travis turned back to face Linda. "Okay mean archaeologist. Make it quick. You've kept me waiting two weeks after all."

Travis noted a curious something flicker behind Linda's eyes. "Okay. I'll hurry."

"Goddammitt!!!"

"Coming Mr. Walters!"

As Linda made her stumbling way to the Walters' front door, Travis joined Corey on the sidewalk. "All she'll tell me so far is that it's big news."

Corey was staring not at Keith's property but back at his own. "Big huh?"

"Yeah. Whatever that means." Linda was on the porch now with Keith, opening the manilla folder and removing a document. "All Keith's dreams are about to come true, right here and now."

Corey looked back toward Keith's for a moment, but then back again toward his own house. His words were distracted. "Yeah wonder how he's gonna keep it secure."

The light sprinkle had graduated to a light gentle rain. "Looks like Alicia didn't beat the weather after all. She hates to run in the rain."

Corey's attention now turned to a group of young black men walking up the sidewalk, three or four houses away from reaching Corey's. "No. Rain's good. Less crime committed when it rains. Well documented."

Up on the porch, Linda was reading to Keith from her papers; then Travis was surprised to see Keith suddenly snatched the sheets from her hand and throw them on the ground. Linda was backing up in alarm; all that could be heard was the enraged man spluttering in outrage at the imperiled archaeologist.

Travis strained to hear. "What the hell did she say to him?"

"Yeah I wonder." But Corey's head had been turned once again back to his side of Crested Boulder, his eyebrows raised by the appearance of two new teenage boys walking up the sidewalk in the general direction of Corey's house but from the opposite direction of the three young men who continued to draw near as well. Back at the Walters', Keith was up in her face; Travis watched with real concern for her safety as Linda found her chance to duck under his waving arms, scoop up the papers and scurry down off the porch, then run across the muddy mine field and out to the sidewalk. Meanwhile, Keith paced angrily back and forth across his porch, still roaring incoherencies but mingling them frequently with all-too-clear *FUCKs* and *GODDAMNs*.

"Jesus Christ Linda what was all that?"

Panting, Linda reclaimed her composure. "What a maniac! A maniac!"

"I thought you said you had big news for him."

"I did! I do!" The swivel on Corey's head twisted yet again, this time to watch a car pull into Sheila's driveway next door to his own house and deposit four teenage boys into Sheila's yard. Having perceived this new threat, Corey quickly glanced up and down Crested Boulder; the first two groups were growing nearer and converging, which Ralph had noticed as well, the big dog now pacing expectantly back and forth along the length of his fence and wagging his tail.

"So it's my turn now, tell me!"

"Okay. The bones. Well, we've determined that the- "

"Corey?" Without so much as a see-you-later, Corey had taken off double-time across the street and back to his house, where, after a quick check of all three groups, he hurried in through his gate and locked it behind him.

"Is he okay?" Meanwhile the rain had intensified, as had Keith's rage, his berserk anger spinning him back and forth across his front stoop like an infuriated dervish.

"Let's get out of the rain. Can we sit in your van?"

"Yeah, come on!" As Travis and Linda jogged toward the refuge of the DNR van's front seat, Corey, with Ralph sitting dutifully by his side in the pouring rain, took up watch in the chair on his front stoop, from where he saw all three groups of young men enter Sheila's house without incident. But his drawn Beretta sat in his lap just in case.

Linda shook muddy raindrops from her report papers. "Okay. The bones."

"Right." Outside the van, the rain fell steadily; through the driver's side window, Travis could see Alicia splashing back home from her run, then slosh up the porch steps and disappear into the Riggins' front door. "So how ancient is Ancient Walters Man?"

Linda smiled mischievously. "Well now I can tell you the part which we knew all along. Not ancient at all. Not like your neighbor hoped."

"You knew that all along?"

"Oh yeah. That much we did know. You have to remember this is Georgia. With our humid climate, and the corrosive clay, unprotected human remains don't survive underground more than like three hundred years."

A twinge of disappointment rose up in Travis, not for his neighbor's bones but for his own. "Okay. So no Walters Man."

"But- " Linda eagerly held up one of her report pages. "- they're *still* old. Almost two hundred years old." Through the windshield, Travis saw Alicia step back out to the porch for something, then head back in. "And when our paleopathologist studied the remains, she found in all six of them bone lesions, a condition called osteomyelitis. Which- " Now Linda stared up at him, her eyes saucers. "- which is attributable to the advanced stages of smallpox." Her voice was quiet, even somber. "They all died of smallpox Travis."

The van was silent, save for the murmur of rain against the windshield. Unnoticed by the two, Keith had left his porch and was now stomping about in the rain in his stocking feet, still shouting obscenities while kicking up mud with each step.

"Wow. Do we know who they were?"

Linda nodded. "We've dated the bones as I've said to be in the two-hundred-year range. So we went back into the land records, and it wasn't difficult to learn who lived in this area then, because there was one family who owned pretty much all the land you can see from here, a seven-hundred acre plantation for more than sixty years up until just after the war, a family named Holman."

"So the skeletons are Holmans."

"No. Well- no. Not really." Thunder had joined in with the rain by now, with flashes of lightning; Keith was thundering in livid accompaniment, a redneck Lear raving at the tempest, now marching with dread purpose in the direction of the street. "There are plenty of Holman family records available, birth and death records, fires, illnesses, all that. We learned that in 1832 there was a smallpox outbreak in north Georgia. And at the Holman plantation that year, the smallpox took six members of the household."

"The household?" Out at the sidewalk, Keith had made it to his historical marker sign; a clap of thunder prompted him to give the sky the finger with both hands in response. "What does 'the household' mean?"

Linda leaned in closer. "'The household' was a genteel word for something else Travis. For *slaves*. And the six Walters skeletons... are all African-American." Grabbing the post of the sign, Keith pulled it from the wet earth with a growl, and began smashing it to bits against a nearby fire hydrant.

"That's kindof incredible! A slave cemetery, right next door!"

"Well, not a cemetery per se. It was clearly a single-event burial site, because the bodies were buried too haphazardly, with no preparation, obviously in a hurry, probably due to fear from the disease. But whoever buried them did take the time to lay them east to west, with their heads pointed west, which was typically how African slaves were buried, so that- "

"- so that when Gabriel blows his horn in Jerusalem they won't have to turn around, they'll already be facing east when they sit up. I read about that."

"Or, so they'd be facing their real home, Africa. Either way. You see? Pretty big news, right?"

"It's amazing! Oh, damn..." A light went on in Travis' head. "That explains Keith!" Looking out through his passenger-side window, Travis and Linda peered through the rain, and saw Keith kicking at the plywood sheets of his never-used walkway as four eyes in his kitchen window watched it all. "I wish you'd've told me first. I could have spared you from being assaulted." Travis watched as Keith escalated his aggression against the walkway, now flipping the sheets of plywood into the air. "And what a shame, he built up such a welcome for their return. But he clearly wasn't prepared for *who* was returning." Travis turned back to Linda. "Wait. *Are* the bones returning?"

Linda sighed with relief. "God no! Can you imagine your neighbor as their caretaker?" Out in the pouring rain, Keith was screaming at the fence he'd built around the hole while smashing it to bits with a shovel. "No, they're being reburied, but we're not sure where yet. We're working with a local African-American historical group to determine the best thing to do. And with the ancestors of the Holman family."

"Sounds like our Linda's gonna be on TV again."

By now, Keith had turned the full barrel of his shovel's rage against the step unit and rail. Linda's eyes deepened. "But here's the worst part Travis. In all those well-kept records of the Holman family and the plantation's history, which included list after list of people's names, names of those who attended dinner parties and weddings and names of local politicians and preachers and names of soldiers and even the names of their horses, guess what those records give us as the names of our six smallpox victims?" Linda read from her report. "'Adult Negro Male. Adult Negro Female. Adolescent Negro Male. Adolescent Negro Female. Infant Male Negro Twins.'" Linda lowered her papers and stared out the windshield. "Objects. Just objects."

Keith was down in the hole now, still smashing and screaming. Travis took note of how the rain had twirled the ends of Linda's ponytail into gentle curls. "Will there be a reburial ceremony?"

Linda smiled back at him. "We've already talked about it." Her eyes seemed to widen, just a little. "You'll come, right?"

"I wouldn't miss it."

The front seat of the van had grown smaller somehow; for several moments, both searched in vain for something to look at other than each other. "Well, I should probably make a break for it and get back to the house."

"Right. Oh wait!" Travis removed his hand from the door, for he was in no hurry. "I need your phone number." She then added quickly, "To call you about the reburial."

"Well of course!" With a quick exchange of numbers, Travis said his goodbyes and, stepping out into the rain, made the dash to his porch, from where he watched the DNR van bounce down the Walters' pock-marked drive and motor off down Crested Boulder.

Next door, an exhausted but still enraged Keith slipped and slided against the muddy walls of his hole in a pitiful effort to escape it, a task rendered more difficult for having just destroyed his step unit. With one foot up over the edge, success seemed his; but then he slipped back down, landing on the wet clay where, flat on his back in the muck, the defeated man unleashed one final, plaintive cry of "fucking niggers!" and, finding himself already in the grave, resigned himself to a death by drowning. Turning toward his front door, Travis' eyes glanced down out of habit to Sheila's phone adapter, and was surprised to see no Sheila phone plugged into it, though he had clearly seen it there when he'd walked over to speak with Linda before the rain. When had she come for it? But there was a bigger mystery, on his mind since Linda's explanation of the bones' identities (or rather, lack of identities). There had been six smallpox deaths among the Holman plantation slaves, and all six victims had been accounted for in Keith's hole. Who then was the mystery child buried next to his koi pond? With this question nagging his thoughts, Travis went indoors, where he knew a happy wife awaited him; but upstairs, where the paint was barely dry on the new renovations, the until-then untested skylight revealed that all was not entirely well, as a steady drip drip drip of rain leaked through and dribbled across the travertine tile.

7

In recent years, astronomers and other cosmologists have theorized that the universe, rather than slowing down in its expansion, is in fact accelerating. The cosmos, rather than a settled, finished thing, barrels ahead in a state of developmental unrest, with movement at breakneck speed its truest nature, despite the illusion of unmoving stillness we see above us in any starlit sky. But while the leading physicists tell us that the vast universe is speeding up, the much smaller universe of Crested Boulder Drive, after so many weeks of upheaval, uprooting and unearthing, seemed finally to be slowing down and settling in for the dog days of summer. A week had transpired since Keith's racist heart had been broken by Linda's news that rainy afternoon; when his own little universe, which along with his fortunes he had seen as steadily expanding, was brought crashing down upon him to the point of implosion. The story of the six skeletons was public now; Linda's predicted return to the local news was accompanied by representatives of the Afro-American Historical and Genealogical Society of Atlanta, who announced that the Holman slaves' remains would be reburied in the Old Marietta Cemetery in a section which was known as the Slave Lot (located, in perfect irony, just across the gravel path from the Confederate Soldier cemetery). A reinterment ceremony at the new grave would take place in three weeks, a day which Travis had already added to his calendar, thanks to the much-awaited text from Linda inviting him. It was a text which served as the first fallen domino of a subsequent cascade of messagings between the two; and while each texter employed prudence and restraint as to content (their shared excitement over the find, anticipation of the reburial, fun facts about archaeology, making fun of Keith Walters, etcetera) their mutually-followed rule of platonic circumspection made neither party unaware of the real fuel which was stoking their texting enthusiasm. As for the loving wife from whom Travis had in recent days begun to hide his phone, Alicia's work upstairs (as well as the contractor's work) was co although a bottle of champagne was opened to celebra the event, Alicia's emotions were mixed; with her domestic bliss having only been so recently born as a direct result of the happy disaster, the recovery from same left her stuck in neutral with her motor still running. It was clear to him that she was looking for something to fill the void but so far, had not found it; meanwhile, although not looking for anything, a steady supply of received texts suggested to Travis that he found something he had not set out to find.

And so, one calm week into the moratorium on trees crashing, bones raising and bullets flying, Travis' truck returned home from a typical day of work where its driver stepped out to see, across the street, Corey, involved in a rather odd-looking outdoor project, something which involved large plastic tarps folded over a clothesline, with Ralph supervising the proceedings. As he crossed the street to investigate, the happy dog ran up to his fence to wait for the head scratching which he knew would escalate, as it always did with his owner's friend, into full-on belly rubbing.

"Drying out some tarps are you?"

“Hey Travis.” It was no longer startling in the least for Travis to see Corey wearing his holstered handgun, permanently attached now as it had become. Travis wondered if he took it off indoors. “Just a mental health measure you might say.”

Travis found Corey’s word choice a coincidental one- recent days had found Travis wondering about his young neighbor in just that light. “Tell me more.”

“Okay, let me tie on this last weight.” Travis looked more closely at the array. A long wire cable had been affixed to two trees which stood fifty feet apart, both trees abutting the fence which separated Corey's property from Sheila's impropriety, creating the look of a long laundry line parallel to the fence, and over that wire had been folded three tarps in succession, each perhaps sixteen feet square. Tied to the corner grommets of each tarp and hanging down to the ground were small weights, presumably to prevent wind from blowing the tarps off the line. "I'll let you be the first to test it. Go up on my porch and sit in my lawn chair."

Leaving off from his ministrations to Ralph's happy belly, Travis obeyed Corey's odd directive. "Okay. Now what?"

Corey crossed his arms. "Look straight ahead, and tell me what you see."

"Tarps. All I see is tarps."

"And what *don't* you see?"

Now it made sense. When Travis looked straight ahead, all he could see, up and down the length of Corey's yard, was a fifty-foot wall of tarps ten feet high. What he could not see- what the design of Corey's tarps meant to spare him from ever seeing again- was Sheila's house or yard.

"You built a wall."

"I built a wall." Ralph sat next to him, wagging his tail in agreement. Travis was sure the dog was smiling.

"Well Corey, since they don't make a tarp big enough to cover her house, this is the next best thing. Good luck with it." Scratching Ralph's dopey head one last time, Travis crossed back home; stepping up onto his porch, he glanced across the way at Keith's now abandoned hole. Standing alone at the hole's edge, and just staring down into it, was Keith's son.

"Whaddya bet he slits his dad's throat before his eighteenth birthday?" Alicia, dressed for a run, had stepped outside to meet him with a kiss. "What's Corey up to across the street?"

"He's making Crested Boulder great again." Turning toward the door, Travis noticed Sheila's phone adapter, still without a phone. "It's funny we haven't seen her phone plugged in since, well, since that day when the archaeologist was here. Not that I'm complaining mind you."

"And we won't see it again either."

Travis followed her into the kitchen. "Really? Why's that?"

"Because I threw it out." With her sweetest smile, Alicia handed him his wine.

"Out. Like, in the garbage thrown out?"

"Like smash it with a hammer and sweep up the pieces in the dustpan thrown out. Felt pretty good." She had said it as a challenge, pure and simple.

"Oh." Travis pretended to look through the mail. "Quite the bold statement."

"You don't approve?"

As Alicia waited for him to blunder into the wrong move that both she and he knew he was about to make, Travis found himself thinking about the live trap he used for catching rats in his yard, a long metal cage which did not kill the unwanted visitor but which, when a triggered plate at the end of the cage was stepped on, brought the door down behind the animal, trapping it in the cage until released unharmed in a nearby park. Travis wondered if the animal, after stepping into the cage, knew in some way as it walked toward the bait at the other end that the trip would not end well, and if it did know, why it continued toward its own doom, just as Travis did now. "There were other choices besides smashing it."

"Like?"

"Like, you could've said 'Travis, tell her to take her phone and not bring it back.'"

"Should I have needed to say that to you?"

"No dear."

"And would you have ever dealt with it if I hadn't dealt with it?"

"Probably not dear."

"Which means you disqualified yourself from making a decision about her phone, am I right?"

"Clearly dear."

Alicia closed in. "And by the way- why is it you're the only one who is allowed to deal with Sheila? This is my house too now." Travis wondered if he heard her correctly. *Now?* Had it really not felt to her that it was her house before? Before when?

"Still, it *was* her phone."

"That her son stole from somebody."

"That her son quite probably stole from somebody. But that's not the point."

"The point" Alicia said, as she took the wine glass from his hand and set it on the counter, "is that since you haven't said no to her, I'll say it for you now." Alicia's sweetest smile returned as she took her victory lap. "Sheila is cut off. For good."

"What about- "

"Not even water!" Having added the punctuation to his sentence, Alicia adjusted her headband and headed out for her run. Three seconds later, her scream made him run to the door, where he saw his wife pointing down in angry shock. There, at the end of the adapter cord, was another phone.

"Holy crap!"

"Get the motherfucking hammer!" But before Alicia could snatch up the phone, Travis beat her to the grab, and held the phone out of her reach. "I'll go over there right now. I'll tell her. I'll go right now and- "

"*GO RIGHT NOW!*" With her hands on her hips, Alicia stood her ground on the porch and waited for her order to be carried out. Travis had not made it to the end of the driveway before a very grim-faced Corey met him at the curb.

"He's back Travis."

"Who?"

Corey's dark voice trembled slightly. "The asshole who sideswiped my truck."

At the mention of the return of Dat Man, the recollection of fire ants caused Travis' scrotum to shrivel. Looking across the street to where Corey was pointing, Travis saw not the black Charger/Challenger of Dat Man's previous Visigothian assaults, but another Chrysler product, a ten year-old paint-oxidized hubcaps-missing tag-applied-for Dodge Sebring, parked on Sheila's gravel driveway. Conspicuously absent however was the sound of screaming or the exchanging of blows.

"That's not the car. How do you know it's him?"

Corey closed his eyes, then continued evenly. "It's that sonofabitch alright. I didn't get his tag number the other time but I saw his face and I knew I'd never forget it. That's him." Though Corey's external composure remained intact, the pressure was clearly building beneath the skin. "I guess he thinks I'm so stupid that he can just come back right next door just because it's not the same car. Well, we'll see."

"What does 'we'll see' mean?"

Corey's eyes were leaden. "We'll see." With that, Corey turned and walked back across the street toward his house. Travis followed close behind.

"What's going on?" By now, Alicia had noticed the developing situation and had walked down the driveway for a better look.

"Go back to the house!" Startled by his hissing urgency, Alicia scampered back to the top of the drive as Travis made it to Corey's gate, just as the latter reached his top porch step and went into his house. A moment later, Corey reappeared, the picture of composure and wielding a huge sledge hammer.

"I'm just gonna go talk to him."

"Wait!" Travis rushed up to block Corey's path to Dat Man's car. "You can't go vigilante Corey. Call the police. Tell 'em he's here and what car he's in. They'll get him."

Again Corey closed his eyes and breathed deeply before responding. "I'm not going vigilante. I just wanna talk. And I already *did* call the police. Do you see any yet? Me neither." In the back, Ralph sat in the grass and waited for someone to play with. "You know as well as I do these cops just roll their eyes when they get Sheila calls. So, I'll just go talk to him."

"Corey, if you push this, *you'll* go to jail, not him!" A visible surge of anger welled up in Corey's throat, and the arm holding the sledge hammer bent slightly at the elbow and rose an inch; but then, Travis could see a countering wave of control rise up as well in the younger man, a wave which met the rage's force and, in a few seconds, overcame it. Corey lowered the hammer and exhaled. "Good. Now put the hammer away and wait for the police." Turning slowly while mumbling "Alright, I'll put the hammer away," Corey marched sullenly back up his steps and into his house. From next door, Travis could hear a man's voice purring like a seductive and inebriated engine, and Sheila's unmistakable cackle laughing in approving tones. But then Travis heard the screen door open behind him once again; turning to face the sound, he saw Corey back out on his porch, this time strolling calmly down his steps and carrying a massive pipe wrench.

"Corey goddammitt- "

"Just a few words. Only take a second."

Travis stepped in front of him, placing his hands on Corey's shoulders. "Don't do it Corey."

Corey's was the visage of innocence. "But I'm not doing anything."

"Don't go over there Corey."

"I only want to talk."

"Go sit on your porch Corey!"

Once again, the eyes filled with steam as the weapon-wielding elbow bent; and once again, Corey's arms relaxed, and an unseen valve released its buildup.

"Thank you Corey." Corey smiled and nodded in surrender. But then suddenly, the smaller man was off like a shot, darting around the surprised realtor like a halfback and running an end-around in the direction of Dat Man's Sebring.

"Corey stop!"

With a twisting lunge, Travis made a desperation dive at the escaping man's legs; one flailing hand found Corey's heel, which was just enough to trip him face-first onto the sidewalk. Crawling atop the struggling Corey, Travis sat on his back and held him down as Ralph hopped and barked from behind his fence, eager to join in the horseplay.

"No pipe wrenches Corey!"

Though kicking and bucking, Corey's voice retained its unsettling calmness. "Please let me up Travis. Please just let me up."

"No!" Travis held on tight and rode out the disobedient colt. "You can't let yourself become like her Corey." He leaned forward and whispered into the back of Corey's head. *"We can't let ourselves become like her."* There was a paroxysm, and then another; but soon, Travis' horse-whispering had its effect, and Corey relaxed, lying limp and prostrate on the cement. "Can I let you up?"

Corey's voice was a resigned whimper. "Fine. You can let me up." Rolling off the defused bomb, Travis sat panting on the grass as Corey brushed himself off and trudged back to his porch. The sound of a creaking door could be heard at Sheila's; once again, it was Dat Man's voice, still idling in a throaty rumble with Sheila mooing unintelligibly. Travis joined Corey, sitting beside him on the steps.

Corey's voice was a defeated drone. "You know the cops aren't coming Travis."

"Yes they are."

"No they aren't."

"Just give 'em a minute!" From next door, the obscene gurgling and cooing could now be heard making its way down Sheila's driveway. Gravel scuffled beneath unseen feet; and then, a moment later, the sound of scuffling gravel was replaced by a car door opening and closing.

Corey's bowed head rose slowly at the sound. "What... what was that?" Across the fence, the Sebring's tired engine rumbled to life. "Is... is he leaving Travis?" Corey was standing now. "He's leaving Travis. My friend is leaving."

"Corey- " But he was down the sidewalk before Travis could intercept him, staring at the fence as if he could see through it.

"Corey you have the description of his car, just give the cops th-"

"SHUT THE FUCK UP YOU HEAR ME SHUT UP!" With a ferocity many times the size of the man, Corey spun back around to square off with Travis, who recoiled at the fearsome transformation of his

young friend. His chest heaved and panted; his nostrils were flared , and his eyes, only moments before lusterless with defeat, now burned with wildness. In an instant, he'd drawn his Beretta, and as Dat Man's car began to back down the drive, a gun-wielding Corey charged out onto Crested Boulder to meet the vehicle with deadly force.

Alicia had watched it all, and shouted from across the street. "I'm calling 911!"

"He alre- no, yeah, call 'em again!"

Unaware of the ambush awaiting him in the street, Dat Man pulled out onto Crested Boulder, and when he straightened the wheel, there was Corey in his way, staring back at him from the end of the car's hood, the large handgun pointed at Dat Man's nose through the cracked windshield. The driver's eyes bulged in terror.

"Yeah! Remember me you goddamn sonofabitch?"

In the yard, Sheila hopped and howled in dismay. "Oh sweet Jesus don' shoot dat man you damn crazy man don' shoot dat man!"

"Citizen's arrest asshole! Get out of the car!" Corey cocked the pistol's hammer. *"Get out of the car!"*

"Corey put it down!" Having taken cover behind the fence, Travis peeked out from around the end of it. "It ain't worth all this!"

In a heartbeat, Dat Man considered his options; choosing retreat, he slammed the car into reverse, crashing the Sebring's rear end straight through the fence and striking the exact spot where, a nanosecond before diving onto the sidewalk to his left, Travis had been crouching. As the car's tires spun in vain to free it from the splintered fence, Corey's weapon remained trained on the windshield. "So, now you drive through my fence too, asshole?"

Sheila ran out to where Travis lay on the sidewalk. "Mistah Diggins call off your fool fren', he cain't shoot dat man we frens agin!"

"Citizen's arrest! Let's go!" But just as Corey stepped up to the driver's side window to make his collar, Dat Man flung himself across the car seat and burst out of the vehicle through the passenger side door and began running along Corey's side of the fence toward h. back yard.

"Bad move dickhead!" Corey was right. The yard was completely fenced in, and

Dat Man had chosen to run not toward freedom but into more fence. The only way out of the yard was through the front gate, where Corey stood his ground with his pistol.

"Travis, 911 says they're on their way!" Alicia was crouched behind Travis' truck, where she hoped no bullets could find her.

"Hear that Corey? They're coming. Put the gun away!"

"Now what dickhead?" Finding himself cornered, Dat Man's prospects took an even worse turn at discovering Ralph, or rather, being discovered by Ralph, whose barking approach Dat Man (mis)interpreted as anything but friendly; with canine teeth on one side and Corey's Beretta on the other, Dat Man saw a refuge, if not an escape- the long line of suspended tarps, behind which he now slipped to separate himself from both dog and man, wrapping himself in a cocoon of the stiff plastic.

"Come out of there you sonofabitch!" The business end of Corey's pistol was pointed now at Dat Man's plastic-wrapped head.

"Goddammit Corey put that gun away!" Out at the gate, Sheila continued to wail and cry; the aim of the Beretta's barrel remained unchanged. "Corey, you got him. He's trapped. The cops are coming. Put the gun away and wait."

"No!" Corey was shaking but still pointed the pistol. "It's not enough to just wait! He deserves more!" Corey turned his face to Travis; it was a face twisted with anguish. "I deserve more."

"Corey- " Travis stepped closer, but carefully. "Think about it: all he did was sideswipe your truck. That's all."

For a moment, Corey froze in place, his wild eyes staring at Travis and his arm shaking while keeping the pistol pointed at Dat Man's head. But then, his eyes blinked, and his elbow dropped; his fury subsiding and his senses returning, Corey lowered the gun, then holstered it, and stood in numb resignation with his arms at his sides.

"Thank you." Ralph was at Travis' side now, wagging his tail in agreement.

"I... got a little crazy I guess." Corey and the cocoon which held Dat Man were quiet and still. It was Sheila, hollering from the gate, who broke the silence.

"IZ ALRIGHT HE DONE PUT DA GUN AWAY YOU KIN RUN NOW!"

It was all the encouragement the encased pupa needed to break out into imago; unwrapping himself in a burst, Dat Man ran down along the tarp toward the front gate.

"Sheila goddammit!"

"Well Mistah Diggins, you said all he done was sideswipe his truck."

For the smallest fraction of a second, Dr. Jekyll watched in shock as Dat Man made for his escape. But in an instant Mr. Hyde was running in pursuit, along the opposite side of the tarp, with Travis at the last moment grabbing Ralph by his leash to prevent him from running along with them that he might keep up with the fun.

"Let it go Corey!" But there was no capping the fire hose this time; ten feet before Dat Man reached the end of the tarp, Corey dove into it, snapping the clothesline and tackling his quarry with the tarp between them. Now the wrestling match on the ground was on, with Dat Man fighting to escape from beneath the tarp and Corey lying atop to keep him in place. But Dat Man was larger and stronger; flipping Corey off him with a lurch, Dat Man stood, though still covered by the tarp, while Corey, on the outside of it and fumbling through the plastic, found an ankle and held on tight.

Ralph squirmed in Travis' grip as he peered up and down the street. "Where the fuck is 911?" Attempting to run, Dat Man felt his ankle twist from Corey's hold, and toppling over, fell upon Corey into a reversal of positions, with Dat Man now on the outside of the tarp and Corey the covered one, buried under Dat Man's weight. All that remained for him was to stand and flee, but Corey, having lost grip of the ankle but finding a wrist instead, gripped it tight through the tarp and held Dat Man atop him, preventing him from standing.

"Lemme go goddammit!"

"Fuck you!" From under the tarp, Corey held fast to the wrist as Dat Man began punching at Corey frantically through the plastic with his one free hand.

"Oh hell it on now!" As Dat Man punched away at where he felt Corey to be, the smaller man held on, clinging more stubbornly with every blow he received. Travis, unable to help his friend since both his hands held back the eager dog, could only watch the street and pray (yes the godless man prayed) for Cobb County's finest to arrive. Then one punch, finding the center of Corey's face with pinpoint accuracy, broke Corey's nose; it was pain unlike any he had ever felt, the kind of pain which, as it rushed red and throbbing through his nerves, told him in no uncertain terms to release the wrist and live to fight another day. But another voice, the same voice to which Corey had succumbed and listened when he made the decision to step in front of Dat Man's car, a voice triggered by a different pain entirely, spoke even more loudly, refusing to be disobeyed. And so, with his one free hand, Corey fumbled about under the tarp for the means to obey it. Nearby, Travis had seen enough; tying Ralph's leash to the gate post, he approached the struggling men. But he had not yet decided- would Travis set Dat Man's ankle free and let him run off? Pull him off Corey but then try to hold him for the police? It was a decision Travis never had the chance to make, for in an instant, Ralph (whose leash's knot, like his owner, had come undone) sprung past him and, determined to share in the humans' fun, leapt onto the unsuspecting back of his owner's new wrestle-buddy and began play-biting at Dat Man's neck and arms. Now it was Sheila's turn to join in the action by pulling on Dat Man's leg in an effort to free him, and it was all the help he needed to wrest himself from Corey's grip; Travis could only stand and watch as Dat Man ran off down Crested Boulder, abandoning his car in the gaping hole of the fence where he had crashed it, it's engine still running and Sheila trailing behind him, moaning and howling. But Ralph ran nowhere, for now, wiggling about beneath his big belly, was his owner, still under the tarp, toward whom Ralph focused all his bouncing, bounding, pawing and play-biting. Watching the big dog frolic happily on top of Corey, Travis could not help but smile with relief, for while a broken fence was maddening, a much worse thing might well have happened; indeed, it was thanks to Corey that disaster had been avoided, for though at first giving in to his worse demons, he had ultimately listened to his better angels and holstered his revolver. But unseen by Travis under the tarp, still feeling the heavy attacking weight upon him and too bleary with pain to think of it as belonging to anyone other than Dat Man, Corey finally found what he'd been looking for, and in obedience to that voice of rage, shot one bullet through the plastic and heard no longer the sound of angels or demons but a single, tortured yelp, and then silence.

The young couple stood in the center of the empty living room, staring down at the floor. The wife bent over to touch it. "So what wood is this?"

Travis opened a blind to let in more light. "It's hand scraped hickory. All new."

"Really nice." With a glance from his wife to follow her lead, the husband bent down as well, nodding in a pretense of understanding what the hell he was touching.

"Everything in the house is so... finished."

"Yes." Travis led them down a short hall and into a bedroom. "The last owner made a number of upgrades over and above a basic renovation."

"Good thing. For us I mean." A sour smile on the man's face suggested he knew what his wife would say next. "My Jason doesn't even own a hand saw."

Jason had learned it was best to just smile along. "Laura's right. I'm not exactly the Bob Vila type."

"Maybe not now. But just wait until you're a homeowner. A house has a way of putting a salt-and-pepper beard and a flannel shirt on all of us."

The couple laughed at Travis' two-hundred forty-seventh telling of his lame Bob Villa joke as they moved into another bedroom. "Second bedroom of three." The afternoon sun streamed in through the west window.

Laura was squinting. "Wow. That's hot. Would need some serious curtains."

"But it would feel great in the winter."

Travis found Jason's optimism annoying. Travis found optimism annoying in general these days. "Nope. No such luck. In the winter the angle of the sun changes. Barely comes in at all."

Jason remained as sunny as the room. "That would suit my wife just fine. She hates Georgia summers. And yet, where is it we live?" His punch line getting no laugh, Jason made the excellent choice of explaining his joke to his audience. "Georgia, right?" A glare from Laura reduced Jason's height two full inches. "Well, not much summer left now anyway. Wow. It's true. Where'd the summer go?"

The showing party moved to the second floor. Climbing the stairs, Travis thought about what Jason said. It was true. The summer was ending. And as far as Travis was concerned, Laura was right- it could not end too quickly. But in truth, the seasons had already changed, three weeks earlier, when the only neighbor on Crested Boulder who loved everybody and only wanted to be loved in return had died in a pool of his own blood and his owner's tears. Yes, the summer ended that day, had turned cold just like that; Greater Sheila had claimed a real casualty this time, two actually, since Corey had for all intents and purposes ceased to exist as much as his dog. But unlike unlucky Ralph, unluckier Corey was left with the aftermath of his thoughts (including the bitter knowledge that the police had arrived after all for the ninety-ninth time and arrested Dat Man only minutes after he had fled down Crested Boulder, thus casting the tragedy in an even more senseless light). How afflicted must those thoughts have been?

Since the accident, Corey no longer spoke of anything, much less about his thought life, so Travis was left with only guesses on the subject. Yes, Corey had "lost it" - but what, specifically had he lost? From what part of him? And what poison had filled the void? Travis had observed the spiraling turn in his neighbor day by day, the escalating paranoia, but to think that its end might result in... for in fact, he knew as no one else that Corey had not shot his best friend accidently, though Travis told the police exactly than when the younger man was too distraught to utter a word of explanation of his own. Accidents were accidents, yes- but Corey's intention was to commit a deadly act. He had straight up attempted to kill Dat Man. And, despite his misidentification of the body mass pressing down on him from the other side of the tarp, he succeeded. In his mind, Corey knew full well, as he touched the trigger, that he was about to kill another man. That it was man's best friend made it no less manslaughter.

"Not one but two motion lights. I like it." Laura's voice brought Travis back to work. He hadn't remembered leaving the upstairs and walking outdoors. " Alarm system, fenced-in yard... and these cameras, they're cloud wifi, right?"

Travis pointed toward the curb. "And note the new mailbox. It's locking."

"Wow. Locking mailbox." Jason made a full 360° turn on the driveway. "It looks like security was a big deal for this seller. Did they have something to worry about?"

"We can't ask Travis that, Jason. Fair Housing Act. He can't comment on neighborhood crime, his answer could be interpreted as discriminatory." Laura beamed with pride at her own knowledge. "Isn't that right Travis?"

"It is. But you can find out about crime in the area yourself online."

Jason pulled at the locked mailbox door to test it. "Prob'ly doesn't matter how much crime there is. It couldn't get through the defenses of this house."

As Laura joined Jason at the mailbox for a private discussion, Travis gave them space and returned his mind to the subject of Corey's mind that fateful afternoon. He recalled the moment when Corey had spun to face him, just before he'd run out into the street with weapon drawn. It was someone other than Corey who stared back at him, a Bizarro of sorts- his body shaking with emotion, his eyes other-worldly, his face a Kabuki mask of fury. It was a previously-unseen Corey displaying a frightening new exterior, suggesting an even more frightening interior. And a question arose for Travis; two questions really, the question itself and the deeper question as to why the question troubled him so: was Corey a level-headed and reasonable man who, when the building stress of his bad experiences became too much, behaved wholly out of character, a sort of temporary insanity, or had the violent, rage-filled monster Travis saw in the street been living in Corey all the while (ie, the real Corey, but suppressed), and were the continual hammer blows of those bad experiences finally enough to shatter his well-constructed but artificial veneer of self-control and set the monster free? Put more simply: did Greater Sheila overwhelm the real Corey, or did Greater Sheila *unleash* the real Corey? As for the second question...

They were in the kitchen now. Laura closed the cabinet doors beneath the sink.

"It's a new dishwasher too. New water heater, new air conditioner... Is there anything in this house that's old?"

Jason's face was buried in his phone, but then popped up at finding something in it. Oh, right! I'm supposed to ask about the plumbing."

Travis knew Laura had seen enough and was sold; he could therefore risk being obtuse to the junior partner. "Sure. Go ahead and ask."

"Um..." Confusion passed across the husband's brow; after quickly checking his phone he was confident once again. "Right. What kind is it and how old is it?

"Also new. All PEX tubing, cheaper than copper and less likely to leak."

Laura nodded. "Of course. Should of known it'd be new too. No wonder the price is higher than I expected for this area." Laura moved her hand across the granite countertop. "It's a new listing. Probably not ready to come down yet are they?"

"Don't be so sure. It's a motivated seller."

The threesome moved down the hallway for the third time; it was a *fait accompli by* this point, with Laura having concluded their time in the kitchen by announcing they'd be making an offer. Passing the downstairs bathroom, Travis caught a glimpse of himself in the cabinet mirror, and it stopped him in his tracks for just a moment. It's funny, he mused, how you choose to look at mirrors every day, and since you're prepared for seeing yourself you're not surprised by the sight; but then, when a mirror suddenly pops up out of nowhere and your face is looking back at you before you can ready yourself for the effect, you can look startling to yourself, shocking even. Those moments, when you're surprised at seeing what you are, perhaps those are the only moments when you truly see yourself, without the obscuring filter of expectation; and as Travis continued to regard himself in that mirror, his memory jumped him back to moments in his past, namely, his encounters with Sheila, when he had behaved "out of character," with yelling and hopping and, albeit without a handgun, with unbridled anger. And it was then that Travis' second question of the day was answered. For if it was true that the real Corey was the savage, primitive beast who'd broken free of his shackles and escaped to wreak havoc that afternoon, then what primitive and dangerous real Travis might be chained in the depths of his own being, also awaiting his day of expression? And how strong were those chains?

Back outside, Travis and Laura stood on the driveway as Jason hung back on the porch, face in phone. "I can't find... what else was it were we supposed to ask?..."

"Whatever it was we covered it Jason." Laura's smile was an apology. "It's our first house. We're kindof excited."

"Well, you should be. It's a good offer, I think you'll get it." It was true of course; Travis knew it was only natural that they should be excited. He also knew it was his job to give them no reason not to be.

"Hey, look!" It was Jason, now out of his phone and looking at the front door. "I finally found something unfinished! This screen door. The frame of the screen isn't painted to match the door."

"You've got a good eye. Yeah, that screen is new too."

"And that fence- " Laura was pointing toward the sidewalk. "The wood at the end of it there is newer than the rest."

Travis forced a laugh. "Oh-oh, they're getting observant. Come on, let's get back to the office before you find out more!" As the couple crawled into his truck and Travis backed down the drive, he was glad they were leaving before being asked about the bare spot in the yard where the dog house used to be. Or before they heard the sound of the dice game which had started up next door.

8

On a tree-covered hill backdropped by the larger hills of Kennesaw and Little Kennesaw Mountains lies the unassuming plot of earth known as the Slave Lot of the Old Marietta Cemetery, a rough-hewn and uneven piece of land where the remains of nineteen slaves and freed blacks were buried during the decade of the Civil War and the two decades preceding it. Unlike the neatly-ordered markers lining the paths of the cemetery proper (an unfortunate word choice, "proper," but accurately chosen, given the historical realities of the antebellum South), the mostly unmarked and anonymous stones comprising the Slave Lot seem strewn by comparison, haphazard and random, jutting akimbo from the sparsely-sodded soil as if having been pushed up to the surface by an accident of seismic upheaval rather than placed from above by a purposeful intelligence. As visitors read from the information sign (planted in the ground with much greater care than any of the stones to which it refers), the Slave Lot is unique in being "the only slave burial ground in any major white Georgia cemetery," an inclusion undertaken in the Christian spirit of Galatians 3:28 in which the apostle Paul reminds the church that "there is neither... slave nor free... but you are all one in Christ Jesus;" and while the sentimental visitor may be warmed by the magnanimous gesture of the owning class at allowing the Slave Lot to exist within their own cemetery's gates, the cynical one cannot help but take note that the Slave Lot's placement on the hill was a strictly segregated one, separated and secluded, ensuring that no grave of the blacks would be allowed to live next door to any grave of the whites, leading that cynic to conclude that the goodly Caucasian believers of the time ascribed a less than literal scriptural meaning to the phrase "all one." But more symbolic even than the Slave Lot's location in relation to the adjacent white persons' interment grounds (and let the name given by the Christian folk of Marietta for the final resting place of human beings,

"Slave Lot," not be overlooked, a name no less callous and impersonal than if it had been "Parking Lot") is it's relationship to the environs surrounding the cemetery. For directly across the road from Slave Lot dwell the three thousand permanent residents of the Marietta Confederate Cemetery, the largest Confederate cemetery south of Richmond, men from every state of the Confederacy, who gave their lives for the cause of preserving their god-given right to buy and bury negroes any damn where they chose. Standing on that dirt road which marks the separation of these opposing contingencies, and then facing the forest-covered (and still to this day, bullet-strewn) Kennesaw Mountain Battlefield, our visitor is provided a sweeping diorama of national shame, with fallen Rebel soldiers at one's left, the slaves who tended their horses at one's right, and directly before them, that silent mountain, staring down upon it all, where the bloodletting which occurred atop it in July of '64 gave sure and somber proof that the end of life inaugurates the end of differences; but a diorama proving just as surely that men may moulder commonly in shared ground yet share in death no common ground.

It was here, at this humble Slave Lot on an already-warm August Sunday morning, where the six unnamed Holman slaves were to be reinterred and given back, if not their names, the acknowledgement of their having once had them. As for the ceremony in store for the one hundred or so attending, the organizers had sought to strike a balance between a fully satisfying event while maintaining simplicity and modest decorum (and to get it over with before the midday sun could climb high enough to spoil things for everybody). Local clergy would speak, promising brevity; introductory comments would be offered by the director of the Metro Atlanta Chapter of the Afro-American Historical and Genealogical Society, and traditional African music would accompany the actual placing of the remains (amounting to six small wooden boxes which lay covered by a cloth upon a nearby bier) into the pre-dug hole around which the celebrants, awaiting the ceremony's beginning, currently sat on folding chairs in the shade of an oversized lawn tent. Perhaps most noteworthy of the planned events would be the delivery of the memorial tribute, offered by none other than Cobb County Magistrate Court Judge Rance Holman, direct descendent of the slaveowning Holmans (with the family's five subsequent non-slaveowning generations laying buried not far from the

Slave Lot, not far geographically at least), a choice of speakers unanimously agreed upon by all as a fitting way to bridge the cultural divide in the name of racial harmony (in that Judge Holman would be the one and only non-African-American participating in the proceedings). Local news crews were present of course, who at the moment were interviewing officials and attendees in general; beside the hole, a large mound of removed dirt stood by, its purpose obvious, when at ceremony's end it would be returned to cover the Slave Lot's six new residents and thus return them to obscurity, putting an eternal end to their brief moment in the sun.

Having finished up her own interview, Linda returned to the shade of the tent and took her seat next to an empty one she was saving for a friend, who upon arriving scanned the crowd for the familiar DNR ball cap and pony tail. Seeing him, she smiled and waved; picking his way between knees and chair backs, Travis sat down beside her.

"You made it!"

"Did you doubt me?" Linda's embarrassed smile was badly concealed. "Have you ever been here before?"

"Oh yes. For another reinterment ceremony as a matter of fact. Right over there." Linda pointed across the small road, toward the Confederate Cemetery. "The remains of four Confederate soldiers were discovered a few years ago on farmland near one of the run-up battles preceding Kennesaw Mountain, the Battle of Kolb's farm. They were all reinterred here, in the Tennessee Section, they were all Tennesseeans." Meanwhile, the last of the organizers were finding their seats; the ceremony was about to begin. "Today's event is quite a bit different than that one, thank god."

"How so?"

Linda squinted, though the sun was not in her face. “Oh it was quite the gala affair. Women in antebellum hoop skirts, men in Confederate uniforms, horse drawn wagons, Confederate flags waving proudly... big opportunity for everyone to get all sentimental and nostalgic about 'the good ol' days'." Linda's gazed fell upon the Slave Lot. "At least nobody's playing dress-up today."

"Here's someone dressed up as a preacher." The ceremony officially began with the pastor of a local A.M.E. church offering an opening prayer, which segued into a brief homily in which the pastor referenced Ezekiel's vison of the dry bones, wherein the Lord promised those dead dry bones that he would "put breath in you, and ye shall live," followed immediately by reminding those assembled how this same Lord resurrected the three-days' dead Jesus from the tomb, culminating in the exhortation, "If, therefore, our Lord so values the bones of those who have passed, shall not we also honor and value these bones today?"

An unintelligible grumble came from Linda's chair. "What's that?" asked Travis.

A fierce whisper answered him. "I said, I don't need *the lord* to tell me that these bones matter, I knew that already!" Looking up, Linda was pleased to read a silent "Amen!" in Travis' smile; meanwhile, the sermon had ended, giving way to the AAHGS of Metro Atlanta director's remarks, a predictably appropriate address which welcomed everyone to the event, acknowledged and thanked all those who had played a role leading up to the reinterment, and offered the AAHGS’s perspective as to its meaning and significance culturally, morally, ethically, historically and all the other "ly's" apropos to such an occasion. Then came the memorial tribute from Judge Holman, sounding much less like a judge than one receiving judgement; his words, delivered with unadorned sincerity and ringing with honest sentiment, expressed what every ear believed to be his heartfelt acknowledgement of "a sorrowful time," as he phrased it, and his family's unfortunate role in aiding and abetting that sorrow, words which celebrated this "better time" which eschewed "bringing together" rather than "driving apart" and held, though not spelled out in so many words, a family's deep apology. With Judge Holman stepping away from the rostrum and retiring behind it next to the covered bier, the drums began to beat; now it had come to the reinterment itself, accompanied by the African ensemble. An elder of the AME church removed the satin cloth, revealing the six caskets, and the casket bearers (five other elders of the church and, in a fitting gesture, Judge Holman himself) carefully lifted the boxes and assembled themselves in a straight line. As they took their first measured steps toward the awaiting hole, a shouted voice rang out from behind the assemblage.

"Some things never change, do they!?"

The seated crowd turned as one; behind them stood an older black man in his 70's, unassuming and unremarkable in physicality and dress, but with eyes glowing like white embers. Upon hearing his outburst, those standing near and around him backed away a step, afraid of something more to follow, and the man obliged them, even more loudly. *"Always gotta be the Slave Lot, don't it?"* The musicians stopped their playing; feeling all eyes upon him now, he straightened his posture to his full height; meanwhile, the two disinterested police officers assigned to the event suddenly awoke from their malaise and began to make their way from the curb toward the man as he continued shouting from his invisible soapbox. *"Why these people in these boxes gotta be done the same way our people got done back in slave times? Why they still, STILL not good enough to lay in the white man's cemetery?"* Now the man saw the officers closing in, and knowing his window of opportunity was about to be slammed shut, hollered out that window as loud and fast as he could. *"How come these people we buryin' today good enough to wipe the Holman baby bottoms but not good enough to lay side by side with the Holmans Mr. Holman? This how we 'honor' them,' by throwin' 'em out of sight out of mind, throwin' 'em down in this place which still calls 'em slaves?! Why there gotta BE a slave lot anyhow? There never shoulda BEEN no place called a Slave Lot in the first place, now you wanna add more to it? They ain't slaves no mo'! They just as dead as every rich white man named Holman layin' out yonder! They ain't slaves no mo! They deserve better than Slave Lot! They deserve better than Slave Lot!"* By now the police officers had reached the impassioned man, whose shouts of *"They ain't slaves no mo'!"* rang out over and over again as he was led away without a struggle. At the bier, the casket-bearers, no less stunned than the seated crowd, stood by awkwardly, still holding their solemn consignments; after a tense nod from the AAHGS director to the pastor, then from the pastor to the casket bearers and musicians, the ceremony resumed, and one by one the small boxes were placed side-by-side in the open earth. Hazarding a brief glance to his left, Travis saw that Linda's attention was split (as was everyone's) between the reinterment and the street, where the police were placing the now-quieted old man against the back of the squad car and frisking him for weapons. Meanwhile, the reinterment proceeded; with all six caskets finally in the ground, the casket-bearers stepped back and stood next to the bier, and a music student from Spelman College stepped up to the rostrum and began an *a cappella* rendition of a traditional 19th-century spiritual. Suddenly, the protestor's voice sprang back to life- shouts of *"Why she gotta sing that ol' slave song!"* were mixed with the singer's notes, and with one eye of each person in the crowd watching, the man was placed in the back seat of the squad car and the door shut, muffling (but not entirely silencing) his objections. Soldiering on despite the distraction, the AME pastor hurried up to the rostrum and, in a voice louder than perhaps was necessary, delivered the final benediction and prayer, thus concluding the reinterment ceremony. The attendees began to stand and mingle; Linda and Travis remained seated.

Linda stared at the squad car holding the protestor. "Are they arresting him?"

"Before they do the reporters need to go over and thank him for their story.

Check it out." Off to one side, three microphones attached to reporters' arms were inches from the face of the AAHGS director, who found herself cornered like a possum against a tree. Out on the street, a man in a suit hurried up to the squad car and tapped on the driver's side window- it was none other than Judge Holman- and after a brief discussion with the officers, the back door of the squad was opened, and the protesting man was brought out, free to go. The judge, his eyes laden with sympathy, extended his hand to the man in conciliation. For a moment, the man stared down at the hand, then up at Judge Holman's apologetic eyes; but after a single shake of his head, the man turned his back and walked away, leaving the hand suspended in space. Linda watched as the man disappeared down the sidewalk and then turned to her companion.

"Travis?"

"Yes?"

"Why there gotta be a slave lot anyhow?"

He stared at the pile of earth which soon would cover the answer to Linda's question. "Wanna take a walk?"

"Let's take a walk."

It was high noon as they strolled through the main grounds of the cemetery, speaking only occasionally, stopping now and then under whatever shade was afforded them and regarding the stones. Behind them in the distance, the burial custodians were covering the Holman slaves.

"I never thanked you for coming out today."

"Thanked *me*?" He plucked a leaf as they passed under a sycamore. "You're the one who needs to be thanked. You're the one who solved their mystery."

"Well, thank the paleopathologist really." Linda paused and pretended to be studying a stone; then blurted, "Why didn't your wife come along?"

It was sudden and out of context, an obvious fact-finding mission; all summer, Travis had made no mention of Alicia's existence to Linda, and due to the question's abrupt appearance, was clearly a subject that had been on Linda's mind but for which she'd found no discreet way of broaching. So discretion be damned.

"Skeletons aren't Alicia's thing."

"That's what I figured."

What had you figured? That skeletons aren't Alicia's thing, or that there was an Alicia? "Yeah, when it comes to uncovered bones and yardwork, she's happy to... look the other way." He had worded it quite consciously; the provocative double-entendre had been absolutely intentional. *What the fuck are you doing right now?*

Linda avoided eye contact, but it hid nothing from him. "Well, looking the other way is convenient." While the trajectory of their conversation had taken a thrilling turn, Travis also found it a little terrifying; feeling it prudent to find a new direction, he noticed a monument he'd seen before on an earlier visit and seized upon its potential.

“So, do you know about this little girl?”

Linda regarded the long white marble slab which lay flat on the earth, with an urn at the foot and at the opposite end, the headstone. "Mary Anne Phagan. No, should I?"

"If you like murder mysteries." He stepped closer to the headstone. "Mary Phagan was a little girl whose family came from Marietta and then moved with her mother down to East Point where she quit school at age ten to go work in a textile mill, and then later a pencil factory on Atlanta's west side, where she worked six days fifty-five hours a week for ten cents an hour, which was big money compared to the mill."

"So much for child labor laws."

"Sadly, the least of her problems." Travis looked at the headstone; he hadn't noticed before that it said it had been erected by the Marietta Chapter of the United Confederate Veterans. "The little girl got laid off at the pencil factory and came in to collect her last pay. They found her the next morning in the basement, raped and strangled to death. After investigating, they focused on the director of the factory, a young Cornell-educated Jewish guy named Leo Frank, and that's who they charged."

Now Linda had moved in close as well to read the sentimental inscription of the flat slab. "Murder mystery you say. So he didn't do it?"

Travis stepped to the side in an effort to stay in the shade. "It was a messy situation. There was a night watchman and the janitor who were suspected as well, 'specially the janitor, but the prosecutor trying to convict Leo Frank said that the black janitor couldn't have done it because the story the janitor told which pinned it on Frank was really complicated, and everybody knew that no black man was smart enough to fabricate a story that was complicated. So he had to be telling the truth."

"Which of course a white jury agreed with."

Travis nodded. "Anyway, they convicted Leo Frank on very little evidence, sentenced him to death, put him in jail- but over the weeks and months more and more facts which seemed to clear him kept coming out until the governor actually made the move of commuting Frank's sentence to life instead of hanging. Let's just say the public at large found the governor's decision... disappointing."

"And how did the people of Georgia express their disappointment?"

"By storming the prison, handcuffing the warden and removing Leo Frank back up to Mary Phagan's family's home town of Marietta and lynching him there. The mob called themselves The Knights Of Mary Phagan."

Linda shook her head. "This country has a disturbing history with groups who call themselves 'Knights.'"

She was cooking in the direct sun; Travis took Linda’s warm arm and drew her into his shade. "That's right, but Leo Frank's guilt or innocence isn't the fascinating part of the story to me. Not anymore anyway."

"What do you mean, not anymore?"

"Not anymore, thanks to you." Her eyes widened; Travis saw it, and poured all he had into them. "Before, I used to be concerned with the justice aspect, you know, like 'was Leo Frank railroaded because of antisemitism?' and 'was the probably-guilty janitor dismissed as a subject because of the flipped-racist thinking that 'oh that negro is too stupid to have invented his elaborate story blaming Leo Frank so it must be the truth?' And yes, those are important questions. But thanks to you... " The sun had migrated, so he turned Linda once again to pull the sunlight out of her eyes "... instead what I'm thinking about is Mary Phagan, this dead little girl buried in the ground, who didn't exist while she was alive but only received love and attention and an expensive stone paid for by strangers because of a sensational crime committed against her. Who was there to value her before she became national news?" For a moment, Linda simply stared back, as if processing his words from a tape delay. But slowly she began to smile, then suddenly wrapped Travis in an appreciative hug under the bough of the sycamore, a hug he was happy to reciprocate. But just as quickly she stepped back as if startled.

"What?"

"This is it then." His brow sought explanation. "My work with the Holman Slaves. It's done." She stood there, sadly and awkwardly, and Travis knew just what was needed.

"Miss Myers." Stiffening to attention, Travis extended his hand to her as the polite gentleman; Linda did not try to conceal her eye-rolling. "It's been an absolute pleasure getting to know you and learning from you and exchanging geeky scientific texts with you. Thank you for a thoroughly wholesome and edifying experience."

Linda took his hand and assumed a similar voice of distant cordiality. "Thank you as well Mr. Riggins. It's always gratifying for those of us in the scientific community when we're able to interact with the public and- " Now Linda dropped both his hand and the play-acting. "- look, can't we still like have lunch now and then, maybe meet for a drink, or, you know... something?"

"Goodbye Miss Myers." Gently taking up her hand once again, Travis looked into her eyes with a warm finality and nodded just once; accepting her fate, Linda nodded and smiled, and after fighting back the impulse for one final hug, walked quickly to the DNR van and, without looking back, climbed in and drove off. As he watched her disappear, Travis took inventory of the event, and determined that he'd carried out his devious plan masterfully: his attendance at the ceremony was a calculated move which clearly impressed her (not to mention the advance work he'd done over weeks of texting during which he repeatedly expressed his "interest" in her chosen field); his telling of the Mary Phagan story, carefully researched in advance and crafted to show off his deep sensibilities concerning right and wrong while simultaneously crediting her for his newfound epiphanies concerning the value of human life; his reprehensible yet strategically-necessary double-mindedness when referring to Alicia; even the firm manner he adopted while "ending" their fledgling relationship, by appearing resolved to remain faithful which only made Linda respect and admire him even more- and thereby find him even more attractive. Yes, the bones were buried, but their phones were not, and at a tactically-chosen future hour, his phone would surprise hers, and the game would resume, the game which Travis was still telling himself was only a harmless amusement and would never graduate to a higher (or lower) level. Having made his way back to his truck parked near the cemetery, Travis climbed in, and through his windshield saw a young man, a gangly long-haired teenager, wearing an ill-fitting black suit and clumsy Sunday shoes, sprinting away from the site of the reinterment and reaching a bus stop just in time, where the young man climbed onto the bus before it continued south on Atlanta Street. Travis was sure it could not have been Keith's son.

\`\`

"I'm bored."

It was early in the evening, both just home from work, and

Alicia was sitting in the sofa sprawled-out like a restless teenager, her knees spread wide and flapping in-and-out with unchanneled energy, arms folded across her Georgia State t-shirt and head thrown back, her eyes staring up at an unresponsive ceiling.

"Wanna help me prune the butterfly bushes?" Travis knew well what an ominous sign it was, whenever Alicia on those rare occasions expressed boredom. It was like a seismologist who, over time, records an increase of tectonic activity above an unstable fault- a pressure-relieving upheaval was inevitable and imminent. "We haven't walked the Chattahoochee Trail in a while. Still early enough, we could go right now."

Alicia squirmed. "Nah. Besides there's a Braves game over there tonight, traffic will suck." She pulled her eyes down from the ceiling and pointed them at Travis. "There's Kennesaw Mountain. I know you like Kennesaw."

"I do like Kennesaw." Now it was Travis who was squirming. Kennesaw? Beneath whose shadow he'd been strolling the cemetery just a few days earlier with Linda at their secret(?) rendezvous/reinterment ceremony? Why would Alicia be suggesting Kennesaw so coincidentally? *And why was she looking at me that way?*

In an instant, Alicia resumed her ceiling stare. "Nah. Too hot still. Besides, that's not what I'm talking about." Relieved to hear that "that's" not what she was talking about, Travis relaxed a bit, but not Alicia- now she popped up onto her feet and paced about the living room. "It's not a 'go for a hike' kind of bored. It's a 'gotta apply myself' kind of bored." Without further explanation he understood, even saw it coming. It had been several weeks since the work was completed upstairs, and thus several weeks since Alicia's hands-on experience of feeling invested in her home which had resulted in the invigorated woman Travis had been so happy to live with of late. The horrors across the street involving Corey and Ralph had knocked her off her pins for a brief time; but with calm restored (and the nice couple moving into Corey's house just last weekend, the new neighbor Laura and Alicia getting on so well that she'd even signed up for Alicia's "Fit Body" boot camp), Alicia had bounced back to her "new normal," and now, like a dairy cow in need of milking, her domestic energy ached for release. Weeding the butterfly bushes would clearly not pull her udder.

"Gotta apply yourself. Like, you mean, around the- "

Instantly Travis realized how naïve he was to think she hadn't already figured it out in advance and planned her strategy. "Have you noticed the windows down here?"

He made a show of looking around the downstairs. "These glass things? That are between me and my bird feeders?"

"The answer, of course, is that no you haven't noticed them. You're a man. You don't care what the fort looks like- all you care is about what's going on *around* the fort, outside it." Alicia glided up to one of the offending portals. "Now, pretend you're not farsighted and you can see with detail things right in front of your face." She lifted a curtain leg with two tentative fingers as if it were a smallpox blanket. "Look at that."

"Holy fuck. How have we been sleeping at night?"

"I know, right?" With an athletic scamper, Alicia bounded back to him and was inches in front of Travis' face. "It doesn't need that much really. Just paint and new window treatments. Find a nice two-tone color combo for the whole room to work off of, you know, I was thinking maybe plum red and plum yellow yes yellow is a plum color, and if you do the walls in the yellow then your window headboards and casings and sills contrasting in the plum red with the inner rails and sashes and grilles back to the yellow, and your curtains would be some blend of the two with a third accent color in there and that could be so many things, a swirly green for example, then pull out all these hideous plastic blinds and- "

"Alright stop!" Like a boxer pummeling her opponent against the ropes who's pulled off by the referee and sent to a neutral corner, Alicia relented, but her victory smirk indicated she was already unlacing her gloves. "Now you know that if the walls go yellow and the windows go plum- wait, did you say they're both plum? No- "

"Yes. Look at a plum, it's yellow inside red outside."

"- plum red and yellow. Then that means the beige carpet- "

"Oh that shit gotta go regardless!" Alicia stood in the center of the living room, arms outstretched, like a conquering Alexander indicating the expanse of her newly-acquired lands. Not receiving (and not expecting to receive) any resistance from her vanquished husband, she plopped back onto the sofa to tie her shoes and then bounced back up. "Okay. Gotta get to the hardware store before they close."

"So I take it you're not bored anymore?"

She was standing before him with her keys. "How can I be bored with this much work to do?" With a kiss she was out the door; after holding onto the sofa for a moment until the dizziness passed, Travis returned to the window, laughing inwardly. It's only right, he told himself, that she should stake her own domain; furthermore, he should have guessed that the gravitational pull of her manifest destiny would expand her upstairs realm in a downstairs direction. Opening the curtains which were now marked for death, Travis glanced out upon that realm which remained his, and saw, as soon as his wife's car passed through the gate and headed off down Crested Boulder, Sheila appear from her hiding place, an overgrown shrub just off the property line at the end of the driveway, emerging from the bush like some disheveled Dryad fallen upon the baddest of times.

"MISTAH DIGGINS, WHEAH YOU AT MISTAH DIGGINS?" He snapped the curtains closed. There were, as there always were at Sheila sightings, two options from which to choose; one, wait her out behind the curtains until she gave up and plodded away like a lost lamb, or two, go out and deal with her nonsense and cut it as short as possible. To wait her out was tempting in the short term, but what's more pathetic than hiding behind the curtains in one's own house? Besides, Travis knew she'd only shuffle back into her bush and waylay him at her first opportunity later in the day. Going out and dealing with her meant, well, having to deal with her, but it brought one head-on with the dreaded inevitable and, though the pain in that moment would be excruciating, suffering it would buy him her riddance for the rest of the day and evening. Probably. At least today she didn't seem to be carrying any uncharged phones.

"Whaddya need Sheila?"

She was listing side-to-side like a leaky bathtub toy at the end of the driveway, a lottery ticket in one hand and her ubiquitous black plastic bag in the other. "Mistah Diggins I feel so bad 'bout that crazy man shooting 'is dawg like dat!" The incident with Corey was more than a month in the past; Sheila's mind still processed it, like it processed everything, in the immediate now. "It get me so nervous I need me cig'rettes to 'lax me Mistah Diggins you got fo' dollahs fo' cig'rettes?"

His wife was miles away by now, but as far as Travis was concerned, her omniscent eye still watched him through the nevermore curtains. "Sheila, no means no. No more anything. You're on your own. I told you that."

Sheila jumped into it as if she'd rehearsed her response for days. "Yeah but you say 'no Sheila sorry not even no watah no mo' not even watah no mo'' but I ain' *axin'* fo' watah I axin' fo' fo' dollahs!"

"No Sheila. No money for cigarettes."

"How 'bout some watah then?"

Travis could feel the top of his head beginning to sweat. "Sheila listen to me. No more water. No more money. No more phone charging. Nothing. Goodbye." After a shooing-off wave of his hand, Travis turned back toward the house; in his mind's eye, he saw Alicia looking out the window and nodding in support.

Meanwhile, Sheila violated Travis' water ban by creating some of her own as the tears rolled down her face. "Mistah Diggins you ain' nevah said no before when I ax fo' ice why you mean now and not gimme no ice?"

"You... you didn't ask me for ice Sheila."

"I know ah din' ax fo' no ice! I ax you fo' fo' dollahs! You got fo' dollahs Mistah- "

"GODDAMMITT SHEILA!" The force of the blast sent the tottering woman reeling. "Just go. GO! I got work to do. You want water? Fine!" Travis snatched up the garden hose which lay curled up next to the drive. "Here. Water!"

With a sour face, Sheila turned away and began shuffling down the driveway toward the sidewalk. "Ah hell no, I don' wan' no nasty-ass hose watah, shee-it, I got me some good-ass bottle watah AN' ice back up at da house inna coolah the chuch gimme." As Sheila turned her prow onto the sidewalk and began chugging upstream, Travis watched as the fingers of Sheila's lottery ticket hand remembered they were holding something; lifting the ticket to eye-level, Sheila squinted the length and breadth of the multi-colored card, and when her eyes determined there was no reason to continue holding it, her hand agreed, and threw the lottery ticket behind her, where it fluttered and landed at the end of Travis' driveway.

"Sheila!" She rolled on, oblivious as stone. "Sheila! Why'd you throw that lottery ticket onto my driveway?"

Without slowing her stride, Sheila's head twisted back toward him. "'Cuz they ain' no money in it Mistah Diggins. Ain' no money." As the simple woman mumbled off in the direction of Iffy Grocery, Travis bent down and, mumbling as well, picked up her litter and walked up the driveway. The sound of crunching gravel next door turned his head; peering across the fence at the Walters', Travis watched a Cobb County police SUV marked "Code Enforcement" dodge the potholes and come to a stop on Keith's deconstructed driveway; stepping out were two people, a tall African-American county police officer and a balding white man with a clipboard. Watching their steps, the men navigated their precarious way up to Keith's porch- but before they could knock on the door, it cracked open, and a single eyeball peered out upon the intruders, just as Travis reached the end of the fence and peeked his eye around as well for a better view.

The clipboard man introduced himself. "Mr. Walters? My name is Trey Miller from the County Code Enforcement office. Can I call you Keith?" The eyeball darted up and down Miller head to toe, pausing on the clipboard. Having received no verbal response, Miller continued. "Mr. Walters, we're here about a safety concern that's been reported." At the words "been reported," the eyeball shot a flame-throwing glance in the direction of the Riggins residence as Miller gestured toward the array of vain attempts made in the search for Walters Man which pock-marked Keith's suburban quagmire. "You've got... quite a lotta holes here in the yard."

The eyeball did not blink. Silent seconds passed.

"Anyway... well, you got all these holes, two feet deep two feet wide, and from what I can see full of water. “ Frequent rains had indeed filled the holes, which now explained to Travis why the mosquitoes had been worse the past several weeks. "Now it's your yard of course and a homeowner can dig and alter the ground and what-not, within depth guidelines and away from buried utilities of course. But this many... this deep... well, anyone coming onto your property is at risk of falling in, slipping in, driving into ‘em. Like I said. Public safety." Now the eyeball took in the African-American cop, which narrowed the eyeball even more. "So- per the code, a property owner has a duty to maintain his property in a reasonably safe condition for others, and what you're probably not aware is, if someone comes onto your property and is injured due to your negligent maintenance of your property, the property owner can be liable for- "

"The county code does not specifically say you can't have holes in your yard." Defiance shone behind the eyeball's white viscosity; confident that he was outside the peripheral view of the half-concealed head, Travis crept along the fence line to be close enough to listen as the eyeball continued its argument. "And since the code says nothing about the holes in my yard I'm not required to fill them."

"Yes, but the safety hazard they- "

"Under the law of premises liability" the eyeball continued, "a property owner does in fact have a legal duty to maintain safe conditions and is liable if negligence can be established. However- " now the eyebrow raised, pulling the eyeball open like a gun turret revealing a 50-caliber gun, " - in order to establish a premises liability case, you need to prove that the property owner owed you a duty of care, that he breached that duty by leaving his property unreasonably dangerous, and that you suffered an injury as a result. But that duty of care depends on the circumstances. Because if someone- "

The police officer stepped up beside Mr. Miller. "Mr. Keith, this ain't a court of law, we're not- "

"- BECAUSE IF SOMEONE CAME ONTO YOUR PROPERTY UNINVITED" continued the eyeball, its glare trained wholly at the cop who, upon feeling the heat of that glare, retreated a step, "then that person is NOT owed a duty of care, and the property owner only has to put up warnings for very dangerous and unreasonable man-made hazards. And since the code doesn't mention holes as dangerous or unreasonable then I am free from liability and I don't have to do shit about them so you can go now. Go on. Go." The eyeball blinked its haughty dismissal; flummoxed, Mr. Miller looked up to the officer, who could only shrug. Miller's glance then fell upon the yawning pit where plywood and scrap wood now lay in place of its six former occupants.

"But then there's the matter of... *that* hole."

In a sweep which narrowly missed knocking Miller's clipboard halfway across the yard, the door swung open, and the full horror of Keith's entirety Jabba-ed its way out of his hut and into the two men's faces. "That hole was an act of God! It's an act of God! I'm not responsible for acts of God!" The whale being fully breached on the porch now, Keith noticed Travis standing near the fence and instantly hollered him down. "Riggins! Hey Riggins! Buddy! Tell 'em! That hole is an act of God!" Keith turned back to the two men and introduced them to his buddy Travis. "That's my asshole neighbor. My tree fell on his house, made the hole." Again Keith shouted at his new best friend. "Riggins, buddy, tell 'em it was an act of God!"

"That hole?" Standing in the yard, Travis considered his options. It was crucial, of course, for him to maintain the peace with his virulent neighbor, given what Travis knew about what Keith knew about the thing no one else knew about but Travis. No temptation to be clever therefore, no burning desire to lampoon the man on his own property, could Travis surrender to, what with a police officer standing right in front of him. And so, Travis swallowed back his first inappropriate answer, then went with another which was even more inappropriate but felt sooo great: "Well, fellas, if there actually was a god, and he was in the business of doing acts, I'm pretty sure he would've spared my house and pushed that tree over onto Keith's shithouse shack."

There was silence on the porch, save the creaky *eereek-eereek* of Keith's open front door. But then a grin began to slice across Keith's face like a long, jagged incision, and in a voice so loud that even buried bones could hear, the petulant man spoke. "So Officer- "Keith made a show of trying to read the policeman's name tag. "- Brantley, Officer Brantley. I know somethin' that maybe you'd like to know too. About my gooood neighbor over there." Now lowered to a whisper too soft for Travis to pick up, Keith spilled his story, pointing now and then to the spot where Travis knew he'd be pointing, knew full well even while the words of his irresistible wise crack were falling out of his mouth- across the fence and directly at the bare patch next to the koi pond. Now the officer was looking back and forth between the bare patch and Travis.

"Mr. Riggins? Is this true what your neighbor's tellin' us?"

It was pointless to do anything but confess. "Um... yeah. It's true."

"Ha!" Keith's victorious fist-pump shook him like a Jello mold.

"You know that means we're gonna need to... take a look."

"I understand." As Travis stepped aside to allow the three men around the fence onto his own property, a fatalistic peace fell upon him at the realization that his secret bones were about to be made public, and in a flash, was reminded of the same feeling he'd experienced upon seeing the giant fallen oak protruding from his second story, that feeling of lightness which replaced the lead weight of anxiety, knowing that the tree, having fallen once, had fallen for the last time ever. Now, similarly, his anxiety was defused because the bones were about to be unearthed, and once above ground, both they and Travis would be exposed, never to be reburied again.

Trudging onto his yard to join the others (he thought of those crime shows where the serial killer makes a plea deal upon agreeing to take the authorities to where he'd buried the remains), Travis decided to just come out with it rather than answer a string of clumsy and embarrassing questions. But he wasn't quick enough; the questions started despite him, beginning with Officer Brantley. "So Mr. Riggins- you dug this?"

"I did dig this, yes."

Now it was Miller's turn. "How deep did you go?"

So why is this Docker's-wearing code enforcement tool asking police questions? "Well, about... a little more than three feet I guess."

The buried child's vertebrae trembled as Keith hopped up and down over it.

"See? See?!!"

Mr. Miller continued. "And you never thought that might be a problem?"

Clearly, Miller was a wanna-be cop who was rejected by the academy. "Okay, yes, I pretty much knew it was a problem, alright?"

Officer Brantley stepped with cruel precision directly onto the bare spot. "Mr. Riggins, you know we have laws about this sort of thing don't you?"

Travis' fears had been well founded; their questions could not have extenuated his pain more if they'd been purposed to do so. It was time to end the ridiculum right now and let the inevitable unfold- his felony concealment of human remains conviction, the destruction of his landscaping by the county, and Alicia's obligatory divorce proceedings. “Look, when I found her it was a total accident, all I was trying to do was- “

“- because you can’t install a fish pond in Cobb County without a permit if the depth is 24” or deeper. That’s the code.” Mr. Miller held up the clipboard and waved it pedantically.

“Yes!” shouted a fist-pumping Keith. “YES!!!”

The two officials stared at Travis grimly as grinning Keith rocked back and forth on his heels, arms folded across his chest. “Wait.” Travis took a long breath and looked from face to face. “You’re here about the koi pond?”

"Thought you'd get away with it didn't you Riggins? Where's your smart-ass jokes now?"

Mr. Miller strolled around the pond's periphery. "Cobb County's got pretty stiff fines for out-of-code fish ponds. Too bad too. This is a nice'n."

Travis could feel the blood returning to his extremities. "My koi pond, wow. Okay. Well, actually, I didn't need a permit, because it's less than 24" deep."

"But you said you dug more than three feet."

"Yes, but then I filled it back in just enough to make code. Measure it. Only 23" deep." From the back of his belt, Miller produced a tape measure, extending it past the floating lily pads and down into the water. Meanwhile, Keith watched and waited in suspended animation. Miller read it, then shook his head.

"Only 23" deep."

"FUCK!" An upswell of rage turned Keith's head into a tomato; atremble with frustration, the furious man stomped off, splurting expletives with each step. "FUCK! FUCK YOU RIGGINS! FUCKING BULLSHIT! FUCK THIS FUCKING BULLSHIT!"

Mr. Miller called after him. "We'll be back in a bit Mr. Walters to talk some more about your big hole."

"FUCK MY BIG HOLE!"

With the ignominious exit of his neighbor, a relieved Travis was left to wrap things up with the officials. "So we're good here then?"

"We're good." Miller watched the huge koi drifting happily through the dark water, then expanded his view. "Quite the spread you have here."

"Thanks. It's my hobby I suppose."

Officer Brantley kicked his toe across the bare spot, then peered down at Travis with a creased brow. "Wait. Who's 'her'?"

"Her?"

"Her." The big policeman fast-reversed his mind back to an earlier point in their conversation. "You said 'when you found *her* it was an accident.' Who is *her*?"

Travis' throat tightened. "Her. Oh. Oh yeah! *Her.* Well... I was at Lowe's right, just shopping for, oh I don't know, whatever, I'm just shopping, and there *she* was, this very pond, on display! I totally just... found her by accident. Said to myself then and there, I gotta get her into the ground ASAP. And here she is!"

Officer Brantley chuckled. "Gotcha. Okay, we'll leave ya to her."

The two men turned to leave, but then Brantley paused yet again, his face somber. "Um, Mr. Riggins, before we go back over to that neighbor of yours, do you know if he has any firearms?"

Back in the house, Travis changed into his digging clothes with a lightheartedness known only to the miraculously reprieved. It was all over. The little girl's bones, his buried secret, was just that and would remain so. Keith knew nothing after all; tiptoeing around the crazy man had been unnecessary, and now, laughing to himself as he tied his boots, Travis was free to finally finish off the bare spot with what he'd intended to plant there in the first place, the pretty lawn spinner which had been waiting out in the storage shed all these weeks. It remained true that the little girl's mystery would forever go unsolved, but the nagging itch of that unresolved issue was soothed by the resolution of two others- his precious landscaping and nearly-as-precious marriage would live to bloom another day. Stepping out of the house into the inviting sunshine and making his way back to the shed, Travis reflected on anxiety's destructive power, and his deliverance from that anxiety which the twirly multi-colored spinner would symbolize. And as he came around the corner of the koi pond with his happy armload of spinner parts he saw Keith's son sitting on the bare spot, a shovel across his lap.

"I know your secret Mr. Riggins."

9

The paler-than-white face of the young man staring up at Travis was a joyless one, serious beyond his or even Travis' age. "So you think you know something?"

"Don't fuck with me Mr. Riggins," the sullen teenager said, flicking a spider off his leg without breaking eye contact with the adult man. "I saw you holding the skull."

Travis remembered he was still carrying the yard spinner, and dropped it off to the side. "Okay. So have you told anyone?"

The boy didn't smile, but came as close to a smile as a face like his could allow. "Don't you want to know who I am?"

"I know who you are. You're Keith's kid."

"No." Now the young man stood, twitching the stringy blonde hair out of his face and standing his straightest and tallest in an effort to show himself a man, an image compromised by the oversized shovel and the even more oversized sneakers. "That's not who I am. What's my name?"

Travis thought it best to not tell the young man the nicknames he'd thought up over the years for the seldom-seen youth next door he'd never met- Boy Radley, InvisiBilly, The Ghost of Crested Boulder. "I don't know your name. Sorry."

"See? You don't know me." The boy pierced the ground with the point of the shovel, and then leaned onto the upright handle. "It's Devon. But not Walters."

Travis looked nervously over at Keith's. "Not Walters. So are you... adopted?"

Devon's face tilted sarcastically. "Do you really think they'd let somebody like Keith adopt anybody?" Again, Travis hazarded a glance at the windows next door. "Don't worry about him. He won't know I'm here. When he came back from your house he ran straight downstairs to his train room to drink beer and pout. He'll stay there all night." As Travis wondered what a "train room" might be, Devon stared thoughtfully at the bare earth beneath his feet, then continued. "Now that I'm here I could probably stay here all night too." With that, Devon sat on the bare spot, cross-legged, and after a nod from the boy that he should sit as well, Travis had no choice but to join him.

For many seconds, the only sound was the gurgle from the koi pond's fountain. "Do you want something to drink, I think my wife has like Diet Coke or- "

"I've lived here a lot longer than you Mr. Riggins."

Fuck me, he's gonna tell me his whole sad story. But Travis had to listen. Because Devon had seen the skull. "Yeah. Ten years or something, right?"

"Eleven." A blankness passed behind Devon's eyes, as if his vision had turned inward upon a barren landscape. "Since I was four. I played outside all the time. Not like now." Devon's eyes were focused out at the sidewalk, his head turning slowly along its concrete length. "Riding my tricycle. Up and down that sidewalk. Just up and down." He turned one grayish eye back toward Travis; the other remained hidden behind his blonde mop. "Can you imagine, me, some little kid riding a tricycle?"

"Sure. Why not?"

Devon glared poisonously. "Don't talk down to me. The counsellors do that. I see through it every time."

Travis swallowed and nodded. "Right. Sorry. Okay no. Can't imagine you pedaling your little Big Wheel up and down the sidewalk."

"Thank you." Dropping his head forward, Devon seemed to exhale something more than air, then straightened again. "But I did. That was when I was a lot younger. When the neighborhood was different."

"Look, Devon, is there a point to telling me about- "

"Do you wanna know whose bones we're sitting on or not?"

The first robin's song of oncoming evening trilled and bubbled somewhere nearby; the soil beneath Travis' legs seemed shallower now, incapable of bearing his weight. "You know who's buried here?"

"Yes." Devon pulled back the hair from his face with both hands, then returned them to gripping his shovel handle. "But first I gotta tell you about my best friend."

Travis lowered his voice to a whisper. "Holy shit Devon!" The young man was staring ahead as if into an imaginary campfire. "Are you telling me it's your best friend who's buried here?"

Devon spun on Travis and hissed angrily. "*Did I say that?*" Closing his eyes in frustration he shook his head, his hands now in fists, the long hair whipping across his face as he spoke. "Shit! Can one person just *one person* let me tell a story my way *just once* without making up their own ending before I get there?"

"Okay okay I'm sorry! Go ahead."

Devon sighed, then tossed a few blades of the sparse grass into the imaginary campfire. "Like I told you. Used to ride my trike all day up and down this sidewalk. Up to Iffy and back, that was before there were drug dealers in front of it. Store had gum and candy and stuff. Don't know what they have there now. Drugs I guess." Devon's gangly legs were uncrossed now, his feet flat on the ground where he sat, knees up, his arms wrapped around his bony shins. "But I was never there alone. Always with my friend. She rode everywhere with me."

Travis wished they were each holding a beer. "She?"

"Yes." Devon nodded slowly as if confirming his memory. "Same age as me. Went to kindergarten with me. First grade too. Second grade..." Here Devon's voice trailed off across the non-existent embers; seconds later, he was back. "And when we outgrew our trikes we rode our bikes. We were at each other's house all the time, playing with our action figures out in her yard, or my yard, or we'd bury them up to their necks in the sandbox at the church playground... we rode the bus together, sat by each other in school, got in trouble for the same things, we even... we wanted to do a sleep over, but Keith wouldn't have her in our house, and he wouldn't let me stay over at her house, so instead we put up a tent in her front yard, one of her brothers helped us, you know, kinda like a big tarp over a clothesline thing." For a moment the image of Corey's tarp flooded in, but Devon's story pushed it out again. "And we made the tent into like our own little house in the pretend forest, I snuck a blanket and pillow from home, we had flashlights and snacks and our Yu-Gi-Oh cards and we pretended like we were, like, apart from everything, somewhere else. Somebody else." Now Devon turned his grim gray eyes straight at Travis. "And we were raising our baby."

"Devon I hope to hell you mean like a stuffed animal or something."

This time it was an actual smile, albeit a gloomy one. "We had a kitten. A stray she found. And so we called it our baby. We put an old sweater in a cardboard box and called it her bed. And we were a secret yard family." Devon seemed relaxed now, almost at peace. "And it was like the best summer ever." But just like that, the nascent smile retreated into its hiding place. "Until the kitten got run over by a car."

In his peripheral vision, Travis saw the first street light of the evening snap on down the block. "That's messed up Devon."

The young man nodded. "And so, we had a little funeral. And we buried it."

Travis' voice was a whisper once again as Travis tried to fill in the blanks. "Devon man, that's impossible, these here bones are definitely not kitten bones."

"Did I say we buried the kitten here? Did I say that?" Devon kicked at the shovel, knocking it into the imaginary coals. "I told you, let me tell the story without you trying to guess what's next! I know how to do it alright?!" Travis raised one hand in apology, and with the other zippered his lip. Devon continued. "So anyway. We buried it. In *her* yard. Right next to the tarp tent. Which believe it or not was okay because, see, our kitten was still right there at least. I mean yeah, it was squished and shit, but it was still there. We could see where it was that we put her so it wasn't so bad to deal with." Retrieving the

shovel, Devon laid the handle across his lap. "And then on the first day of second grade my friend wasn't at the bus stop."

Travis gave it a moment to settle before daring to advance the story. "So... so what was that then? Did her family move?"

Devon shook his head. "No. Nothing with her family changed. Except her mom who was kindof going crazy on account of her daughter being missing." This time it was Devon who sensed the awkward pause, and rushed ahead before a Travis remark could make it worse. "Just went missing. Gone. Was riding her bike with me on Saturday, didn't come to my house all day Sunday, missed the bus on Monday. Her mom, she was all crying and hollering and what-not, she called the cops, they were driving real slow all around the neighborhood shining their floodlights; her mom and her brothers all searching and calling out, asking me when I saw her last, cops asking me too. And then the week went on, and still she was gone, and every day I sat in class and I didn't even notice who was sitting next to me, because it wasn't her. And we never saw her again."

The catbirds had joined in with the robins' evening song by this time, the shadows of dusk fully overtaking the little bare spot. "Nobody ever found her?"

"No. For a few weeks I'd see police cars here and there, cruising around, then a couple of cops who didn't wear uniforms asking people some questions, but pretty soon, it was just kindof... over with. Her brothers, actually her half-brothers, they said they were gonna find whoever grabbed their sister, gonna kill his ass, blah blah, but there was nobody to find and kill. To this day I can't remember one thing about my whole second grade year. Like it didn't happen." Devon watched an imaginary cinder float off into the evening air. "And pretty soon I was old enough to figure out what 'being dead' was really all about, and that my friend was probably dead somewhere, and I kindof... started to get used to that. But what I couldn't get used to was- " Devon made sure Travis was paying attention before continuing. "- I mean, with the kitten, yeah, she was dead, but there she was, buried in that little hole with the rock we marked it with. But I couldn't see where Monique was. I didn't have anything to, like, connect to. You know what I mean?"

"Her name was Monique?" Devon nodded. "I know what I want to ask next, but I don't want to jump your story."

Devon's eyes seemed to thank his older neighbor, and then the story continued. "I stopped riding my bike for good after Monique was gone. Wouldn't touch it. And when Keith tried to get rid of my old tricycle that I first rode with Monique when we were four I pitched a tantrum, said keep your hands off it, so he just left in there on the stoop. All these years." Travis glanced over at Keith's porch, one item of his junk heap now explained. "I kinda stopped wanting to do anything after that really. My mom, she thought I was like autistic and shit; she was like this old hippy who liked this guy Neil Young who she heard set up model trains for his kids who had cerebral palsy and so she set one up for me too, thinking maybe Keith and I could bond and shit by playing trains. But he didn't like playing with some fucking sad quiet kid and I knew he didn't wanna be around me, so I left the train alone like everything else, which is when he just started getting into the model train by himself. It became his place to go hide. I didn't care. It was better for everybody when he went off to hide."

It was late enough now that the hardware store would be closing; Travis wanted no interruptions from Alicia or anyone else before the story ended. "I think it's time to explain the shovel Devon."

The young man grimaced. "It is." For the first time while telling his story, Devon now stood, and began pacing back and forth across the bare spot, gesturing with the shovel now and then for emphasis. "So one day a couple of months ago I'm looking out the window, and it's like just about this time of day, and I see you Mr. Riggins. Right here. Kneeling down at the hole you dug. And I see you lift up a skull Mr. Riggins. And I could tell it wasn't grown-up size. It was a child's skull. That's when I knew."

“So you *are* saying that you think your friend is buried here.”

"Yes. I'm saying it *now.* Wasn't it better that I told my whole story first before I came out and said it?”

Travis was used to always doing the driving; now he was learning how to be a passenger. “But how can you be sure it’s her?"

"Oh I'm sure. You were holding Monique. I could feel it."

Travis thought back five years, recalling the state of neglected abandon in which he first saw his property before making his offer. "Was anyone living here at the time?"

"No. It was one of those dark empty houses that wasn’t lived in and wasn’t for sale. Until it was, and then you came." With the last crepuscular glow of the evening losing it grip, Devon scanned Travis' lush landscaping. "It didn't look like this back then. Just a gnarly shit dump. You know, like Keith's yard." Travis resisted laughing at Devon's one and only joke. "But now you got it so beautiful. It's like something out of a movie. And now that I know Monique is here- " the young man looked down on the bare spot, then up to Travis, "- it kindof feels good to know she's in this, like, special garden, with flowers all around her and a fountain and everything. It's like it was all put here just for her. Like somebody cared about her."

Here and there, the first lights of the evening pin-pricked the deepening dark. "So when all the skeletons were found in your yard... what did you think then?"

"That maybe I was wrong. That your bones and them were all a group. But then they proved they were the slaves' bones, and that there were only six and they found them all, so yours were something different and that made me even more sure." Devon shook his head bitterly. "Those slaves' bones... stupid Keith, thinking they were like the missing link or something, I learned on the internet that bones that old couldn't survive in this dirt. I just let him believe it though, you go asshole, just make a fool of yourself. Big fucking joke on him when they were "just niggers," right?"

Now Travis remembered where he had last seen Devon's feet, though not in the same shoes. "You were at the reinterment ceremony weren't you?"

Devon's pacing skidded to a stop. "It was weird. It was like they..." He closed his eyes for a moment, and then resumed. "So they were here all along, right, this was where they lived, way before us, and we kinda moved in on top of them, uninvited. It was like all this time they let us live here, without complaining. So when the tree forced them up, it was like... like I owed them something, you know? Like I had to say goodbye to them and, you know- apologize." He breathed in the cool of the evening air, then looked back to Travis. "Now you know why I don't call myself a Walters."

It was dark enough to be called night now; the solar lights lining Travis' walking path had turned themselves on, providing just enough illumination for the two men to still see the main points of each other's faces. Then bright headlights outshone everything- it was Alicia's car turning into the driveway, pulling past Travis' truck and into the garage. No one sitting on the bare spot moved or made a sound as Alicia came out of the garage, followed by the clicking of the front door which let them know they were alone again. "Mrs. Riggins doesn't know about the bones. Does she?"

Travis laughed for the first time of the entire conversation. "You guessed right. She's not exactly an archaeology buff."

"But I know you are."

"Why's that?"

"'Cause I see how you like hanging out with that lady archaeologist."

With Alicia's walk up the Riggins' porch the motion light had been triggered awake to greet her, but it was Devon's observation which made Travis feel illuminated. "Oh yeah. Linda Myers. Nice person."

"So anyway..." Devon repositioned his grip on the shovel handle. "...we have to tell the police you know. About the bones. It's, like, why I'm here and stuff."

"I know Devon." It was true. There was no hiding or avoiding anymore. What would happen to Travis' home and happiness was simply going to have to happen, koi pond and marriage be damned. "We'll call the county tomorrow."

"But: we dig her up right now." Devon jumped to his feet, his shovel ready.

"Let's let the police do that Devon."

"But I gotta see Monique again!" In the pale glow of the solar lights, Devon seemed smaller than before. "I've been waiting eight years."

Across the street, another motion light snapped into brightness over at the new neighbors' house, one which had been installed a lifetime ago by Corey. "The police really need to do the re-digging Devon, to handle it like a crime scene. But I promise you'll be here when they do." Now the light across the street outlined a silhouette, one which moved slowly up the sidewalk and neared the new neighbors' house. "We better call it a night Devon. Don't need any neighbors seein' us out here creepin' around in the dark with a shovel."

Devon gazed across the street at the advancing silhouette. "Oh it's nobody to worry about. Just Monique's mom."

Travis had bent over to pick up the spinner parts, but straightened up quickly once again. "Monique's mom?"

"Yeah." Across the street, the shuffling silhouette now came into clear outline against the glare of the motion light. "Miss Sheila. Monique's mom."

\\

Sitting at his desk at the real estate office the next morning, Travis felt better about himself than he had in a long while. True to his word to young Devon, he'd begun his day with a call to the Cobb County police department, where a desk cop had taken his report of human bones being found in his yard and listened to Travis' suggestion that perhaps they could be the remains of the missing Glavin girl from eight years earlier (as to why he'd reburied the bones, Travis would explain to the police that he didn't want them exposed to the elements so he reburied them for safe measure, a plausible story which would conveniently omit the problematic detail that the reburying occurred months rather than hours before his calling them in). It was a brief and businesslike phone call, more like reporting the finding of a lost wallet than finding a human being; the officer's reaction over the phone had been non-existent, and when Travis gave Sheila's address as the home of the missing little girl, he wondered if it was his imagination when, after giving the officer the number 1413, he detected a dismissive sigh at the other end of the line. The call had ended with a weary "okay sir, we'll have someone follow up " in a tone which signified to Travis that the addendum "sooner or later" was to be tacitly understood.

Still he knew he had (finally) done the right thing, despite the officer's lack of forensic enthusiasm. As for the collateral damage which would certainly follow, both physical and interpersonal, Travis marveled at how less traumatic it all seemed in his mind today, now that he had no choice in preventing it, providing him yet another object lesson of how much easier on the emotions it was to fix a problem than to fixate upon it. Things would be replanted and repaired- no big deal. And as for Alicia, he was sure he'd exaggerated what her reaction was going be. Yes, she'll be creeped out and pissed off- but no, she will not serve him divorce papers. Besides, these bones would be up and gone quickly, with none of the prolongation of the Walters Man event, since this was simply a one-off burial. But at this Travis tripped over a speed bump: *was* it just a one-off burial? How could he be sure? Devon's theory about the bones, despite his passionate certainty, was only that really, a theory. Perhaps the two properties, which generations ago had been all one under the Holman name, contained more slave remains than the smallpox victims. Was it not possible that the area had once been a version of the Slave Lot, where slaves had been buried for years before (and even after) the six found at Keith's, and lay scattered therefore all about and beneath the Riggins' property, the little girl under the bare spot being but one of those many? The thought of his horticultural heaven becoming pock-mocked with exploratory holes like his neighbor's perforated plot was nauseating; it would of course be within Travis' rights to refuse the DNR his permission to dig up the yard, but there would be the expectation, from both the historical and the archaeological communities, for him to "do the right thing" and submit his half-acre to the shovels (and knowing Alicia's general disregard for Travis' gardenic Eden, he was sure she'd want the whole place dug up as well, for the peace of mind of knowing she wasn't sleeping above any below-ground sleepers). Insofar as the "archaeological community" was concerned, Travis was at least honest enough with himself to admit that it amounted to one person and one person only: Linda Myers. What would she think of him if he were to deny them/her access to the treasures the land held, simply for the sake of shrubbery? He had impressed her so with his well-calculated display of compassionate sensibilities as regarding human worth and honoring those humble souls who society discards, etc. etc., values which of course he really did believe in but, more importantly to his cause, were simpatico with hers- all the progress he'd made with her therefore (*progress, Travis? To where exactly?)* would come screeching to a halt upon her seeing him for the lawn-worshipper he really was. Yes, Travis' morning at the office had begun with good feelings- but as thoughts like these began to infiltrate his mind, the afternoon found him seriously wondering just how good he would still be feeling after shovels had been set to soil.

But as for shovels, no amount of trepidation on Travis' part could make him deny the shovel of his earnest new friend Devon. What an extraordinary encounter it had been the evening before, and what an extraordinary young man! How incongruous that such a sensitive and perceptive soul could have sprouted and bloomed in the infertile barrens of the Walters' gloomy greenhouse; a dark flower he was, but a bold one, a black orchid most rare. Replaying in his mind their sitting-on-the-bare-spot colloquy, Travis realized it represented not only the most engaging encounter he'd ever enjoyed with a neighbor these five years, but the *only* neighborly encounter which he could describe as engaging, period. This sullen and somber teenager, so cynical beyond his years about so many things, was anything but cynical concerning his devotion to his lost friend, a devotion as pure as platinum and just as solid; the sort of devotion, Travis admitted, which he himself could not boast of ever holding for anyone. Leaving his house for work that morning, he had seen those devoted eyes peering out at him through a Walters window, eyes which he could no longer mistake for any other Walters eyes after having studied their contents so deeply the night before; eyes which watched and waited for the only news the boy cared to learn, the confirmation of what he believed to be the bones' identity. It was Travis' sincere wish as well that the bones might be proven to be hers and so end the mystery- in order to both fill the hole in Devon's heart and to prevent more holes from appearing in his pristine lawn.

It was later that same afternoon, upon returning to the office after his last showing of the day, when Travis' cell phone vibrated in his pocket.

"Hello dear."

"So did you think I wouldn't find out about her you sonofabitch?" It was a somewhat less cordial greeting than Travis was accustomed to receiving from his wife.

"Excuse me?"

He could tell from the sound of her voice that Alicia was outdoors. *"This is one hell of a way for me to find out. How long have you been hiding her from me?"*

Linda! Alicia's found out about Linda! Panic washed through Travis as he added things up in a nanosecond. Somehow she must have met Linda at the house today; maybe thinking Travis was home, she came by, and was snagged by his wife before she could leave and then grilled with questions; knowing Linda, she was probably too guileless to lie about the texting and hanging together at the reinterment. He was doomed. "Her?", he pretended. Who's 'her'?"

"Just stop it asshole! Stop it!"

"Alicia, there's nothing funny going on with her, I can explain the whole- "

"Nothing funny!? I'll say it's not fucking funny!" Travis could almost hear the swigging of the chardonnay bottle glug-glugging down her throat. "*Well she's still here if you want to come see her*

before she's gone, far be it from me to get between the two of you." With that, the phone clicked dead; a minute later he was in his truck, speeding toward the reckoning which awaited him at home.

Upon turning the corner of his block, Travis felt the lining of his stomach curdle, for the very sight which for his entire drive was the one he most dreaded to see was the first which came into view: Linda's DNR van. So it was true. His dalliance had been found out. But as he neared, an even more gut-curdling sight took precedent over the first- two Cobb County police cars, and officers unrolling yellow "Crime Scene" tape. What crime of passion had his enraged wife committed? But no- standing nearby in the yard was Linda, not murdered in the least, and not far from her Alicia, clearly not disposed to committing any such murder. *The bones!* Well of course! Now it was stupidly obvious: the cops were here already for the bones. But all that explained was the police presence. It still didn't explain...

"So when were you going to tell me about her?" But it was Linda who was asking this time, not Alicia.

"Her. As in- ?"

"As in the girl you've been hiding from me."

Now Alicia came up as well. "Right. The missing little girl the cops told us about. *That you dug up in our front yard!"*

The sudden gear-shifting was making Travis dizzy. "Alicia, this is Linda Myers, as seen on TV. Linda, this is my wife Alicia."

But the two women had already taken care of such formalities and spoke amongst themselves. "Alicia, how long ago did you say he dug the hole?"

"Back in the spring, before the tree came down!"

"And he didn't tell you what was in it ever since?"

"Ever since!" The two women glared at him, shaking their heads in disgust. From across the yard, the cop who seemed to be in charge of the investigation was approaching. Travis quickly determined that a procedural briefing was in order.

"Okayfeelfreetobemadatmel'llexplainsoonbutpleasedon'ttellthis coplhidthebones goddamntellmeyoudidn'talreadytellhimthatl- "

"Mr. Riggins?" It was one Chief Detective George McGill of the Cobb County Police Department, 6th Precinct. "First of all, wanna thank you for reporting what you found here in your yard. Must've been quite a shock."

"Oh believe me it was." *The bones were kindof surprising too.*

"Your wife and Miss Myers told us you buried the remains back up after you found 'em yesterday, really glad you did, what with the rain we got overnight. Might've compromised the evidence." Travis hazarded a glance at the women and tried to thank them with his eyes.

"Yes, well, I just thought it was the right thing to do." As both women shot him daggers, Travis kept it moving along. "It didn't seem ya'll were all that interested when I called it in this morning."

Detective McGill watched as two DNR shovelers carefully began their work (*well of course dummy, THAT'S why Linda's here, the cops called the DNR at the report of human remains, duh),* then turned back to Travis. "Oh you definitely got our attention with this one Mr. Riggins. This case goes back to 2012. Back then this investigation was our Number One priority, was for months really, we put everything we had into solving it but, well..." The detective sighed, but then regrouped. "Anyway, this could be huge."

"She was my best friend." Devon had silently crept up beside the group. Travis was grateful that the boy had not brought along his shovel.

"Well son" said McGill, "we can't be sure it's her yet, or even if it's a little girl, or a little boy. Miss Myers' people will be helping us with the identification. But if it is her..." A crowd of Crested Boulderisians had gathered out on the sidewalk and were craning their necks. "... this would be as big a break in a Cobb County cold case as we've had in ten years. But before we get too excited we'll need to deal with the obvious coincidence of this being found right next to the house where the slave remains were removed." The detective stared over at Keith's house and shook his head. "Glad we're over here for all this and not over there. My guys tell me your neighbor's no treat to deal with." Devon nodded in confirmation.

"Detective McGill!" It was one of the DNR diggers.

"Well?" The two shovelers' nods confirmed grim findings; setting their shovels aside, they resumed working instead with small hand spades and brushes. The detective turned back to his audience. "Alright. Time to see what we have."

Alicia, for one, had seen enough. "Okay, don't need to see bones, I'm out of here." Alicia shook Linda's hand and exchanged with her a "nice to meet you," then narrowed her eyes on Travis. "We'll talk later." As Alicia went back indoors, McGill turned his attention to Devon.

"You were her best friend you say?"

"Yes." Devon stared at the archaeologists' brushes as they removed the dirt. "We rode tricycles together."

The detective smiled. "Small world isn't it? Well son, if it's your friend Brittany, we'll know soon enough."

McGill turned, but paused at the sound of Travis' voice behind him. "Brittany?"

The detective nodded. "Brittany. You know." Travis' face revealed that the name meant nothing to him. McGill was amazed. "Brittany Ketterson! The daughter of state senator Tom Ketterson, who disappeared from East Cobb in 2012? Biggest local story of the year." Devon's eyebrows raised in protest; a side-look from Travis checked him. "Believe me, when Dispatch told us you called this morning, every investigator in the office sat up straight in his chair. All of north Georgia was lookin' for her back in the day. And if we've found her now" said McGill, looking first into Devon's confused face and then into Travis', "we'll have you to thank Mr. Riggins." With a polite nod to Linda, Detective McGill returned to the dig site, just as the first television news teams rolled up on the curb and began setting up for interviews.

"Who the hell is Brittany!?" Devon's face was equal parts outrage and disgust.

"Devon, man, when I called I told them Monique not- "

"Who's Monique?" Travis had nearly forgotten that Linda had remained.

"Linda, this is my neighbor, Devon Wal- Devon."

"Her name is Monique not Brittany!"

When Travis was finally able to reduce Devon's decibel level to one which didn't attract the attention of blue uniforms and TV microphones, Travis began the task of damage control for both Linda and his upset young neighbor. He confessed to Linda that he had, in fact, found the bones in the spring; how the "shock" of the discovery had "made him not think clearly," leading him to the foolish and short-sighted decision to rebury them (only temporarily he assured her, a complete falsehood but he assured her of it nonetheless), and how his conscience was stabbed by Devon's story of his long-missing cycle-buddy (which was true, but the fact that he was finally doing the right thing now only because the boy had brought his own shovel and threatened to do it himself was a detail he shrewdly omitted). Sensing that his repentant line of bullshit was making a positive effect by softening Linda's anger and pulling her sympathies back, Travis turned his mollifying skills toward Devon. Yes, it did seem that the primary interest of the police was this Ketterson cold case and not the Gavins one, but Travis assured him that no matter who the police thought or hoped they had in the grave, the scientific testing- and here he commended Linda to the boy for her team's archaeological skills- would show the truth of the remains' identity; and if that identity proved to be Monique, it would lead not only to his little friend receiving the dignity which she deserved in death but, perhaps, the long-denied justice for the crime committed against her in life. To Travis' relief, his efforts on both fronts were successful: Devon's anger was assuaged, and Linda's affections were well on the way to being restored; just in time, as it turned out, for them to observe Linda's colleagues and the forensic investigators snap photo after photo of the now fully-exposed skeleton, then lift it carefully and still intact (save for the separated skull, which, when brought up to the light, Travis could feel his young friend yearning to hold in his own hands) and placed in the back of the DNR van.

"Where are they taking her Travis?"

"You mean, *if* it's her."

"Where are they taking Monique?"

"To the medical examiner's office, Devon." As Linda explained the procedures to him as they walked toward the DNR van, Travis noticed that the TV crews had picked her out in the crowd and were closing in. "And actually, my team won't be doing the work. It'll be forensic anthropologists who will be heading up the examination."

"Forensic anthropologists." Devon rolled the words about in his head for a moment and wasn't sure if he liked them. "Will you be there too?"

Linda smiled down at the stringy blonde orchid. "I'll be checking in every day."

"Mizz Myers!" A microphone had found her; now it was joined by two more.

"Okay, hang on, lemme finish up here." The reporters and camera people stepped back just a little; Linda turned back to Travis, her demeanor softer than the one which had greeted him a half hour earlier, to be sure, but still retaining some reservation. Devon turned away in some embarrassment, sensing that what was to follow was not meant for his ears. "It's really great, your helping out Devon with this. It obviously means everything to him."

"He still has the tricycle Linda." Her brows creased, seeking more explanation. "That they used to ride together when they were four. He wouldn't let his dad throw it out. He's kept it, just like he's kept her." It was another strategically-delivered exhalation of sentiment, blown from his mouth like a warm breeze, wafting across the last remnant of permafrost on Linda's face and melting it away. Her thaw was complete. The full springtime of Linda's smile had returned.

As she started toward the interviewers, a hand pulled Linda back by the arm.

"Miss Linda?"

"Yes Devon?"

"Tell the forensic anth- what was it?"

"Anthropologists."

"Anthropologists. Tell them that her name is Monique. Not Brittany."

Linda's head tilted sympathetically. "Devon, that's not how they work. They're scientists, they just give the remains a case number. They don't use names."

Devon's eyes narrowed darkly. "Like at the Slave Lot?"

"Mizz Myers, could we get you for thirty seconds please?" Pulled into the media circle, Linda's apologetic eyes remained on Devon as her mouth dutifully responded to the reporters' questions. Meanwhile, the crowd on the sidewalk had grown to several dozen; from among the murmur and mumbles, one unmistakable voice rose with shrill clarity above the others.

"WHUD YOU DIG UP NOW WIT' YO' DIGGIN' IN DAT YAHD MISTAH DIGGINS?"

Devon took an uneasy step or two toward his own house. "Gotta go."

Travis' Sheila-dar picked her out in the crowd, shuffling and side-stepping her way to the front row. "Why, what's up?"

"Can't stay. That's Miss Sheila. She doesn't like to see me." Behind them, the doors of the DNR van slammed shut, its cargo now loaded.

"You mean, ever since- "

"Ever since." As Sheila worked her way closer along the sidewalk, Devon moved sideways so that Travis' body blocked her view of the boy. "Every time she saw me after Monique disappeared, she'd start into crying and moaning and remembering. So I hide from her, so that it doesn't take her back to that place."

"WHUD THEY FINE DOWN IN DAT HOLE MISTAH DIGGINS?"

"See ya." Slinking off like a teenage ninja, Devon ran along the fence row, then slipped around it into his own yard. Four eyes peering through Walters curtains observed his approach, then disappeared from the window as the slapping front screen door swallowed him into the house.

Sheila stood hollering in Travis' yard, oblivious to the various workers and authorities crisscrossing around her as they wrapped up their respective tasks. It was classic Sheila as always, standing in the way of others who had something useful to do; old habit told Travis to make her move along and get out of their way. But then it struck him: for the first time in all his history with Sheila, here was the first time when she more than anyone possessed the right to be standing here; more right, if Devon's theory about the bones was correct, to be standing in Travis' yard than even Travis himself. Depending on who'd been loaded into the DNR van, all these people should be getting the fuck out of the way of Sheila Gavins. A wave of compassion, one he couldn't fully suppress, surged up nauseously within him; a compassion which he resented bitterly for the complicating guilt it now caused him.

"You dig too gott damm much in yo' yahd Mistah Diggins. I done TOLL you dat a thousan' times!"

She had never told him that even one time of course, let alone a thousand times; whether she imagined she had done so or, like so many words which bubbled out of Sheila's mouth, they'd simply taken shape and rolled unchecked past her tongue without being truth-checked by her brain before proceeding. But it was a great relief to Travis *that* she'd said it, for it confirmed for him that Sheila was still out of touch with reality, and, if Sheila was still out of touch with reality, then he could continue to dismiss her as bat-shit crazy, compassion be damned. "It's very busy over here right now Sheila. Please get out of the way." Besides, he had more important matters which required his attention at the moment, like scanning across the hubbub to find Linda once again, to touch base with her and say his goodbyes.

"You need t' quit diggin' Mistah Diggins. Leave whass buried down in th' groun' buried down in th' groun'."

It was more of the same from Sheila, yet something about it twisted with the turn of a new hook; Travis turned back to look at her, but she was gone, in a sense; it was a Sheila somehow removed who remained, floating, or perhaps sinking, her murky eyes transfixed on a wakeful dream, out of time and apart from the here-and-now. "If it buried down undah then it buried an' gone, down wheah th' devil take it, an' when th' devil take he don' gib back, don' nevah gib back, the devil holds on an' won' leh go. The devil holds on an' won' leh go."

Now the red and blue lights of the squad cars came to life; the ignition of the DNR van started up as the reporters headed off toward their vehicles. Sheila remained, lost in the private nowhere her mind had wandered into. "Don' be diggin' up whut th' devil holds, devil holds on an' won' leh go. Th' devil won' leh go. Th' devil won' leh go." Still muttering, her feet began to move as if by sleepwalking, propelling her forward like a tottering wind-up robot; not aimlessly though, but inexorably toward her intended object, the now-vacated open grave.

"Sheila, wait!"

Rushing up to intercept her, Travis blocked her way, but the mumbling woman's feet continued toward their goal. "Th' devil won' leh go Mistah Diggins. The devil won' leh go." In his peripheral vision, Travis saw the DNR van moving even with him now, backing down the drive, and seated in the passenger side nearest him, Linda's face. But even nearer to him was Sheila's face, which pleaded for help he couldn't provide. "The devil won' leh me go Mistah Diggins. The devil won' leh me go. Tell the devil leh me go. Tell the devil leh me go."

"Come on Sheila." Taking her gently by the shoulders (but it truth, not gently; it was simply his loathing to make contact which rendered his approach tentative and thus made his touch appear gentle and compassionate, and from Linda's admiring viewpoint through the window, gentle and compassionate indeed), Travis turned Sheila away from the grave and back toward the sidewalk, and walked the gibbering woman across his lawn toward the assembled onlookers.

But when Travis left her with the group it did not envelope her as one of their own, but rather, split in two like the Red Sea, leaving Sheila to languish alone like an abandoned island between the divided waters.

"Tell the devil leh me go Mistah Diggins."

"Sheila do you... do you want some water?"

"You dig too much Mistah Diggins. You dig too gott damm much."

"I'll get you some water." Turning back toward the house, Travis noticed the DNR van was no longer beside him; looking down the driveway, there it was, leaving his gate and merging onto Crested Boulder. As it drove slowly away with police escort, he saw a smiling and reconquered Linda waving goodbye. Her conqueror waved back. Then, realizing he'd forgotten to take Sheila's grimy water bottle to refill it, Travis turned to find her. But she was gone. The parted waters had closed back in. The island of sidewalk was no more. Meanwhile, behind his kitchen window, Alicia closed the blinds and turned away. She'd seen enough.

10

To examine mankind's attitude toward the autumn season is to consider yet another example of the human species' contrary- or at the very least, counterintuitive- relationship with the natural world. Fall is that time of the year when Death and Dormancy, having been sent packing at winter's end and put out of sight and out of mind throughout the spring and summer, press their noses once more against October's window and begin tapping on the glass, reminding us that their return all along was inevitable. Garden annuals wither and droop onto the ground, ashamed of the sudden onset of wrinkles in their faces; leaves, feeling their blood drying up altogether, understand that they've overstayed their welcome and release their useless grips, surrendering to gravity, and the garden spider, having enjoyed the spoils of her six-month reign of terror as apex predator of the shrubbery, is overthrown by just one chilling frost, her suddenly brittle legs no longer able to spin their way out of oblivion's web. Birds flee the scene altogether, mammals and reptiles hunker down in hibernation, and fish slow themselves to a state so unmoving as to resemble death itself. With the disappearance of food, the loss of daylight and the ever-nearing advance of an all-encompassing cold, autumn announces to the natural world in no uncertain terms, "The End is Near!", and no creature which hears that end-times pronouncement considers for a moment that there's anything for them to do but submit. Except for Man. For while the natural world hears in the breeze of autumn the choking gasps of a dying year, the human animal views autumn as a beginning rather than an end, a time of re-energizing and a stirring to life. For example, fall is the time of harvest for most of the human world, the single-most celebrated yearly event which human history has ever known, when, unlike in the natural world, more food will be available to Earth's dominant species than at any other time of the year. What's more, the fall marks the end of summer's strangling oppression, when people can once again step out of their homes and not feel the magnifying glass of the sun focused squarely on their smoldering heads. For most students, fall is the beginning of the school year, not the end of it; fall marks as well the triumphant return of America's true national pastime, football of the oblong variety, and rekindles in all (well, in most) the anticipation of what's euphemistically referred to as "the holiday season," what with its butternut-spiced optimisms and wooly-sweatered snugly feelings of renewed good will. In short, human beings hear in autumn's arrival the wake-up call of reveille, not the mournful lights-out of taps; autumn rings in the inauguration of hope for a more pleasant few months than the miserable months which came just before it, the sort of hope which, as people enjoy brisk walks in fresh cool air or sips of Schwarzbier lagers around bonfires, convinces them that the winter which looms just around the corner will surely be a pleasant three months as well. And when that winter finally arrives and kicks their asses unmercifully, those same hopeful dreamers will in a moment change their minds and long for the heat of summer to be tapping on their window glass again.

But as Travis sat in his truck with the windows down on the first delightfully cool afternoon of late September, parked on his driveway home from work and in no hurry to leave the temperate pleasure of his breezy cab, he knew for certain he would not be longing for summer to return anytime soon no matter how harsh the winter to come; summer, for all he cared, could remain displaced by autumns and winters indefinitely. It had been a long and trying hot season for the Riggins family, what with giant tree attacks and slaughtered dogs and unceasing Sheilas and surly neighbors, and a seemingly inexhaustible supply of human remains quaking underfoot. The summer had created a strain on many fronts, a strain which had left its stifling effects; but today, with the soft air blowing through his open windows like the gentlest sweep of a broom, Travis could feel that strain lifting off and drifting away as he considered the many ways that things were looking up. To begin with, his mystery bones, as disruptive events go, were no more; no more were they disruptive that is, for in yet another reminder to him that our worries are almost always greater than our realities, the investigators and diggers had been able to remove all the remains and evidence they needed without so much as displacing a spoonful of dirt more than what Travis had dug out originally. In fact, despite the score of police, scientists and media who had invaded Travis' property, no indication remained that anyone beside the homeowner had ever been in the yard, for not a flower was trampled, not a flagstone overturned, and the precious koi pond, whose destruction Travis had accepted as a foregone conclusion, had been avoided entirely, his lazing fish feeling nary a ripple of vibration in their water the entire time. All that remained to attest to the great goat rodeo that had taken place was the same unaltered original hole, which the police had asked Travis to refrain from refilling so long as the investigation continued. Which at today's date still did; no word had come from the authorities yet as to the skeleton's identity. But here too was an example of how things were looking up: Linda had texted Travis only the day before that a news announcement would be made within a couple of days, prompting him to relay this update to an excited Devon, instructing him not to miss the eleven o'clock news each night. It had been the lead story on that same eleven o'clock news back on the evening of the skeleton's removal, a story which recalled the Brittany Ketterson disappearance of 2012, including photos of the little white girl and interviews with the detectives who had worked the case at that time. Linda, of course, had done a fine job once again with her brief interview which followed, now having become a veteran before the camera; Travis texted his congratulations to her the next day, which prompted a dam burst of texts back and forth from each phone; here then was yet another encouragement, albeit an illicit one, the electronic confirmation that all things were well again in the forbidden Land Of The Linda.

Then there was the positive turn as regarding his actual wife, whose traumatic stress following the revelation of the bones had proven as minimal as the dig site's. The dreaded shrew-taming Travis assumed would be required in order to talk Alicia down from her anger ledge over his coverup turned out to be unnecessary; all that needed doing was to simply explain to her (after first removing the cork from the wine bottle of course) that it was she and only she he had in mind when he'd kept his secret from her, deciding it was best to say nothing in order to spare her delicate emotions (he had used the actual word "delicate," said it with a straight face even), knowing how distraught she'd have been if he told her what lurked beneath the sod *(And babe, wasn't I right? Just look at how upset you were!)* In no time she was obsessing happily once again over window treatments and paint, distracted by the indoors from unpleasantries outdoors. Even in her home improvement project Travis found new reasons to be cheerful; having been struck one day by the frightening reality that, unless he intervened, he'd soon be living in a house with plum red and plum yellow windows, he had devised an ingenious strategy for steering her from such madness. Rather than making the rookie husband blunder of objecting outright to her choices, Travis determined he would surreptitiously undermine her confidence in her color scheme with the time-proven opposite approach: praise her design concepts to the skies with enthusiastic endorsement, understanding full well that anything her husband thought was fabulous must necessarily be a terrible idea. With comments such as "Goddamn, it's gonna be SO GREAT having the only windows in the neighborhood that look like a rainbow Pride flag!" and "I can't believe *everybody* isn't turning their windows into rainbows!" she began second-guessing herself almost instantly, and after just a few days of hearing him express his abiding love for the plum family, Alicia determined that this family could not be allowed to live in her home after all, moving her to opt for a more tasteful palette indicative of a forest rather than a fruit basket- for which Travis made sure to seal the deal by expressing his preference for the plum, thereby guaranteeing Alicia would stick with the new plumless plan. Yes, the onset of autumn was bringing the promise of better, calmer colors in general for Travis, himself having endured an all-too colorful summer and now longing for the blessed blandness of a drama-free winter.

His reverie was broken by the braying of an ass in his passenger-side window. "Whatchoo doin' sittin' in yo' truck Mistah Diggins?"

"Hey Sheila." Now the breeze in his cab had become his enemy; it carried the reek of stale beer and neglected hygiene. "Need something?"

Sheila hitched up her pants as she leaned her head in through the window. "You know it done got col' out t'day winnah-time comin', gotta light me mah cannels t'night."

"You light your candles every night. In order to see. Not because it's cold. Right?"

Her eyes bugged wide as she responded to the stupidest man on earth. "Hell yeah I light my cannels evah night! Thass wah I need fo' dollahs fo' cannels!"

A crow squawked "Amen" in support. "How many times Sheila? I told you, no more four dollars." Her mouth opened, but Travis was quicker. "And not three dollars and not two dollars either."

Sheila backed a step to regroup, and when her eyes rolled back into her head in search of her next tack, she found it. "Den I need fahrwood fo' when I burn mah fahr. Gon' be gettin' col' out soon." For many more years than Travis had lived on Crested Boulder, Sheila had burned firewood indoors, presumably in a fireplace, throughout the winter, the fierce orange glow a familiar sight behind her front window at all hours of the night, flames which always appeared much much larger than any standard fireplace should or could contain. To Travis, it was perfect Sheila irony, knowing that for decades her crumbling, never-inspected chimney belched like a blast furnace night after night without incident, while Travis' own fireplace, despite being professionally swept and serviced on an annual basis by a CSIA certified chimney sweep, managed to backfire into a small but smoky creosote fire just one winter earlier, setting off the Riggins' smoke alarms and bringing out the fire department who admonished him to "do a better job maintaining his flue." How Sheila's house of sticks and straws came through her nightly conflagrations uncinderized was beyond his understanding; but then again, if Sheila herself continued to awaken each day herself still intact and unburnt by the equally frequent firestorms of her life, why shouldn't her matchbox home do so as well? "Well it's not gonna be cold enough for you to need a fire for a few weeks, but yes, I'll bring you over some wood this evening."

As always, Sheila's gratitude was effusive. "So you gonna gib me fo' dollahs now fo' cig'rettes?"

"For cigarettes? I thought you said for candles."

Sheila's arms flapped in frustration. "THASS HOW I LIGHT MAH CIG'RETTES, WITHUH CANNELS! Gottdamm Mistah Diggins you a hahd man t' talk sinse to!" Exasperated with Travis' inability to focus, Sheila mumbled defeatedly as she shuffled away from the truck and gallumphed her way down the driveway; turning her rudder sidewalk-ward, she raised her arm in a conciliatory wave goodbye. But as Travis watched more closely, he realized Sheila's wave was more functional than friendly, as from her grimy fingers another spent lottery ticket fluttered down onto his driveway.

"Goddammitt Sheila!" But it was spoken for his own ears only, under his breath, knowing that remonstrating Sheila for throwing litter would do as much good as commanding a parade horse to not shit in the street. Picking up the crumpled ticket, Travis turned back up his driveway; glancing across the fence he saw the same person he always saw these days without fail, each afternoon upon arriving home from work- Devon, standing on his dad's porch, checking in with Travis for news about the bones.

"Hey Mr. Riggins."

"Hey."

"Anything from Miss Linda?"

It always bothered Travis when Devon said Linda's name out loud, especially when he shouted it. "No. Nothing yet. Keep watching the news." Devon nodded, then trudged back into his parents' house. Heading into his own, Travis was hit by the smell of latex paint and the crunch of plastic underneath his feet; in the adjoining living room,

Alicia stood on a wobbly stepladder, rolling a soft yellow color onto the walls.

"If you screw the extension pole onto your roller you can reach the top of that wall without a ladder and you get better leverage which means you don't have to push so hard and then won't get a neckache."

Alicia stopped rolling; turning on the ladder to face him, Travis saw that her face was speckled with several million tiny yellow dots. "I'm not that dumb Travis. I know that. I couldn't find the stick." She backed down the ladder and reloaded her roller in the paint pan which sat on the drop cloth next to her, letting the excess drip off before moving it away from the tray. "But I couldn't wait 'til you got home and found it for me. I got my ratchet-ride class to teach tonight remember? Needed to get one coat on at least." With the paint-laden roller sagging and still dripping, Alicia climbed her ladder again and resumed speckling her face.

"The stick's out in the shed. I'll go get it for you." Crossing into the kitchen on his way toward the French doors, Travis felt his pocket vibrate, which prompted him to holler back at Alicia. "Should have texted me, I'd have told you where it was." Checking his phone, it was what he always hoped to see these days- a text from Linda: *"Finally some news! Watch tonight channel 4. Is not everything but something! How are you?"*

Travis smiled at Linda's improved spelling of "you." In her first texts to him it was "u," but Travis had told her that was 4 kids. Grownups need 2 spell out their words. *"I'm great. Will Devon be happy with the news?"* Her response was non-committal:

"Film at 11"

"I was gonna text you, but I know you already get so many texts." The sound of Alicia's voice four feet away nearly sent Travis' phone into the ceiling fan. She stood in the archway between the living room and the kitchen. "Because of your work. From clients and such." She was wiping paint speckles off her face with a sopping-wet rag. "Done for today. But I'll be happy to use that extension stick for the second coat."

"I'll go get it now so that you'll have it." Escaping into the back yard, Travis headed toward the shed, where his eye fell upon his woodpile, reminding him with a pinching pain of Sheila's firewood. The madwoman would be back for it, of that he was certain. Knowing it was better to dispense with Sheila on his own terms rather than hers, Travis took up an armload of the wood and carried it to the front yard. His plan would be to secretly stage the firewood near the curb for now until Alicia left to go teach her class, and then, in direct defiance of his wife's imposed embargo against Greater Sheila, deliver the unsanctioned cargo himself to 1413 that evening. Placing the wood in an inconspicuous spot near the curb, Travis stood upright to see Laura and Jason, his newest neighbors/clients, waving at him from across the street. Travis reciprocated, and his impulse was to cross the street and chat them up in a neighborly way. But it was an impulse he resisted when he noticed sitting next to them the third member of the family who he'd not yet had the pleasure of meeting, and indeed felt no pleasure to meet, at least for the indeterminate near future: a big friendly-looking dog.

"Very nice people, Brother Jason and Sister Laura." It was the good Sister Beulah and the nearly-as-good Pastor Kenneth, arrayed in full proselytizing splendor before Travis on the sidewalk. "Christian people. Love the Lord with all their hearts."

"You've met them already?"

"Oh yes." As the new dog retrieved a ball at the spot where the old dog bled to death, Laura and Jason expanded their waving to include their fellow believers. "Expecting them to visit us this Sunday worship. They already have their home church but we're gonna steal 'em just this one time."

Travis' decision to not chat up the new neighbors was looking better by the second. "Okay, well, back to work for me then."

"The Lord has used you mightily for shining light in the darkness, Brother Travis."

Sister Beulah's pronouncement turned Travis back around. "Say what?"

"The Lord's hand. It's been upon you." Now it was the pastor who stepped up to the pulpit. "The first heavenly sign was revealed through the great tree, ripped out of the ground by the mighty hand of God to bring up to the light those poor lost souls who had been buried in slavery's bondage."

"It was god's will to crush my house?"

"'Yes, but remember the words of Hosea: 'He hath torn AND he hath healed us!'" Sister Beulah chimed in exuberantly. "'He has smitten, AND he hath binded us up!'"

"Actually it was the insurance company who hath binded us up but- "

"- and now," continued the Pastor, "we see how the hand of God has guided your shovel Brother Travis, removing the earthen shroud of sin and darkness which had covered the bones of that poor little girl all these years, buried there in hate so long ago but never forgotten, not by God or by man."

Travis stepped closer to the evangelists, hoping that closing the distance might encourage them to lower their voices. "You realize we don't know for sure if it's the little girl yet, right?"

"But *God* knows it's that little girl." Sister Beulah pointed her Bible heavenward, not lowering her outside voice in the least. "God has always known, and has waited, in His timing, for this day when your shovel would reopen the book of secrets that's been closed so long and bring our troubled Sister Sheila peace and closure."

"Amen!"

"Okay hold on." Travis felt the blood rise in his gullet. "Please tell me you didn't

tell Sheila who you think was removed from that hole. You didn't, right?"

Sister Beulah was positively cheerful. "Why yes we did, praise Jesus."

Travis struggled to keep his response measured. “So thanks to you, Sheila is now walking around in the belief that the remains of her missing daughter have been found, even though the medical examiner hasn’t said a word about it yet?”

Pastor Kenneth came to the aid of his assailed partner. "You forget Brother Travis, that we, Sheila's church family, were here in 2012 and lived through it with her and prayed through it with her. The medical examiner wasn’t here prayin’, we were. So we know the truth about those bones the Lord revealed to you. We know this is an answer to those prayers."

“And what if you’re wrong? Did that ever cross your mind?”

Although many inches shorter in stature, Sister Beulah looked down upon Travis with an impenetrable, condescending smile and spoke with the finality of last rites. “Brother Travis, what doesn't seem to cross *your* mind is that the Lord God is in charge, that the Lord knows all, more than any mere man, and that it was the Lord’s will that we tell His truth to Sister Sheila, because the Lord-”

“FUCK THE LORD!” It was loud enough that even Jason’s dog dropped his ball and looked across the street. Pulling his voice back to a choleric whisper, Travis got up in their faces close enough for the toes of his sneakers to be stabbed by the pastor’s pointed wingtips. “Who the hell do you think you two are, messing with that already messed-up head of hers, tearin’ off all her old scabs that aren’t healed, just ‘cause you think you know something when you and your god don’t know shit! It’s for the scientists to determine who that skeleton is. But instead you go blabbin’ things you don’t know and get her all worked up. *It’s not fair to Sheila!*”

Sister Beulah held her ground. “Since when did you start caring about Sheila?’

“I DON’T care about Sheila!”

“Hey there neighbors!” Having suddenly materialized next to them on the sidewalk was Jason, with Laura and New Dog right behind. “What are we discussing so loudly over here?”

"We were just testifying, Brother Jason" explained Pastor Kenneth, "to the miracle which God is doing in Brother Travis' hole."

"Oh, right! The one where they found Sister Sheila's daughter."

"You mean you told the new neighbors too?"

"Amen Brother Travis!"

"GODDAMMITT!"

Jason called after Travis who was already stomping his way back to the house. "You don't need to take the Lord's name in vain like that."

"Oh shut up, I already sold you the house. I can say what I want to now."

The lead story that night on the 11 o'clock news was in fact the breaking development in the Brittany Ketterson case, which featured the official announcement of the medical examiner's and forensic anthropologist's findings as to the identity of the skeletal remains. Standing behind the podium as the law enforcement representative was the same Detective McGill who Travis remembered as the investigator he'd met the afternoon when the remains were removed; and while McGill had told Travis that day that he'd participated in the 2012 investigation of Brittany's disappearance, he hadn't told Travis what the news pointed out this evening- that Detective McGill was the chief investigator on the case back in 2012, and had now resumed those responsibilities. Alicia, home from teaching her spin class, watched along with Travis; and when Det. McGill uttered the devastating determination- as personally devastating to him, arguably, as it was to the Ketterson family- that the remains were in fact those of a girl the correct approximate age of young Brittany, but, conclusively, not those of the state senator's missing daughter, Alicia twisted uneasily on the sofa.

"So... they don't know who it is now?"

"Doesn't sound like it. Or if they do they're not saying yet."

Her brow furrowed. "But... that's bad! I mean, this was supposed to end it. They would prove it was her and then move on. We'd move on. The hole would get filled and no more shit with bones. But now-

" Alicia turned to Travis and stared him through. "- this means they might be out here again looking for more clues to figure out who this mystery girl was. Right?"

"There's that chance."

"Fuck." Alicia stood and paced back and forth across the plastic drop cloths which remained for the 2nd coat. "So I still get to live with an open damn grave in my yard and a murder mystery right outside my bedroom window. Great." After finding no relief from her agitation by walking about, Alicia plopped heavily back down next to Travis. "So. Who do you think it was who used to live in those bones?"

"I have literally no clue." Which was the truth; Travis really did no longer have any earthly, or unearthly, idea as to the identity of the mysterious little skeleton. Because one crucial fact which Travis had heard in the forensic findings as reported by Det. McGill made it painfully clear to him that the deceased little girl, while proven to the investigators not to be little Brittany, could not be little Monique either. *And Devon must have just heard the same thing too!*

"Well I'm too wired now to sleep." Alicia stood with her hands on her hips, awkwardly planted in the center of the living room, then with sudden resolve took up her wine glass from the end table and threw back the last gulp. "Fuck it. Don't care that it's almost midnight. I'm painting the 2nd coat." Alicia glanced about at her paint tools; then, "Did you bring in my extension stick?"

Travis leapt to his feet. "Totally forgot! I'll go get it." It was just what he needed, his wife's sudden burst of nocturnal energy, for it provided him an excuse to go outside in the middle of night and secretly meet up with the boy who had certainly just heard the bad news about Monique and would be waiting for Travis at their graveside rendezvous. Sure enough, Devon was waiting when Travis rounded the koi pond.

"Travis, what took you so long?"

"So I guess this means you saw the news." Devon nodded, eagerly in fact; despite the minimal illumination provided by the solar lights,

Travis could see an odd dark patch under Devon's left eye. "What's that on your face?"

Devon shook his head dismissively. "Nothing. Just Keith."

"What do you mean, 'just Keith?'"

"He caught me talking to you today. When I was out on the porch."

"The sonofabitch punched you?"

Devon shrugged his shoulders. "It's okay. I punched him back." The young man stood a little taller and seemed to brighten. "Anyway. So did you hear? It's not that Brittany girl!"

"Well, no. But- "

"That's great news right?" For some reason, Devon seemed in high spirits, elated even. *Hadn't he paid attention to the whole story?*

"But that's as far as they went Devon, that it *wasn't* the Brittany Ketterson girl. They didn't say who it was."

"Well, no, they didn't come right out and say it's Monique, but come on, it's obvious now!" Devon was up on his toes, his whisper nearly giddy with energy. "The detective said it, a young girl, same age as Monique, buried there the same time and stuff that Monique disappeared. It's her for sure!"

"Devon..."

"And now the anthrowhatevers and Miss Linda, they'll be able to prove it!"

As Devon stood in the darkened garden, his face more brightly aglow than all the solar lights which surrounded him, Travis realized it was the only time since he'd known the previously sullen boy that he'd ever seen him smile quite so broadly or as often. "Devon, I don't know how you missed it, but they won't be proving it at all."

Devon laughed in the clueless grownup's face. "You're crazy Travis! I didn't miss anything! Why won't they be able to prove it?"

The cicadas and tree frogs, who had provided their humming drone the entire time in accompaniment to the conversation, now dialed it down several clicks, as if curious themselves to learn Travis' meaning. He spoke slowly and simply, too simply even, to make sure it penetrated the naive teenager's ecstatic veneer. "Because Devon, the detective said the remains of the girl they found was African-American. She was *African-American*. So it couldn't be Monique, Devon. Because Monique's mom is Sheila. And you know as well as I do that Sheila is white."

\\

Beneath the ebony cover of the moonless midnight the little pathway lights glowed more sharply than ever, the upward angle of their beams casting the boy's and the man's features in eerily elongated masks of black and white; between them, the empty grave lay at their feet like an obsidian pool, its opaque stillness creating an illusion of impenetrability, an inky glaze which seemed to conceal hidden depths of bottomless mystery beneath its surface. For the moment, Travis stared into the half-illuminated face of the young man, curious to determine what ripples of reaction had been effected there by his sobering words. And to Travis' surprise, that face was still smiling back at him brightly.

"Devon, you get it don't you? The remains were of a black girl, so it couldn't be Monique because Sheila couldn't be her mother."

Despite the darkness of the garden, Travis saw Devon's eyes rolling with amused exasperation. "Dang Travis, you think I don't know that Miss Sheila is white? You think I'm stupid?"

"No I definitely don't think you're stupid but- "

"That was the best part of the news story, when they said that about the bones!" Devon tossed the hair back out of his eyes and laughed. "You really don't know much about Miss Sheila, do you Travis?"

Travis sighed. "I try to know as little as possible, to be honest."

"Sit." With a sudden drop, Devon plopped himself onto the ground, and nodded for Travis to do the same. The two neighbors sat on the edge of the hole, their legs and feet dangling down into it. "So. You look around and see all of Monique's white half-brothers and you assume shit."

"Half-brothers?"

Devon smiled sarcastically. "See? Thing One you don't know. Yeah. Half- brothers. Her half-brothers all got this dad or that dad and what-not, but Monique's dad was somebody else. Monique's dad... " At this point Devon hung fire, and with a teasing raising of the eyebrows extended the palm of his hand, the gesture for Travis to finish the sentence.

"... was black?" Grinning broadly, Devon nodded. "You're sure?"

"Am I sure???" Again, Devon flicked the hair out of his face. "Travis, who grew up in this neighborhood, you or me? Yes, Monique's dad was black. That's Thing Two you didn't know. You never saw him 'cause he got thrown in jail before you lived here, when Monique was like five or something." Devon stared down into the hole, rocking back and forth almost imperceptively. "It messed Monique up real bad when her dad got put away. I could tell. She was real sad for a while after that. She didn't get back to happy again until we started playing our yard family game under the blanket-tent." Now Devon looked up at his older friend. "It messed up Miss Sheila real bad too."

"When Monique's dad went to jail?"

Devon nodded. "Monique got all sad and moody, but Miss Sheila, she got pissed-off when they took him away. Really angry and mean. That's when all her yelling and shit started. Blaming white people for not havin' a husband around the house anymore, even though she herself was white. It made her like... it made her, you know, start acting... the way she does now. It sounds messed up but it's true Travis. It was like- I thought about this later, when I got older- it was like by talking like that it was her protest, you know, showing people what side she was on. Didn't you ever wonder why she talks like she does?"

It had long been a point of curious fascination to Travis; an unspoken and somewhat shameful fascination on his part, the whys and wherefores behind the inexplicable speaking style which proceeded from his neighbor's mouth (in fact, when Travis had first met her, he was sure it was an act, some horrible racist mockery which she was performing, but time had proven to him without a doubt that it was just the way she spoke, who knew why. Until now). The various men Sheila had caroused with over the five years that Travis had known her had all been black, and he had assumed it was just “her thing,” a preference for black men, which had in turn resulted in a preference (and an affinity for) black culture. But what Devon now told him revealed much deeper roots entirely. “What got Monique’s dad sent to jail?”

“Drugs” said Devon, with a “what else?” shrug of the shoulders. “At least that’s what her half-brothers said it was. Don’t know when he’s getting out. If ever.”

As Devon picked up bits of dry leaf and threw them methodically into the hole, contemplating each one before releasing it, Travis reflected back to the news story. “So if Monique’s dad was black, then that would account for the African-American features of the skull they talked about, the formation of the nasal region and the teeth and the eye orbits. Devon, did Monique look more like a black girl or a white girl to you?”

The young man stopped throwing the leaf bits and stared back at Travis. “She looked more like a Monique girl to me.”

Travis winced. “Sorry.”

“But- ask Keith what she looked like to *him*.” Devon was throwing the leaf bits again, but whipping them into the hole angrily. “Now you see why she couldn’t do a sleepover at my house.”

"Thing Three I didn't know."

Another rare Devon smile appeared, and with it, he brightened once again. "But see, that's the point Travis! The skeleton was a black girl, and Monique was a black girl! Black enough to match what the experts found out anyway. So like I said, it's all making sense now! That's Monique who they have, you know it too. Admit it!"

Travis laughed self-consciously. "You're making a believer out of me Devon."

"And all that's left now is for the scientists to do like the DNA stuff and the police do their stuff and prove what happened to her!" Devon's arms were folded across his chest, and he rocked back and forth where he sat, like an eager little boy the night before Christmas. "Eight years Travis. Everybody just forgot about her for eight years. But I didn't forget. I never stopped thinking about her. All these eight years. I never forgot about her."

"You fo'got abou' me Mistah Diggins."

Sheila stood behind them, in the shadows, swaying side-to-side under the trellis.

"Shit!" Travis quickly pulled his dangling legs out of the hole and scooted back. Devon, however, remained just as he was, staring straight forward and completely still.

"You fo'got abou' mah fahwood. You dinn' brang it."

"Oh- right. Sorry." For several moments, all three said nothing more, with Devon staring ahead like a seated statue and Sheila swaying beneath the trellis' ivy like a visiting specter. Soon the creepiness became too much for Travis, who scrambled to his feet with nervous energy. "I set your wood out earlier, it's up next to- "

"How'd it get eight years so fass?" Now Sheila was staring at the hole, still swaying, off in a dream. Her eyes then drifted down to the back of the young man before her feet. "Ain't seen you 'roun inna long time." With that, Devon slowly raised his head, and then stood at the edge of the hole, eventually turning and facing Monique's mom.

"Miss Sheila."

"Deron." Not a smile really, but a gaze of wonder more or less, crept across Sheila's features. "You all growed up. You Mistah Deron now." Once again, Sheila's drifting eyes fell upon the hole. "Ah used to have fahrwood. But iss gone now. Iss all gone. Wheah mah fahrwood go to?" She was looking back and forth between the two men, her eyes pleading along with her deteriorated voice. "Didjoo fine mah fahrwood? Didjoo fine it fo' me?"

"Travis?" Now it was Devon's eyes and voice which were pleading. "Where's Miss Sheila's firewood?"

As the little pathway lights began to lose their charge and fade to a timid glow, Travis stayed behind at the curb and watched as Devon and Sheila, the former whose arms were stacked with wood and the latter trailing close behind, crossed Crested Boulder and trudged up the crumbling driveway; through a broken-paned window of the ruined house at the top of that driveway, a lone candle could be seen burning inside, the only flickering exception to an otherwise unlit world. At another window but of a different house a pair of eyes watched the proceedings, then disappeared behind curtains which angrily snapped shut. Travis looked on from across the street as Devon set the firewood down at the spot where Sheila pointed; then, as Sheila shambled up to her broken front door, Devon followed her, and both went inside. Watching through the window as Devon's shadow followed Sheila's and they passed across the candle's dim backlighting, Travis thought of how he'd never once been inside where Sheila lived, and had always shuddered at the thought. But this young man Devon, he was there, right there; not only had he been in the dwelling before and knew its secrets, it was clear that he was not prevented by fear or revulsion or misunderstanding to be at ease within its walls. Whatever horrors might be seen in that house now, Devon had seen it in much different times. Did he see that house today as he had seen it then? Was he seeing a very different Miss Sheila?

As the two shadows flickered back and forth across the dim yellow of the candle, Travis felt an odd trembling; but it was only his phone, vibrating with a text. His heart leapt like the little candle flame, knowing it was Linda, checking in after the big TV news story to get his reaction. He had much to tell her, about Devon and Monique and Monique's father, and yes, about Monique's mother. He had much else to tell her too, things he knew he shouldn't tell her and no doubt wouldn't, but things which, when he thought of them, made his phone vibrate that much more happily. Pulling the phone out of his pocket, he checked the screen, and read her text:

"Never mind with the stick, u don't need 2 bring it. I'm done."

11

For any visitor of the Cobb County Police Department's 6th Precinct, it wouldn't leap out as obvious what activity took place within its drably-painted walls. The surroundings were barely distinguishable from any other office setting: modestly-appointed workspaces partitioned by a maze of half-height cubicle walls, the desks in those cubes topped with a predictable array of computers and file cabinets and printers and fax machines (yes, fax machines, an otherwise extinct dinosaur kept alive by law enforcement), and the staff going about their tasks, phone calls and data entry and coffee-refilling and small-talk, in the same manner as so many millions of other folks whose butts were assigned to office chairs in mundane operations anywhere. Indeed, if it weren't for the American and State of Georgia flags on display and the fact that so many of the employed were armed with prominently-displayed weapons, our visitor would have little reason to assume that the business at hand was anything as exciting or dramatic as crime fighting. But despite its aura of ordinariness, the unremarkable appearance of the place and its easy-going, untroubled atmosphere, the reason for the existence of the 6th precinct office was that all things in the 6th precinct were not in fact so untroubled. It was trouble which made up the business day of the 6th precinct- the prevention of trouble, people getting in trouble, people getting out of trouble, people making trouble, people filing complaints against people who troubled them- and so, from the highest ranking captain down to the lowest ranking clerk, the job description of every 6th precinct employee could be reduced down to one common denominator: trouble processing. Without the existence of a troubled 6th precinct, the trouble processors would not get paid. And nobody there seemed too troubled by that.

Travis definitely didn't want any trouble this morning at the 6th precinct. All he wanted were some answers. A month had transpired since the announcement of whose bones they were not, and no further updates had been provided as to whose bones they were. It had been a particularly slow-moving month for him, for twice each day- when he left for work in the morning, and when he came home in the afternoon- Devon would be standing on his parents' porch, his eyes asking the same question they always asked. And for all those twice-a-days, Travis would shake his head- no, he had learned nothing new. He'd continued to watch the local news without fail, and had kept in contact with Linda in case she knew of any progress (not that the topic of dead bones was required for Travis to stay in touch with Linda; his interest in Linda's very much-alive bones was reason enough to remain faithful with his texting). Now, having grown frustrated with so many days of no resolution from the authorities and wearying of having nothing to deliver to the boy but head-shakes, Travis had come to the precinct office, if only to have it told to him explicitly that no breakthroughs had been made rather than continuing with the tacit assumption of same. It was Detective McGill, the lead investigator he'd met the day of the bones' removal, with whom he requested to speak this morning, and given the fact that it was on his property where the bones had been found, he was confident McGill would acknowledge that he was entitled to a few minutes of the detective's time, especially considering the gratitude which McGill had expressed that day toward Travis for making the report. While at first he intended to simply call the detective on the phone, he'd thought it better to come to the precinct in-person, deciding that a face-to-face would give him a much more satisfying experience than a telephone's detached distance could provide. What's more, a one-on-one would allow Travis to employ what he considered his secret weapon: his irresistible real estate salesman charm, a talent which went wasted over the phone lines. Except of course when he was texting archaeologists.

"Mr. Riggins! It's Riggins, right?" It was Detective McGill, in his shirtsleeves and wearing his shoulder-holstered .38, offering his hand to Travis.

"Riggins, yes. Travis. Nice to see you again Detective."

"They told me you were out here. You could have just called, but hey, come on back, I got a minute. Want a bad cup of coffee?" The older man weaved Travis through the cubicles where plainclothes officers and non-police office workers sat, speaking on headsets or typing into computers, now and then glancing up; it struck Travis that several of those who looked at him seemed to recognize him, as if perhaps they'd been at his house the day the remains were removed, and it was those eyes, the ones reflecting familiarity, which seemed the quickest to look away from him and return to their laptops. After a visit to the breakroom for their coffees, McGill led them back to his corner cubicle, which was only slightly larger than the ones surrounding it but clearly bore the lived-in look of being occupied by the same person for decades. "Here, have a seat. Now you see the fancy office they give you after twenty-nine years a detective." Sitting heavily behind his desk, McGill glanced at his cell phone, then politely flipped it over, screen down. He smiled up at Travis expansively. "So! Dug up anything else of interest in that yard of yours lately?"

Travis was quick on the draw. "Man, I got skeletons poppin' up all over the place. They must know it's Halloween."

The detective laughed, then added, "Well I hope these new ones are wearin' name tags, it'll make my job a lot easier!" Both men laughed; then, McGill stood and walked across his cubicle to a metal file cabinet, and from a drawer removed without having to search for it an oversized manilla envelope. Returning with it and sitting again, McGill dropped the envelope in front of him; a label on the front read *Ketterson, Brittany Elaine.* "Guess I don't need to tell ya, it was a big disappointment when the tests came back negative on those bones."

Travis raised an eyebrow. "Negative for what?"

The detective's coffee cup paused before touching his lips. "Well no. Not tested negative really. I meant that the tests showed the bones weren't, you know, the girl we hoped it was." Travis' brow wrinkled; again McGill's cup was lowered before drinking, and he shook his head. "*Hoped.* Bad word choice. Of course we don't 'hope' someone is found dead, you understand. It's just that this case here...

well, that whole cabinet is files of this same investigation, was such a high-profile cold case for so long, we got somewhat... hope-full in a police way when you called."

"Totally understand." As McGill completed his twice-interrupted slurp of coffee, Travis saw in his peripheral vision another dress shirt and shoulder-holster approach McGill's cubicle , but then wheel about quickly just as it came even with Travis' shoulder and depart in the opposite direction. "Alright. So where is it now?"

McGill's face made a queer turn. "Where's what?"

"The investigation. Where is it now, where do you stand with it?"

"Oh, the investigation. Yes. Well..." Both the detective's hands rested on the envelope, clasped together. "As you can imagine, the forensic anthropologist's findings pretty much shot the investigation totally out of the water. Again. With the bones not being the senator's daughter's, we're right back to where we left off in 2012."

Travis was beginning to wonder if he and the detective were sitting in the same room. "No. The *ongoing* investigation. Into the identity of the bones that I dug up."

The tiniest twitch fluttered behind McGill's eyes, but then the smile returned. "Sorry, I'm slow. Yes, the investigation. Well... " The detective leaned back in his chair and stretched his legs. "There's a standard process we go through with cases like this. We have the scientific data from the forensics of course. Then it's a matter of checking as to what other missing persons were reported in the area at around the same time, of similar age, sex, etcetera, and start comparing and eliminating. It's painstaking work, as you might imagine."

"It's mostly a matter of DNA right? You find a missing girl that age and from that time frame, take DNA from her surviving family, compare it against the bones."

Detective McGill raised his coffee cup to Travis in a toast. "Mr. Riggins, your TV viewing has made you a fine detective!"

"Thanks." Travis waited this time for McGill to complete his coffee slurp, then continued. "So have you gotten DNA samples from the family?"

The detective burped rather loudly. "Damn, sorry. Which family?"

"Monique Gavins' family."

"Monique Gavins. Not familiar."

Now it was Travis who smiled, but only after a calming breath. "When I first called about the bones, what I told the officer, you have all that on file, right?"

"I'm sure we do..." McGill opened up the Ketterson file envelope in front of him, and in no time found the phone record. "Ah. And here we go. You called September 12th, 9:18 am, spoke with Officer Clevinger, and... there it is, just as you said. Monique Gavins. Mother Sheila Gavins, who lives at 1413 Crested Boulder. That's very close to your address isn't it?"

Travis successfully fought off an aggressive impulse to roll his eyes. "Just across the street." He was glad for the coffee, for it gave his hands something to hold to disguise his growing restlessness. "I'm guessing you didn't work that disappearance case back in '12. You probably would have remembered it if you had."

"Exactly. We work so many cases." The old detective closed his eyes and began rubbing his forehead. "Sometimes they start to run together a little. I'll need to check the records." But then his eyes opened, wide and cheery, as he held up the record of Travis' initial phone call. "But we've got it now, right? That's the main thing." Taking up a spiral notepad, the detective began to scribble. "Okay. We got the mother living at 1413, so we'll need to get a DNA sample from her ASAP."

"And then compare it with the bones, right?"

There was no reaction from Mcgill as he continued to write; but then, something set a hook in his thoughts. "Wait a minute. Sheila Gavins? Oh hell Travis, we know her. Our guys've been to that house a hun'erd times. But ain't she a white woman though? 'Cause you know, those bones- "

"- Yes," Travis interrupted. "But Monique's dad is black. Pernell Gavins. He's in jail here in Atlanta. Pretty easy for you to get his DNA too. Is what I'm guessing."

Another broad grin from McGill was forthcoming. "You have definitely done your police work Mr. Riggins! Tellin' ya, if you ever need a job... but just to warn ya, the pay is terrible!" Detective McGill laughed at his own dumb joke and then carefully tore the sheet from his notebook, slipping it into the Brittany Ketterson file. Standing abruptly, he offered his hand, signifying the end of the interview. "Well this has been great. I owe you once again Mr. Riggins."

Travis rose as well and shook the detective's hand. "Don't mention it Detective." It was all wrapping up too quickly for Travis; something itched in his mind which he couldn't identify, and he looked for some kind of prolongation until he could pin it down. "So, um... will I be a pest if I come back in, say... a week?"

"We're here to serve."

"Okay. Thanks." Still bothered by the brain itch but out of stalling ideas, Travis turned to leave, and noticed another detective approaching McGill's workspace, who upon seeing Travis made an inexplicably awkward turn in the opposite direction, just as the first detective had. Then suddenly the itch revealed itself, and Travis scratched it with one last question for the detective. "You just put the notes in the envelope, yes?"

"Yes."

"Which was one of the Ketterson envelopes. Why?" McGill's face was stone. "Shouldn't it instead go into some sort of new Jane Doe file, since they're not Brittany Ketterson's? You *have* started a Jane Doe file for the bones, haven't you?"

In the click of a moment, the detective's good-natured friendliness vanished entirely; now he was a cop, and not a happy one. "Mr. Riggins, how long did you say you've lived at your house?"

"Five years. Why?"

"Five years." McGill's eyes narrowed. "Just a couple of years after the report says those bones were buried. In what later became your yard."

It was a nervous tickle which made him laugh involuntarily. "Um... okay. And?"

The detective continued evenly and slowly. "It was a vacant lot before you bought the house. We know because we checked the records Mr. Riggins. A great place for someone to bury something they didn't want found, at least until that someone maybe realizes that some other someone could buy the house and then find it. So maybe the someone who did the burying gets nervous and buys the house himself. In order to keep an eye on it. So that no one will dig up the you-know-what."

Travis' throat began to tighten. "This is ridiculous. I'm the one who dug up the you-know-what and reported it to you-know-who!"

McGill was undeterred. "Exactly. *After* the code enforcement officer paid you a little visit." As Travis stood dumbfounded, McGill referred to notes which he'd just pulled from the envelope. "- a visit concerning your koi pond. He was asking questions, about the depth, wasn't that it?"

"You actually *investigated* me? About my stupid pond?"

The detective's eyes did not blink. "The officer, he was standing right on top of your secret there. Right under his feet." Now McGill came around the desk until he and Travis were only inches apart. The detective held the notes in Travis' face. "It's funny what paranoia will make a person do Mr. Riggins. It makes you panic. Think crazy things. Like make a person think that Code Enforcement and his asshole next-door neighbor who by the way we asked him about you and boooy did he have a lot to say, paranoia makes him think that maybe they'll start poking around that koi pond, and he decides 'Hey, instead of them finding my little secret and me having to explain dead girl's bones, what if I just dig them up myself and *pretend* to find the skeleton and report it like a good upstanding citizen, and that way turn the suspicion away from me?'"

"This is so fucking absu- "

"- BECAUSE he thinks to himself, why not? He thinks, 'Hey, it's been eight years, if there was ever any evidence of me down there it's gone now, it's just dry bones that's left. *So what* if they learn who the bones belonged to eight years later! There's nothing down there anymore to prove who buried 'em in my yard. So just let 'em find 'em!"

Having finished his performance, Detective McGill retreated a step, as if preparing to take a bow. Travis stared back in amazement. "You put that much time and thought and work into making me out as a suspect? *Me*?"

The detective's smile this time was unlike his others; this one was venomous.

"Well it just goes to show you, Mr. Riggins, that we actually do our jobs around here at the precinct. We ain't just bumbling about with wrong files and not remembering missing children from 2012 and losing stuff and what-not." With a self-satisfied spin on his heels, McGill sauntered back to his chair and sat, his arms folded across the holster on his chest. "And since we are in fact doing our jobs here, you should probably just let us do 'em, and leave your Jane Doe for us to figure out. Or else the next time you come visit us it might be because we... *invited* you. If you follow me. Go on home now Mr. Riggins." With a patronizing wave-off, Travis found himself dismissed; recovering from his paralysis to make an inglorious retreat, Travis turned to leave the cubicle, and immediately felt the sensation of a dozen pairs of eyes avoiding him as if he were the Medusa, yet watching his every move. The styrofoam coffee cup was still in his hand; turning back to face McGill, he set it on the desk.

"If you ever get around to collecting DNA, here's some from your lead suspect."

When Travis drove back to his neighborhood after work, the first thing he noticed on Crested Boulder was Devon at Sheila's house, standing beside her on the rotted remains of her front porch. Only a month ago any sighting of Devon whatsoever would have been as likely a Yeti at a Falcons game, let alone hanging out with Sheila; of late though it was an everyday occurrence, for since that night with the firewood an old bridge seemed to have rebuilt itself, and now, the young man had taken up the habit of helping Sheila with odd jobs around her house, jobs such as a fifteen year-old boy could accomplish. Simple things, amounting to little more than carrying this and moving that; no task which appeared to Travis so substantive to be called actual maintenance, no repairing work, unless repairing the bond between an incongruous pair of people could be counted, the retying of a knot which time and tragedy had unraveled. But today was a little different; today, Devon was nailing a panel of plywood onto Sheila's broken front door. Travis had seen that plywood before. It was the same chunk of wood which he'd carried to Sheila's house months earlier, the plywood which at one time concealed the bones which might be her daughter's. As his truck passed the house, Devon saw it and came running across the street to meet Travis in his driveway.

"Looks like you've got a repair project goin' on over at Sh- "

"Didjoo go to the police this morning?" Travis had told him the night before about his planned visit with McGill; the boy had likely lain awake the entire night as a result. "Wha'd you find out?"

"Well, I asked the det- "

"Wait, hang on- "Devon aimed his voice across the street. "Sorry Miss Sheila, I'll be right back!" He spun back to Travis. "Okay, wha'd they say?" During his drive home, Travis had sorted out in his mind what he would tell the boy from what he wouldn't; hoping it wasn't a lie, he told Devon that the police were about to begin the DNA testing of Monique's family. He also told him what his first move had been following his interview with McGill: to text Linda and ask her to get involved as well. What he didn't tell Devon was why he'd texted her. His experience at the precinct had been bizarre to say the least; it smelled of something rottener than the standard-issue bureaucratic sluggishness he feared he might encounter, had expected to encounter even. Why in hell had McGill concocted the elaborate insanity which made Travis out to be a child killer, a story which McGill himself surely did not believe for a moment? Sure, Travis had called him out on a point of procedure or two, but did that justify the detective to accuse him of murder? Had Travis crossed some line and kicked a hidden tripwire to make the detective respond so disproportionately? And not just Detective McGill, but everyone at the station seemed to know something which only Travis didn't. Or was he just imagining things about the atmosphere of the office- was his the disproportionate reaction, borne of paranoia? At all events, he had texted Linda to intervene in any way she could, knowing her relationship with both the case and with law enforcement gave her access to doors Travis couldn't open. Paranoia or no, something funny lay buried at the 6th precinct; perhaps his archaeologist friend could dig it up.

"So how come they haven't done the DNA testing already by now? It's been more than a month!"

"Devon my man, I asked the detective that very same question. The wheels turn slowly I'm afraid." Looking over Devon's shoulder, Travis saw Sheila across the street, inspecting the work which the young man had been performing on her door with the toe of her shoe. "You've been over at 1413 a lot lately. How is your- " It was not a subject which Travis was ever comfortable broaching with the boy. "- what's your dad say about you helping Sheila?"

Predictably, Devon's face soured. "He's not sayin' nothing now. I bribed him. Look." Devon pointed to the Walters' front yard, where he noticed that the dozens of holes about which the code enforcement officer had brought the county's complaint were now all filled. "That shut him up at least for a while."

"And what about talking to me? I mean, aren't you afraid of another black eye?"

Devon stared over at his house, as if offering himself willingly to whoever might be watching him in the windows. "It takes more than a punch in the face to keep me away from Monique." He looked back at Travis. "Hitting me didn't keep me away from her when I was seven. It won't now either."

"Mistah Diggins, why you take mah helpuh away from me, he fixin' mah fron' doh!" Sheila had materialized at the end of the driveway, a swaying apparition holding a hammer in one hand and a tall 40oz in the other. "You sen' 'im on back t' me, Mistah Deron fin'ly puttin' up that wood you nevah done nuttin' wit'."

Devon turned to Travis apologetically. "Um, yeah, Miss Sheila told me you brought her that plywood. She's been telling me how you help her out. Or used to." He grinned at Travis a little sheepishly, then whispered, "When she asked for four dollars and I said I didn't have it, she said you never give her four dollars any more either."

"That's right, no more with the f- " Travis' pocket trembled. "Hang on..." As Travis checked his phone, Sheila pulled on Devon's arm.

"Come on, you still got hammerin' to do on that doh."

"Alright. Travis, I'm heading back over to- "

"Hold up. Read this text from Linda." Travis handed his phone to Devon.

"At 6 precinct police station right now. Holy shit you won't believe what I found out. The assholes!"

Devon stared up at Travis. "What does she mean?"

"No idea." Travis' reply to Linda was immediate: *"???"*

Meanwhile, Sheila pulled harder on Devon's sleeve. "Mistah Deron come on, I got bullet-ho windahs need fixin' too!"

Devon remained focused on the phone. "Who are the assholes? The police?"

"Hell yeah the po-leece assholes! Now come on back!"

As Travis stared helplessly at the unresponsive screen, Devon became insistent. "Wha'd she find out Travis? Wha'd she find out?"

"Devon, how should- "

"I got mo' cold beer at th' house you old enough t' drink, come on!"

The empty screen of the cellphone stretched each second into eternities. "Whatever's going on at the police station... she probably can't check her phone..."

"We gotta go then!" Devon pointed frantically at Travis' phone. "We gotta go there now!"

"Tha's right, we gotta go, come on!" Once again, Sheila pulled on the boy's arm.

"Devon, she didn't say for us to go down there."

"Tha's right, don' go down theah, don' go down theah..."

"But she found out something!" The more that Sheila pulled and protested, the more the young man persisted, oblivious of the pleading woman. "This might be what we've been waiting for Travis! You know it could be!"

Sheila's hold upon Devon was weakening; she was mumbling now. "What I bin waitin' fo' Mistah Deron. Is what I bin waitin' fo'."

"We can't just 'go down there' Devon- "

"No you cain't. You cain't go down theah..."

"Let's give Linda just a little more time to answer my te-"

With a throw of his arm, Devon finally broke loose of Sheila; the recoil sent her backpeddling. "No Travis! I've been looking at my old tricycle on my porch every day for eight years! You can't make me wait any longer! We're goin' down there!"

"Ah cain't..." Still reeling from being shaken off, Sheila now lost her battle against gravity, and with a crumpling thud, fell to the sidewalk, her can of beer washing her grimy jeans and the curb with suds.

"Miss Sheila!" Hurrying to her side, Devon attempted to bring Sheila back to her feet, but the inebriated woman's wooziness wouldn’t permit it; reproaching himself for his callousness, Devon knelt down beside her, and vainly wiped at the beer on her pantleg, as Travis only watched from where he had not moved, useless as tits on a bull. "I'm sorry Miss Sheila. I just got excited about- “ Sheila's vacant eyes gazed up at him to complete the thought, but Devon spared her the finish. "Miss Sheila, we'll get you back to your house, and then me and Travis, we have to leave for a little bit." Devon's eyes turned back up and zeroed in on Travis'. "We have to leave, now, don't we Travis?"

Sheila patted Devon with her paw. "Mistah Deron, you come right back from yo' bidness with Mistah Diggins and hep me. You gotta hep me Deron. Mistah Diggins don' hep me no mo'. You mah only fren' now."

As Travis sped through the Smyrna streets toward the 6th precinct (the irony was not lost on him, that if a cop pulled him over for speeding his excuse was that he was fleeing *to* the police), Devon held Travis' phone to watch it for any new Linda texts.

"We got a problem Devon."

"What's that?"

They were only a block away from the station. "If Linda doesn't text me back she won't know we're coming. We need to text her again and see if she's- "

"Yes!!!" Glancing over, there was Devon, smiling victoriously and holding Travis' phone aloft like a trophy. "While you were driving I texted her on your phone like I was you. She just answered. She said she's meeting you outside!" Now Travis was pulling into the precinct's parking lot, and there was the familiar DNR van, with Linda standing beside it. Upon seeing his truck come to a stop, Linda walked up briskly.

"I can't believe you came down here!" Stepping out of his truck to meet her, Travis could see at a glance that Linda was several clicks past upset, and her first words confirmed it. "These stupid incompetent motherfucking assholes, you won't believe what they did!" At that moment, Devon stepped out of the truck as well.

"Hi Miss Linda."

The sight of Devon stopped Linda in her tracks. "Hey. Hi Devon."

"What's... what's going on?"

Travis' face was asking her the same thing. "Travis, could I... talk to you for a second?" Keeping her distance from the truck where Devon stood, Linda waited for Travis to come to her. Linda's voice was a whisper. "Travis, I didn't know you were bringing Devon, your text only mentioned you!"

"Devon sent it. As me, from my phone." Linda rolled her eyes. "So what if he's here Linda, I don't get it! What's the deal? Incompetent motherfuckers?"

Linda glanced back at the station, then continued in her whisper. "Well I did like you asked, started asking this person and that person, people I knew close to the investigation, and got nothing, until finally..." Linda looked over Travis' shoulder at Devon. "Oh how the hell are we gonna tell him?!"

"Tell him what?" Just then, Detective McGill and another official-looking man in a shirt and tie emerged from the station. Recognizing Travis with Linda, McGill approached them warily.

"I thought we agreed Miss Myers, not to tell the whole world."

"I didn't agree to anything of the kind."

"But won't you agree that Mr. Riggins here is only on a need-to-know basis?"

"I think he needs to know as much as anybody!"

"Linda..." The man in the shirt and tie now stepped up. "We did say it would be best to hold off talking about it until the detective's people can first make a statement."

"So now you want to hush it up too Steve? Does that mean that you're admitting the medical examiner's office is to blame?"

"I told you it wasn't us, we followed every protocol."

"Well it wasn't us at DNR, it was between your forensics team or the police!"

Now McGill pointed at Travis. "Well regardless who it was you don't need to be blabbing to the property owner out in the police parking lot!"

"Nobody's blabbed anything to me yet, I- "

"You lost Monique." The sound of Devon's voice rendered everyone else silent. He studied all their faces. "You lost her. Didn't you?"

The medical examiner whispered to McGill. "Who's the kid?"

"The next-door neighbor."

Travis looked to Linda for confirmation. "Is it true?"

Linda stepped away from the three men and faced the boy. "Devon... Somehow, we don't know how, yet, Monique... I mean, the remains, are... missing."

McGill shook his head. "Jesus Christ she *is* gonna tell the whole world..."

Travis now stood beside Linda. "Missing? What does 'missing' mean?"

"It means" said Linda, unable to look him in the eye, "that in the... handling, the transporting from... here to there, between agencies, or... the remains never - "now she looked up at Travis, her eyes full of anguish "- never ended up *with* anyone."

"That's impossible."

"Exactly what I said."

As the penny dropped, Travis spun on McGill. "So that's what was behind all the weirdness this morning. Trying to scare the fuck out of me to make me quit asking questions. Because you knew *then* that the bones were missing!"

"I don't need to listen to this." The detective turned back toward the precinct, with the medical examiner following right behind.

Travis pursued them step-for-step. "It's why you haven't bothered with a Jane Doe file for the bones! Because their *aren't* any bones anymore! It's why you haven't done any DNA testing of Monique's family yet! Why test when you got no bones to compare the DNA to, right?!"

McGill spun around to face him. "Riggins, I'd advise you to back a little damn off if I was you. You're not in your own yard now. You're in my yard."

Linda grabbed her friend by the arm. "Travis, don't make it worse."

Once again Detective McGill and the examiner turned back toward the station, but again they were deterred; not by a voice this time, but by a person, standing directly in their path.

"That was my best frlend you threw away."

"Devon!" Caught up in his own anger, Travis had forgotten about the one who had even more. "Get back here son!"

A surprised McGill could only stammer. "Look, kid- "

"I know what happened. Even a kid like me knows what happened." Devon tossed the hair out of his face and stared at the veteran detective with the fearlessness of a mother bear. "I saw you at Travis' house that day. I saw you on TV. I saw how you were all excited about finding that missing white girl, and when it turned out to be not your little white girl, you didn't care anymore about them bones. They were just some ol' nigger bones to you police. Half-nigger anyway. Tell me I'm wrong!"

By now McGill had recovered enough from the shock of Devon's assault to get away from it; but when he moved to go around the skinny young man, Devon side-stepped in front of him, blocking the door. "Riggins, get this kid out of my way!"

Devon was leaning into McGill now, begging for a fight. "Or else what? You gonna arrest me? Hit me? Go ahead! I get hit all the time!" Incredibly, Devon stepped up even closer now, so close he could have touched the detective's holster. "So how white did Monique have to be for you to not lose her? Like maybe three-quarters white? Would that have been enough for you to care about my friend? Or is it just the hundred percent white kids like Brittany you don't throw in the garbage? Are they the only ones that get to be on the eleven o'clock news?"

The old detective hadn't lasted so long on the force by making a habit of matching anger with anger; and so, even as Devon's rage rang at full-volume, McGill muted his entirely. "Young man, I am very sorry about the loss... your loss. Of your friend. Monique." This last he uttered uneasily, possessing no confidence that he had remembered the girl's name correctly. But the sound of it in Devon's ear was enough to bring him off the ledge, for until that point it had been his intention to pull the gun from the detective's holster and blow first the old man's head across the pavement and then his own; but now,

Devon relented, and only stood limp as a ragdoll with his head hanging, his straggly hair falling back into his face.

"Eight years. I held onto her for eight years. And you couldn't hold onto her for two months."

Devon waited alone back at the truck as Travis took his time walking Linda across the parking lot toward the DNR van.

"Is he going to be alright you think?"

Travis smiled. "He's a tough kid. He'll be fine. If he doesn't kill his dad that is."

"I can't believe he really hits him."

"No telling what all goes on behind the curtains of that house." They were close to reaching the van now; Travis slowed their walking even more. "What's worst about this whole fiasco isn't not knowing what happened to Monique. I don't think Devon really cared about knowing who did what to her. Probably didn't even want to know. All he cared about was that it *was* her." Despite the slowest walk of all time they had reached the van, but instead of walking to the driver's side, Linda went around to the passenger side and leaned up against the door, arms crossed, intent on listening to all Travis had to say. She was in no hurry to leave either, and so Travis took it as his cue. "See, before the bones, Devon hid himself away like some shut-in, a recluse. But when Monique was found - yeah I know it wasn't proven, but as far as he was concerned, she was found- it was like he was found again too. Going across the street and helping Monique's mom Sheila. Talking to me every day. Even smiling now and then. And now that she's re-disappeared... I wonder if he'll disappear again too."

The anxiety in Linda's eyes caused by the McGill confrontation was gone now, replaced by warmth. "You've been a better dad to that kid these last few weeks than his dad. You know that right?"

"Well... it's a pretty low bar." *Keep the bullshit flowin' Travis! She's lovin' it!*

"And the way you gave it to McGill just now! I almost started cheering you."

"Wouldn't have been a very good idea."

"No I guess not."

"No."

They laughed self-consciously at the non-existent joke; then, they found themselves quiet for several awkward seconds, a silence broken by Linda who spoke to what they were both thinking.

"So... I guess my work at the Riggins dig is completed."

Travis' heart leapt at the regret he heard in her voice. "Wow. I suppose so. Who needs an archaeologist around when there aren't any bones left, right?" Their eyes met, and neither one dared look away. "Guess I need to start digging in my yard again ASAP."

Linda's response wasn't the joke he expected. "That might solve our problem."

"Do we have a problem?"

"I think we do."

Travis had imagined this very moment- imagined it frequently, whenever he thought of her really- when things between the two of them might come to that terrifying and exciting "next move" phase, the big showdown, when an unmistakable line would present itself in the sand which demanded the courage- and the foolishness- to kiss their way across it. It was the great romantic swan dive, the cinematic fantasy of the reckless, impulsive plunge, which regular guys who sell houses and drive pickup trucks and actually love their wives seldom experience. Now it was here. But his Bogart and Bacall mouth-to-mouth fantasy had not included the parking lot of a cop shop or Devon watching from his truck. The kiss, he realized with great disappointment and even greater relief, was out of the question.

"How about lunch this week?"

"That would be great."

"I'll text you."

"Okay."

After an entirely appropriate hug goodbye, Travis floated across the lot back to his truck. It was the kind of restrained embrace which grownups exchange all the time, or at least that's how he hoped it would appear from an observer's point of view; but for Travis and

Linda, it signified their first and only physical contact besides a handshake, and was thereby a landmark. As hugs go, it was one which he was sure wouldn't require an explanation for Devon. Still, Travis had one prepared, just to proactively defuse it.

"Okay Devon, now before you make some- " But the truck was empty. Devon was gone.

\`\`

When Travis left the police station late that afternoon, he did not drive straight home, but rather cruised up and down the streets between the precinct and Crested Boulder, searching for a walking Devon. No mop of straggly hair was anywhere to be seen; once home, he hurried up his front steps, hoping his appearance would trigger their porch ritual, but the Walters' front door remained unopened. Travis' mind was a sea of overflow as he opened his own door, flooded from two directions: one, from concern over the emotional state of the troubled young man, and two, from guilty-giddy anticipation of the next chapter with the troubling young woman. And now, stepping inside, he fully expected a facefull of trouble from the old lady. But before Travis's mouth had a chance to explain where he'd been all afternoon, it was kissed into submission by a pair of wine-pickled lips.

"It's done!" Stepping back from her ambushed husband, Alicia stood there proudly, one hand holding her wine glass and the other gesturing about the room like a Versailles tour guide. "The downstairs is *done*! The cornice valances finally came in at the decorator's and I put them up this afternoon." Alicia rotated in a wobbly 360° around the room, her tour guide hand pointing out each finished window. "Look at these fabulous fuckers!"

Travis nodded appreciatively. "Well done! So it's all finished now, everything?"

"Everything! Paint, carpet, windows, crown molding, floor moldings, all of it." Alicia emptied her glass, then held it aloft triumphantly. "No more beige! No more boring! No more somebody else's colors instead of mine!" Travis paid his respects to Alicia's handiwork in every direction, and when he faced front again, he found Alicia extending to him a glass of wine of his own. "Okay we have to toast."

"Agreed," said Travis, taking the glass. "To my wife, who saved her family from the horrors of plum red and plum yellow."

"No." Alicia came closer, nearly as close as Linda had been just an hour before. "Not to your wife. To my husband. Who let me change whatever I wanted and spend whatever I wanted upstairs and downstairs both and who puts up with me when I'm cranky and when I'm a bitch which is always and never complains even when I paint the house at midnight and who is the best husband ever and who I love."

"And I love my wife." Travis kissed her, and drank up both his wine and what she'd said. It caught him by surprise of course, as most pre-written speeches which are recited to us out of the blue are surprising; as speeches go, he was sure she'd meant it, but it was at the end, the two phrases following "paint the house at midnight," where he thought he'd heard something more than just an expression of her heart- what he heard was a statement of determination, as if by saying it aloud it would convince herself that what she said was true and would remain true. But he knew that at least one part of what she'd said was not true. "You give me too much credit for being such a good husband. I never even lifted a finger while you did all this by yourself."

"True. Couldn't even bring me the roller stick." Her little shot surprised him as much as her speech had; having delivered it with a smile, Alicia sat expansively on the sofa. "But you were distracted that night by Your Sheila. Who could blame you?"

There was a way Alicia formed her mouth which always indicated whether her jabs were merely jokes or something more sinister; if it was the latter, the façade of an upturned smile built upon a poorly-disguised grimace foundation would appear, and if such facial engineering was detected, responding with a joke meant certain death for the responder. Travis studied her face under the light which she'd turned up to show off the room's new color scheme, but the glare disguised the truth. He opted for safety. "She has a way of ambushing a person out of frickin' nowhere. But I didn't help her that night you know. Devon next door did." Bringing himself within range of retaliation, Travis sat next to her. "I don't help her anymore you know. I don't."

For several interminable moments, Alicia stared back sphinxlike, betraying no thought or emotion, deadly or otherwise. Then her smile snapped back on. "And that's another reason why I'm toasting my husband tonight!" She clinked his glass. "Because he's going to keep it that way."

"Amen." They drank, and Travis inwardly celebrated surviving his interview at the Bridge Of Death. He was feeling more unafraid by the moment.

"Would you like a little refill my dear?"

"Yes please!" He walked Alicia's glass to where she'd left the bottle on an end table. He poured as she spoke. "Because we have one more toast to make."

"Fantastic. To whom?"

"To my husband's girlfriend."

Travis had just lifted the filled glasses; somehow he set them back down on the table without dumping them onto the rug. "Which husband, and which girlfriend?"

Alicia sat back with both hands on her stomach, her face tilted up, laughing out loud. "Oh! Oh man! You should have seen your face! God it was good!" Travis stood frozen, terrified of speaking or moving. "You know. Your anthropologist or whatever she is. With the little ball cap and perky tail. I mean pony tail."

"Linda Myers. The archaeologist." She nodded happily as Travis sat next to her again. "Okay Alicia. I don't know when you decided to take up fiction writing, but not only is that Linda Myers woman not my girlfriend, she is also *not my girlfriend*."

"Swear on a stack of bones?"

"Stop it!"

Alicia bounced with glee. "Oh I know she's not your girlfriendl You already have fruit tree girlfriends and koi pond girlfriends and bird feeder girlfriends. Where would you find time for a bone girlfriend?" She ratcheted his discomfort by running a finger through his hair and around his face. "She may not be your girlfriend, but you are her boyfriend! In *her* mind. I saw her that day when they took the bones, sitting in her little van, driving off and waving at you all sad like she was leaving her summer boyfriend behind and going back to her all-girls' boarding school. I almost felt sorry for her."

Travis pulled a tickling finger out of his earhole. "Good god..."

"Now, you *did* wave back at her." Travis couldn't remember; had he been that careless? "But you were just being polite." Alicia pulled her feet up onto the sofa, her hands resting on Travis' leg. "Oh Travis, who could blame her? With your real estate salesman charm and fly haircut and all?" She leaned in. "You think a wife doesn't notice what other women are up to?" He imagined- at least he hoped he was only imagining- that he saw something else glimmering behind her eyes, as if they were telling him they noticed what husbands were up to as well. "It's okay that nerdy bone-ologists have crushes on you Travis. As long as you leave her bones alone." Then she kissed him as he sat in numbed silence, not trusting anything which might come out of his own mouth. "Now, get up and bring us those wine glasses. I have one more thing to show you."

Resupplied with chardonnay, Alicia took Travis by the hand, and when they reached the upstairs bedroom, Alicia turned on the light. "Notice anything different?"

"I do... this wine, it's not the shitty Yellowtail you usually drink."

Alicia smacked him on his non-glass-holding arm. "Shut up. Look at the bed." Doing as she requested, Travis noticed the change right away.

"The bedspread. New, right?"

"Correction: old. Really old." Hovering reverently at the foot of the bed, Alicia spoke in solemn tones. "This... is an original 1904 Catherine Evans Whitener tufted chenille bedspread which she herself stitched in Dalton Georgia, handed down from my great-great grandmother to my great-grandmother to my grandmother and to my mother and now to me. *1904* Travis!" She walked to the dimmer switch, twisting it until the museum lighting best captured the artifact's essence. "As you can see it's in mint condition. Not a stain, not a tear, not a body fluid, nothing. Preserved like new by one old lady after another after another until finally your old lady has it."

Travis stepped closer to pretend he understood what he was looking at. "Wow, check out the stitching in the- "

"GET BACK WITH THAT WINE!" Recoiling in terror, Travis covered the glass with his hand. "You get one drop on that comforter and we're through!"

"Jeez, sorry!" Leaving her own glass on the dresser, Alicia smoothed out an already-smooth corner of the spread. "We won't sleep under it very often of course. It's not for everyday to say the least. Just special occasions. Like tonight." Taking his wine glass and setting it down safely next to hers on the dresser, she led him to the end of the bed where they both sat. "The truth is, this comforter has been mine for a few years. My mom said I could take it when I moved into my own house. But until now..." Alicia looked up at him and held his hand. "- until now it hasn't felt so much like my house. But like I told you, all that's changed, now that you've let me make my mark on it. Now, this is my home. So the comforter finally has a home here too." She kissed him, and Travis remembered why he had married her in the first place. "Okay. Now this bedspread's gotta come off for about twenty minutes. We have bad things to do."

Later that night, when it was safe to return the venerated comforter to the bed and Travis lay beneath it beside his happily-sleeping wife, he reviewed the day's events and performed a quick inventory of his psychological and emotional condition. As to his wife's impromptu housewarming party, it once again confirmed that Alicia, even in his weak moments of blonde temptation, was the woman he actually loved. How she'd piqued his guilt this evening in this way and in that, as if telepathically reading all his adulterous shortcomings and in one stroke accusing him and forgiving him. Then there was Linda, the object of his indiscretions, or rather, his dreamt-of indiscretions. Sure, he liked her, and she clearly like him; still, it was nothing more than childishness on his part to fool around with Linda in such an irresponsible way, and while brushing his teeth before bedtime, Travis determined that he would make an end of the thing once and for all by texting Linda in the morning and telling her that they should forego the illicit lunch they'd discussed; and when his phone had vibrated on the bathroom sink a minute later as he rinsed out his mouth, a sticky-sweet "goodnight" text from Linda expressing her excitement about their upcoming first date, Travis seized the moment and took decisive action by instantly forgetting any thought of ending the affair and instead naming the time and place for that lunch at a cozy (code for "secluded, where people could hide") spot just off the Marietta Square. Staring up now at the dark ceiling, with thoughts of pony tails dancing in his head, the wine sent Travis off to sleep, his last thought being not of the woman he loved nor of the teenager for whom he was worried, but rather, that a lunch, after all, is nothing more than lunch really.

Standing on the edge of the muddy hole which now held trash instead of discarded human beings, the teenager about whom sleeping Travis was not at the moment worried threw the last of his father's model trains and pieces of broken track into the excavated void, hurling curses at each little engine and car as they shattered at the bottom against clay and broken plywood. The father was in no condition to play with his toys or do anything else at the moment, thanks to his son; but it was not with toys or trains or derailed fathers or muddy holes which the young man was concerned, but another sort of hole entirely, one which, since it could never be fully emptied, he would instead try to cover forever in an effort to obliterate all memory of its ever existing. He was up on the porch; now he was back at the hole, carrying his old tricycle which he had pedaled alongside his first girlfriend's trike so many times, so many years before. And after throwing the tricycle into the hole (why hold onto it any longer, since others had not cared enough to hold onto his girl?), the young man took up the shovel and began to dig next to the big hole, throwing scoops of earth into the big hole, over the tricycle, over his memory, shovel after shovel of earth to make the emptiness of the big hole go away. But despite his efforts, the hole could not be filled; the big hole was too big, too full of so much unfillable nothing, too deep for the young man's shovel to have an effect. Understanding at last that this hole which could never be emptied could also never be filled, the young man sat on the ground, his feet dangling over the edge of all that lay before him, where he began to cry, shedding tears for a make-believe house they'd built under a tarp and for a baby kitten they'd buried and promised they would always remember; the young man cried as only an eight year-old boy can cry for a lost little girl whose name was forgotten by everyone else but a name which he, because he could never forget her name, would never speak again.

12

When the sun rose the next morning Travis was less than thrilled to see it; it was Saturday morning after all, and with no property showings it was to be a true day off, a day to sleep in at least a little. But when Alicia had jumped up at dawn, even though her first class wasn't until 10, Travis found himself being rolled out of the sack and onto the floor so that his eager wife could show him "how the angle of the sunrise bounced off the raised tufting of the comforter's chenille." Before his eyes were fully open therefore the now-remarkable bed was already made; when Alicia headed out the door for work, he had asked her when the first tour groups would be coming in to see it and if it meant he'd have to put on a proper pair of pants. Now, he stood with his coffee, looking out through the newly-treated front window, scanning the neighborhood and feeling not too bad despite the effects of the cheap chardonnay and his pre-dawn rousting. Across the street, Brother Jason and Sister Laura were raking leaves, supervised by their dog, and as he watched them, the triple emollients of decent coffee, no hangover and cool fall weather soothed Travis' attitude to the point that he almost considered crossing the street and finally introducing himself to the resident of the new doghouse which stood where Ralph's used to be. As far as his chores, Travis had an unusually short list, what with the growing season at an end; it then occurred to him that today might be a good day to finally fill in The Hole, now that there'd be no further investigative activity in it- at which point the events with Devon at the police station the afternoon before flooded back, along with guilt for temporarily forgetting them. In an instant, his caffeinated tranquility was replaced by renewed concern for the young man, wondering how he was dealing today with what had clearly been a shattering experience in the precinct parking lot. Their communication platform for weeks had been their respective front porches, so Travis stepped outside, hoping to see Devon standing across. But who he saw on the

Walters front porch was not Devon but Keith, staring right back at him, with not one but two black eyes, a stare which communicated both a fierce accusation and, strangely, an appeal of some kind, but for what Travis could not begin to guess. After several uncomfortable moments locked in this mutual gaze, Keith blinked, or rather, winced, then turned away and shuffled back into his house. Travis' eye then fell to the big hole, in which he saw the broken shrapnel of a model train set, a shovel and a twisted tricycle. It was all Travis could do to resist walking around the fence to the edge of the hole to check if Devon was at the bottom as well. What Travis did decide, however, was to forego filling his own hole for now, out of consideration for his young friend's emotional state which, from the looks of Keith's face, must be just as bruised; and who knew, perhaps letting Devon be the one to fill the former grave would give him a semblance of closure, a way for him to make some gesture of saying the goodbyes which had been so cruelly deprived him. Travis would keep his shovel next to the koi pond just in case.

When Travis turned to go back indoors, a sight nearly as startling as Keith's puffy face stopped him in his steps; there, laying on the floor of the porch, was a cell phone, plugged into the wall outlet. It was an ancient flip phone, and there was of course no doubt as to the phone's owner. Hadn't he made it clear to Sheila the last time, no more phone charging, ever? At least, Travis thought to himself with relief, it was he who'd found it and not Alicia, for her reaction might well have peeled the brand-new paint right off the walls. Picking up the phone, Travis thought about his next move; and just as he decided he would hide Sheila's phone by taking it indoors with him and in that way mess with her head, the owner of that phone commenced to mess with his.

"Mistah Diggins is mah phone chawged yet?"

Sheila lumbered up the drive as Travis held up Exhibit A. "What the hell is this?"

Her head fell to one side in disbelief. "Goddamm Mistah Riggins, I jus' tol' you I was chawgin' mah phone so whatchoo think it is?"

"No. I mean, I told you before, no more phone charging. Do you remember?"

"Hell yeah I remembuh! You said 'Sheila you cain't chawge no mo' phones.'"

"Then...?"

"Mah son got me a new phone so now I gotta chawge it." Having disarmed Travis with her trademark reasoning, Sheila moved onto her second agenda item. "You got watah fo' my watah bottle Mistah Diggins?"

With one move, Travis yanked the adapter from the outlet and held it and the phone out to Sheila. "Here. Get it out of here." Sheila made no move to take it, responding only with a vacant stare, her drifting eyes unable to make landing. But Travis wasn't having it. "I told you, no more phones and no more water. And I meant it." He thrust the phone in her face and shooed her away with his arm. "So go on."

Now the vacant eyes took on a new aspect; something glimmered in them as her face began to crumble, and then the mooncalf eyes moistened. "Mistah Deron, he been chawgin' mah phone fo' me an' givin' me watah. Buh he didn' come hep me t'day."

Travis rolled his eyes at the maudlin woman. "Sheila, Devon had a bad night last night. He'll be over to see you."

"No Mistah Diggins." Now the tears fell freely. "I tole you yeste'day when you took 'im from me, bring Mistah Deron back t' me but you dinnit, now he gone 'an nobody heah to chawge mah phone an' gimme watah." Travis stood by helplessly as Sheila's lament ran its course. "I knew if you took 'im I'd nevah see 'im agin. Now I loss Mistah Diggins and Mistah Deron bofe. Now I loss ever'body." Travis heard something extra in Sheila's "ever'body" which seemed to include more someones than just himself and Devon. And somehow it was all his fault. Her face still wet, Sheila took the phone from Travis and retreated down the driveway. "Ever'body bin took away from me now. Ever'body took away."

"Sheila. Wait." The pathetic shuffling came to a stop. "Here. Gimme the phone. And your water bottle."

Sniffing back her tears, Sheila handed him the items along with her gratitude. "Don' gimme none o' that nasty-ass gahden hose watah now, I want good watah." Five minutes later, with her bottle refilled with good water and her phone refilling with Riggins electricity, Sheila floated off down Crested Boulder, leaving Travis to pick up the lottery ticket which she'd dropped on his driveway and to reflect on Devon's current status as missing in action. Although he'd meant it when he told Sheila that Devon's no-show at 1413 was only temporary, Travis remembered the concern he'd expressed the day before to Linda, that the second traumatic disappearance of Monique from Devon's life might result in him disappearing as well; and while he had said those words mostly from the ulterior motive of impressing Linda with his depth of compassion, he knew that this boy had indeed hidden himself from the light of day all the years he'd known him, and so the idea that he might retire once again behind the curtains and revert to Boy Radley was a distinct possibility. And while the losing of Monique (it was everyone's assumption now that it really had been Monique) was a cruel blow, it had meant the loss of a girl already dead and gone; but a Devon disappeared once again behind closed doors would mean the loss of someone who had only just recently come alive.

An hour later (a period filled by texts with Linda texts and keeping his coffee away from the bedspread), Travis noted the time, and realized his wife's return from teaching her class was imminent; remembering Sheila's charging cell phone and that it could by no means still be there when his wife arrived, he stepped out onto the porch to check if it was still plugged in. It was of course. Grabbing it up with perturbation, he looked across the street and saw the phone's owner puttering about in her yard and yelling at no one and everyone. "Sheila! Come get this phone or I'm throwing it!"

Sheila clambered up the drive. "Don' know why you gotta be so mean I jus' chawgin' my phone like you tol' me to."

"Take it." Travis pointed at the phone as she approached, and when he looked at it again, he saw its screen vibrating and turning blue. "You got a text Sheila." Looking down at the screen, he read silently the following message, all in caps:

"*I KNOW U HOME BITCH I KNOW WHAT U BEEN UP TO"*

Travis gestured down at the phone. "Looks like you got a friend." Without unplugging it from the wall, Sheila looked down at the screen, and then jumped away from it, her ashen face turning even ashier.

"Oh goddamm no! Oh goddamm no!"

"No what?" Travis regretted asking before the question was out of his mouth.

"Oh goddamm no! Izz him again!"

"Who?"

"DAT MAN!"

Upon hearing the words "DAT MAN," Travis' heart was inundated by a flood of delightful memories. "Dat Man. Isn't he in jail?"

Sheila rocked side-to-side in agitation. "He *was*. Don' you see? He out now!" As she crept back up to the phone, it again popped up with blue light, triggering another of Sheila's pitiful wails while pointing at the phone in terror. "No no godDAMM no!"

"But they just put him in jail didn't they?"

Sheila's face twisted. "Jus' put in? Sheee-it, he always been in jail."

Travis was falling behinder by the moment. "What does 'always' mean?" Once again the phone trembled on the floor of the porch, and both Sheila and Travis leaned over to read the new text.

"I KNOW WHAT YOU BEEN UP TO WIT HIM."

Sheila howled and backed away from the vibrating device. "Oh shit! Oh shit! You see dat Mistah Diggins? He know all about what I been up to with Dat Man!"

"But- " Travis pointed down at the phone once again, "- *that's* Dat Man."

"HAIL no it ain't!" Sheila was on fire with exasperation. "Dat Man still in jail!"

"But you just said- "

"An' now dat man comin' aftah me because of Dat Man!"

"Goddammit Sheilah! Are there *two* Dat Man's now?"

"TWO Dat Man's?" Sheila was apoplectic. "If theah was two Dat Man's den mah husban' would kill me two times!"

Travis tried to shake the cobwebs from his head. "Wait- your husband?" He pointed yet again at the phone. "*That's* your husband?"

Sheila held her face in her hands and shook her head. "Nah nah nah Mistah Diggins, why you so stupid, *that* ain't mah husban'! Tha's mah *phone*! Mah husban' the one sendin' the tex' *on* mah phone!" The phone blinked angrily again, sending Sheila into paroxysms. "An' now dat man comin' to kill me ovah Dat Man!" As Travis finally began to pull bits of truth out of Sheila's tangled hairball, the phone continued spitting its blue light of accusation upon the afflicted woman, who wrung her hands pitifully while dancing side to side.

He had heard enough. "Look Sheila. Hate it for you, but you need to go deal with it. At home. Not here." The thought of Alicia's impending return added to his urgency. "Quick, take your phone, let's go. Go!" Seeing that the woman was immobilized, Travis threw his hands up in the air and strode over to the phone himself; but when he bent to take it up, the crackling pop of splintering wood straightened him to standing.

"What the hell- "

"Izz mah husban' right theah! Look!"

Following the pointing of Sheila's crooked finger, Travis looked across Crested Boulder; hulking across Sheila's front stoop was a large figure at her door, but "at her door" by no means captured the image- the man was going like hell at her door, kicking it in and shattering into small pieces the sheet of plywood which Devon only recently nailed up, his feet well on his way to completely destroying it. "That's your husband?"

"He not due to git out til nex' year!" Sheila said, as the man tore the last of the plywood off the door with his bare hands and threw it across the yard with a guttural roar. "He mus' be out early fo' good behav'or."

"Clearly." With the door reduced to kindling wood, the enraged husband stomped into the house; from inside, his *ursa arctos horribilis* bellering could be heard all the way over at 1418. "Okay. Getting my phone, calling the police."

"DON' CALL NO GOTT DAMM PO-LEECE! Po-leece jus' upset 'im!" Sheila hid behind a corner post of Travis' porch to make herself invisible. "Jus' let 'im go bout izz bidness an' when he sees ahm not theah he be gone. He cain't fuck up mah shit mah shit already fucked up. Jus' let 'im go 'bout izz bidness an' he be gone."

Marveling at Sheila's uncharacteristically reasonable assessment of things, Travis nodded and hid behind the other corner post. His voice was a conspiratorial whisper. "Right. Just wait him out. Besides, Devon will fix up whatever he breaks." Just then, the husband emerged from the house, guzzling from a forty-ounce bottle of beer.

Sheila was off the porch and screaming before Travis could hold her back. "MUTHAFUCKA DON' *TELL* ME YOU STEALIN' MAH FOHTIES!"

"Sheila, shut up!"

Incredibly, the husband was the only person in the 30080 zip code who hadn't heard her. But she set about fixing that by increasing the decibels. "LEE MAH BEER ALONE! YO GOTT DAMM STEPSON BOUGHT ME DEM BEERS DEY AIN'T FO' YOU T' TAKE MUTHAFUCKA!"

Travis pulled her by the arm. "Sheila, shut up, don't bring him over here!"

"YOU BES' NOT TAKE MAH CIG'RETTES NEITHUH!"

"*SHEILA!*" Having lost all patience, Travis hollered her name; and it was this of all things which the husband finally heard and which attracted the behemoth's attention.

"Goddamn Mistah Diggins now look whatchoo done! He gonna come ovah heah!" Sure enough, after looking about to discern from where his estranged wife's name had been uttered, his eyes landed on Sheila, and the furious man set off in her direction, loping across

Crested Boulder with no regard for oncoming traffic, daring the cars to make the mistake of running into him. "Oh shit, dat man got e'en biggah in jail!"

"Bitch I know whatchoo bin up to wit dat man!" Having made it across to the sidewalk, the husband noticed Travis. "Who this muthafuckah?"

"None yo' gott damm bidness! Now gimme tha beah back, I didn' say you could have none." It was strange to Travis, how she'd been shaken with fear by her husband's texts only a moment before, but now, finding herself within his literal striking distance, she was utterly fearless, ready to grapple with the powerful man hand-to-hand if necessary. It reminded him how he'd lived in terror at the thought of the tree hitting his house, and how that fear was instantly defused when he found its branches protruding from his upstairs. But unlike that tree, this wild oak's limbs were still swinging. Sheila stepped up to her husband, one hand on her hip and the other pointing at Travis. "This my fren' Mistah Diggins. He hep' me out sometimes, chawgin' up mah phone."

The husband glared at Travis. "Your fren', huh? I jus' BET he chawges yo' phone, he give it a good chawge don' he?" *Well, at least they're talking,* thought Travis. From the battering the husband gave to the front door, Travis assumed that nothing but more battering could possibly follow. But now, things had simmered to mere shit-slinging. They all might live another day after all. "How many othuh gott damm fren's o' yours bin chawgin' you up while I bin locked away ho?"

Sheila leaned in, right up to her husband's face, and when she did, a feeling of dread passed through Travis in anticipation of her reply, a foreboding which proved warranted. "Well put it dis way daddy," Sheila taunted, her creaking hips twitching side-to-side obscenely, "You ain't the *only* muthafuckah bin bangin' in mah fron doh."

At this, the man-bear raised up to his full height, his eyes reignited with rage. "Fuck you ho! You wantchor beer back? Here, bitch!" Suddenly the husband rushed up to Travis' truck and smashed the bottle against the back bumper, shattering glass everywhere but leaving the jagged neck of the bottle in his hand, the remnant so perfectly weaponized as to suggest he'd performed this trick before, and often. "I gotchor fohtie ounce!" And as Travis watched in frozen horror, the husband stepped up to Sheila and, with businesslike efficiency, sliced once and then again across Sheila's face with the knife-edged bottle in an "X" pattern, cutting both her face and her forearms which she'd raised, albeit too late, in defense. "There bitch! How you like your beer bottle now?" Screaming, Sheila turned her bleeding face away from him; the man repeated his "X" slashing, cutting into the back of her neck, back, head and shoulders.

"There's your beer bottle! There!" As the husband hacked away at Sheila (who by now had fallen into a sobbing lump), Travis considered his options. Finding his phone to call 911 would allow the crazy man that much more time to slash. No, he needed to intervene now. But he had no weapon; then he saw lying nearby the garden hose, with the spray nozzle screwed onto the end- and the water to the hose was turned on and ready to go. Running to it, Travis picked up the hose and, getting as close to the slashing man as he dared, turned the water full blast directly into the husband's face.

"Ahhh! Fuuuck!" It was distraction enough to interrupt his attack on Sheila, at least for the moment; then, before the man had a chance to recover, Travis played out several feet of the hose and, wielding the hose and metal spray nozzle like a modern-day version of the medieval flail, swung the hose high in an overhead loop, which brought the sharp spray nozzle crashing down onto the husband's melon.

"Shit!" As the husband staggered back holding his head, Sheila rolled off to the side of the driveway, bleeding and moaning in the grass. But in a second the husband had recovered, and, feeling his own blood on his hand, turned his wrath toward Travis. "Bad move muthafuckah. Real bad move." Squaring off in the driveway like gladiators, Travis and the husband circled each other slowly, the latter armed with the jagged weaponry of back alley warfare, the former accessorized with garden tools. And, like in the gladiatorial arena of ancient Rome, there now appeared Christians.

"Sister Sheila!" It was Sister Beulah, along with Pastor Kenneth. "What in the..." Sister B. looked upon the deadly standoff on the driveway and recognized the aggressor. "Oh dear Jesus it's that man of hers out of jail! Pastor call 911!"

"Already on the phone Sister!"

"Fuck you niggahs too!" As the husband slashed away at Travis, the brave homeowner countered with parrying swipes of the nozzle and hose, just enough to block the sharp edges of the bottle. "Call the po-leece, don'' give a fuck!" With the sparring continuing back-and-forth, Sister Beulah rushed to Sheila, whose entire upper body was by now wrapped in a wreath of red.

"We need to get you to the 'mergency room baby!"

Dazed and weak, Sheila could only mumble from where she sat in the grass, her face wearing a mask of blood. "Git mah... call mah son... mah... go call..."

"We'll call everybody, let's get you to the hospital first." Then the evangelist felt her own face dripping, and horrified that it might be Sheila's blood, touched it with her hand; but it was water, water which was spurting from tiny cuts here and there in Travis' hose from the slashes of the bottle. Travis saw what was happening to the hose, and knew in less than no time it would be completely severed and he'd be defenseless.

Sheila's husband knew it too and intensified his slashing. "So you been kickin' in her front doh while I been away, zat right muthafuckah?" All Travis could do was back away toward his porch in an effort to reduce the number of hits to his hose; then, a blur of red streaked past him and stumbled up onto the porch steps.

"Sister Sheila!"

"Gotta call mah son!" In a burst of frantic energy, Sheila, despite her wounds, had scrambled to her feet and propelled herself to the porch where her phone was charging. Seeing her get past him, the husband faked one way then went the other, rushing up onto the steps and leaving Travis and his hose behind on the pavement.

"Come 'ere bitch!" With a lunging strike the husband jabbed the bottle's edge into Sheila's back; with a moan she fell, up against the front door. From behind, Travis grabbed desperately onto the murderous man's ankle and pulled him away from the fallen woman, enough to cause the next few slashes with the bottle to fall just short of their mark. Meanwhile, the valorous Pastor Kenneth prayed as Sister Beulah screamed.

"The police are coming Sister Sheila! Get inside, behind the door!"

"Wait, what?!" Travis shouted, as he held on for dear life to the writhing serpent which was the husband's pantleg. "No Sheila, don't go in my house!"

"It's your only chance Sister!" It was true- with no way off the porch thanks to the swinging knife of glass preventing retreat and the wall of the house stopping Sheila from going any further in that direction, there seemed no refuge other than opening the door which she was shoved up against and escaping inside. And Travis knew it.

But still he protested. "Just stay down Sheila! The cops are coming!" Then the husband made another huge lunge from the top step, this time slicing deeply into the back of Sheila's leg.

"Get up Sister Sheila! Go in!"

"I'm killin' you bitch!"

"Stay down Sheila!"

"No, get up! Go in!"

"Stay down!"

"Get up Sister Sheila! Go in! Get up ! Go in!"

With the last of her strength, Sheila found the means to stand. Dizzy now from blood loss, she mumbled aloud Sister Beulah's commands. "Go...get... in go... up go..." Fumbling for the door, her hand found the handle; again the slicing glass caught the back of her leg, which seemed to provide her the propulsion necessary to open the door and throw herself indoors, falling as she mumbled. "Get... in... in... go... up..."

"Get back here bitch!" With Sheila safely behind the door beyond his reach, the husband turned his full fury upon the man pulling his pantleg. "Killin' yo' ass nex'!" A moment later Travis found himself on his back at the bottom of the porch steps, pinned down by the husband who straddled him while stabbing and flailing his sharp weapon. By now the hose was little more than a mass of perforated plastic, and as the husband slashed into it through the spurting water in an effort to reach the human face behind it, Travis could only bunch it into protective coils and, by absorbing the blows, hope to to block the crazed man's slashing arm in the process.

"Where the fuck are the police?"

"They're on their way Brother Travis!" Now the two men were rolling about the driveway, a twisting, grappling, cursing and slashing knot of wet confusion; but rather than running out of steam, the husband seemed to be growing more violent and vicious in his attacks. "Pastor, do something to help Brother Travis!"

Pastor Kenneth's courageous voice rang out from the sidewalk. "I am Sister! Been prayin' the whole time!" There was little hose remaining now to protect Travis from the stronger man's glass knife, and as he felt his energy depleting and the blur of the bottle getting nearer to his nose, Travis' thoughts wandered to an incongruous place, in the way brains sometimes do when under extreme duress- Travis now realized who it was that was trying to kill him, and he took this opportunity to introduce himself.

"We found your daughter!"

The husband's arm stopped in mid-slash. "Whatchoo say?"

Travis was panting. "We found Monique!"

"My little girl?" The hand holding the bottle dropped harmlessly to the ground.

"Yes. In my yard."

"Monique?..." Travis felt the muscles which had been pressing against him relaxing and releasing now, the steel coils softening, the man who pinned him down reduced to little more than a small, dead weight. "Monique." The father of the lost little girl sat back, his eyes adrift, and he exhaled a long, rasping breath, as if not having breathed in years at which point he fell like a lump to one side, knocked stone-cold unconscious by a single blow to the temple from Sister Beulah's leather-bound Bible.

Three minutes later, the scene had changed dramatically. The subdued husband was conscious now, but not a free man, thanks to the assistance of yet more Christian soldiers on the scene; now he sat on the sidewalk against Travis' gate, pinned there by Brother Jason and Sister Laura's dog, who growled at the perp with snapping jaws, straining at the end of his leash held tightly by both owners. The approaching sirens could be heard in the distance now, from the ambulance and the Cobb County police. But just as the emergency vehicles were coming into view on Crested Boulder, another vehicle beat them to the address; and as that car pulled in past blood-splattered man, barking dog and highly agitated Christians, its driver came to a stop just short of a shredded mess of gushing garden hose which held Travis, dazed, soaked and exhausted, sitting on the driveway and extricating himself from an entanglement which, as the driver's face clearly told him, was only going to get more entangling.

"Hi dear. How was class?"

As Alicia stepped away from her car and saw the approaching red and blue lights, Sister Beulah ran up to Travis and pulled at the remaining hose. "Oh thank Jesus Brother Travis, you ain't hurt, and now the ambulance is finally here."

"Why is an ambulance here?"

Travis was standing now. "Alicia, while you were gone- "

"Brother Travis," Sister Beulah interrupted, pointing to the front door, "we gotta go in there and check on Sister Sheila."

The ambulance was parked on the street now, and the EMT's were removing a gurney from the back of it. Alicia stepped up to Travis. "Sheila?" *In there?*"

"I told her not to, I- " Not waiting for his answer, Alicia marched up the driveway and onto the porch. In a flash, Travis imagined the next few seconds- perhaps the final seconds- of his life, how Alicia would open the door and find a bloody Sheila in a lump in the foyer. She was at the door now, and before going in, Alicia glanced down and saw Sheila's phone, still plugged in and mocking her with its blinking blue LED. Ripping it from the wall, Alicia glared at Travis, then threw the phone into the shrubs. Just then the EMT's came rushing up the driveway, carrying the gurney.

"Ma'am, we need to get past and get in, so please- "

"Back off! I go in first!" Alicia stood at the top of the steps and blocked their way. "This is MY house!" As the EMT's cowered at the bottom of the steps, Alicia threw open the front door, and there, lying across the foyer, was no one. She glanced about- there was no corpse of Sheila to be seen, not in the living room, not in the kitchen, nowhere.

Then she saw the open door leading to the upstairs.

For Sheila had done her best to do what Sister Beulah told her to do. "Get up Sister Sheila! Go in!" She had repeated those words to herself, to get up off the porch and go in, and in her diminished state she'd done her best, to get up and go in. But the words had turned and twisted in her short-circuiting mind as shock began to take its toll and her consciousness betrayed her, and though the words she repeated to herself kept her moving forward, they changed just a little, until they were no longer get up and go in, but get in... and *go up*. Which she'd done. All the way up to the bedroom, where, after following the trail of blood to the top of the stairs, Alicia now looked on in horror at the spot where Sheila, still inconveniently bleeding, had chosen to collapse; saw her lying atop the antique comforter, the dark red spreading in every direction, creating rivulets in and out through the tufted chenille and obliterating so much more than expert craftsmanship and a hundred years of heritage could ever account for.

13

In the weeks that followed, an unfamiliar calm fell upon those residential properties upon which had taken place The Battle Of Crested Boulder, a welcome respite to the rancor; quiet permeated for once, due to the fact that the noisiest of that battle's belligerents had either been silenced or removed, or both. Foremost amongst them of course had been Sheila's husband who, when the neighbors' dog released the man into police custody (a red-letter day for law enforcement, representing their landmark 100th Greater Sheila visit), had been overheard muttering to himself "Ain't nevah gettin' outta jail this time," a pronouncement no doubt true due to the severity of his crimes. And while Travis had been one of his victims, it was not the man's violence which had impressed itself most upon his recollection of the events, but rather, the sensitive spot Travis had touched, quite by accident, at the mention of the man's lost daughter. Had it struck him to hurl the name of Monique at his assailant as a defusing tactic, he'd have gone for it sooner, but that hadn't been Travis' motive; at the mention of her name the man had instantly surrendered to something more powerful within him than even the demons of his rage. And it complicated things for Travis, for up until the moment when Monique's father had, upon hearing her name, once again *become* Monique's father, it had been easy for him to categorize the man as a wholly malevolent force, a bad guy of the baddest variety. But in those startling moments just before Sister Beulah struck him down with the word of God, Travis had seen another man sitting on top of him, not a malevolent or a bad man at all, but one possessing, and possessed by, love. It was this duality, his disparate behaviors which defied simple one-dimensional categorization and which made defining the man more problematic, which caused Travis trouble when he thought about him afterward. For he knew that Pernell Gavins (yes, the man even had a name, yet another troublesome fact which humanized the monster) was sitting in jail now, which was where he needed to be of course; yet he also knew that Pernell, as he sat handcuffed in the back of the patrol unit that afternoon on his way to the station, must have wondered the entire ride- and all the next day, and the next, and certainly still wondered- what the hell that guy with the garden hose meant when he said "We found Monique in my yard." What did he imagine "in my yard" meant? Travis hadn't said "buried there." Did he think Travis meant a living, breathing Monique was found wandering about his lawn? It occurred to him that no more was said to Pernell than those few cryptic words, nothing else had been explained to him (and the arresting officers, part and parcel to the lost bone coverup, were of course not divulging). Now this man sat in jail, an old wound, perhaps his deepest ever, ripped wide open again, his mind and heart thrust once again into the confusion and frustration which must have been his constant torment eight years earlier when his girl was taken from him, but now with a strange new twist added to that confusion. And the more Travis thought about this man and his situation- this man who could not so conveniently be dismissed as "just" a bad guy- the more it troubled him, until he came to the conclusion that he would have to do something about it, visit him in jail, tell him all that had transpired, not only to perform a service for Pernell but for himself too, that being, to unload his burdened conscience. For Travis's priorities were unchanged- "make himself feel better" was still No. One on the list. So a humanitarian trip to the county jail was in order.

As for the murderer's victim, she was not- murdered that is. No, Sheila had been sliced, diced, flayed and filleted by her husband's broken bottle, but every wound had missed the major arteries and were of the flesh wound variety, vascularly dramatic to be sure and resulting in no small loss of that vascularity, but after three days in the ICU, Sheila was released, wrapped like a ghetto mummy in bandages and sent back home to recuperate (but in truth, three days of no smoking no drugs hospital food instead of fried pork rinds and IV fluid instead of malt liquor left her healthier at her dismissal than she'd been before her attack). Sheila's most shattering injury was not to her person but to her demolished front door; an injury which remained untreated, since Devon had not yet been seen, confirming Travis' fears that the lost bones ordeal had indeed thrown the young man into seclusion again (in the aftermath of the bottle attack, while the authorities were performing their duties, he had glanced over at the Walters' and saw the mandatory window eyes, but no eye-dentification of them could be made). With Devon out of the picture, Travis had a new problem, or rather, an old problem with a new, intensifying wrinkle: having so gallantly "saved Sheila's life," Travis's status had been upgraded to that of Her Hero, and in the absence of her previous hero Devon, Her New Hero was now Her Only Hero, which meant that her outpouring of love toward him- as well as her outreach for help from him- had risen to unprecedented heights. Sheila hovered constantly now, a fixed figure at the end of Travis' driveway, her bandages fluttering in the November breeze as she waved one hand high in praise of Her Hero and held the other hand out for, well, for dollars usually, fo' to be exact; and despite his determination to continue refusing the woman, the trauma she endured made her unrefusable, to the point that he'd even relented to allow Sheila to plug yet another antique flip-phone into the same porch outlet from which Alicia had so unceremoniously uninstalled the last one. It was in direct violation of all he'd promised his wife of course, as were all of the assistances he was now extending to Sheila. But in the aftermath following the cataclysmic events of the bloody day in question, a new standard operating procedure had been adopted at the Riggins home as touching all matters Sheila; or, more accurately, the old s.o.p. had been discontinued and not replaced by a new one. For Travis had much bigger problems than procedural ones with Alicia. His bigger problem was that Alicia had left him.

Upon discovering the dead body of the comforter beneath the bleeding body of Sheila, Alicia's first impulse had been to find a knife and stab her a few more times. And then stab her husband. But convinced that the woman was already dead- and resolved that the man on the driveway was as good as dead, to her- she had instead stepped aside to allow the EMT's to do their job, then went down to the kitchen, walking past her wine and stopping instead at the liquor cabinet, where Alicia took up Travis' most expensive and least empty bottle of single-malt scotch and sat with it on the sofa, draining its contents while in a dazed stupor of shock which her ensuing inebriation did not alleviate in the least. When she was finally able to stand, it was only to grab enough gear for her to spend the night elsewhere, leaving Travis to perform the cleanup. And while he found it a fairly easy though utterly disgusting thing to restore the condition of the house, there was nothing within his power he could do to restore their home. Alicia was gone, and she'd made it clear she was never coming back. That it was beyond reconciliation was obvious to him, despite the fact that neither he nor even Sheila could be accused of any crime more than being the victims of a shit-storm tsunami. The drowning event represented yet another miserable instance of The Sheila Effect, in which Sheila herself does not do the horrible thing per se but without a Sheila the thing would not have occurred. And Travis, as always, had invited none of it. All he wanted- all he'd ever wanted for the last five years from this poisonous, parasitic woman- was to be left alone to enjoy his lovely home and his lovely wife and his lovely life that he'd cultivated so carefully. No, he hadn't been the perfect husband, but it wasn't because of his domestic imperfections that his wife had walked out. It was a maddening irony that, yes, there was "the other woman" with whom he was secretly cultivating an illicit bond which, if learned by his wife, would legitimately provide her the reason to end it all, and yet this woman had not factored into the proceedings; instead, Travis had been abandoned because of "the OTHER other woman," one with whom he wanted to cultivate nothing, illicit or otherwise! But the fact remained: although Travis knew his relationship with Sheila did not warrant being left by his wife, she'd left him over Sheila regardless- he had simply not done enough to eradicate Sheila from Alicia's presence. For as any gardener knows, success doesn't only depend of the beauty of the flowers which the he plants, but his ability to keep out the weeds.

Travis had failed to rid his garden of the most invasive weed of all, and so the blood, despite his latex cleanup gloves, was on his hands.

Then there was the matter of the actual other woman. In lieu of the disaster, Travis had decided their lunch should probably be postponed for the time being, for obvious reasons, but not texting her until deciding, firstly, that he should tell Linda up-front that Alicia had left him, and then secondly, settling upon the way to do the telling which was most advantageous to his ambitions with Linda. His approach was strategic: he began his text with an overview of all Travis had endured for five years from Sheila (underscoring of course the many ways Travis had generously provided the unfortunate woman comfort and assistance); he then related the horrific details of that Saturday's horror show and how no reasonable spouse could have expected him to have done more to prevent the unfolding of those grim events; then finally, after documenting Alicia's many exasperations over the years with Sheila's plight (carefully avoiding any mention of *himself* being exasperated by Sheila), punctuating the texting by telling Linda he'd been rendered wifeless. The tactic worked; Linda's text response had been wholly sympathetic, that after all the charitable outreach and selfless attentiveness he'd extended toward Sheila over the years, how unfair it was for him to now receive as his reward in his lowest hour the loss of his wife's support (*Travis, that man might have killed you!* Linda had typed). But immediately following this most successful of text exchanges, it was followed by several days of electronic silence, as if each party was aware that further communication would be perceived as an escalation, a signal acknowledging to the other that, well, the thing they both had on their minds was more possible now than ever, so, how 'bout it?; and as such, neither wanted to be the one to reach out too soon, before a respectably appropriate "grieving of his marriage" period had elapsed. Linda was the brave one to break the silence, brave yet discrete, texting him simply that, hey, if you need to talk about anything, I'm here. So the next day, Linda was in fact there, with him at their rescheduled lunch, during which the conversational floodgates were opened to every subject save one, that being, the whole reason they were there. But despite their sidesteps to avoid their mutually-shared preoccupation, the subject of their relationship silently devoured their minds the entire lunch, to the point that the unspoken thoughts of their romantic desires were louder than the voiced words of the approved topics (primary among them was Devon, and their concern over Travis' not seeing him since the precinct fiasco). By the time the check arrived, each knew where they stood with the other; driving home, Travis could feel his guilt diminishing and his confidence growing about Linda, thinking so far as to envision, ever so vaguely, something which might even be called a future with her. And he was even more confident that she could be counted on once again to make the next move.

It was later that same day of the lunch, nearly six weeks after the carnage of the comforter, when Travis arrived home from work; as was now the rule, Sheila awaited him at the end of his driveway, expressing her love for Her Hero while expressing her need for anything Her Hero had to give. Although he'd grudgingly returned the word "yes" to his vocabulary now that he was no longer required to answer to his Higher Power, Travis had found ways to temper those "yesses" with certain regulatory "no's" as well, if only to make him feel a little less of a sap; for example, while he'd sometimes acquiesce to Sheila's four dollar request, he would haggle it down to two dollars, take it or leave it. Which she always took. He would also cut not only the amount in half but the frequency- if he said yes to her the last time, he'd say no to her the next, a give-and-take which Sheila also accepted (and adjusted to, by simply asking for money twice as often) and began to even expect. "Mistah Diggins I know you gimme me two dollahs las' time so you gonna say no dis time but anyway you got fo' dollahs for mah candles e'en though you only gonna gimme two win I ax fo' fo'?" And so it went. On one day, the first Friday after Alicia had left which found Travis feeling particularly low, it was as if the strange woman somehow sensed his dolor and came out randomly with "Mistah Diggins we bofe need a stiff drank, you got some good liquor in yo' house?" Which of course he did, and was so caught off guard that he'd poured out shots for each of them, throwing them back as they stood by the gate, at the very spot where Pernell had created the "X" which hadn't yet fully left Sheila's face. It had become their Friday happy hour routine now (she also showed up on Tuesday for the drink, to which per their understanding he always said no); by drinking with his enemy, the same enemy he still wished would one night just go to sleep and not wake up again, he found something in the contradictory civility of their ritual which was nostalgic, almost chivalrous, a time-honored respect for one's adversary, as when rival Civil War generals who once upon a time engaged in "gentlemanly warfare" would send their forces out to slaughter each other, but then after the battle send emissaries to the other side with an exchange of gifts (which occurred at Travis' very own Kennesaw Mountain following the battle of the same name). This particular day being Friday, therefore, Travis had produced the Jameson and the shot glasses (when he told her that it was Irish whisky, Sheila had answered without awareness of the pun, "well irish you gimme a little mo"), and after their shots Sheila had wandered off, leaving in her wake the mandatory tossed lottery ticket on his driveway. As he bent over for it, a familiar voice which he was certain he would never hear again gave him a startle.

"Some shit never changes." It was Corey, sitting behind the wheel of his still-scratched truck which was parked on the curb. The unoccupied spot on the seat beside him was achingly conspicuous.

Travis walked up to Corey's open window. "Wow. Long time."

Corey grunted, then watched as Sheila made her way onto her property. "Still cleaning up after her fucking mess, are you?"

"Busted. So, what brings you back to- " He stopped himself before saying "the scene of the crime" "- the old neighborhood?"

Corey glanced over at his old house, then quickly looked back. "I saw the news a few weeks back. About those bones. In your yard, right?"

"Yep. That was me."

"Some senator's daughter or something who was missing?"

Travis shook his head. "Nah. Turned out not to be. They, well, they never determined whose bones they were." He stepped up closer to the window. "But between you and me, I'm pretty sure I know whose they were."

Corey nodded. "So do I. Sheila's daughter."

Travis stared back dumbfounded. "How do you- "

"Remember the day we met, at the house with the realtor? I told you then I'd done my research about next door. Well..." Corey stared through narrowed eyes over at 1413. "...that was one of the things I learned. About her missing kid." Travis found himself without a next thing to say. Corey was not so reticent. "You think she did it?"

Travis was sure he'd heard him incorrectly. "She?" Corey only stared back.

"Sheila? Did she...?" Now Corey nodded. "To her own daughter?"

"Why not? She's responsible for everything ain't she? Everything she touches she kills. She killed my dog, didn't she?" Again, Travis was stumped for a response; but again, Corey sailed ahead without a bump. "So, how's Alicia?"

Travis was almost glad to tell him, just to counter the imbalance of Corey's misery with some of his own. "Alicia. Yeah. Well, she left me."

"Left? Like, 'gone' left?"

"Like 'gone' left."

He found it curious that Corey's face reflected no surprise at the news; all he did was look across the street again. Finally he spoke. "She left because of Sheila." His eyes returned to Travis'. "Didn't she?" Travis face confirmed everything. "Right. The bitch kills everybody." With each unanswerable comment from Corey, Travis' discomfort grew. More was to follow. "So what are you gonna do about it?"

"About 'it'?"

"About Sheila Gavins."

Silent seconds passed. "There's nothing really... *to* do, is there?"

Now the trace of a smile curled the corners of Corey's mouth as he continued to stare across the street. "Oh, there's shit you could do. For a start..." He turned back to Travis. "... you could stop havin' drinks with her." Travis forgot he was holding the shot glasses. "Havin' a little party with the bitch who killed my dog?"

Travis felt ill at once. "Oh. These. No, this was just- "

"Or was one of those shots poisoned? Hers maybe?" Once again, Travis had no response, but Corey had already started up his truck, and without looking back at Travis again, squealed his tires and drove off; and as the truck flew past Sheila's, a 40-oz bottle in a paper bag came flying out Corey's open window, landing like a Molotov cocktail in her yard. Sheila waddled out of her house like a spider checking what had landed on her web, then after picking it up, she sniffed the bottle and drank down the remaining drips. Travis considered Corey's "one of 'em was poisoned" remark as he watched the truck speed away, and decided conclusively that at least one of 'em certainly was.

On Saturday, Travis was raking leaves in the front yard, remarking to himself what a relatively minor chore it was this autumn with Keith's giant oak no longer contributing to the task. Yes, it had created quite the disruption when it came crashing down, but now, with his raking job having been made so easy, he was actually enjoying the aftermath of the disaster, and could now look forward next spring to some big white blossoms on his previously-shrouded little dogwood. There were advantages to no longer be living beneath the big tree, and Travis couldn’t help but draw parallels with his domestic situation. As with the tree, the crashing down of his marriage created a significant initial impact, but as he’d come to learn, the calamities we dread can be less of a problem than the dread itself. For to his surprise, the emotional desperation which he assumed would devastate him by Alicia's absence just hadn't materialized; six weeks following her exit, Travis found himself dealing with it, simple as that. He had his low moments, yes, but all-in-all he was okay and functioning perfectly well. He was in fact feeling just a little guilty at how sensibly and rationally he was bearing up on the whole. He’d resigned himself to his new reality, that he would carry on as a single guy; Alicia's income hadn't been that much anyway (in truth, it was not his own financial situation which concerned him, but how she would get by on her low-paying job at the gym), and now, without wifely responsibilities, he'd be able to attack his sales work that much more aggressively and make the kind of money which an un-wived wage earner might earn. Of course there were messy details to be resolved, but with no children to complicate things, it would be a clean enough break. In short, he would be fine. And while Travis was heartened by the stress-free and manageable cleanup following the fall of his domestic tree, what buoyed him most was the new tree sprouting in its place, the Linda tree, from which he permitted himself to take more and more encouragement as each fresh twig appeared. To be sure, if the ledger of his thoughts consisted of a "Losing Alicia" column and a "Winning Linda" column, the latter would be the longer, with new entries being added to their developing story, a story fast becoming more than an aspirational "if and when" but a "now."

It was just that column of his mind which Travis was reading from as he raked the yard that Saturday, thinking of what he might text to Linda to elicit an electronic smile, then imagining her response, and ultimately, how the back-and-forth would lead to, well, who could tell what, an intrepid suggestion from one of them about a first actual date perhaps? Down the street, an unusual amount of hoo-ha and hell-raising was taking place at 1413, decidedly celebratory in nature, a full-blown party in the middle of the afternoon. Cars were driving up one after another, parking along Crested Boulder nearly all the way to the Iffy Grocery, and others were pulled off the pavement, in the yard, anywhere a car could fit. Music thumped from the open trunk of one car, making its back-end bounce and vibrate in rhythm, causing any human back-end within its blast zone to bounce as well; one armload of food after another was being carried in through Sheila's still-broke front door, more coolers and trays (and human occupants) than the tiny hovel might have been thought able to accommodate. Despite the wall of noise which mushroom-clouded out of the chaos, one high and howling voice could be heard above it all- that of Sheila's, who was clearly feeling no pain and reveling in her role of mistress of ceremonies. Grateful that his house was upwind (and that, curiously, he'd found no tossed lottery ticket that morning at the end of his driveway for him to pick up), Travis ignored the bacchanal and continued raking; just then, a white courier van pulled up next to him, stopping at the curb. As he tried to remember what Amazon delivery it might be, the driver jumped out of the van, carrying an envelope.

"Travis Riggins?"

"That's me."

The young man held out the envelope; Travis took it, at which point the deliverer added, "You've been served." As the driver jumped back into his van and drove off, Travis opened the envelope, and pulled out legal documents; the top page read "IN THE SUPERIOR COURT OF COBB COUNTY, STATE OF GEORGIA," and then, "Petitioner: Alicia Riggins. Respondent: Travis Riggins." He'd been expecting the divorce papers for weeks, but only vaguely, subconsciously; intellectually he was aware of the procedure and that being served was a part of it, so the intellectual component of him was not surprised. But another part of him, an emotional side, had not been similarly briefed in advance, for as he stood near the curb with the papers in one hand and his rake in the other, a crumbling sort of implosion began, initiating from somewhere deep and buried, like the first ominous subterranean tremors of a coal mine cave-in. Upon reading his name and her name, and the cold legalese which now linked them, ironically linked them, in a way which even his intellectual mind had not been prepared to see, that intellect began to shut down, bit by bit, as the emotional cave-in proceeded in earnest, burying more and more of his reasonable mind and filling all the chambers of his psyche with panic. It was real now. His marriage was ending. The woman he had shared a life with for more than five years was gone and would not be back. The feeling of it, the emotional feeling of a part of him removed, the visceral sensation of loss, which he was convinced he had eluded, now was everything in a moment; the detailed contents of the papers were of no matter to Travis, for his eyes could not read them anyway and did not need to read them, and how he continued to hold the papers was a mystery, for he felt no control over his hands. It was this, the feeling of no control, which held him immobilized, the crushing realization that control belonged to Alicia and that he controlled nothing. What a fool he saw himself as now, what an immature child, pretending these weeks that he was on some extended vacation, a lark in the park with a perky blonde, as though he'd eventually recover from his foolishness after sowing his oats and then return unscathed to his real life, the life which really mattered. No, Alicia was his real life, and his real life was gone now- these papers in his hand guaranteed it. And no extended vacation was going to compensate for that.

As Travis' paralysis held him statue-like on the curb, the good Sister Beulah and Pastor Kenneth, having just come from the raucous party house down the street, approached him merrily, with Sister Beulah taking the lead. "Brother Travis, ain't this a blessed day which the Lord has made?"

He was too disarmed for sarcasm. "No."

Pastor Kenneth raised his Bible as he pointed back toward 1413. "God answers prayer, Brother Travis. Our prayers and Sister Sheila's prayers. She ain't told you yet?"

"Told me what?"

Now Sister Beulah's Bible was raised in praise as well. "Sister Sheila won the lottery this morning! Seventy-eight hundred, cash money! God is *good*!"

Travis could hear Sheila's cackling laughter above the party noise as a ball of lead dropped into his gut. "Sheila won the lottery?"

"Praise Jesus!" Sister Beulah shook her head and laughed. "Seventy-eight hundred, I swear, it's more money than Sister Sheila ever held in her life."

"Seventy-eight hundred dollars..." Travis' stumbling brain bounced from divorce papers to the sound of Sheila's voice and back again. "And she has her cash already?"

Pastor Kenneth stepped up proudly. "That's right Travis. You see, when Sister Sheila told us she won we put her in the church van right then and drove her ourselves, right down to the Georgia Lottery Office on Williams Street. She signed the forms and got her cash. Same day!"

"Praise God!"

"How 'bout that." Again, Travis felt the divorce papers in his hand. "Great that you helped her out and all."

"Well the poor thing certainly deserves a little help" Sister Beulah intoned, as the pastor nodded in harmony, "after all she's been through."

"One storm after another."

"As you know as well as anyone, Brother Travis."

"Storms." Travis stared numbly across the street at the revelers, his ability to do any more than that buried beneath the avalanche. "Sheila. And her storms."

Sister Beulah clapped her hands brightly, as if shooing away the building clouds of Travis' mood. "Well! We'll get along now and let you get back to your work Brother Travis." Taking a step down the sidewalk, the godly woman turned back. "Oh and say hello to Miss Alicia for us. We haven't seen her lately." And with that, they were gone, leaving Travis standing on the curb to smell the barbecue and the weed smoke wafting his way, the prevailing winds having turned in a decidedly different direction.

He was still there, many hours later that same evening, sitting on the tailgate of his truck, enjoying the good times with his bottle of Jameson as the party up the street grew bigger and happier in every way. It was the funniest joke of all time, that much Travis knew, and its hilarity only increased each time Jameson got tilted. Here was His Sheila, the ever-festering human pimple perched upon Crested Boulder's butt cheek, a swollen zit which pops itself on a regular basis and with disregard for aim squirts its corrosive puss into the face of anyone within range of its eruption- and is this open sore cauterized shut after her many years of zit-spraying? Hell no. The chancre is rewarded by Providence with thousands of free dollars. Pure comedy, have a drink. Then there was the timing of her party, another joke, surely an intentional one played on him by this same asshole Providence, that her good fortune should be delivered into her hands just as Travis' bad fortune was literally being delivered into his, and that her celebration should occur right in his gobsmacked face. More laughs. Have a drink. But there were still more levels to the laughter. Not only was the one hand of Providence handing out blessings to this woman just as the other was fisting Travis up the ass, but this very woman *was the thrust behind the fisting*. Sheila, Queen of the Lottery, The Happiest Woman In Smyrna Georgia, she and she alone was the one who had destroyed his marriage. A laugh riot. Drink some more. Sheila, the wellspring of all calamity, whose mere existence seemed to bring destruction to pass (hadn't Corey said "everything she touches she kills?"), was now riding the crest of her Big Lucky Break, just as Travis was wallowing in his Sheila-made brokenness. It was laugh-out-loud funny, drink-straight-from-the-bottle funny; this offscouring of a soul who perpetuated, merely perpetuated from one day to the next with the existential blindness of mold, who applied no effort whatsoever to life's required tasks, who prepared for nothing, planned for nothing, never thought before she spoke and never aimed before swinging, now had Providence swinging her way, while the prudent and responsible Coreys and Travis' and Alicias of the world who tried, actually *tried,* to live with intentional purpose, were left blood-stained and miserable in her careless wake. Sheila had done nothing whatsoever to earn her fortune. Fortune? For a man of Travis' financial condition, seventy-eight hundred dollars was not life-changing. But for Sheila, it absolutely was- for Sheila, it was the windfall of a lifetime, the Irish Sweepstakes, for the simple reason that it felt that way to her. Yes, it *felt* to her like it was everything, and for Sheila, a being who did not examine beyond her feelings, her feelings constituted the whole of her reality. Sheila, therefore, was now rich as Croesus, and at the expense of impoverished Travis. And this provided yet another belly-laugh irony for him, the subjectivity of perception- since Sheila possessed nothing all her life, she had acclimated herself to her abject state, so that it only required adding a very little to that nothing to make her feel like a queen; but while Travis could boast of exponentially greater wealth (not just money but stability, solidity, comfort, security), he had become inured to that wealth, so that now he was like the junkie for whom his daily dose, though appearing considerable to someone else, no longer got him high, his needle giving him nothing now but relief from dope sickness and maintenance of a humdrum disenchantment. Travis *felt* poor, by comparison, and so he was poor; Sheila felt rich, and so she was. Travis and Jameson both laughed at this observation (he was beginning to think that maybe the fucking bottle was only laughing at him, not with him, but he couldn't be sure because he'd been drinking after all), and this concept of wealth's relativity gave Jameson some new material for his comedy routine: he told Travis the one about the guy who had a good job with a steady income, a nice home, a very sexy truck and a 4-star Kelley Blue Book-rated wife, but then lost the wife, and felt crushed despite still having the rest, and how this same guy had this trash neighbor across the street who had no job, no income, a shit shack, junk in her trunk and a bottle-slashing husband, but because she had nothing to lose didn't feel crushed at all even when the husband crushed her with the bottle because she been crushed her whole life so she was okay with that, and Jameson's punch line was probably gonna be some shit about that trash neighbor winning the lottery but Travis jammed Jameson into his mouth before he had a chance to say it.

But as soon as Jameson pulled himself out of Travis' mouth he went back to his damn jokes. His next one was the one about this whole idea of Providence. Of course there was no such thing as Providence and Travis knew it. Providence had always been a code word for God, that guys like Thomas Jefferson used because they didn't really believe in God but couldn't admit it publicly so they gave people a concession to appease them; instead of mentioning God and Jesus specifically the Jeffersonian doubters just referred to this vague Providence entity as the Higher Power who we all counted on to make shit go right. Well Travis wasn't a politician like Jefferson and so he had no trouble saying right out loud that there was no god and no Providence, but when he looked at how things had played out, with the perfect storm of Sheila's windfall and her party and the divorce papers and the messengers of Sister Sheila's good news being the damn evangelists no less, it struck him that only an almighty god could coordinate such a perfectly articulated effort at fucking with his head in such an articulated way, a real asshole of an almighty god too, and that today's events looked very suspiciously like that almighty god was giving him a nice "Gotcha!", as if paying Travis back for being bad-mouthed by him and being told he didn't exist all these years. And when Jameson suggested that maybe Travis had been wrong after all about all this "no god" stuff, Travis decided Jameson needed to wrap his act up and get off the stage, which he did when Travis finally finished off the bottle. He sat there on his tailgate with his head spinning, and felt himself starting to fade; and just as the noise of the party down the street were beginning to sound like a mocking lullaby telling him to go to sleep, the empty Jameson lost his grip and went rolling off the end of the tailgate and crashed onto the driveway, shattering into pieces, leaving Jameson's neck all jagged just the way Pernell's 40oz looked on that other Saturday right at this very spot. Travis thought it was a pretty fitting way to end a pretty shitty night. But dammit if a new bottle named

Glenfiddich didn't step up and volunteer to keep the shit-show going by jumping up onto the stage and telling some jokes of his own.

His routine began on the subject of gratitude, about all the instances when Travis had helped Sheila and gotten no thanks in return, and Glenfiddich nearly used up all his set time on that list alone. But while he never received any thanks, Travis could nevertheless always count on getting paid back in the form of some kind of shit-bomb blowing up in his face, the old cliché of no good deed going unpunished. What's more, Sheila lacked the governing mechanism which Travis had assumed was built into all people, that internal device which checks a person from availing another's generosity too many times, the braking system which screeches polite people to a halt before wearing out their welcome. But Sheila's brake pads were worn away, or never existed; she just kept coming at whatever it was she wanted to get, without shame, and because Travis was a good person- which he knew was a euphemism for a weak person- he had made the mistake of saying yes, which conditioned her to return over and over again to her yes-man. And of course it followed that any time he dared say no, he became the asshole. Helping Sheila was a thankless trap, but time had proven he couldn't keep himself from falling into it. He'd say no which would push the teary-face button so he'd say yes instead and he'd be right back where he didn't want to be. Glenfiddich's routine was starting to sound pretty redundant because Travis had already been over all this so many times before in his mind without Glenfiddich's help, but Glenfiddich then pointed out how it was a little different this time: this time the Sheila trap had cost him his wife, the same wife who never had any problem whatsoever saying no to Sheila, who had never been stupid enough to exchange even Word One with Sheila (it was amazing but true- in five years his wife had somehow managed to learn everything she knew about her nemesis purely second-hand, through Travis' encounters, without ever hearing it straight from the horse's ass' mouth). Alicia had no problem taking Sheila's cellphone and throwing it into the shrubs. And because Travis hadn't been smart enough to throw Sheila into the shrubs, she'd paid him back by getting him divorced.

Unfair! This was the word which Glenfiddich was pouring down Travis' throat now, the new direction of his act. It was all unfair! Unfair how the people in the world who gave a shit like Travis were victimized by the don't-give-a-shitters like Sheila; unfair that she could feel so rich with so little while he felt so poor with so much;

unfair that having nothing to lose meant losing all fear of losing what you don't have; unfair that the givers in the world were repaid by the takers with even more taking and without so much as a thank-you. The laughs were coming loud and fast now from the audience in his drunk head, from the drunk party down the street, from Glenfiddich every time he was turned bottoms-up; it was like Glenfiddich's routine had reached its big finale, like a fireworks show when they shoot every rocket remaining at the end, and Glenfiddich's rapid-fire rocket show consisted of all the unfairnesses which he was recalling to Travis' mind one after the other, not just the ones done to him but to everyone around him: it was unfair that Corey worked so hard on his home only to have his living in it spoiled by idiots; it was unfair that a really good dog was killed, and unfair for Corey to have to live with being the one who killed him; it was unfair for Devon to have Keith for a father, and unfair for him to have lost the same friend twice; it was unfair that Monique's life had been taken from her, and then have her death taken from her as well; it was unfair for Alicia that she had to walk into the worst "Welcome Home" greeting anyone could imagine; it was unfair to Sheila that she was attacked by her husband...

"What?"

Travis had said it out loud, said it to Glenfiddich, and it must have been exactly what Glenfiddich wanted him to say because the smart-ass bottle had already dropped the mic in triumph and left the stage, rolling over empty next to Travis and laying beside him on the tailgate, and he was just staring up at Travis now with a big satisfied smile on his glassy face. Glenfiddich's last joke had put an end to the firework show, seemed to have put an end to everything, because even the party house had just like that gone quiet; the only thing Travis could hear were the words of that last joke repeating in his head. "It was unfair to Sheila that she was attacked by her husband." What besides Glenfiddich made him say it? Did it mean then that he truly felt, in the place where he now feared might be lurking humanlike feelings, that Sheila could be a victim just as Corey and

Devon and Monique and Alicia had been? Or had the alcohol only tricked him into blurting out something he really didn't believe? And now that it had come blurting out, regardless of how he felt about it, was it true? *Was* Sheila a victim?

Eager to get away from the cyclopic hole in Glenfiddich's neck which kept leering up at him accusatorily, Travis slid off the tailgate and began a thought-sorting inebriated meander about his night-shrouded landscape. *Was Sheila a victim?* Troubling as it was, it seemed right off that the answer was a clear "yes." Of course Sheila was a victim. No suggestive remark she could have made to Pernell about her front door or her back door or any other door warranted taking a bottle to her face. Pernell had been the victimizer, and Sheila the victim. Building on that, Travis expanded his view of the unfortunate woman, and realized that she'd no doubt been victimized her entire life by so many more jagged bottles, figurative and literal. What legacy of disadvantagement must have been bestowed upon Sheila from early on, what lack of opportunity and choice must have been her birthright? Wasn't this the explanation for what she became and where she'd ended up? For Travis to then suggest that one such as Sheila had not been victimized by life itself would be to willfully ignore the obvious. Yes, Sheila was a victim; and as he walked the grounds of his compound and allowed the full weight of this realization to settle, a new word appeared in his mind, one which he'd never associated with Sheila but which now loomed large and insistent: sympathy. Yes. Sheila deserved- he was unable to bring himself to say it, and so Glenfiddich shouted it for him- Sheila deserved his sympathy, despite the ill treatment she had served him. Here then was a real dilemma, a moral conundrum; for if there'd been one foundation stone upon which Travis' attitude toward Sheila had been built these five years, it was resentment, and of late, with Alicia's Sheila-induced departure, he had built upon that Sheila Resentment foundation stone a towering fortress of Sheila Blame. Resentment and blame were the only responses Travis had ever deigned to offer the wretch. Resenting and blaming Sheila had vented him of his bile and provided him a perverse sort of compensation for the troubles she brought him. Resenting and blaming Sheila fueled Travis' sense of superiority, a better-than-thou feeling he wasn't proud of but not made any less real by his shame at feeling it. But if sympathy for this same Sheila were allowed to infiltrate, to muddy those pure and free-flowing streams of resentment and blame and, with its cross-current, mix itself into the message and transform his mind and heart into murky, indecisive pools, then the ground beneath Travis' feet would collapse into a sinkhole. For if sympathy found a foothold in Travis' attitude toward Sheila, then dismissing her outright could no longer be an option for his conscience; and if his attitude toward Sheila needed overhauling, then he could only wonder, no, he was afraid to wonder, how much else in his life, in his relationships with people and the world at large, might also require overhauling. Black-or-white, thumbs-up or thumbs-down, this had been Travis' simplified approach to everyone and everything. This one is a good neighbor, that's a bad neighbor, a good client, a bad client, a really good archaeologist, a bad police captain, etcetera. But to now be required to process Sheila in terms which were not so simply black or white- to be forced to see her as, well, mixed- meant the greater world must be viewed as mixed as well, and would demand of Travis that he engage that world with a mix of wisdom and discernment along with the resentment, tolerance and compassion along with the blame, a spectrum of sensibilities which he was not sure he possessed nor sure he even wanted to possess. This troublesome fissure of sympathy bubbling up through the newly-appearing cracks in his resolve presented a real threat to the integrity of his foundation, and the terrifying prospect of so much unstable earth beneath his feet now had his legs feeling wobblier than the combined efforts of Jameson and Glenfiddich had been capable of producing.

Across the street the cars were one by one leaving the extinguished party; the orange glow of Sheila's indoor campfire could be seen through her front window, silhouetting the last departing stragglers as they shuffled out into the early AM dark. Travis' perambulations meanwhile had taken him into his dew-blanketed back yard, still on his feet despite the alcohol and the late hour, unable to call it a night so long as his moral dilemma remained unresolved. There would be no sleeping until one thing or the other had taken place: either his long-established foundation of judgmental simplicity would be restored intact or it would be shattered utterly, leaving him in need of a total rebuild. A total rebuild? Surely he was exaggerating his present predicament. There was no way his attitude toward this insignificant flotsam of a woman could be central to his psychological health and his ability to successfully function with others of his species. The discomfiting softening towards her which he was experiencing, the way that he was, well, humanizing her, this was certainly just a symptom of heightened vulnerability brought on by the concerted attack of Alicia's leaving, the divorce papers, Sheila's lottery windfall and a shitload of 80-proof comedy. And so, determined to restore his default settings and get his mind right, Travis accelerated his meandering to pacing, then set himself to the mental task of pulling the invasive weeds of sympathy out of his psyche's garden so that the familiar flowers of resentment and blame could blossom once again without entanglement. A decent night's sleep depended on it.

In order to perform a self-exorcism of the sympathy demon, Travis determined it needful to analyze the demon fully, deconstruct it if you will, that he might come to learn his enemy better and, by so doing, defuse its power with the greater power of reason. Despite his lack of personal experience with the substance, he estimated sympathy's composition to be about ninety-five percent emotion, since it could be described as the *feelings* of pity and sorrow for another (he guessed the remaining five percent of sympathy's makeup to be mostly saline, in the form of tears). The misfortune which had triggered his "feelings of pity and sorrow" for Sheila had initially been her victimization at the hands of Pernell, and then his understanding of Sheila's entire life as a victim. Valid reasons to garner sympathy to be sure, making her no less but probably no greater deserving of sympathy than Corey, Devon, Monique *et al*. And it was this "*et al*" which gave Travis pause, the "and others": who comprised this "and others" group deserving sympathy? Well it was obvious- the "and others" group should really be called "and everyone," because it was. No one, he realized, has ever lived without having been victimized by something or someone in their lives, whether by twists of fate, circumstances of birth, the cruelties of bad parents, the honest mistakes of good parents, disease, bad luck, clergy, teachers, nature, nurture, accident or intent. The most despotic tyrants, guilty of crimes against humanity, the enslavers of nations, have been done wrong sometime in their lives, enduring mean babysitters or scoliotic spines or any of the other various injustices which universally beset every member of the species in various degrees of severity. In viewing the world this way, he now imagined sprawled out before him a pathetic sea of humanity, everyone sharing the common denominator of victimization, crying up toward the heavens like billions of baby birds from their nests to receive their grub of sympathy. But what did receiving sympathy mean? What should it mean? With Sheila, Travis' discovery of having feelings of sympathy toward her presented a threat to his psychological *status quo* because they sent him down a slippery slope, to wit: if Sheila deserved sympathy, then perhaps she deserved forgiveness; and if sympathy and forgiveness were permitted to push their way in, wouldn't they necessarily push out resentment and blame in the process? *And what would be left of him without his resentment and blame?* Absolving Sheila of guilt for her torments was abhorrent to his sense of justice. But then a new thought struck him, such an obvious one that he marveled at his denseness for not stumbling upon it sooner: what did feelings of sympathy have to do with the withholding of justice? Nothing whatsoever! Dealing with wrongdoers involves no connection between the sympathy we may feel for them and the justice we mete out to them for their wrongs. Those same despotic tyrants, victims themselves though they may be, are not spared the consequences for their crimes just because their daddies left them at the age of three. No, sympathy was not an action-item in the response to bad behavior; justice was the action-item for bad behavior, and the proper one at that, while sympathy was merely "the feeling of pity and sorrow" over the misfortunes in that poor tyrant's life which had contributed to his bad behavior. Travis saw that the separate streams of justice and sympathy did not collide and in so doing end each other's ability to flow, but rather, they flowed parallel, in their respective channels; and with that being the case, it was also true that the streams of resentment and blame (feeder tributaries of justice, let's face it) could flow side-by-side next to the stream of sympathy. This meant he could feel sympathy for poor Sheila but *go right on resenting and blaming her too*. Yes! This newly-sprung sickening-sweet stream of sympathy didn't need to be diked, it simply needed its own dedicated canal to flow through so as not to pollute the more rational one next to it. Travis' river of hatred had been restored to its original purity! His powers of reason had saved the day, or rather, the night. Now he could sleep soundly.

Yet Travis still could not sleep, or rather, would not sleep, despite Jameson's and Glenfiddich's lingering efforts to send him to bed. It was time for a victory lap around the gardenias. Now that his river of hate was once again free to flow without womanish cross-currents of sympathy swirling the stream, it gushed with renewed fervor, and Travis rode the swirls. Too stoked on himself to stay more than a sentence with any one metaphor, he jumped off it and went with another- he was on a roll, an emotional roll uphill, the sort of transporting surge of energy some experience when, after hitting bottom following a spiral, we mope about on the floor in a puddle of self-pity, but then, employing a combination of self-encouragements, rallying cries, rationalizations, excuses and other assorted lies, we find our way back onto our feet and soar skyward once again, not just freed from our depression but downright defiant, our wings flapping and our beaks crowing, powered by a battery of self-righteousness. Travis was flapping and crowing in like manner at this pre-dawn hour, strutting down his flagstone pathway like some conquering egret, his self-affirming adrenalin not satisfied with simply having slain the Gavin Gorgon but in his bloodlust now parading its severed head on a pike. Who was this Sheila after all, who'd caused him so much grief, who had precipitated the end of his marriage and, even more unforgivably, engaged his sympathy? Fuck Sheila! Sheila was an agent of destruction, nothing more. No attribute other than destruction one could be credited to her, none. Her children were all petty criminals and failures in general. Her careless footprint on the planet was trailed with litter. *Fuck her!* The neighborhood looked worse because of her, smelled worse because of her, sounded much much worse because of her and in every way was worse Because Of Her. She'd only been allowed to prosecute her reign of terror because good honest people had granted her a forbearance she did not deserve. How an industrious, productive, beauty-cultivating and contributing person like Travis could have endured her as patiently as he had all these years was a testament to his better breeding. *Better breeding goddammit!* Had he answered her in kind when Sheila chased off his wife? Had he kicked down her front door? Cut her with a bottle? Taken revenge in any way? No! Here then was another unfairness, one which he found most maddening of all, that having been victimized, he was held in check from responding in kind by his high standards of neighborly comportment, while Sheila, the victimizer, suffered no such behavioral restriction since she possessed no standards of any kind whatsoever. *Fuck that bitch!* Yes, Sheila was destruction personified. What good then is anything which only destroyed? What good... is any*one* who only destroyed? A phrase commonly used refers to a person as a "valued member of the community." So what earns one this designation of "valued?" By dispensing havoc and blight? No! As his walkabout trotted him back and forth across the trampled corpse of his defeated enemy, it was this concept of value which consumed his Sheila-thoughts as her eulogy rolled out in his mind. Sheila was NOT a "valued member of the community." Travis, Corey, Devon, the Alicia formerly known as his wife, these community members demonstrated value in their respective ways; even the two goddamn evangelists were valued, for their intentions were good. The good sister and the pastor were trying to save souls, and so the community found them worth saving. But Sheila- well, Sheila was not worth saving.

Travis stopped in his tracks. "Sheila was not worth saving." He repeated the sentence, then played back the tape of his rantings and ravings which had brought him to that end point. It had come out easily, unforced and natural, the conclusion that she was not worth saving. An ominous internal quiet now replaced his mania, an eerie calm which matched the dark silence of the predawn neighborhood. "Not worth saving." It reminded him of when he and Alicia had cleaned out the basement, as they gathered up the broken flower pots and dried-out paint cans and other bits of junk and say "not worth saving," then throw them onto the trash pile. Travis understood that he'd just thrown Sheila upon this same junkheap, an image which conjured newsreel footage from the liberation of Dachau showing the bodies piled at the crematorium awaiting incineration. Only fit to be incinerated- was this how he thought of Sheila? And if so, then who- no, what- did that make him? What began as a victory lap had run him face-first into the wall of yet another crisis of morality, just when he thought he'd sorted things out and settled the matter. Travis had effectively reduced Sheila to garbage, and by so doing had reduced himself to something even lower. Feeling the exhaustion of the late/early hour, the walking and the first throbs of a Sunday morning hangover, Travis sat on the stone bench next to the pond and, closing his eyes, allowed a flashlight to shine into this new subterranean cavern in his soul which his manic explorations had uncovered that he might better understand its contents. It was a dangerous place he'd found, this previously unearthed patch of self, that much he already knew; to be judging human beings as having value or no value was abominable to him, yet he was clearly doing just that with Sheila. That he possessed such a mechanism alarmed him, and as he looked back upon his attitudes towards others over the years he discovered that he'd always done it, had always more or less assessed people by their value like so many cuts of meat at the market; had done it, albeit subconsciously, consistently, and this alarmed him all the more. He was reminded of the significant role value played in his chosen line of work, real estate, and how absurdly subjective he found the principles of value and how unfairly they were applied. Now here he was, applying his own subjective principles of lower value and higher value, but applying them to human beings, not bungalows. Once again his prospects of peaceful sleep were in peril, and so, just as he'd done when his shovel had disturbed the buried nest of sympathy, Travis faced the problem of human valuation head-on, and straightaway confirmed that two contradictory statements were true: one, that his intellect fully believed that all human beings were of equal value, "created equal" as per the aforementioned Jefferson, and two, that his emotions didn't buy that shit for a minute. What was he to do with this revelation of his double-mindedness, his heart-vs-mind-edness? If his mind was so resolved, then why wasn't his mind able to pull his heart on board? And if his heart was opposed to his mind, did that suggest it was his mind that had it wrong? His exhaustion was comprehensive now, mentally and physically; he wished his emotions and his mind could thrash out their differences on their own without his help, that he could just sit here on his bench and await the outcome, without himself doing any of the heavy lifting. And it was as if his energy-depleted consciousness had thrown in the towel and handed the battle over to his subconscious, for he now imagined the two halves of his discordant psyche were having just that conversation, with himself as witness.

Emotions, too impatient not to speak first, began by insisting that neither Thomas Jefferson or anyone else could convince him that Sheila had any value. "Just look at what she is! Look at what she isn't!"

Mind was more reasonable. "Look Emotions," he said, "I understand why you feel that way. But I think it's because you're not aware of the two types of value."

"Two types?" Feeling a new line of bullshit developing, Emotions' eyes narrowed suspiciously. "Go on."

"Well," began Mind, "there are two types of value by which any person can be considered: intrinsic and earned. By intrinsic value, we're not talking about the similar-sounding terminology used in commodities trading or how the term is used in real estate. The intrinsic value of humans refers to the natural, just-by-being human value that everyone is born with. It's not merited or earned. It's just there."

"The kind which that slave-owning hypocrite Jefferson wrote about?"

"Exactly. So anyway, because it's innate and not earned, Sheila possesses just as much intrinsic value as any Nobel Prize winner or philanthropist."

"Whatever. So the other value, you have to earn it in order to get it I suppose."

Mind nodded his container. "Correct, Emotions. That's why it's called earned value, which means simply, the value which one does in fact merit, based on how much value that person brings to the world."

Emotions grunted. "That mangy cow doesn't have any of that kind of value."

"Well Emotions, you may indeed *feel* that. But: no matter how strongly you or anyone may feel that the Sheilas of the world have accrued no earned value, this in no way diminishes or cancels a person's intrinsic value. Their intrinsic value is their humanity, their gift from birth, and they can in no way forfeit it no matter what horrible, low-value things they do or what valuable things they don't do."

"Great. So now you're gonna tell me this means the death penalty is wrong. *Because it's not wrong dammit!*"

Mind remained non-combative. "Let's leave that issue for another time. The point, Emotions, is that every person should be considered in the light of these two separate criterions of value, the intrinsic and the earned. Which means- "

Wait," Emotions butted in. "I think I get it! Which means that you, Mind, can keep right on with knowing that Sheila has intrinsic value, but I meanwhile can go on knowing- well, feeling, since feeling is my way of knowing- that she has no damn *earned* value at all! Right?"

"That's it Emotions. And if we can find a way to stay in our separate lanes in that regard, then-"

At this point Travis, who began only half-listening but had gradually tuned them in with his full attention, now picked up the baton and ran with it. "- then it means that if the two of you can stay in your separate lanes- your separate streams, right?- then it can work out the same way I worked it out with the Resentment/Blame and Sympathy streams. Because just as I could know that Sheila is a sympathetic figure but go right on feeling all my hatred for the bitch, I can also *know* that she has intrinsic human value but go on *feeling* that she's a worthless piece of shit. "It's brilliant!" He was off the bench and pacing again. "Taking it a step further: if I acknowledge her intrinsic value, her right to exist, then for me to say she's 'not worth saving' is fine, because it doesn't mean I'm saying she should be incinerated in a gas oven or anything, it's just a *feeling* I have, it's not an action item, it's just an expression of my *feeling* that she has no earned value *which she doesn't*. I can say she's a worthless piece of shit and feel okay about it! *Yes!*" With the weight of his inner conflict lifted, Travis felt lighter than air and, despite the heaviness of his hangover, did a little leap of celebration, and nearly slid himself into the open bone pit. Catching himself at the edge, he laughed at his silliness, then observed the metaphor, at how he'd quite nearly fallen into the hole which he himself had dug. What he might have found in that hole he did not think further upon, nor did he guess how far down it might have dropped him. But he'd pulled himself up and stayed above ground, despite the downward pull of Jameson and Glenfiddich, and most of all, despite Sheila. Was there some hole waiting to pull her down, some reckoning, a misadventure? Of course there would be; there were always holes opening up beneath Sheila, for her trajectory was ever downward, no matter how many lottery tickets might raise her in the moment. But when that next inevitable hole gobbled her, Travis would not be responsible for pulling her out. It would be a hole she'd dug for herself after all, that much he could count on. He would sympathize, but his sympathy would be of the above ground, hands-free variety. And now it was time for him to be sleeping soundly, high atop an upstairs bed.

14

By the time he finally made it back to the house in the predawn gray that Sunday morning Travis had felt, well, not exactly buoyant, thanks to the Booze Brothers' after-hours show, but not that much worse for wear otherwise, satisfied that he was well on the way toward a full recovery from the shocks of his emotionally tumultuous Saturday. Head and heart seemed in better agreement now; and when he'd made the upstairs climb and fallen into bed, he stayed conscious long enough to perform a quick rundown of the major bullet points of his life and where he stood with each: his divorce- he would need to find a lawyer Monday morning, fairly routine, it would all take care of itself; Linda- steady as she goes, one step at a time, she's waaay into me, victory is assured; dealing with Sheila- found my balance now, sympathy detected but effectively defused, separate streams and all that, pipeline of hate flowing at full capacity once again; my house and yard- felt some of those flagstones wobbling under foot while walking around, gotta fix that, also the apple trees and roses are dormant now, need to prune back the new growth next weekend. And is it finally time to fill in the hole? This last question propped his eyes open as it reminded him of Devon, who Travis had still not seen since that day at the precinct. It had gotten to the point that he'd nearly considered the desperate approach of knocking on Keith's door and asking if Devon could come out and play, but the prospect of any further interviews with his creepy neighbor prevented him from taking that step; besides, Travis' presence on Walters property might serve to reignite Keith's brutality toward his son and blacken the boy's eye again. As he drifted off, he realized that in all his weeks of being friends with Devon it never occurred to him to get his cell phone number, or give him his own, so that they might communicate by texting. Texting... need to text Linda in the morning... Linda...

It was nearly noon when the earth's gravity pulled a head-throbbing Travis downstairs to face what was left of Sunday. His cell phone rang; not trusting what his voice might sound like in his recuperative state, he hoped it wasn't Linda. It was a number not known to him, but being a real estate agent, all calls had to be taken.

"Hello?" Sure enough, it came out a croak.

"*Hell of a party last night.*" It was a man's voice, vaguely familiar.

"Who's this?"

Many silent seconds passed, until Travis was about to hang up. Then, *"Did your friend tell you how much money she won?"*

Now he recognized the voice. "Corey?"

Again, the caller's response was delayed. "*Seventy-eight hundred bucks. How long you think it'll take her to piss it away?*"

"Um... yeah, no tellin'." Another pause followed, lasting years.

"*You saw the fucking campfire she had burnin' all night in that house?*"

"I did. Yes."

"*Didn'tchoo once tell me...*" The voice trailed away, and for a few exasperating moments Travis heard only breathing. "- *didn'tchoo once tell me you had your chimney swept out professionally, like regularly, and still you got a creosote fire in it?*"

"That's right."

"*Fire department came out and everything?*"

"Yeah."

Once again, the long pause. "*Reckon that bitch ever gets her chimney swept?*"

He remembered having told the story to Corey, months earlier. "Not likely. It's a miracle."

"*What's a fucking miracle?*" The words were spit like a burst of blow darts.

"That... her house hasn't burned down yet?"

Now the caller went back to the silent pause. "*Yeah. It's a miracle.*" More wordless seconds. "*Must be nice. To be so lucky.*"

"Must be." Silence.

"*Ain't fair.*" Silence again.

"Nope." Still more silence.

"*How long's it gonna last you think?*"

"How long's what gonna last?"

It was the longest pause of all. "*Her luck.*"

"Corey..." But he'd hung up. Travis stared at his phone as if Corey were inside it. *Quite a party last night.* Had he been there? Of course not. But he must have been somewhere nearby, watching it. Where he could keep an eye on it. *WTF?* And Sheila's lottery money. How did he know *that?* Corey's disembodied voice had been imbued with the disattachment of omnipresence, catching Travis off guard while he was vulnerable in the throes of his hangover fog; and while that fog gradually lifted as the day wore on, the menacing residue which the phone call had deposited did not depart but grew more leaden, settling into Travis' thought life in a most unsettling manner.

On Monday, Travis called the office of a divorce attorney he'd picked from an internet search the night before (that same evening he had texted Linda to tell her about the served papers, and her response had been predictably supportive and restrained), and on Thursday he was sitting in the office of one Gary Martindale of The Vinings Family Law Group. That he disliked the man from the start didn't surprise him in the least; Travis disliked all attorneys right from the start, and continued to dislike them right up to the finish. Had Travis' legal matter been a more complicated one, liking his attorney may have mattered more; with a matter as quick and simple as his divorce would be, Travis could hold his nose for a consultation or two.

"Well Mr. Riggins, this is pretty cut-and-dried." Martindale flipped through the papers while nodding his mostly-bald head. "No children, that's always the most difficult thing in these matters."

"Not even a dog" Travis added. "I always wanted a dog, she didn't. So we negotiated a deal, if no dogs then no kids either. Worked out for the best it looks like."

Martindale's smile seemed to cause his mouth considerable pain. "Worked out for the best." As he scanned the documents he kept on nodding; Travis resisted the impulse to grab onto the bobbing melon and hold it still. "No maintenance being asked, so you won't need to negotiate that. But- " Finally Martindale's head came to a stop.

"- didn't you say your wife doesn't earn very much?"

"Not as much as me, no."

"Ah, this explains it." Once again Martindale's head resumed its bobble. "It's the settlement of the property. She's leaving it at that. Okay."

Travis stared back as if the words were foreign. "Settlement of the property?"

"Right. In the Request For Relief."

"The... which?"

Now Martindale looked at Travis for the first time. "The Request For Relief. The settlement of the property." Travis raised his eyebrows. "You haven't read this?"

"Um..."

It had long been a subject of chagrin for Travis, a phobia which had developed over the years, of not reading documents of any kind which pertained to his affairs until it became absolutely necessary to do so. It was childish and ridiculous and he knew it; nevertheless, he bore a nightmarish terror at setting eyes upon any written materials, printed or electronic, which pertained to his grownup responsibilities, a morbidly unreasonable avoidance of opening a letter or an account website for fear that he'd then learn some surprising and disastrous information about himself, even when the likelihood of such a discovery was low or even non-existent. Innocuous matters such as renewal notices for auto registration or insurance policies, banking and credit card websites, utilities bills and routine tax documents, everyday realities such as these he avoided like peanut allergies, daring to approach them only when the terror of what might happen if he kept avoiding them outgrew the terror of looking at them- and thus himself- in the eye. The irony was that every day as a realtor Travis plunged head-first into purchase agreements, buyer's agent agreements, home inspection reports, seller disclosures, closing disclosures, etc., reading them carefully and dodging no word or phrase, never dreaming to delay or avoid- but on his clients' behalf, not his own. What made his behavior even sillier was that he wasn't the sort of man who let his affairs get out of control, and so had no tangible reason to be afraid of seeing the details of them. How did not opening a letter make its contents exist any less? If dealing with it was inevitable, why not deal with it at once rather than later, and thereby get ahead of whatever the thing was instead of behind? With every letter he delayed opening and website he put off logging into, he knew what awaited him there, but knowing or not knowing the contents was not the point. No, the fear was not of *what* he would see, but *of seeing,* period, the small unnerving shock of finding the tiny mirror which lurked in each envelope, each account page, which when gazed into reflected a picture of himself. And so, with his divorce papers, he had followed his s.o.p. of not reading them until an attorney read it for him; now, Martindale did just that, as Travis avoided eye contact out of embarrassment.

"Here in the Request For Relief section, it has her demands for the settlement of the property."

The word "demands" hit Travis like an ominous missile. "Which are?"

Martindale was nodding again. "Pretty standard. Selling the house and dividing the proceeds. That's what she's accepting instead of maintenance." He looked up at Travis. "You weren't planning on staying in the house were you?"

"Well, yeah. Of course."

"Then you're aware that you need to buy her out." Martindale peered back at him with the supercilious smirk of the very wealthy. "Do you have that much cash?"

Travis was glad he was already sitting down. "No."

This time Martindale's smile could not have said "Of course you don't" any more than if he'd used those very words. "Did you think she was just gonna give it to you?"

"I was thinking... jesus christ, what *was* I thinking?" Travis sat back, incredulous at the full picture of his own stupidity upon which he now gazed. As a realtor, he'd dealt frequently with clients who were divorcing, and understood the mechanics of property resolution quite well. That the papers could have been served to him therefore and his first thought, his very first thought, had not immediately been "holy shit I'm losing my house" was beyond absurd. But it was true. He hadn't considered it until now. And not having thought about it was Sheila's fault somehow. He didn't know why but it was.

Driving back to work after the consultation, Travis allowed the full weight of what he had learned to settle in. Well of course Alicia wanted the house to be sold off. What other choice did she have? After Sheila had so definitively marked her territory with her bodily fluids, Alicia wouldn't possibly consider remaining in it one day longer; no matter how much of herself Alicia had poured into the renovation, it all came to naught when Sheila poured so much of herself all over it. What's more, Alicia would need her half of the money from the sale to get on her feet financially. For Travis to buy out her interest in the home and thereby remain in it he would need several hundred thousand dollars cash up front, which of course he didn't have (Martindale's smart-ass comment had been *she's not gonna put you on a payment plan you know*). Alicia knew full well that Travis was not that liquid; he could almost hear her saying "If I'm getting run out of my house, then he's getting run out of his house too." Thinking back, he remembered how he'd thought himself so generous when he had supported Alicia's desire to upgrade both the upstairs and downstairs, so glad to pay many thousands so that she'd feel like it was her home and not just his, and how it had seemed such a good investment, both in the property and in *his relationship with his wife*; and now, having spent those many thousands *for her*, he had not only reduced his buying power by depleting himself financially, but with that upgrade had raised the value of the house considerably higher, putting it that much farther out of his reach to buy out the wife who was leaving him! Truly the madness had come full circle: the house had not felt like home to Alicia- then it did- and then it didn't once again; yet now it was so much her home that it was in her power to make it Travis' home no more, no matter how he felt.

How he felt- yes, this is what occupied him as he left Martindale's, not the mundane practicalities of his situation, but on his feelings of home and impending loss of same. 1418 Crested Boulder Drive was so much more than the address where he lived- 1418 Crested Boulder Drive *was* Travis. He had purchased it when it was a neglected nothing and re-created it in His own image. It was not that Travis identified with his home and its environs; this half-acre was his identity, was him as indivisibly as any of his other body parts, and the thought of it being chopped away struck him as no less a matter of amputation than had the Settlement Of Property demanded his right lung be removed. Snapshots of his handiwork swiped across his mind: the shrubbery, the stonework and iron gate, the koi pond, the kinetic sculptures, the arches and arbors and pathways lined with café lights, each image a beauty and a torture, each a victory and a loss. For his life to no longer continue on that spot of earth was not so much an exile as an extermination, and of course Alicia fully knew it. He saw more than simple self-interest in her demand that the house be sold- he saw vindictiveness, not just self-preservation but revenge, not a defensive move on her part but an unprovoked attack. Yes, it *was* unprovoked, for what, really, had Travis done to her? What had been his great unpardonable sin? Had he abused her? Threatened her? Lied to her? Cheated on her? (for he'd only gone so far as being double-minded but not yet so far as double-dipping). Had he *invited* Sheila into the house? Was he the one who bled all over the gramma blanket? And so what if Sheila had? Was this so very terminal? *Bleeding?* To throw away a marriage of five years and destroy the life of a man who considered cheating on you but hadn't actually? *Over some bloody bled-on blanket???* It was insanity, pure insanity, and the longer Travis thought about it, the more insane Alicia appeared. The spiteful woman had lost her mind; she'd flipped over nothings, the cumulative effect of this nothing and that nothing and all those other little nothings, and when added together they only proved the first rule of arithmetic, that nothing plus nothing equals nothing at all. That they were all Sheila nothings exonerated him even more fully from having committed any irreconcilable crimes. But as he considered just how many Sheila nothings there were, he found his attitude about-facing as he remembered what that same cumulative effect of Sheila's nothings had done to him; how it had so corroded the walls of his tolerance over time that he'd become the one who fantasized hearing one day the happy news of Sheila's painless demise, or, what the hell, painful if necessary, and thus put an end to the endlessly repeating interactions with this worthless- but *intrinsically valuable* of course- woman. And if Sheila's nothings had wrecked such havoc upon him, then maybe the sum of her nothings added up to something after all, and Alicia's escape might be understood as not so very unprovoked. For if the destructive powers of Greater Sheila had sent such a one as Corey to the dark place where he presently resided, it was no great stretch to see how it could send Alicia away to hers. And now Travis was being sent away too.

For the rest of the day, Travis did his best to focus on work to take his mind off his unfolding domestic disaster. But if a man were to hope that his job would help him forget his troubles then he couldn't have chosen a worse profession, since "focusing on work" meant assisting one happy couple after another in their giddy search for their dream home, or selling their old dream home to go look for an even dreamier one; with each "Oh, Gary, just look at this big back yard!" and "Ohmygod what a delicious dining room!", Travis felt a twinge of queasiness, and by the mid afternoon found himself wanting to retire from the realty game and never facilitate the pursuit of another dream ever again. But a measure of relief arrived, in the form of a text from Linda, just a friendly "hello how are you?" sort of thing, with thankfully no references to his divorce or his meeting with Martindale. In a matter of just a few back-and-forths with her, his mood had lightened appreciably; by the end of their exchange, they had even (finally!) agreed upon the itinerary of their first real date, dinner and a play on Saturday night. And so, thanks to the intervention of Linda and their first date to look forward to, Travis had mostly talked himself off his ledge by the end of the day, at least the extreme edge of it, so that, by the time he was driving home, the pain of his impending homelessness had been reduced down from excruciating to a somewhat manageable ache.

As he approached the turn to put him onto Crested Boulder, Travis narrowed his eyes in preparation for a new strategy he'd decided upon during the drive. Obsessed as he was about the care and preservation of his suburban Shangri La, his returning-home habit for five years had been, from the first moment the property came into sight, to soak in every visible detail of house and yard, every tree, shutter, shingle and stone, slowing the roll of his approach to extend his viewing time, and thus perform a thorough drive-by inspection before turning onto the driveway. It was not so much to check if anything amiss, for nothing ever was, save the occasional burned out café light bulb or perhaps an oak tree in his roof. No, the inspection was not one of scrutiny, but of adoration; he had given his all toward 1418's magazine-worthy curb appeal, and so he made sure each day without fail to retake the mental snapshot of his home every time it came within view, determining to never take its loveliness for granted, subconsciously preparing himself perhaps for some time when he might lose sight of it forever. And now, this morning, that time had come, but in the cruelest way; for if the earth had opened and the whole half acre was swallowed in a second, it would be an instant death, over and done with, but until the house was sold, he would remain immersed in it, surrounded by the splendor which his own hands had wrought while knowing it would soon belong to another. During that time he would no longer be the master of 1418, but its impermanent ghost, lingering about irrelevantly and haunting the grounds. And so, to survive the emotional torture of remaining in the presence of the loved one he was soon to lose forever, Travis set upon weaning himself from his daily drive-up inspection, to prevent his eyes from feasting upon its beauty and by so doing reduce his hunger for it; he would live out his remaining days at 1418 in a tunnel vision, eyes front, no more worshipping glances upon camellia blossoms or shimmering goldfish or wrens in the birdbath or sunlight on the weathervane. His mind would know, of course, that beauty surrounded him everywhere, but he would trick his mind- he was so very skilled at tricking his mind after all- and with enough practice at doing what he was convinced most other people did all the time anyway, that being, to pay no attention to the beauty all around them and to somnambulate through life wearing blinders, Travis was confident that he could pass these weeks of house arrest not exactly torment-free but in a state of semi-detached numbness. With his vision limited therefore to the three feet directly in front of the hood of his truck, Travis made the turn through his gate, parked, and with eyes turned to the ground marched toward his house with nary a sidelong glance- and nearly tripped over a broken flower pot on the sidewalk.

Travis recognized at once the shards of terra cotta strewn about at his feet. They had comprised one of two matching 10" pots which sat on the left and right sideboards of his arbor chaise swing which was set in a few feet from the sidewalk. But how had the pot fallen and rolled off? Finding himself forced to already break his resolve of suspending all visual inspections of his disappearing kingdom, Travis turned his eyes reluctantly to the swing, and saw that the eye bolt which secured one of the two chains into the roof of the arbor had torn completely out, and so the swing had fallen down at that end, the arm of the swing having smashed the terra cotta pot as it fell, knocking the pot to the sidewalk. Inspecting the swing more closely, he could see that moisture had rotted the wood into which the bolt had been screwed; a whole new roof plank therefore would be needed to replace the rotted one and the eye bolts and chains could then be resecured into it. It was an easy fix as fixes go; he had several more of the 8' planks in his shed, perfectly dry and ready to use. After picking up the broken chunks of earthenware from the sidewalk and throwing them into the trash, Travis went indoors and headed toward the laundry room where hung his yard work clothes. But as he was changing his pants, a question came to his mind, one which he'd never asked himself even one time in the past five years, a previously unimaginable question but which presented itself now as all too obvious in regards to the swing: why bother fixing it? What was the point? He had built the arbor from a kit two years earlier, had bolted up those chains and sat on that swing (alone of course) enjoying his handiwork dozens of times. But it was his no longer for all intents and purposes. Now it belonged to the next guy. Travis let his pants fall to the floor as he considered this new and frightening attitude which had crept into his being, and having made entry, it swung wide the gate and allowed a rush of its fellows to join, some of whom being the following: Why then fix those loose flagstone steps? Why prune the roses? Why rake the leaves? Why fill the bone hole? Why feed the koi? Why not let them die? Why... *do anything?* At this last, an electrified tingle of panic trickled through his limbs as his down spiral continued in a progression toward despair. "Why should I maintain the property for someone else? What futility is that? I've already told myself to not look at its beauty any longer, so why fight off ugliness? What's the point of creating beauty when it can be taken away and given to someone else? Let it go to hell! Let the next someone make his own beauty, like I did!" Then came a darker turn: "And if it's futile for me to maintain the property, if it's futile for me to create beauty which can't be mine, if it's futile to do anything at all for 1418, and if *all my identity* is wrapped up in 1418... then I, Travis Riggins, am futility! Travis Riggins no longer *has any point!"* But darker still was to follow: "And if I have no point... then why go on living? If what I am is gone, then why remain? If I'm no longer fixing swings then I AM no longer!" By this point the panic was no mere trickling tingle, it was a numbing pulse, holding him hostage in the laundry room with his pants around his ankles. Had it really come to this? Was this the ultimate action-item to which his logic had brought him? Travis felt himself at a crossroads of existence. In a bleak vision, he now saw the end of his stewardship of 1418 and the end of his human life as inseparably paired, walking together, eyes front and oblivious, wearing their new who-gives-a-shit what-does-it-matter blinders, ignoring broken swings and overgrown roses and wobbly flagstones as they stroll toward oblivion. Perhaps the eyebolt on the other side of the swing had not rotted yet. Perhaps it was still strong enough for him to suspend a rope and tie a noose that could

"*NO GODDAMMITT! I STILL GIVE A SHIT!*" With a spin and a shout, Travis shook himself from his torpor and, seeing his saws and hammers hanging on the wall across the laundry room, made a life-affirming lunge for them, and forgetting that his pants were still around his ankles, hurtled himself head-first into the wall, bringing the tools crashing down on top of him. Undeterred, he took up the ones he needed and, pants now up and ready for business, ran back out to the arbor, where in a flurry of extension cords and prybars and screwdrivers and curses he attacked the repairing of the arbor swing. As he was cutting the new plank down to size with his circular saw, a tapping on his shoulder nearly caused the spinning blade to jump up into his face.

"Goddamn Mister Diggins, you 'bout cut mah leg off!"

"What the fuck Sheila?!" She had retreated back to the sidewalk, away from the sawblade. "You don't tap on somebody when- "

"Whatchoo done wit Mistah Deron?"

"Excuse me?"

Sheila crossed her arms belligerently. "You took Mistah Deron an' he nevah come back. I got shit need done. Wheah he bin?"

It was never a good time for Sheila's abrupt selfishness, but now was worse than ever. Travis took up the saw. "Sheila I got shit I need done too. So you need to go on."

But she did not go on. Instead, she went on. "Mah fron' doh still need fixin'. You need come ovah fix mah doh."

Travis stared incredulously. "I? I need to fix your door?"

Now she mumbled, as if not wanting him to hear but making sure he did. "Less me git all cut up in 'is driveway then he won' ev'n fix mah doh..."

"I *let you* get cut up? That's what I did?"

"Tha's right."

"*And* I gotta fix your door?"

"Yes you do Mistah Diggins."

For a moment, he could only marvel at the miracle which swayed before him, arms crossed in petulance. She was incredible. She was insane. She was inscrutable. She was Sheila. For a pleasurable moment, Travis imagined himself starting up the saw saw and chasing her down the sidewalk with it. Returning reluctantly to the real world, he repositioned his glasses and leaned over the plank once more. "Ok, back to work."

"THEN you come fix mah doh."

"I'M NOT FIXING YOUR MOTHERFUCKING DOOR!" He had screamed it at the top of his voice, a blast which would have sent a lesser adversary recoiling in shock. But all Travis had done was speak at the volume level Sheila was most comfortable with, and so she remained unmoved. Again he turned back to his work, waving her off. "Why not just go pay somebody to fix your stupid door, with all the money you won on Saturday?"

"Shee-it, ain't got that money no mo'."

Travis looked up. "What?"

"Hail no. That money gone!" Sheila shook her head and, to Travis' amazement, laughed.

"Almost eight thousand dollars, right?" She nodded, matter-of-fact. "How is it all gone? In less than a week?"

Sheila pursed her brow as if it were the stupidest question in the world. "Spint. Stole. Lost." She shrugged. "Gone."

Travis put down the saw. "Some of it was stolen you say?"

"Tha's right."

"And you lost some of it?"

"Prob'ly stole too. Aftah it got lost."

"How much did you get to spend?"

Sheila's yellow eyes lit up. "You see that muhfuckin' party we had Sat'day night?

BIG-ass party!" Sheila grinned triumphantly. "THA'S what I spint."

"And... you're not mad?"

"Hell yeah I'm mad! *I'm mad you ain't fixin' mah fron' doh!"* As Sheila rocked and swayed, Travis took in the full measure of injustice which now revealed itself as he contrasted Sheila's state of being against his own. Here was Travis, experiencing a major loss (though still in his home its loss was but a certainty), sufficiently distraught by it to be despairing of life itself; and here was Sheila, also experiencing a loss, no less than the fortune of her life, which having miraculously appeared, had vanished in a matter of days and left her with nothing to show but one loud party. But unlike him, Sheila is unphased, easy-come-easy-go, the sailing of her ship not disturbed in the slightest and carrying on with disaffected nonchalance, no more and no less happy than any other time in her insensate existence. And Sheila's advantage over him was more than a merely emotional one: while he'd worked so hard to maintain and beautify the home in which his entire being was inextricably interwoven, the home where he'd done all the right things and so *deserved to keep it*, Travis was losing it; while Sheila, who cared for nothing, worked at nothing, thought of nothing and deserved nothing was keeping her everything, that "everything" being her home of twenty-five years. Yes, Sheila was keeping her home. The same Sheila who was making Travis lose his.

"If you jus' gonna sit there on the groun' you might's well jus' come fix mah doh."

That's right you stupid cow. I'm sittin' on the ground taking a break from fixing the home I don't get to keep while you don't do shit except tell me I need to come fix your house which you do get to keep. He shooed her off. "Go home Sheila."

Appearing to accept defeat, Sheila began shuffling away down Travis' walk, but then turned back to him one last time. "You got fo' dollahs fo' candles?"

Before he'd even realized it, Travis was on his feet and chasing Sheila down the sidewalk with the running circular saw, a high-pitched scream emanating from both its whirring blade and his own mouth. "GO HOME SHEILA! GO HOME NOW!"

"Aiaieeeeieeieaaaeee! Muhfuckah crazy!" Thrusting the saw at the fleeing woman like it was a cattle prod, Travis ran her down the walk; upon reaching the full length of the extension cord, the saw's plug popped out of it, shutting down the blade. Hearing the silence, Sheila stopped running and looked back. "Looks you ain't got no powah no mo' Mistah Diggins." With that she resumed her shuffling, and at the end of the driveway, Travis saw fluttering down from her hand a crumpled piece of paper. It was a lottery ticket. He watched her disappear down the street, the shuffling figure becoming smaller and smaller, a diminishing rag pile thrown against the darkening horizon. And as he stared, the tiny speck of Sheila slowly began to grow in his mind, expanding upward and outward, but shapeless now, her amorphous girth spreading itself bloblike over her yard, then over her sidewalk, even oozing across Crested Boulder, until her sticky essence had breached his own property's boundary line and covered his yard and everything else which was his, just as Sheila always did, one bloblike way or another. And now it was Travis who was shrinking as his bones turned to concrete, and soon he was unable to move, cemented to the spot where his power had been unplugged, surrounded by a growing sea of lottery tickets and divorce papers and four-dollar bills which rose up on all sides of the powerless lump of stone which he'd become. Then came what felt like a click; and this click inside him triggered a shifting, like subterranean plates scraping along a fault line, a fracture occurring deep within his sanity and destabilizing his surface, making any next step terrifying and treacherous; and that shifting opened up fissures and cracks through which escaped the steam of an overheated imagination, noxious clouds of brutality and bitter reprisals, hissing pockets of gaseous vapors which awaited only a match to light them and make them explode. Four dollars for candles was what she'd asked for. It was a reasonable enough request. Just four dollars, and the match would be lit, and her poisonous vapors would explode, and the house would be gone, burnt to the ground, a torment to his eyes no longer. He could see it all, the beautiful dream of what could be- the dark little lump of a house which mocked him by its very existence, stubbornly refusing to go away year after year, suddenly lit up in a flash and sent to hell, a celebration of all-consuming orange, and its resident blob, this insignificant Sheila, finally evicted and sent running from the flames in one glorious moment of scorched earth reparation. Travis stood in his yard for a long time, minutes, days, enjoying the fireworks show in his mind, watching the little embers sailing off into the dark sky up and away from the charred house, which by now had been reduced to merely the largest of the embers, glowing like a coal but soon to glow no longer. And it was real in his mind, real enough for him to take comfort from its incendiary warmth; and like a campfire which burns for a time but then cools, and must be stoked to bring it back to life, Travis relit Sheila's conflagration again and again by replaying it mentally, imagining the cold dark house, the igniting, the woman running away, the roaring flames, then all dark again, this sequence repeating and repeating, each re-viewing sending heat through his veins like so many hits of smack. And when the buzz of replaying the fire scene began to lose its edge, he found a way to increase the high- by imagining not only the fire but how he might go about setting it.

It would be so easy! No security cameras, no lighting of any kind, easy access/ easy escape and, best of all, a dry tinderbox of a house. For the remainder of that Thursday night, Travis fantasized, surrendering to his crime lust and obsessing over the details of the "what if"; how he could creep unseen through the scruffy woods behind Sheila's house while carrying the gas can, then soak the house all around, then light the match, then slip back into the woods and be home in barely a minute. He pictured a night when Sister Beulah and the pastor would drive up to Sheila's house in the church van to carry her on her errands (for while arson was within the realm of his imagination, murder was not, so she would have to be gone from the house). And besides, Sheila's survival was an essential component of his fantasy, for if Sheila died in the blaze, she wouldn't be able to gaze sadly upon the ashes the next day and feel the pain of loss which Travis now felt when he looked upon the scene of his own, figuratively speaking, upcoming fire, only a matter of weeks remaining until he would be burned by Alicia's demands. That pain, the pain of loss, was what Sheila needed to feel if justice was to be served. And this marked a change in his attitude, for in times before, he hadn't wanted any pain, even of the emotional variety, to come to Sheila, only her peaceful and eternal removal, for back then he didn't truly hate her (or hadn't acknowledged his hatred yet). But oh, he hated the fuck out of her now, oh yes, hated her definitely, completely, purely; his epiphany about the separate streams of resentment and blame and sympathy and justice had provided him the how-to for unlimited hating. No, it was not the burn of flames Sheila needed to feel, but the burn of loss-- and Travis' vengeful eyes needed to *see* her feeling it. The money shot of his fantasy's climax depended on it.

What happens to a man when his firewall is breached and he becomes infected with the malware of his own dark thoughts? Is it enough for such a man to establish a boundary of separate coexistence between his imagination and his real intentions, that is, to allow his mind to paint the picture of himself doing the worst sorts of deeds but to resolve that the painting will remain mounted on the wall, never granted the freedom of stepping out of its frame and achieving its follow-through in three-dimensional fullness? This was the deal Travis struck with himself, and once again, following the example of his separate streams, he saw no conflict between the two operations remaining in their swim lanes, understanding that a man could not be convicted simply for the thoughts in his head. And so those thoughts raced unchecked; they sustained him, if a poison could be thought of as providing sustenance, the way that people who find themselves in unrelenting pain attempt to send their mind to another place, an imagined other world where pain does not exist, in order to detach from the pain which does. The fact that pain not only existed in Travis' "other place" but was a vital feature of it was immaterial, since the imagined pain was not his; no, his fire fantasy made his own impending doom a little less dour, and so, for the remainder of Thursday, as he showed homes to clients on Friday, then into the weekend, Travis saw in everything the happy flames, saw the even happier ashen aftermath, saw his happiness made complete with Sheila standing helplessly amongst the cinders, finally brought down as low as himself. And in this way his sustaining stream of poison kept him afloat.

It was at home on Saturday, just before sundown, while he was in his yard pruning the next owner's stupid fucking apple trees, when he heard Sheila across the street, all alone but laughing and singing and carrying on, clearly high as hell from some white powder or other and loving life, her fortune gone but having a big 'ol time, a celebration apropos of nothing. Travis' blood boiled anew. How could she taunt him in this way? Did she not know that her house was burning down in his mind? Was she not aware of the justice he was meting out to her? *YOUR HOUSE IS ON FIRE YOU STUPID BITCH!* And it was this perceived taunting, this bold effrontery which provoked the next click, the next shifting in Travis' grinding gears, resulting in his fantasy taking on a decidedly ill-advised new aspect: role-play. For as he watched the intoxicated woman capering about her yard and whooping it up, Travis' river of poison was fed by the runoff from a "two can play it that way" tributary. Stomping angrily indoors, he changed into all-black clothing, including a black knit beanie and black boots, then hurried down to the kitchen where he found a box of matches. Heading back outdoors thusly dressed and equipped he hurried to his shed, where his two-gallon gas can sat beside the lawn mower. Taking up the full can, he carried it and the matches (at the last moment also grabbing a stack of old newspapers saved, appropriately enough, for kindling bonfires) to the front of the house, and as the drug-fueled Sheila happily waved and hollered at non-existent people passing by on the sidewalk, Travis set the gas can, matches and stack of paper at the very end of his driveway, conspicuously displayed (it was nearly dark by now, but the streetlight illuminated his presentation like stage lighting), then stood behind it all with his hands on his hips, staring across the street in the direction of his adversary. His silent thoughts hollered at her. *"Hey! Hey party girl! See this? Do you? Yeah, that's right- it's a gas can and matches and dry paper. And you see how I'm dressed? Yeah! Like a ninja. A fucking NINJA! You see what I could do if I wanted to? I can burn your house down bitch! You chase away my wife and you take away my home, well I can make you homeless too bitch! It would be SO EASY! You see me? Do you SEE ME?"* As his thoughts shouted their threats, Sheila kept on partying, inconsiderately ignoring him, pretending (yes she was pretending, he was certain of it) to be completely unaware of the wrath he was mentally hurling her way (for five years he could not step into his yard without her eyes finding him without fail- now he was begging for her to look his way... and she was *ignoring* him?) For several minutes he stood like that, a grim monument to mental illness, as Sheila danced with her apparitions, oblivious to his telepathic attack; the sensible faction of his mind, a minority party by this point, told him that his little stunt was insane, but goddammit, it was *something to do* instead of standing there taking it! But over the span of those minutes, the surge of irrationality which had pushed him into his silly gesture of unvoiced retaliation began to ebb, and with the Sensible Party reestablishing a majority, he now took the full measure of just how ridiculous he looked, and was suddenly terrified by the prospect of being seen by his neighbors. Gazing down sheepishly at the gas can, matches and newspapers, Travis gathered them all up in a hurry, ready to carry the objects of his shame back to the shed as quickly as he could. But before he could head toward the back yard, the headlights of a vehicle caught his eye- it was the Church of God of Prophecy's van pulling onto Sheila's drive, there to pick her up for an errand... just as he had imagined in his fantasy.

Still holding his armload of incendiaries, Travis stared at the van from his driveway, frozen by dread. How could this be happening?

How had Sister Beulah and the pastor picked this of all nights to take Sheila away from her house, with himself standing here with gasoline and matches, and with darkness conveniently offering its cover? Had they in fact picked this night, or had this night picked him? For here he was, already in costume for his role, all his props assembled, and his stage directions pre-rehearsed and clear. The big overhead spotlight had dimmed in readiness, and his scene partners across the street were following their scripts and making *exeunt*. Travis saw himself performing the entire scene, in much clearer detail now than his fantasy had revealed it to him- there went the church van, driving away with Sheila; here he was crossing Crested Boulder beneath the burned out street light, glad now that all his calls to Georgia Power about fixing it had been ignored, and now he was slipping behind Laura and Jason's fence; next he was in Sheila's back yard, so dark, impenetrably dark yet he had penetrated, and he was at the house; now pouring the gas, placing the papers, then striking a single match at each of the four walls; dashing back behind the fence, re-crossing the unlit street... and here he stood, returned again to the driveway which he had never left, still holding the evidence of a non-existent crime, the church van however having driven away for real, and the empty house remaining, unburned as ever. His breaths were short and shallow, for he was winded as if having actually performed the stealthy circuit invented by his mind, or observed by his mind, he had no confidence in either explanation, for what was real and what was invention had slipped a little in certainty. *But this was all just madness!* Shaking free from his self-hypnosis, Travis made a stumbling run to the shed, where he dumped gas can, matches and newspaper inside it and locked the door. He then ran up to the house, where, once his breathing returned to normal, he walked to the liquor cabinet for a much-needed dose of comic relief to help him forget it all. But before the booze could be uncorked, a glow of orange turned his eyes toward the front window. Looking across the street, he stared upon the impossible. The orange glow was flame. Sheila's house was on fire.

He was out of the house and on the driveway now, hiding hunkered down behind his truck, peering over it to watch the giant orange fireball which 1413 had become. He smelled his hands. There was no gas smell. But how *could* there be any gas smell? He had not set the fire. But of course he had. There it was after all, the identical twin of what his mind had seen all weekend. Where were the gas can, the matches and the paper? Had there even been a gas can and matches and paper? And had he only imagined the black clothing? No- he was still wearing it all. He was not imagining. He had imagined, but now he wasn't. Had someone called the fire department yet? Should he report the fire he started? They would be coming soon, the fire trucks. There were no sirens yet, but the fire trucks would be coming. He imagined what the sirens would sound like. Or was he really hearing them? Either way, they'd be coming. Coming for the fire, and coming to get him. And again he fell into dreaming- how strange, a part of his mind observed, that stress and panic always set him to dreaming- he was dreaming now of the firemen, coming to put out the fire, how they would walk into the fire and come back out of it, all on fire themselves now, and in their anger at being set on fire they would turn away from putting out the fire and instead seek out the one who had turned them into fire, to mete out justice; now they were coming for him, they were the fire, and they were coming for him. For in his dream he saw the fire coming across Sheila's bright orange yard, crossing Crested Boulder, the fire clearly coming toward him, headed for the spot where he was hiding. The brightness of the fire would reveal him. In his dream, the fire was coming to find him out. And he knew he was dreaming, and he shook his head to wake himself. Now he could hear the sirens in the distance, but he could still see the bright orange at the end of his driveway. He was awake now and not dreaming. The fire was standing at the end of his driveway, and it spoke.

"Mistah Diggins, ah need- ah need..."

Sheila stood in the driveway wreathed in orange, her face and hair aflame, her ragged clothing an enveloping torch fueled by her incinerated flesh. And still she spoke. "Mistah Diggins... hep me... Mistah Diggins..." Travis raced to the house and turned on the spigot connected to the garden hose; hurrying back to the nozzle, he sprayed the burning woman, who by now had crumpled into a smoking ball onto the concrete. The fire was out in seconds, but the damage had been done- Sheila lay on the driveway wide-eyed, shaking violently, with great clumps of flesh missing from all parts of her body. Travis stood over her helplessly; now the fire trucks were at her house, and neighbors up and down Crested Boulder were walking towards the scene, staring at the tree-high flames. But no one looked toward Travis' driveway; he had extinguished Sheila before the neighbors appeared. Nevertheless, the still-smoldering woman would need to be moved before someone saw her. In a panic, Travis grabbed her melted shoes, hot to the touch, and began pulling, dragging her off the driveway, small bits of charred clothing being left behind as she was scraped across the pavement. Finally she was out of sight from the street, laid out on the grass in a smear of wet ashes. But what now? Of course he knew his next move must be to run across the street and tell the firemen that the owner of the house was lying in a singed heap in his front yard and that an ambulance was needed. But how would he explain it? Why was she in his yard of all places? Travis knew he hadn't set the fire... or had he? Too much was happening at once, waves of overload swamped him and prevented him from thinking clearly. Then he heard Sheila moan, and he leaned over her disfigured face.

"Sheila, I'm gonna go get help right now." But now police cars had joined the operation. Travis remained where he was.

"You spruh- sprayed me wi-wit watah." Her eyes were glassy, and the trembling made her words nearly unintelligible.

"Just hold on Sheila."

"Mi- Mistah Di-Diggins?"

"Yes?

"Thankoo." At this, the trembling stopped, as did her suffering once and for all.

Two hours later, the fire at 1413 had burned itself down to a simmering glow, the fire hoses keeping the remaining hotspots in check as the crowd which had watched it all from across the street returned to their homes. Also leaving the scene was an empty ambulance; no one had been discovered either injured or deceased, for the owner of the house hadn't yet been located, neither when the responders first reached the scene nor as the smoke, per the cliché, was clearing. The owner of 1418 was missing too, as far as Linda was concerned, for he'd stood her up at the restaurant for their date that night, and her texts and phone calls to him had gone unanswered. He had more pressing matters to attend to; and as the emergency crews were finishing up their work for the night, Travis was completing his too, as he tossed the final shovelfuls of earth to fill the hole which had once held Monique's bones but was now the resting place of her mother's. He'd left the hole empty for the day when Devon might fill it himself, but clearly Devon had already buried that chapter of his life away forever, having retreated into his father's house and not being seen outside it all these weeks. No, this hole belonged to no one but Travis now, and he alone would be forever responsible for its contents, no matter who the next owner might be, or any future owners forever. He was otherwise losing everything, but this spot would never be taken from him, for Sheila had made it his forever. This legacy was her gift to him.

As Travis lay down the shovel next to the koi pond, his phone vibrated; it would be Linda calling again, unaware that he no longer possessed the ability to speak to her. Checking the number, he saw it wasn't hers after all, but still it was one he recognized. Despite his fear, or perhaps because of it, he answered.

"Corey?" For several seconds there was only silence. But then...

"*Thank you.*"

Nothing more followed. Travis pocketed his phone and looked across the street at the remains of Sheila's home, smoldering like charcoal under the night sky just as he had imagined it could. No- as he imagined it *would*. For he'd done it somehow. He had burned down the house. He had killed Sheila. And now he knew for certain that he did the deed, for Corey had watched him do it and called to thank him for it. Sheila had thanked him too with her last words, she who had never been grateful for anything. So many people were thankful for Travis this fine evening. Truly he had proven his value.

15

On Sunday morning, Travis awoke to a boozeless hangover, since he had not partaken of a single drop the night before, or at least couldn't remember having done so. All the torpor and thick-headedness of a hangover was there, complete with throbbing headache, as well as that all-too familiar post-inebriate uncertainty of the drunken events, not only what those events were, but how they could possibly have happened, behaviors in which no one could imagine engaging without the facilitation of drink. So as soon as he was downstairs Travis threw on a jacket and shoes and, with no certainty as to what he might discover, set out into his yard to prove whether he had dreamt all of it, none of it or part of it. Upon opening the front door, one thing was clear- there had been a house fire, for he could smell it, and there across the street was the visual proof. The fire marshal's red car and an unmarked police unit were there at the moment, and an inspector along with two detectives were sifting through the ashes, obviously looking for clues as to the cause of the blaze. *Ask me, gentlemen! It was arson! I used gasoline and newspapers at all four walls! Or maybe I didn't.* It was this thought which sent him back to the shed, where after opening it, he saw the gas can exactly where he had remembered setting it, still completely full of gasoline, and the unused newspapers and a full box of matches. How had he burned the house then? Feeling his phone in his pocket, Travis checked the call history from the night before, and saw listed there the calls from Linda, then the last call of the night, Corey's number, and the sight of it gave him a chill. Of all the evening's dreadful details, Corey's call had seemed to him on the morning after the most likely one for him to have only imagined, for Corey's cryptic voice had appeared out of the ether, spirit-like, as if it had emanated from Travis' disturbed mind rather than from a telephone. But here was the record of the call. Corey's call had been as real as the rest of it. Putting his phone away, Travis walked toward the spot he most dreaded, and saw next to the koi pond the hole which was hole no longer, filled in just as he'd remembered himself doing, and the shovel laying beside it. The shovel bothered him, the direction toward the mounded earth in which the handle lay, like it was pointing out to the world what he had sought so desperately to conceal. He grabbed the accusatory shovel and tossed it into the bushes, then stared back at what his recollection from the night before told him was now, once again, an occupied grave. And it was a grave of course, there was no doubt about it, since there could be no reason otherwise for him to have filled in the hole unless the concealment of his murder had necessitated it. But of all the horrific occurrences in question, the murder was the one which he most wished to unbelieve; and so, taking up the shovel once again, he began digging into the still-loose soil, until the shovel turned over a scorched and rigid human hand, proof-positive that his nightmare had been a wakeful one. He covered the hand again with earth.

That evening, Travis surfed the local TV news shows to see if any mention was being made about the fire, but none of the stations covered it; no mention of the fire turned up online either. The effects of his befuddlement hangover were mostly gone now, and though he was still experiencing post-traumatic shock, it was not so acute as earlier in the day. With head cleared and emotions settled, the conclusion that he himself had actually started the fire began to sound less and less plausible to him, not so much because he couldn't remember having done it (his distrust in his ability to separate reality from imagination was steadily growing) but based on the absence of physical evidence linking him to the crime. Still, when bedtime arrived, Travis' sickness over the whole matter remained nauseating enough to kill the idea of getting any quality sleep. What he needed was yet more concrete evidence of his innocence if he hoped to close his eyes. Heading downstairs and opening the kitchen cabinet where he kept the household matches, Travis grabbed an unopened box; taking the box with him outdoors to the back yard, he opened the shed and found the box of matches from the night before. First he opened the brand new box from the kitchen and counted the matches- fifty total, just as the label indicated. He then counted the matches in the box from the night before, and there were fifty as well. Clearly, none of the matches from the Saturday night box had been used. A little laugh, not quite audible but still a laugh, passed through him, as he took in the full ridiculous view of himself standing outside in the cold in his robe and slippers counting matches, a laugh which created the ripple effect of two sensations which had up to this point eluded him, one, relief, and the other, a return of sanity. Of course he hadn't started the fire! He had not lost his mind the night before when he'd seen the church van pull up to Sheila's house. Yes, at that point his imagination had taken flight in a disturbing-as-fuck role-play as an arsonist, but his gasoline, matches, newspaper and, most importantly, his feet, had never left his driveway. It was a remarkable coincidence that Sheila's house had burned, true, but that's all it was; hadn't he marveled these past five years that it hadn't burned to the ground sooner? But what of the fuckery of Corey's phone call, thanking him for doing the deed? Totally explainable: obviously, Corey had seen the house burning, obsessed as he had become with spying on Sheila, and simply assumed Travis was responsible and so made the call; or, since it had become obvious over these weeks that Corey's mental state had deteriorated into mania, perhaps the phone call was his idea of a sick joke, not believing Travis had done it at all but looking to drag him into the torment of his own disease. No, Travis now understood: he was guilty of wishing it so, but not of making it so. *He was not guilty!* With this self-pronouncement of his innocence he was able to sleep, and slept well. On Monday he got through his work day with only a minimum of upset (his only queasiness occurring when he slipped up one time and allowed his eyes to glance at the mounded bare spot). By Tuesday his constitution was sound enough to finally text Linda, apologizing about the missed date with the explanation of the fire (but not providing the most gruesome details of course), an explanation which not only restored his good standing but actually elevated it thanks to the sympathy she felt for him at having to watch the home of "Monique's poor unlucky mom" burn to the ground. By Thursday his emotional equilibrium had been restored to the point that he found himself untroubled to be showing unburnt homes to optimistic dreamers, for with each day he'd not only recovered incrementally from the shock of his Saturday night but had grown more resigned to the eventuality of his moving out. Simply put, the thought of leaving 1418 was just not as troubling as it was before- now that the former owner of 1413 was sharing the address with him.

It was in the afternoon on Sunday, a week and a day after the fire, when Travis was upstairs and heard what was an unfamiliar sound for a Sunday, that of his doorbell ringing. Before he could catch himself he thought of only one thing: *what the fuck does Sheila want now*? Wincing from the sting of this old conditioned response, he then felt a twinge of alarm; for while he'd recovered at least the veneer of normalcy in his life, Travis knew that, eventually, questions would be asked about the disappearance of Sheila. Was this then the police, finally paying him a visit? Looking out the upstairs window he saw no car in his driveway; whoever was ringing the bell was on foot. Yes, it was probably the police, having parked their car down the block and were going door-to-door asking questions. Steeling himself for the next five uncomfortable minutes, he came down, and upon opening the front door saw not the police but an assemblage no less dispiriting, that of his neighbors Jason and Laura standing behind the duo of Sister Beulah and Pastor Kenneth, all four heavily armed with Bibles and sad looks.

"Good afternoon brother Travis." It was Pastor Kenneth, not Sister Beulah, who uncharacteristically took the lead. "I hope we're not troubling you."

"Not at all..." He waited, but the gloomy faces only stared back at him. *Okay, let's get this over with*. "So, what's up?"

The pastor spoke in grave tones as Sister B. maintained her uncustomary quiet. "Brother Travis, we've just come from service, where we lifted up in prayer those who've been passing through troubling times." An "amen" murmured from the nodding heads of Jason and Laura. "And now we're obeying our Lord by visiting the afflicted."

"And I'm one of them?"

Again it was the pastor who responded. "We were all shocked and saddened by what happened to Sister Sheila in the fire."

"Happened to her?"

"Yes. Her passing."

Travis wondered if his dismay was visible. "So she... she did die in the fire then?"

"Oh yes."

Travis resisted an impulse to look at the bare spot. "Then are you saying... they found her?"

Pastor Kenneth shook his head. "Oh no. They'll never find her. There couldn't be nothing left after a fire like that. But she *was* in there. Sister Sheila is nothing but ashes now. Ashes to ashes, dust to dust. Mortal eyes will never rest on her again."

"Ashes to ashes." It was Sister Beulah's trembling voice which echoed the pastor's words, and Travis noticed a thin streak of tears dribbling down from each of her eyes. "And it's my fault she's not here with us today. Oh Lord forgive me, it's my fault!" With these words, the trickle of tears became a full-on flood, as the grieving woman wept and wailed in earnest. "Why did I leave you there that night!?"

Sister Laura hugged the older woman, who continued to sob in her arms. "No Sister Beulah, it wasn't your fault, don't say that!"

Travis addressed the men in a whisper. "How does she mean it was her fault?"

Jason answered, matching Travis' subdued volume. "That night the pastor and Beulah had come to the house to take Sheila to the women's center for a shower."

"We always tried to put her in contact with running water and soap at least once a month" added Pastor Kenneth.

"But when they went to pick her up that evening, Sheila was so intoxicated she couldn't even step into the van. They had to leave her in the house to sleep it off."

"We should have taken her by the feet and dragged her into that van!" As Sister Beulah's fellow believers consoled her, Travis processed this new information. So that explained what he'd seen that fateful night, when the van turned up Sheila's drive. He hadn't imagined seeing it parked there- he'd assumed correctly that it had come to carry her off on some errand, but he had then lost himself in his arson fantasy, his eyes failing to notice that Sheila never boarded the van at all, and his powers of observation were not restored until he came out of his dream, when he saw the van driving away. Had he known she hadn't left the house he'd have cut short his fantasy of burning it down. *But what does it matter what I saw or what I imagined? I didn't set the fire!*

"And so Brother," said the pastor, bringing him back to awareness, "we know that you will feel the lost of Sister Sheila just as deeply as we all do. She always told us how close the two of you were."

"And such bad timing" added Laura, "just before Christmas, and what with your divorce and all."

Travis started. "You know about that?"

Laura nodded sheepishly. "Alicia's my boot camp instructor, remember?"

He couldn't change the subject fast enough; with his front porch overrun by these know-it-alls, he hoped they might know one more thing which he was desperate to learn. "So I noticed, the day after the blaze, the investigators over there doing their inspection. I suppose they determined it was accidental, from Sheila's candles and how she burned firewood in that rotten fireplace and such. Yes?"

"No." Pastor Kenneth was shaking his head. "Fire marshal already determined it was intentional. Very obvious he said. He found hotspots at every wall, pour patterns for accelerant, he even had this little hand-held device, what he call it, a hydrocarbon sniffer, to test the vapors. It pretty much proved that whoever set it used gasoline."

"And... do they also know who set the fire?"

Again Pastor Kenneth shook his head. "No, not yet. Lots of undesirables hung about poor Sister Sheila's house, you know as well as we do 'bout that. But the police have started talking to people in the neighborhood." Travis felt naked, clothed only by his see-through conscience. "Any guess as to who'd want to do it, Brother Travis?"

He pretended to search the air. "Who, wow. No, I couldn't imagine anyb- "

"It don't matter who did it! We all did it! We're all guilty!" Though calmed temporarily by Laura, Sister Beulah's mournful wail now whimpered more miserably than before. "I did it, you did it, you and you did it, Brother Travis did it. We all did it! We are all guilty!"

Once again, the younger woman dealt comfort. "No Beulah, no. None of us started that fire."

"She's right sister" intoned the pastor. "Someone out there has gasoline on his hands, and that person- "

"No! You're not seeing it as God sees it!" It was a shout this time which carried the sister's words, not a whimper; gone was the mournful wail, replaced by the full voice of the prophetess, gearing up for a pronouncement of woe, the tears in her eyes dried in an instant by the brimstone fierceness of the spiritual eruption which carried her. "You all can say that there's someone out there with gasoline on his hands, and yes, there is. And you can say that none of us lit those matches, and that's true as well. But let me remind you of the story of Cain, the first murderer, who slew his brother Abel, and how the Lord approached Cain afterward and asked him, "Cain, where is Abel your brother?", and Cain answered the Lord his God brusquely, saying "Am I my brother's keeper?" This murderous Cain, the first of all murderers, killer of his own brother mind you, thought he could simply brush away the evil he'd done by telling Almighty God that it was not his job to keep track of his brother. *And for this Cain was exiled from the land, accursed in the eyes of God forever!* And the

pastor and myself, what did we do that terrible night? Did we not look down upon Sister Sheila, held in bondage by the demon of drunkenness, as nothing more than a sinner lost in her sin who was ungrateful and underserving of our charity, and did we not that evening in our heart-of-hearts say, "Am I my sister's keeper?" and then abandon her to her fate? *How then are the pastor and myself not accursed as was Cain?* And all of us, before that terrible night, whenever we would walk by that house and shake our heads, knowing full well where her ways were leading her, did we not also dismiss Sister Sheila with "Am I my sister's keeper?" and go about our careless ways? We two were not good Samaritans that night when we left our sister to die in flames. We were led not by the voice of the Almighty but the spirit of Cain, the first murderer, the first to abandon his brother. And let us not forget what the Lord God pronounced to Cain when he discovered what he'd done to Abel: *The blood of your brother cries out to me from the ground.* Yes, and now the blood of Sister Sheila cries out from the ashes, cries in my ear as it should in all our ears, crying "Why didst thou forsake me? *Why were you not my keeper?"* Now the impassioned woman held up her hands for all to see. "People of the Lord, these hands are covered by gasoline. These hands have lit that age-old fire which first burned in Cain and still burns today. *Our hands smell of gasoline today! All our hands!"* At this, the anointing spirit released its hold on her; the godly woman's ignited eyes cooled again, and she exhaled, exhausted from her exhortation. Her three companions stared at the ground. "Pastor," said Sister Beulah, her composed self once again, "I think you should preach that next Sunday. If you don't I will. Good day Brother Travis, the Lord be with you." And with that, Sister Beulah turned and strode off toward the sidewalk, as the others nodded their goodbyes to Travis and hurried off to keep pace with their prophet.

Left behind in their wake, Travis sat in what was soon to be someone else's living room and took inventory of all he'd learned and what he hadn't. The fire marshal's conclusion that the house had been intentionally burned, though not exactly a surprise, was also not what he'd expected to hear either, making him realize that he hadn't really been sure what he expected to hear about the fire's cause, given his own uncertainty as touching his responsibility for it. But if he still found himself on the fence somehow as to his blame, learning from Pastor Kenneth that it had been burned in the exact same manner as he'd rehearsed it in his head did nothing to tilt him away from the "guilty" side of it. For how could such a coincidence exist? Who on earth imagines a fire, then watches it come true? It was folly of the highest order to have gone so far as dress himself in arsonist's attire and array at his feet on the driveway the very implements of his imagined crime; and having performed such a gruesome ceremony, this outward manifestation of his internal anger, it was now proving no easy feat for him to shake himself awake from the spell under which that ill-advised hands-on experience still held him. He'd gone to such neurotic extremes to prove his innocence to himself- checking the undisturbed pile of unburned newspapers, confirming the fullness of the gas can, even counting and re-counting the untouched matches in the never-opened matchbox- yet some unsilenceable voice which cared not for the certainty of the above evidences, continued to whisper accusations to his guilty heart. *Why won't it shut up?* Something more conclusive needed to be done, he decided, some "once and for all" act of guilt purging- or guilt proving, if such a verdict awaited- to satisfy his troubled soul and put a stop to its blameful murmurings for good. It was then that such an act suggested itself, one which, though creepier and more neurotic than any of his previous behaviors, would settle things in his mind with certainty. But it would have to wait until nightfall.

By six PM Sunday evening the winter sun had disappeared; and after deleting without listening to it a voicemail from Linda (a voice of reason was a distraction at this point) he set about his task. Gathering up the newspaper, matches and gas can and bringing it all to the top of his driveway, Travis went indoors and re-emerged minutes later, changed into his now familiar arsonist outfit. For a few moments he simply stood there, immersing himself in the feeling of the clothes and the visual picture of the fire-starting implements at his feet. Satisfied that this first preparatory phase of his mission had been fully recorded in the database of his senses, Travis proceeded to the next step of his plan by gathering up the incendiaries and stepping out toward the unlit curb, walking to the darkest crossing of Crested Boulder and standing under the burned-out street light. With no traffic in sight he crossed the road, slipping along the tree line along the side of Jason and Laura's house, just as he'd pictured himself doing in his dream a week before, and upon reaching their back fence, moved slowly and silently behind their back yard toward his destination, Sheila's property, all the while his sensory antennae tuned to their highest calibration of awareness and with him even stopping now and then to consciously record each step of the experience. Soon he was at the end of what was formerly Corey's fence, and he stood at the property line across which lay the blackened remains of the oven where its owner had been roasted alive. The lingering smell of the ash annoyed him, for it was a recent addition, a smell he would not have been smelling on that night if indeed he'd been there and so it was a pollutant now, tainting the purity of his scientific method. But still he persisted in his mission; after first referring in his mind how her unburned home would have appeared to him that night he crept carefully into the rubble-strewn yard and stopped at the nearest of the walls. Setting crumpled-up balls of newspaper at the base of the wall's charred remains, Travis poured the gas, and made sure its pungent scent left its effect in his nostrils before moving to the next wall, then the final two, repeating the newspaper/ gasoline sequence at each, taking his time to allow none of his actions to go unrecorded by his perceptions. Having made the full circuit of the foundation, Travis stood at what would have been- or perhaps what had been- the fourth and final corner of his gas-pouring. All that remained was to light the matches, the one and only portion of his rite which he did not follow through with now, for obvious reasons; still, he took it as far as he possibly could, going so far as to open the box, remove a handful matches, and pantomime the lighting of them and touching them against the gas-soaked paper. There was no reason to actually light the matches anyway, because by this point Travis had already learned what he needed to know. For in all this he'd been conducting an elaborate test: what he had sought to prove or disprove with his bizarre reenactment ritual was evidence of sensory recall, of having once before performed these deeds, to jolt back into consciousness that which his subconscious may have suppressed. But in each phase of his macabre dumbshow, despite having kept his awareness highly tuned throughout, nothing had triggered in his mind of having been that actor before, other than within the vague dreamscape of his non-corporeal fantasy. The matter was finally settled. Travis had not set the fire. The accusing voice was silent.

Feeling not only the perfect fool but dangerously exposed as he stood at the scene of an arson dressed in black and holding matches and gasoline, Travis tucked his tail to leave; looking across the burned-out home and out upon Crested Boulder to ensure no one was out and about before beginning his return trip, his gaze caught an unusual shape near the center of the burned rubble, silhouetted by the spare lighting from the street which defined its outline amongst the non-distinctive clumps of char. There, resting on the scorched floor in what would have been a bedroom of the home, sat a small metal frame, its most identifying characteristic being a large spokey wheel, and at the back of the framework, two smaller wheels. Despite the absence of the little seat and the plastic pedals which had surely been melted away by the flames, Travis recognized the frame as belonging to a tricycle. His heart skipped. Why was there a tricycle of all things amidst this ruin, found inside the house no less, not out in the yard where one might expect it? His heart provided the answers- surely it had been Monique's trike, the one she must have pedaled alongside Devon when they had been inseparable so many years earlier. This was why the relic had been discovered in a bedroom of the house. Her mother had no doubt saved it all these years, following her little girl's disappearance, unwilling to part with it; Sheila had not allowed the trike to sit derelict out in the yard but had brought it indoors where it could live safe and sound, protected from the elements, providing the lifeless object the sort of care which that mother wasn't able to provide its rider while she had lived. This bedroom then, where the trike sat, had it been Monique's? Had Sheila arranged the room as a memorial to her daughter, with the tricycle its centerpiece, a fond remembrance in lieu of the headstone which was never to be? Had she perhaps gone so far as to maintain the room, keeping it neat and orderly, in sharp contrast to the decay and filth surrounding it, like a tomb in the jungle not visible to the outside world because of the vines that had covered and consumed it, but still intact on the inside, perfectly pristine in the sealed-off sepulcher? For Travis, the little trike and its imagined backstory held his fascination, causing him to momentarily forget about his getaway and focus instead on the inner sanctum which, thanks to the violation of the flames, had been laid open here before him.

He was picking his way through the debris now, across the burned out bits, finally making it to the center of the small home, to that bedroom where he stood before the tricycle. Travis stared at it for several minutes, the powers of his imagination no longer dedicated to the sordid details of an imagined arson but focusing upon a very different sort of fire, the one which no doubt burned in the heart of Sheila for Monique, burning in secret for years, like those coal mine fires beneath the earth which, instead of attempts being made to extinguish them, are left to burn in perpetuity, unperceived on the surface but for wisps of smoke escaping through cracks in the earth. Gazing upon the little tricycle, his mind following it down the sidewalk of Sheila's private hell, Travis thought of how the shattered mother must have stood in this very spot so many times before, staring at the trike just as he stared now, thinking about her lost little girl, just as Travis thought about both girl and mother in this moment; and as his meditation of mourning echoed in unison with that of Sheila's ghost, an epiphany of oneness, of their shared humanity, illuminated for him a vision of the immolated woman as he'd never seen her, or had chosen not to see her. She was real to him in this place, real in a way she'd never been real before, for now he stood, figuratively and literally, where she had stood, and was seeing what she had seen through her eyes; and what he saw was Sheila as an actual human woman, equipped with emotions and thoughts and joys and pains of loss, just as he as a human man was equipped. Gone now was the illusion which he'd maintained all these years, that of some vast gulf of separation existing between their states of being; what Travis had considered before as nothing but an unpleasant intellectual fact, that of their mutual humanness, stood before him now as a fully-dimensional and visceral truth, represented in the testament of the burned trike, this symbolic marker which spoke to him of their undeniable sameness. He'd been forced unwillingly to touch Sheila, when he had taken up her body and planted it in her daughter's vacated grave; now, standing before that daughter's incinerated toy, he was forced even more unwillingly to be touched by Sheila in return.

Unable to continue gazing at the thing which was causing him increasing upset the longer he looked at it, Travis averted his moist eyes; and after drying them enough for his vision to focus again, he allowed those eyes to travel across the street, where they fell upon his own home and property. He blinked, and blinked again- it seemed his eyes were still not quite back to normal, for what he gazed at, familiar things like his truck, his landscaping, his mailbox, his home itself, appeared different somehow, almost as if they weren't his own and he was seeing them for the first time. Rubbing his eyes, he tried to recalibrate them by looking here and there, all about him, cleansing his eyes' palate so to speak, then finally back at 1418- still, it was someone else's address and not his own which came into view. Headlights approached on Crested Boulder, and as the car passed by he dropped down to avoid being seen; and as he hunkered down on the fire-ravaged floor, he found himself staring straight ahead once again at the little trike, his face so close to it that it seemed as if the metal frame was staring back at him. And as Travis and trike regarded one another, he began to understand the phenomena which was playing these tricks on his vision. It was not his eyes, nor the objects across the street upon which they gazed, which were different, but his vantage point which had changed. Returning to his feet and looking out across the street again, Travis realized that he'd never been in this place before, had never stood where Sheila stood and so had never seen the surrounding world as she had seen it all her life. But it was not the world in general which had been cast in a new perspective so suddenly, but his own specific one, the world he knew so intimately and which he'd always assumed he had taken in with all-knowing understanding; his experience now was much like that of the astronaut who, when his module separates from the earth's gravitation to begin its orbit, looks out upon his blue planet for the first time and is able to see his familiar home as the rest of the universe sees it and is arrested by its ironic unfamiliarity. For five years Sheila's home had been a distant and accursed outpost, as inhospitable an asteroid as he could imagine, but he'd landed there now and by so doing had separated himself from his own gravitational pull; now he stood on Planet Sheila, in her daughter's bedroom, looking out across the moonlit horizon upon Planet Diggins. And just as Monique's trike had opened up to him a new vision of Sheila, the picture now presented to him of the place which he thought he'd known so well was revealing a new vision of himself. Who was this man who lived at 1418?

Who was this man indeed? As Travis stared across the street at the suddenly foreign land which was his half-acre, he imagined he was watching himself going about his business there, watching Travis stride down his driveway in his yard clothes, coming out to check the mail; and as the clad-in-black trespassing Travis watched the imaginary one, he sketched in his mind the picture of how that Travis would have appeared to Sheila, standing in this bedroom and looking out its window: tall, fit, younger than she, physically energetic, confident in his bearing, a decisive-looking formidable someone who anyone would recognize at a glance as a man who maintained an unwavering control over an impressive domain. She would have seen a man who always had four dollars in his pocket, a man with water and ice and firewood to give, with phone-charging power to share, who could be generous and caring even if he was sometimes firm with her, even angry now and then. Travis watched himself across the street, giving ice to Sheila who he imagined was also there with him, then watched his imaginary self shoo her away with a brusque gesture and retreat up his driveway. He'd never watched himself do that before, the shooing away thing; he wasn't surprised to see himself wave her off like that, he'd always known of course that he did it, but still, watching himself in the very act, watching from the vantage point of Sheila's own house, redefined the effect somehow, as if it were being performed by someone else and not him. He found it an unpleasant thing to watch himself doing it, like actors who cannot bear to watch their own performances in films. But Real Travis continued to watch his imagined movie; he watched as Imaginary Travis stomped up his driveway, then bent over to pick up a crumpled lottery ticket, at which point he turned and, with the departing Imaginary Sheila's back to him, gave her the finger with both hands. Only Real Travis saw this on the expanded screen of his mind, the real Travis who now stood in Sheila's home, in her dead daughter's bedroom, next to her dead daughter's tricycle. Only the Real Travis saw the true nature of Imaginary Travis, the one which was giving the double fuck-you fingers to the mother of a dead child. But Real Travis understood that the film was not fiction, but a documentary- at one time these imaginary actors had been all-too real; these things had in fact happened, the shooings and the refusals and the brusque dismissals and the flippings of the fingers, and worse. The film was bad and getting no better, but Travis was rivetted to it, closing his eyes now in order to see it more clearly. He watched as the no longer Imaginary Travis was spraying the burning Sheila with the garden hose, and he saw that he sprayed her not out of concern for her pain, but so that no witness would see the flames; saw how he dragged her to the grass not to care for her but to move her out of sight. Yes, this film was no fiction. For its format had changed; since it was a documentary, it was no longer satisfied with showing just the external performances, but the behind-the-scenes making of the film. Now the camera was an investigative tool, one which began to reveal to him the internal motives of its central character and the true nature of the actor who played him. This was no longer an Imaginary Travis who the Real Travis was watching. He who was being watched now was The Most Real Travis who could no longer hide from the eyes of God

FOR in the beginning there dwelleth in the land a most real Travis, and he was called Travis of the Garden, for a garden of great beauty he did create in his own image.

2 It was by the toil of his hands that the garden came to be; and this man took great joy in his work and toiled in pleasure amongst the garden's trees and flowers day and night.

3 And in the barren wastelands east of the garden there dwelt a woman; this woman was Sheila, and she was trouble and a vexation upon Travis of the Garden.

4 So numerous were the vexations of this Sheila unto the gardener that he did pray to the god in whom he believed not, praying both in earnest and in vain, that the god might grant his wish that this Sheila might take to bed one day and never awaken, so as to die, and therefore trouble him no more.

5 And thus did he pray unto his false god, beseeching him in the weariness of his soul, "Am I my neighbor's keeper, oh Lord?"

6 "Must I pray for this woman's health and happiness, she who is but a thorn in my flesh? For I have much work to perform day and night which this Sheila interrupts, and there is no place for such a woman in my perfect garden." And thus did Travis of the Garden pray continually to the god who did not exist.

7 Now it came to pass in those days that a great fire did arise in the wastelands of the east.

8 And consumed in this fire was the woman Sheila, bringing abundant quiet to the land.

9 Then arising from the ashes of this great fire was a new man, who was called Travis of the Fire. And his eyes were sorely blind.

10 Now as this Travis of the Fire stood in his blindness amidst the ashes, there appeareth before him a camera, and this camera was God. For what is God, but that which bringeth vision?

11 And the camera imparted vision unto Travis of the Fire, whose eyes did then see; and Travis of the Fire was sore afraid, speaking unto the camera, "Great Camera, what hast thou to show me, that thou hast appeared before me in this place where ash doth cover the land, and have blest mine eyes with sight?"

12 At this the camera did speak unto the man, saying "Travis of the Fire, come, and I will show thee a man, that thou mayest judge him as thou wilt." Then the camera pointed toward the garden untouched by fire, where Travis of the Garden dwelleth.

13 Then did Travis of the Fire exclaim, "O Camera, this man is familiar to me, and I know him well." To which the camera answered, saying unto him, "Bullshit."

14 Now it did happen that Travis of the Fire observed this Travis of the Garden, as he went about his labors, and saw also the woman Sheila who did perish in the fire; and he asked of the camera, "O Camera, how is it that I am seeing this one who has died?" And the camera made the man of fire to understand that these were visions of the past.

15 Then the man of the fire observed, as the woman Sheila approached the garden, that the keeper of the garden was most brave and valiant of manner,

16 hiding from the woman by crouching low among thickets of shrubbery and trembling there in terror until she passed, praying silently for her death. And seeing this man behave in such a way caused Travis of the Fire to turn his eyes away, for he was ashamed that the eyes of the camera should let him look upon such a man.

17 And seeing the man of fire's shame, the camera spoke unto him, saying "O man amongst the ashes, through my lens will I now show you deeds more shameful still, and cowardly thoughts which dwell within this gardener's heart. Prepare thy sight."

18 Thus having spoke, the camera led Travis of the Fire into the garden, where he did behold all that the gardener had planted therein. And the man of the fire marveled aloud to the camera, saying, "What a garden this gardener has planted, trees and flowers of every kind." But the gardener noticed not that he had visitors. That he was not seen by the gardener amazed Travis of the Fire; and he asked of the camera, "O camera, how is it that this man seeth me not?"

19 To this the camera replied, "Do not wonder at the blindness of this Travis of the Garden, at how we walk amongst his garden unobserved by him. For this gardener hath planted not just trees and flowers of every kind, digging into the soil and placing his seeds into the earth, but he hath planted himself beneath the soil as well, covered thusly where he seeth only himself and believeth himself to lie unseen and hidden. But look now, for my lens shall unearth Travis of the Garden, and reveal him where he hides." And through a miracle of the camera's lens, Travis of the Fire now looked upon the gardener who was buried in the soil, and looked as well upon all the secrets that were buried within the gardener.

20 So the lens did first reveal a woman, and this woman was the gardener's wife. And the gardener had deceived his wife because of another woman, and buried his deception in shallow soil so as to hide it.

21 And this other woman was indeed hidden from the gardener's wife, for his wife did not see where Travis of the Garden had buried his deception; but planted thusly, the deception had sprouted in the gardener's soil, rising up out of the ground as a shrub, lovely in its appearance and with fruit which tempteth;

22 but Travis of the Fire saw that the roots of the lovely deception were shallow and sickly, and to eat of them was death.

23 Then did the lens of the camera turn to yet another of the gardener's deceptions, buried in the same soil but deeper. It too was the deception of a woman. But as the first was the gardener's wife who had been deceived with another woman who had grown unseen in the gardener's soil, this second deception was of that very woman herself, who was also deceived by the gardener.

24 For Travis of the Fire now saw how the gardener had planted and nurtured the lovely new shrub of the deadly roots, watering her and pruning her with great care, and how the lovely shrub had grown under the care of the gardener, growing upward, towards his face, and that she had thought him good;

25 but the camera showed the man of the fire that the water which the gardener had given the deadly shrub was thick with sugar, intoxicating in sweetness but unsustaining, and the pruning had only shaped the shrub into his own image, just as he had shaped the leaves of every other tree and flower which grew in the gardener's garden. For Travis of the Garden loved no image but his own.

26 And Travis of the Fire was ashamed to see the gardener in such a way.

27 Then did the camera turn its lens yet again, this time upon a young man, a lad who was the gardener's neighbor. And the young man's father was born of beasts, and was fierce.

28 And the young man had once flowered as a small sprig of green, and next to him had grown another such sprig who was a girl. And these two sprigs had blossomed in happiness,

29 until one day when the blossoming girl was plucked away to disappear and wither, returning unto the earth. And so the boy of tender green did also wither at the root, his seed returning dormant to his father's fallow soil.

30 But lo, the lens of the camera then showed the man of fire how Travis of the Garden had taken pity on the forsaken seed of the young man, and had watered it, not with the sugared poison he had watered the lovely shrub, but with good water, that which gave the young man life. And thus did the young man sprout tender leaves and blossom a second time.

31 Then the camera said unto Travis of the Fire, "Watch now, man of the fire, and note how this gardener tendeth his young crop." And upon the camera's saying, the man of fire watched as the gardener became distracted by the cares of this world, given over completely to the deceptions of his women and the allure of his own image. And thus did the gardener forsake the resurrected sapling by watering it no more,

32 leaving the resurrected sapling thirsty of heart, so that it withered as it had withered before, returning to dust once again beneath his father's broken soil. And Travis of the Fire was ashamed even so.

AND so it was therefore that the lens of the camera did unearth Travis of the Garden, removing the shallow earth under which he had buried himself, so as to reveal the secrets of his soul.

2 Whereupon the man of fire did cry out unto the camera, "O Camera, you have troubled me greatly by showing me these visions, such shameful acts performed by this wicked man of the garden.

3 But the camera silenced Travis of the Fire by saying unto him "Withhold thy judgement, man of the fire, for thou hast seen but only the beginning. For to this point thou hast observed only the actions of this gardener. Now shall I unearth for you the greater shame, which lieth in his thoughts."

4 Then did the camera take Travis of the Fire up to a great height, high above the garden, where below them lay its beauty as it was created by the skill of the gardener's hand and his care.

5 And through the camera's lens the man of the fire did see from high above two great rivers, unable to be seen when standing in the garden, for there the rivers had been hidden by the trees; and these rivers were perfect in their symmetry, flowing side by side within their channels. And the garden was irrigated far and wide by their waters.

6 And Travis of the Fire was amazed by the greatness of the two rivers, saying unto the camera, "O Camera, you have brought me to this high place that I may see into the shamefulness of the gardener's thoughts, yet here I gaze upon two mighty rivers of which there could be no shame." And the man of the fire was greatly confused.

7 To which the camera replied unto him, "Man of the fire, thine eyes are but young and unpracticed. Look closer upon the trees and flowers of the garden, and mark ye." Then did Travis of the Fire look with greater intent upon all which greweth in the garden, and was amazed to see that the leaves were not of green as they had appeared to him before, but gray of pallor, as if thirsty unto death. "Camera, thou hast shewn me a mystery. For if these mighty rivers irrigate the garden both far and wide, why then are its trees and flowers gray in color and not green?"

8 At this the camera spake again. "Now man of the fire, with thine better eyes look as well upon the rivers." And once again the man of the fire stared with great intent, and saw not the water of life but water gray as ash, swirling in anger and filled with all foul things. And the rivers were sewers, running with all offscouring, sending foul smells even to their high place.

9 Now Travis of the Fire was sickened by what he had been shewn; then did he cast his eyes upon a woeful thing which floated upon the water, and it was one who had drowned. And it was the woman Sheila which had perished in the great fire.

10 But ere the man of fire could ask how this could be, the camera gave its answer. "You see the woman Sheila, whom thou believest to have burned in the great fire. But see now, the woman Sheila did not burn, but rather drowned. For these waters do not give life, but drown it, as fire doth drown life. Thus the woman Sheila was not burned by drowning fire, but drowned by burning water." And it was a riddle to the ears of the frightened man.

11 Then was Travis of the Fire most ashamed, for he himself had been born of fire. "Great Camera, what be the names of these foul rivers, so impressive at a glance but so deadly in their firey truth?" And the camera gave him answer, that one river was named Sympathy, and the other Hate. And it was in River Sympathy in which the body of drowned Sheila floated.

12 Again did the man of the fire cry out in his confusion. "O Camera, how could this be? For no one born of man hath ever drowned in sympathy!"

13 Once more spake the wise camera. "Travis of the Fire, thine eyes are beginning to see. Turn them once more therefore upon the center of the garden, to its very heart, and behold." And the man of the fire obeyed,

14 upon which did the man observe a spring, gushing its waters in all directions. Travis of the Fire had seen not the spring while he had looked upon the garden from below, for then his eyes had been enamored by the impressive trees, which from on high appeared to him now as nothings.

15 And the man of the fire studied the waters as they gushed from the spring, and saw that these waters were the source of both rivers, forming and feeding each.

16 Now at the sight of this the man of the fire trembled, then spake unto the camera. "Wise Camera, mine eyes do now begin to see indeed; and though I fear what may be thine answer, tell me, great camera, whose lens misseth nothing, what is the meaning of this spring?"

17 To which the camera replied, "Travis of the Fire, thou seest the rivers of the garden, how they flow as separate streams. And so did Travis of the Garden create them, River Sympathy and River Hate, both in his own image.

18 "For this gardener had known of both waters within him, but stirred into one as a sea of confusion; and the woman Sheila had waded about in the murky sea made of the sympathy and made of the hate. And thus was she baptized in each.

19 "And it tormented the gardener that she waded freely about in the waters which he had made in his own likeness, and not in the likeness of her.

20 "So Travis of the Garden created the rivers, separating the waters of sympathy from the waters of hate; and this separation the gardener effected in his thoughts, believing he was God of the waters as he had believed himself to be God of Sheila.

21 "And so did the gardener believe he had separated the waters of hate from the waters of sympathy. By doing so he believed that hate could remain in his garden to flow freely, since sympathy remained there too.

22 "But as thou seest, o man of the fire, but one spring feedeth both streams, and that spring is most foul at its source. Therefore his waters of sympathy and hate remain mixed, despite the separate rivers. And so, though his hate may be sympathetic, his sympathy is also hateful. Thusly hath Travis of the Garden created a fool's paradise.

23 "Seest now, man of the fire, the nature of this gardener's heart? For he did not wish his neighbor to have clean water; nay, he did not wish her water at all; he denied her water, and more than this, prayed that fire might come to her, and that she might perish.

24 "And because the water of his garden was that of drowning fire, his prayer was answered.

25 "He had prayed most earnestly that Sheila might never enter his garden, yet now she remains there forever, ashes returned to ashes.

26 "And understand a great truth, O Travis of the Fire: this is the first man of the garden, who planted every tree and flower from the beginning and so within it groweth everything from the first. All death was planted by him, watered by the foul spring, and thus all death grows from within him. There is no death brought to the world which did not grow from this garden. He hath allowed his seeds to blow, even to the wastelands where they have sprouted and bloomed into the very flames which hath brought you forth. This then is the harvest of the gardener."

27 Now did the man of the fire weep bitterly at all he had learned from the camera; then did he ask of the camera, "Great Camera, what must happen now to this cruel Travis of the Garden?"

28 Then did the lens of the camera grow dark with its reply. "Thou hast seen how Travis of the Garden had thought to keep

the woman Sheila away from his paradise, but that she remaineth still.

29 "For she is of the earth, and hath now returned to it, planted there by the gardener even as he hath planted all else. Therefore Sheila has inherited the earth, and the garden shall forever more belong to Sheila.

30 "As for this gardener, he will now be driven away from it forever, exiled unto the wastelands, never to tend the trees and flowers of his garden again.

31 "For I have unearthed to you the nature of Travis of the Garden, and have told thee of his judgement. Even as he is unearthed and made an outcast, so then does Sheila remain in the earth forever."

32 Then with trembling voice did Travis of the Fire speak unto the oracle. "O great and good Camera, whose lens misseth naught, tell me, for I am now ready to hear it, am I not of the fire and of the garden both?"

33 And the camera replieth, "Yes, man of the fire. I have but shown you yourself. For this Travis of the Garden is you, who could not see the sickly forest beyond the trees."

34 To which the man of the fire asked, "Then is this gardener's judgement my judgement as well?"

It was the cold night air and the drone of a distant siren which brought Travis back to his senses; and when he remembered where he was and why he was there, he found himself kneeling once again before the burned tricycle. And when he touched it, an epiphany of sense memory which had been his reason for coming to this place now flooded through him, but it was not the memory he had anticipated. For when he touched the tricycle, Travis was holding the tiny skull of Monique once again.

16

Winter is by-and-large a non-event in the Georgia Piedmont. It's true that a seasonal period which meteorologists signify as winter occurs between the December solstice and the March equinox; it is also true that temperatures fall, as does snow on infrequent occasions. Still, demonstrable facts such as these do not an event make, if one applies the criterion that, to qualify as an event, it must have a beginning and ending. The most identifying trait of Atlanta's winter, one which ironically makes it unidentifiable, is its indecisiveness. By virtue of the fact that winter never quite makes up its mind whether it really wants to occur it is never fully accepted as a force to be reckoned with and is therefore not taken seriously. Winter in the north, on the other hand, does not peer in through the window and timidly tap on the glass; winter in the north kicks in your door, drops its ass into your favorite chair and demands you bring it a beer, and sustains its chairbound tyranny for four unbroken months. For this reason, the northern winter's existence is as undeniable as its horror is inescapable (it's true there are many people living in those regions who genuinely enjoy their relentless winters; we shall not devote ourselves to a discussion of mental illness). But in Atlanta, winter drops in now and then just to remind you that it can be an asshole when it feels like it, lifting its leg onto you with a single inch of snow to cancel flights and close down interstates, a joke whose punchline is that it all melts away the very next day. And by coming and going without arriving or staying, the winter season slips past unnoticed, its first half disguised as extended autumn, its second half as preliminary spring, inspiring the equally unimpressed natural world to pass those days of humdrum half-heartedness in a state not so much befitting of hibernation as it is somnambulation.

The world of Crested Boulder was no less a sleep-walk in late December; it was as if its human denizens (those few who remained, since the fire had served to scatter the diaspora of Greater Sheila across Greater Atlanta and beyond) were simply waiting indoors for everything- the dreary season, the drearier street, all memory of the jarring events which had taken place during the months before- to just go away. No longer did the air carry the unsettling odor of house fire, thanks to several rainy days; the jagged edges of the burned-out shell had softened, shriveled down to a scar, amorphous and forlorn, less shocking in appearance each day as the sight became more familiar, so that, after less than a week and a half, it had already begun to blend into the everyday landscape as just another neglected lot on a street where neglect was the norm. No effort had yet been made to clean up the property, not even to raze the bits which remained, which could have been explained by the fact that the investigation into the arson- and into the mystery surrounding the disappearance of the property's sole resident- was still ongoing, but this did not appear to be the case. With the fire marshal having made the determination early on that the blaze had been intentionally set, the neighbors surrounding had awaited the inevitable visits from the authorities to question them, but such visits hadn't come. If efforts were being made to solve the crime, they were invisible to say the least; with no signs of any follow-up underway, it was as if the police were shrugging off the fire as not so much a crime needing to be solved but a conclusion needing to be accepted, the natural and logical punctuation stop to 1413's book of troubled history. After more than a hundred trips to the house, the weary first-responders could rest in the certainty that they, finally, had been the last responders. And a forgotten Crested Boulder offered no response to that.

No response. This was the overall theme pervading Crested Boulder's muted December as it lay in state, waiting to be replaced by the promise of an even less remarkable January. No response, no news, no winter, no event- and of all these absent features, none was more conspicuous than no Sheila. That the neighborhood's facelessness coincided with the disappearance of its most recognizable face couldn't be dismissed as coincidence. It was profound, the effect of her absence from the block, her absence specifically and of Greater Sheila in general. What other factor but her absence was more responsible for the way things were now, or more accurately, were no more? Of course, "the way things were now" was a better thing in many ways: no screaming sirens, no screaming people, no Dat Men, no bloody comforters, etc. But while Sheila's removal had brought an unprecedented peace and quiet to the land, it had left in its place an emptiness, an uninhabited void (beyond the obvious 40X40 void of charred debris), a neighborhood transformed into a not-quite abandoned Chernobyl, one which those very people who desired Sheila to be gone would not have anticipated and, now that Chernobyl had occurred, were surprised that the ensuing blandness could feel just as toxic as the continuous nuclear meltdown she'd stoked for so many years. There could be no argument of course that peace and quiet was a desirable thing, and that a peace-disturbing broad spectrum of criminal activity was not. And yet, Crested Boulder had been what it was to those who called it home because of Sheila more than they could ever have realized or admitted- with no Sheila, there was no Crested Boulder, despite what the street sign indicated. Oh, there was still business, as usual, but by no means business as usual. Human activity was still observable, but the activity was decidedly less human. True, Sheila Gavins had unwittingly (or rather, half-wittingly) served as a magnet for criminal enterprise, but now that she was gone, so was the magnetism. And without the magnet, Crested Boulder's remaining bits were adrift.

One of those drifting bits awoke on Monday morning feeling much much better than he had the night before. It had been quite the upsetting evening for Travis, what with his arsonist cosplay visit to Sheila's burned house and the strange and disturbing thoughts which were aroused by him being there, unsteadying ones to be sure. But the nocturnal expedition had at least satisfied him, finally, as to his guilt or innocence for the fire; had done more than that even, for it provided him the incontrovertible proof of who the guilty party was. It was more than he'd expected to learn, and now that he knew it, it only remained for him to decide what to do with that information. Someone would need to be told of course. But that could wait just a little longer, first things first. For Travis, feeling rosy and refreshed upon waking up, had decided that he would take a well-earned day off from work, a mental health day of sorts, and reconnect with who and where he was, just to straighten out his internal wiring after all the tangling of late. Cleaning out the cobwebs could only do him good.

And so, as he set off down the sidewalk pedaling his tricycle, Travis surveyed the trees which lined both sides of the street, their branches burned away and leafless, bearing the charred bodies of birds still sitting in their incinerated nests, and thought the trees much prettier than any of trees he'd known in the garden ("the" garden now, not "his," having been cast out of it into exile). His first stop on his neighborhood rounds would be the church, to say his good mornings to his friends Beulah and Pastor Kenneth. As he pedaled up to the church's front walk he saw them both standing at the front steps, with the church behind them entirely engulfed in flames. Sister Beulah waved and smiled as Travis, fully naked as always, stood up from the trike.

"Brother Travis!" Behind her, the pastor waved hello as a tongue of flame began to crawl across his shoulder. "Not at work this Monday morning?"

"Nope. Takin' a mental health day." Somewhere inside the burning church Travis could hear the tortured screams of anguished voices beyond number. "Nice burn you got goin' today."

Sister Beulah looked back at the church with admiration. "Thank you Travis. We must all strive to be our brothers' keepers. And that's where we keep 'em."

Travis nodded an "amen" as he sprayed piss across Beulah's wedge pumps. "I wanted to thank you again for teaching me who it is who's doing all the burning."

"Glad to help." Brother Kenneth was mumbling in glossolalia now, the tongue of flame having slurped itself entirely around his smoldering head. As Travis shook off the last few last drips onto her nylons, Beulah gestured toward the burning church. "Brother Travis, now that you're finally here, come on in and pay the Lord a visit."

"Can't sister. Got more stops." By now he'd already sat his bare ass back on the tricycle seat and turned the wheel to leave. "Besides," Travis said, tucking his balls between his legs, "I'm all out of piss. Have a great day you two!"

As he pedaled off down the sidewalk, Beulah turned to see Pastor Kenneth now head-to-toe in flames but uncomplaining, still praying patiently in tongues. She shook her head at him critically. "Pastor, you gonna need to pray better than that."

Having crossed Crested Boulder, Travis pedaled back in the direction he had just come from, until he was in front of the burned-out shell of what used to be Corey's house, where Ralph lay panting on his side in the front yard, bleeding and whimpering pitifully. Travis parked his tricycle on the sidewalk, then sat beside Ralph in the rust-brown grass. "Hey Ralph."

"Hi Travis." His blood was streaming across the yard in two distinct rivers. "I'm still shot."

"I know. Does it hurt?"

Ralph whimpered. "Yeah."

Travis looked next door at what had once been Sheila's burned house where the new church was being built. "You see what they're doing over there Ralph?"

But Ralph ignored the question, still whimpering in pain. "Travis, why did Corey shoot me?"

"Because somebody told him to."

"Do you know who told him to shoot me?"

"Yes."

Pedaling off again down Crested Boulder, Travis turned into the parking lot of the burned-out Spliffy Grocery where, sitting on the curb next to it and drinking from a 40oz in a paper bag was a cryptically old wino who Travis had known all his life but had never spoken to. Thinking it was as good a time as any, Travis sat between him and a roasted cadaver who offered no objections. "Howdy old man."

"Fuck you young man."

The wino took a swig from the 40 and made a face. "Whatcha drinkin' there old man?"

The wino's squinty eyes ran up and down Travis and saw that he was naked, and that his eyes were zippered shut. The old man reached up and pulled open the zippers. "There, dumb ass. Now you can see what I'm drinkin'."

Now that his eyes were open, Travis was able to smell the foul contents of the bottle, an aroma so powerful as to make the cadaver roll away a few feet. "Goddam man. That shit'll kill you."

The wino raised his singed eyebrows and stared into Travis' unzipped eyes. "Hey I know you. Ain'tchoo the one they call Mistah Diggins, who use to keep the garden?"

"Yep."

Now the old man cackled like a squeaky water pump. "Ha! How 'bout that!" He took another swig and made a face. "I used to have a garden to. Got kicked out of it, same as you."

"What got you kicked out?"

The old man thrust the 40 in Travis' face. "Drinkin' this shit, fool!"

Just in front of them, another tricycle pedaled past on the sidewalk, one without a rider. Travis looked back at the 40. "Can I try it?"

The wino handed the grimy bag to Travis. "Suit yourself."

Travis took a drink, and made a worse face than any the wino had made. The cadaver giggled as Travis spit. "Fuck me! What the hell is this?"

The wino looked at Travis as if he were stupid. "Why that some nasty-ass garden hose water you're drinkin'. Don't tell me you never drank none before."

Travis handed the bottle back to the old man. "Who gave it to you?"

The old man reached up and zipped Travis' eyes shut again, then whispered, "Same one who gives it to us all. You know who gives it. Just as well as I do."

When Travis had finished peeing in the shrubs next to the koi pond, he re-tied his bathrobe around his pajamas and, taking up his leaf blower, dried the shrubs and the growth around them until there was no sign remaining of his moisture, the shrubs and earth now drier than before he had pissed. It was the least he could do, to make no more polluted water than he had already. Sitting again on the stone bench, he stared off across his yard, and imagined in his mind his phone ringing. He was glad that he'd left his phone in the house; work would be calling him, and he had no intention of answering and explaining why he was a no-show. It struck him as funny, that the office would be calling him, that they'd be wondering where he was and wanting him to be there, at work. How could they want him in the office? Didn't they know who he was working for now? Shaking his head, he looked beyond Monique's burnt tricycle which he'd placed on the bare spot atop her mother's grave, and stared across the street at Sheila's burnt house. It was such a strange feeling, now that the mystery of the fire was solved; strange but necessary, like the sight of the koi pond next to him, completely drained and thoroughly dried out (it took three big towels for him to dry out the last of the wetness), the giant fish still laying trapped in the tomb which had held their poisoned water, his precious koi dead now, mostly, an orange tail now and then flipping in vain, dry gills heaving, dying, asking him why, just as Ralph had. At least Travis knew why now, knew what was behind all the killing and burning and death. Or rather, who was behind it. Now he knew who the sonofabitch was.

After blowing away a leaf which had drifted onto the bare spot so close to the trike that it was in danger of touching it, Travis sat on his bench to resume his watch; as he began to explain to the koi the ancient reasons which were responsible for their murder, a non-descript car turned up Travis' driveway and parked behind his truck. Stepping out of it were two men whose arrival did not surprise Travis in the least- it was Detective McGill, accompanied by another detective Travis remembered from his visit to the precinct. The men made their way up the walk, headed toward the front door.

"I'm over here."

Turning toward the direction of the voice, McGill and his partner made their way to the bench, then stood beside it, expecting Travis to stand and greet them. But he remained seated. After an awkward pause, McGill began. "Mr. Riggins. You remember me of course? This is my colleague, Detective Larson." No acknowledgement was forthcoming from the man on the bench, just a nod; recounting the less than cordial encounter which they'd shared at the precinct weeks before, McGill sought to break the ice. "Pretty cold morning to be sittin' outside. Am I right?"

"Yeah, well... I've been kicked out of the garden."

"Oh. Right..." Embarrassed, McGill glanced back to his partner, then fumbled on. "Yes, um, sorry about that... we, um, heard that you're getting divorced and all."

Travis raised an eyebrow. "Getting divorced?" Then a light from his distant past was switched on. "Right. I am getting divorced." McGill felt Larson's elbow poking him; looking at him, he followed the line of Larson's vision, where both detectives stared in silence, first at the flopping fish in the dry koi pond, then at the charred tricycle sitting atop the bare spot which had been the reason for McGill's first visit to the Riggins home. He turned uncomfortably back to Travis, who continued gazing out into space. "We, um, first went to your office, they said you hadn't come in to work." Now he smiled. "Starting your Christmas break early?"

Suddenly Travis grabbed his leaf blower and popped up from the bench, startling the two detectives who backed away a step, their right hands moving instinctively toward their weapons; after blowing away a new leaf which had nearly touched the charred tricycle, Travis calmly sat back down and stared off in the direction of Sheila's house once again. "Just takin' a mental health day."

Relaxing their hands, the two detectives looked at each other uneasily. Mcgill proceeded warily. "Well all righty then. The reason why we're here- "

"I know why you're here." Now Travis was staring up at them. "I've been waiting for you."

After another look between the police officers, it was Larson who took it up this time. "Then maybe you can help us Mr. Riggins."

Travis nodded gravely. "I can help you, Detective- Larson did you say? Yes. I'm just the person to help you." Once again he stared off across the street. "Because I know who's responsible."

Once more, the detectives exchanged glances; McGill nudged Larson to stay the course with his questioning. "Yes, well, Mr. Riggins, we pretty much already know who's responsible for your neighbor's disappearance."

Travis looked up to Larson with surprise. "You already know who's responsible?"

Now he stared off toward Sheila's again, nodding. "Well yes. Of course you do. I'm the slow one to just find out, not you." It was true. Everybody else had already figured out who was responsible before he ever did. Beulah knew. Ralph knew. The camera knew. The tricycle knew. Random winos at the store knew. Corey knew, because Corey had called him afterward to thank him. Why shouldn't the cops know too?

"At this point" continued Larson, as one part of his brain wondered at Travis' odd behavior, "it's disappearing *to where* which is the question now. "

"Is that the question?" The two detectives nodded. Travis paused for a moment, then stood and began walking off without a word toward his back yard.

"Where are you going?"

"To get my shovel."

"Riggins, stop!" The impatient edge of McGill's voice turned Travis around to face them. "Now I don't know what's wrong with you this morning, but we're here because of a missing person report. And like Larson said, we already know who's responsible for the missing person's being missing. His father."

Travis repeated McGill's words in his mind to make sure he'd heard them correctly. "His?"

"Your friend next door. Devon Walters. He's been missing nearly two months."

For the first time all morning, Travis felt the cold air blowing through his robe. "Devon is... missing?"

It was Larson's turn again. "Yep. We're pretty sure he ran away. Had a big fight with his old man back on, when did the mother say they had their fight McGill?"

McGill couldn't resist another glance at the mounded bare spot. "That day when Mr. Riggins here and the boy were at the precinct, a few weeks ago."

"Right." Larson glanced over at the Walters' and shook his head. "The dad, well, he's no picnic, that guy. Hard to blame the kid for taking off. But he's only fifteen."

"His mom told us,"continued McGill, "that he didn't really have any friends to run away to, no money of course. She said his only friend she knew of was you, Riggins."

"So that's why we're here. To see if you got some idea where he might've gone."

Feeling a numbness in his fingers and toes, Travis sat again on the bench, and when he sat, an even greater numbness, one of guilt, began to flood his entire body. Devon had run away, and he hadn't paid attention enough to know about it. In a rush of memory he thought back to that day at the precinct, when Devon had learned how Monique's remains had been lost, and how, at that lowest point for the young man, Travis had gone off sniffing after Linda, leaving Devon alone back in the truck. And that's when he'd jumped out and taken off. That's when Devon ran away. Yes, he had first walked back to his father's house, long enough for their confrontation which resulted in blows being landed by each. But in his heart, Devon's running away had commenced when he left the precinct parking lot, running away from the only friend he thought he could count on, the friend who had forgotten him and let him down. Now, Devon had gone missing- but only because Travis had gone missing first, and had stayed missing, caught up in his pathetic world of adulterous games and arsonous dreams and the tending of his whole filthy weedy garden, watering it with his poisonous, deadly, nasty-ass hose water. For more than a month he had assumed Devon was in his father's house- just one knock on his door and he'd have learned otherwise. But no. Travis was too busy to knock. Devon ran away alright, but he hadn't run away from Keith. He had run away from Travis. And now, like Travis, Devon had become an exile. But in a larger sense, more than running away from his father or from Travis, Devon had been forced into exile by the father of all deadly water, the first exile, the first murderer, the one who Travis was working for and was responsible for all the death and exile and burning.

"Riggins?"

Travis could barely hear McGill's voice over the roaring of the flames which were now pouring out of every window of the Walters' home. "What?"

"Why were you getting your shovel?"

Travis turned to face the two men. "It wasn't Devon's dad who was responsible for him running away."

"Who was it then?"

Travis glanced back at the burning home to see Devon, Keith and his mother burst from the house screaming, and then riding their tricycles down Crested Boulder, all of them human torches. "Cain."

McGill stepped closer. "Cain?" Travis nodded. "Is that a neighbor, some friend of his at school?"

"Cain." Travis walked toward them slowly. "You know. Cain. The first murderer."

Larson was not smiling. "You mean like from the Bible ? That Cain?"

Travis laughed and clapped his hands, sharing Larson's disbelief. "I know, right?

Cain! From Beulah's fucking Bible! That big book of fairy tales about some god that doesn't even exist!" Now the laughter ceased as Travis' eyes grew wider, reflecting his sudden desperation of getting through to the detectives. "But- that fucker Cain, he *does* exist. Cain, that motherfucker, he's real, and he was the first to do it, and he's still doing it." Travis spun about in a full circle, arms outstretched. "I mean, just look around! He's doing all of it!" Then bringing his voice down conspiratorially, Travis whispered to the apprehensive detectives. "And he's doing all of it *through me*!"

McGill's patience was at an end. "Riggins, you been drinkin' this morning?"

"I have not been drinking, detective McGill," said Travis with dignity, standing as tall as he was able, "and more important, I have not been watering. Not anymore." He fired off a burst from his leaf blower to underscore it. "No more watering for me. I've done enough watering for that asshole Cain. Hasn't my water burned enough? I mean, just look!" As Travis ran to the fence and pointed at the unburned Walters home, two pairs of eyes quickly disappeared behind the curtains. Travis shook his head angrily, then gave the finger to what was left of 1413 across the street. "That fucking Cain! It was him all along! Thanks to my water!"

He was pacing about the yard now, muttering angrily under his breath about Cain and Beulah and the garden and Devon being on fire; Larson intercepted Travis and got in his face. "Hey! Earth to Riggins! This isn't a game we're playing. We're looking for your neighbor! What we don't need is- "

"Forget it Donnie." McGill had already turned and was headed back toward the car. "He's off his damn nut. He doesn't know where the kid went."

As Larson stomped off to join his partner, Travis stared numbly at the flames which covered the house next door, mumbling to himself. "He's right. I don't know where the kid went. I don't." Still staring at the Walters', his gaze rested on the front porch; for the first time in weeks he was reminded that Devon's old tricycle was no longer there, and he felt a thorn pierce his heart, and rather than remembering that it had been thrown into the big hole, thought instead, "My only begotten son has pedaled away." By now the detectives had reached the car, and Travis ran to them, shouting and waving. "It was Cain who made him run away! Do you hear me? Cain! Cain is behind everything! Cain sent Devon away. Cain is burning Keith's house! Cain killed Corey's dog! Cain made my wife leave me!"

"That's great Mr. Riggins, that's great. Okay, you can go get your shovel and dig in your bath robe out in the cold. Have a nice day." With both men back inside the unmarked vehicle, Larson began backing it down the driveway.

Travis followed the car, shouting after it. "It was Cain who burned down Sheila's house! I was there so I know! It was Cain who killed Monique! It was Cain who killed Sheila! Ask Corey, he knows! He called Cain to thank him! I can prove it, come see, in the ground! Come see what I mean!" But the car backed out onto Crested Boulder, then drove off, leaving Travis standing at the end of his driveway. He watched it disappear down the street, and once it was gone, there was no more traffic to be seen in either direction, no cars, no one walking on the empty sidewalks, nothing. It made perfect sense to Travis that no one would be out on a day like this. It was much too hot to be outdoors, what with all the flames.

\`\`

The sunlight was angling into its five o'clock slant as the cars sped up and down Crested Boulder at the end of the working day, their drivers happy that another Monday could be checked off and left behind in their rear-view mirrors. The afternoon had warmed up nicely from its chilly beginnings; its was still one full season too soon for gardeners to start thinking of planting of course, but the thought was a tempting one nevertheless. Travis, who'd remained out in the yard hours after the departure of the two detectives and was still wearing his bath robe, could have told his fellow gardeners that the ground was plenty soft enough for planting, even for December, for he had just finished burying in that soft ground the last of his dead koi (well, not quite dead, but he couldn't watch them flopping anymore); and with the intention of returning the shovel to its hanging place in the shed, he turned toward the back yard. But before taking a step, his glance fell upon the driveway, where he saw yet another visitor pull in and park behind his truck, not a detective's car this time, but some sporty-looking Mazda Miata he'd never seen before. Stepping out of it was a young woman, blonde and slender, and when she turned so that Travis could see her face, he was shocked to recognize the mystery woman as Linda; shocked, for every aspect of her appearance now enjoyed the benefit of a makeover. He first noticed her hair, falling about her shoulders instead of disguised by the default ponytail, longer and more voluminous than he'd ever guessed her DNR ball cap could contain, and it reminded him of her first television interview, how he'd fantasized then of how her hair might look thusly liberated, a fantasy which paled in comparison to the shimmering reality before him. Gone were the non-descript, unisex khaki work clothes; in their place were sleek jeans and low heels, a combination which lengthened her slim athletic legs by several miles. Tastefully subtle touches of makeup gave her face a cosmopolitan glow, and when she finally saw him near the bench, she waved and smiled; it was an "aware of its own brilliance" smile, providing yet another glowing feature to an overall effect which was transformative and entirely alluring. For the fresh and wholesome "regular girl" he'd first been attracted to was still there, fully intact, not obliterated by her renovations in the least but enhanced, the way by which the glow of a simple clear finish can bring out the grain and natural beauty of blonde maple. Immobilized by the avatar of this new Linda standing before him, Travis could only stand with concrete feet as the stunning image walked toward him. Tossing the shovel to the side, he resigned himself to whatever fate was about to be his.

At length, the image spoke. "Not sure who should be more surprised- you to see me in heels, or me to see you outdoors in your bath robe. Are you home sick?"

Although the concrete had made its way up to his neck he was still able to shake his head. "No. I'm not sick." *And I'm not home.*

"That's good." Her eyes were fixed upon his, and he had no choice but to let them do what they wanted. "Because if you were sick then I couldn't get any closer to you." With deliberation, Linda took a step in his direction; Travis retreated, and she stopped in her tracks, revising her strategy. "I stopped at Sheila's first. I hadn't seen it since... it happened. It's terrible. Did she- did they ever find her?"

"Nobody knows where she is." *Which is true. Because I'm nobody.*

Still somewhat uneasy with Linda's proximity, Travis stepped to the side a few feet, and when he did, Linda caught her breath at the sight which his sidestep revealed atop the bare spot behind him. "Ohmygod! Where did that burned tricycle... is that...?"

"Yes. It's Monique's."

"You brought it here. From the fire."

Yes, I brought it from the fire. My new boss gave it to me as my reward. For having killed her.

"That's beautiful. I mean, not "beautiful" in the- you know what I mean." Walking away from the bare spot, Travis sat on the stone bench; hoping it was perhaps his silent way of asking her to sit beside him, she took the chance. "How's Devon?"

Travis' smile was wrinkled with irony. "So you remember Devon, do you?"

"Of course! How could I forget about Devon?" A dark glare suddenly replaced the smile, and Linda could almost feel his temperature rising. "Did I- did I say something wro- "

"Devon ran away."

Her hands covered her mouth in shock. "No!"

Travis turned his glare directly at her. "What do you mean 'no?'" he said, now pointing at the Walters' front porch. "Do you see his tricycle anymore?" With a startling burst, Travis leapt up from the bench and walked off a few feet, his back to Linda, who now rose in agitation, standing beside the bench in limbo.

"I'm sorry, I shouldn't have come. It was stupid of me." After hastily adjusting her tight jeans, Linda took a clumsy step or two in her unfamiliar heels toward the driveway. "I should have gotten the hint when you stood me up. I should have quit bothering you." There was a crack in her voice now, as the first tears found their way to the surface. "With everything you're going through, with Devon, and the fire, and your wife, my god, you have a fucking wife, what am I even doing here?" The tears were flowing freely now, as Linda stood derelict at the walk, forlorn and pitiful in her big-girl clothes. Startled by the sound of her sobs, he turned, and the sight of her, no longer a hottie in heels with shimmering hair, but his friend, the girl with the smiling ponytail and khaki ballcap, pulled him out of his mood, out of his exile and back into the moment. Walking up to the weeping woman, he took her hands.

"Come on. I'm sorry. Come on, let's sit down again."

As Travis led Linda back to the bench, she wiped a tear or two from her face.

Sitting once again, she managed a laugh at her own expense. "God! Look at me! What a mess. Just what you need right now. You must think- "

"I think you're beautiful." Now she smiled, her face brightening despite the smearing eye makeup. Something within him brightened just a little as well, something which had recently gone dark, which had gone away altogether. "I'm- I don't know, I guess I'm just a little fucked in the head lately."

"Of course you are! How could you not be?" It was Travis who ventured something resembling a laugh now, a small one, but enough to relax him noticeably. Linda could see the anxiety disappearing from his face, could feel the tension leaving his hands. He looked up to her, and his eyes, which up to this point had stared past her, through her, now gazed directly into hers, resting there peacefully. It was her Travis again, the one she was in love with. Again she laughed. "I guess I'm not very good at being patient. I tend to... I tend to go after what I want." It was bold, the boldest thing either had ever said to the other, but it was met with no resistance; it seemed to warm him, for his color was back. "I didn't misread the signs then, after all?"

"No."

She touched his face, and enjoyed its unshaven roughness. "Then you're not mad that I came by?"

He kissed her; and when he awoke, he blinked his eyes, and he saw, to his utter amazement, Linda, the actual Linda, sitting beside him on the bench, her makeup streaked with tears, her still-open lips smiling back at him, and her hand in his. His dream then had been real. She really was here. Travis could feel that his own lips were smiling back at her as she spoke. "Okay. That's much better."

"I'm sorry I went missing."

"You mean... our date two Saturdays ago?"

"That too."

They kissed again, and when Linda sat back against the bench, she giggled like a schoolgirl, her eyes avoiding him in embarrassment. "Okay. This is a first for me."

"What? You've never kissed a guy in a bath robe sitting outside in December?"

"Not that." Once again, Linda ran her fingers across Travis' unshaven cheek. "I've never kissed a black guy."

"Well, to tell you the truth... "Travis gazed back at her, his brow furrowed with thought, "I've never kissed a black guy either."

"Shut up!" Linda punched his arm playfully; all the tension between them was gone now, and she stretched out her legs to celebrate it. "You know, it's about time I kissed a black guy. All these local good-ol' boys drive me nuts." Her hands flew to her face with exasperation as she shook her head. "Arrrghghg! Listen to me! Now it sounds like I only like you *because* you're black!"

He took her hands again to calm her. "So tell me- why *do* you like me?"

She laughed. "Oh, now I gotta come out and give you a list?"

"Yeah. I could use some positive reinforcement."

Linda kissed him again, and then paused in thought. "Why do I like you?" She sat back for a moment and considered it; then turning to him, she proceeded, evenly and deliberately. "I'll tell you why I like you Travis. Not why I love you, even though I know I do. I love you because... well, who knows what love is. All I know about loving you is that it made me put on makeup and come after someone who stood me up and wouldn't answer my calls. But why I *like* you, that I know for sure." She stood and paced the garden, sorting her thoughts. "I like you because... because you're a first for me. Not my first black boyfriend, forget that silliness. You're something other than just a boyfriend. You're my first..." Having moved away several steps, Linda now turned back to face him. "Do you remember, at Kennesaw, at the reinterment ceremony?

Like a photograph dropped from the sky and fluttering onto his lap, Travis took up the image of that day and stared at it; it was a picture which unfolded like a film, and he saw himself moving through it, the star of it, and the actor was the smooth operator, strolling her down the cemetery path and winning her with his well-rehearsed moves and calculated words. Travis of the Fire cringed at the sight. "Sure. I remember."

"I never told you but... that was one of the best days of my life, Travis." He was still watching the film of that day, but was also watching the girl holding the camera, who glided past him now, the unsuspecting innocent in big-girl heels who moved like a timid deer across his garden. "I saw you that day in a way I hadn't seen you before. I saw, well- I felt as if I saw all of you. The real you, fully revealed." At this, he felt a jarring shift of direction, both in the film and in himself; it was he who was now being led down the path, by the camera in Linda's hands which conducted him. "We were walking in the cemetery that day, but it felt more like a garden, and you and I were new to each other then, in the beginning of you and me *why did she say I was fully revealed?* and we came to the grave of that girl who was murdered, Mary Phagan. Remember?"

"Yes, I remember" *that she was murdered by the black janitor why would she say I was fully revealed?*

"And you explained to me her story, how unjust it was" *unjust to her? unjust to the innocent man who was convicted? unjust that they believed that nigger janitor's lying story because they knew no nigger was smart enough to make up so good a lie? unjust that the white jury thought that way? unjust of a nigger like me to allow this innocent deer to lead us along through this garden?*

"And you had so much sympathy for that poor white girl" *which poor white girl oh the one in the cemetery but which one in the cemetery please continue my deer* even though in that Jim Crow time there was no sympathy for people who looked like you *even though he was guilty beside the river of sympathy* still you had sympathy for her.

Travis felt one of his faces smile. "I remember."

Linda looked off into the air, as if remembering it too; Travis could see that she had lost her big-girl heels in the water when she had crossed the rivers in order to step into his garden, and now she was barefoot. "That day it struck me that I'd never before met anyone quite like you *who was guilty both of me was guilty a foot in each river* black or white. You were someone who didn't see black or white. You saw people *as rivers* as people. You saw value in people *intrinsic and earned* just for being people." *intrinsic is earned what else are you going to lose in these waters?*

She was growing more and more animated by the moment, carried away by the current of her heart's outpouring. "You were outraged at the lynching of the white man falsely accused of the murder... because the lynching was murder too *dead rivers* Murder of any kind, black or white, you're outraged by it. Because you're a man who is all about life, who values life *burns away and is gone like water down the drain* Wait- what happened to all your koi?"

"They drowned."

She regarded him queerly, then laughed and shrugged it off. "Okaaay..." Looking off across the fence, she saw the Walters house, which set her back on track again. "Oh, and then there's Devon! Travis, ohmygod *why hast thou forsaken him* the way you took that kid under your arm when you found the bones, how you took up the cause of proving they were the bones of Devon's little friend *very little friend is what I was* for him, even though the police mishandled *by my hands* the bones *in and out of my hands* still, even though the police couldn't keep hold of her *not my neighbor's keeper* you kept hold of him, and now that he's run away I can't imagine how much pain it's caused you" *caused by me fully revealed the camera showing me once again in the garden*

She had been pacing energetically, her words rolling and tumbling, but now she paused; she was fully naked now, soft and pink and very new, and she stood before him as her camera refocused on him, holding him hostage within the frame of the shot. "I see you so clearly Travis, what you're made of *fire, garden and holy water* and I see how good your heart is, how you were so gentle with poor Sheila *gently and carefully dumping her into* pouring your generosity *shoveling generous earth* over her defending her when she was attacked *attacking her when she was defenseless.* Travis could only watch the opening and closing of her mouth, for he was no longer able to hear her, his attention captured by the nakedness of her feet, or rather, by the nakedness of the place where her feet were planted, for Linda was standing unaware and unashamed on the bare spot *remove thy shoes for thou standeth on holy ground*

THEN didst the camera restore unto Travis of the Garden his power to hear. "So I guess when I say you're the first, I'm saying that you're the first *man*, Travis. I mean, my first real man, a complete man and thus art thou completely revealed to me "I know who you are Travis. I see you for who you are for naught which lies under the ground remaineth hidden from the camera's lens. I've gotten to know you, the man. I know your goodness, and I know how unfair it is that now you're losing everything, your wife, your home, your beautiful garden thou knowest not all of it. But listen to me..." sitting beside him on the bench once again, Travis felt his hands in hers Great Camera, what be'st the meaning of this woman's nakedness? "...this isn't the end for you Travis. You know that, right? You have to make this the beginning of all water, the poisonous spring in the center of the garden. It's been hell, and there will probably be hell to come, but soon you'll be a new man. And it will be time to start your new life and to drink of the water was death, for it gave no life A new home, a new garden. You're young, we're young- no keep me out of it for now did the woman speak according to a vision of a second garden I'm getting ahead of myself- you're young, and you have time to remake all this beauty that you're leaving behind the woman now stood a shadow, ancient and timeless, whose terrible name was known unto Travis of the Garden beautiful again in that new garden.

AND when his eyes had opened, he saw that he too was naked; and he spake unto the woman, saying to her, A new garden?

Linda let go of Travis' hands and leaned back. "Why are you talking like that?"

Then did the shadow nod, and spake unto Travis in silence; thus did Travis repeat the shadow's silent words to the woman:

Thou wouldst have me plant a new garden from the beginning, O woman, even as I planted the first garden, from which I was sent away to dwell in the wasteland forever?

She was nervous now; the way he was staring at her made her feel almost naked. "Travis, this isn't funny. Please stop it."

Now did the shadow anoint Travis of the Garden with its spirit, quickening the mortal man's strength, and therefore also his words:

You have come unto me, woman, in thy nakedness, and have spoken kindly words of love as a balm, that your honeyed words might soothe me, telling sweetly of thy hopes for a new garden "Travis, this is a very bad joke, what's wrong with you?" that I might plant and raise up this second garden in mine own image, to replace the first garden of my murderous shame, and thou wouldst place yourself beside me in that second garden "I'm leaving! Let go of me dammitt!" as its first woman, there to dwell beside me, the second garden's first man.

And by this you would have me forget my murders of the first garden "Travis, what's come over you!" to wash my hands of them. Thus you would have me begin anew.

But thou forgettest that I am he, Travis of the Garden, who carries the spirit of murder where so ever he goeth. "Get- get off me!" I am borne of his spirit, the first murderer, whose timeless ancient shadow stands behind thee even now, anointing me with his spirit. "You're hurting me Travis!"

For know this O woman: in this second garden I would do naught but kill again and again, for this is the nature of the spirit I carry within me. It is why my judgement has been thus, to be exiled from the garden to live forever in the wasteland, where I might murder no more.

Yet with thy alluring nakedness "I thought you loved me Travis!" and honeyed words thou wouldst seduce Travis of the Garden, even as I did seduce thee in the land of Kennesaw, and would whisper into my ear that I should plant again, grow again, and murder again. "Somebody! Somebody, hel- " And thou wouldst presume to reign in murder beside me in that garden.

But know this, Temptress- I am not only Travis of the Garden, but Tr- lay right there, lay down, temptress! - Travis of the Fire, who by the lens of the camera now has eyes which see beyond the poisoned trees. And I know that the water of my garden only kills. And therefore had I resolved never to kill again.

Yet if I am to turn my hand away shut your fucking mouth you whore! from murder at last, I must murder one last time, that she who wouldst seduce me into planting a new garden of murder might be forever silenced.

THEREFORE, thou, Woman of Temptation, whose desire it is to be the first woman of the second garden, receive thy judgement, from the stay on the fucking ground! from the spirit of Cain, the first murderer, who anointeth me with the fire of judgement. Now I do burn thee, temptress! Be thou consumed by the ancient fire! Burn!

Standing beside the bench, his chest heaving and panting, Travis stared at Sheila's bare spot, beside the tricycle, where he had lain Linda down on the ground, where she had been consumed by the fire and returned to the earth forever, and was no more. And after scrambling up off the wet dirt and jumping into her car, cold and shivering, completely soaked with water from her mud-caked hair down to her ruined heels, Linda sped away, leaving Travis the eternal murderer standing at the spot where he had committed his latest killing, still holding the deadly garden hose.

17

On Tuesday, the warmish weather which had but timidly poked its head into the quiet neighborhood of Crested Boulder the day before now strutted all the way in with a defiant summery swagger, as if intent on never leaving; the calendar did not confirm summer's arrival of course, pointing out that it was still December, but it was summer all the same with shirtsleeve temperatures, warm enough that the first wriggle-hatched wave of opportunistic mosquitoes seized their chance to buzz about in a seasonally inappropriate celebration of life. The people also celebrated the "lovely" weather like so many seasonally-inappropriate buzzing humans, glorying in the comfortable air and finding nothing but delight at being able to open their windows and let in the outdoors. But intelligent people knew better; intelligent people could not enjoy the lovely day at face-value, for they detected something ominous behind the pretty face of premature warmth and were not seduced by its pleasantness, understanding that destructive powers were at work which contributed to the all-too real mirage, powers which were global in their causes and their effects. This heat, which had rousted the insect world awake so early in its winter sleep and had inflamed the jonquils and phlox into blooming as if it were April was unnatural, and foretold that a terrible price would be paid, and in truth, was being paid already. And yet, perhaps it was not so very unnatural, this December summer, for it was happening in nature after all, with nature's full if not approving participation. Rather, it seemed as if nature's very nature was in the process of changing, albeit against its will, within the crucible in which mankind had entrapped it. Nature was a fire now, and all of creation had become its fuel.

And if someone had told Travis that his little part of this neo-natural world was just a bit warmer even than the rest of it, he wouldn't have argued the point. Things had gotten a little overheated the day before, to be sure. He was decidedly cooler now, but the cooling had come much too late for him to reverse the unpleasantness. He had overheated, and he had fucked up. Linda was gone and would not be coming back, and Travis understood it was for the best. He had more than just burned that bridge, he had napalmed it, what with his biblically-disproportionate blunder of a water stunt. It had seemed right enough at the time, but of late, so many wrong things seemed right during the on again/off again heat waves of his recent brain-boilings. At all events, he'd proven beyond argument that he didn't deserve a woman like Linda, nor even a woman like Alicia. And inversely, those women (and at least one other unlucky woman) surely didn't deserve the misfortune of ever knowing a man like him. It struck him as such a shameful irony, on this calmer and more rational Tuesday morning, that on one hand, he had learned so much in the past week and a half about good and bad, about truth and untruth, about God and man, and more than anything, about himself, but on the other, he'd taken what he had learned and twisted it all so very badly, falling headlong into spiritual hallucinations and mystic transportations and overreactive flights of fancy, entertaining whatever neurotic and paranoic impulse entered his overloaded brain. His behavior had been reprehensible these past several days; but upon awaking the morning after, Travis had found his clarity of thinking restored and his mental processes cooled, and he'd been able at last to analyze his bad behaviors from a more rational perspective, not just his behavior over this recent period of his life but over his adult life in general, back to times before any houses had been burned down by the power of his imagination or girlfriends had been burned down by the power of his garden hose. It was this earlier history, his "before the fire" history, upon which his no-longer inflamed mental faculties were primarily focused today. For while the role which Travis of the past played exhibited far less flair for the dramatic than the Travis of the past few days, it was this former Travis who today's Travis had come to realize was the leading actor in the play which told the story of his life, and whose character arc provided the primary reason for why the play had deteriorated into such a tragi-farce.

It was just that sordid theatrical offering which Travis contemplated as he looked out the window, sipping his coffee and shaking his head with chagrin at how he'd ended up where he was, yet grateful for being granted the opportunity to view it all from the perspective of his new-found lucidity. That story, his pre-fire story, retold itself to him now in stark contrast to the mercurial highs and lows of these recent days of madness, milder in manner but no less shameful in the telling. He saw that pre-fire story as a prolonged litany of secret misbehaviors and subtle crimes, some in deed but many more in thought (he understood now that there was no difference between the two, none whatsoever), a life of crimes against humanity for which he'd never been tried, let alone convicted. He saw that his entire pathetic life had been one big covert action, himself operating as an undercover sinner while impersonating a saint, disguised by respectable-looking habits and impeccable outward conduct. As he sipped his coffee, he reflected with bitter self-loathing upon Dat Man, and how superior not only to that unfortunate gentleman he had thought himself, but also more highly evolved than Sheila's other Dat Man, her husband Pernell; indeed, Travis had bought into the delusion that the long litany of Dat Men who Sheila suffered all her life were mere Neanderthals compared to Travis' lofty *homo sapien*-ness. But now, in this aftermath of his mad days, he had made the painful realization that he was in no way above the Dat Men, but was one of them, himself only the latest Dat Man of the many Dat Men who had victimized Sheila, he not with door-kickings and beatings and broken bottles but with judgmental guile, petty refusals and liberal dispensations of condescension and self-centeredness. No, Travis was not only no better a Dat Man than the others, but a worse one, if for no other reason than this: none of the others had ever burned her alive until she no longer lived. But Travis had done just that, perhaps not in deed, but definitely in thought (no difference between the two, none whatsoever). This better-balanced Tuesday morning had allowed Travis to see it all with a new clarity, and to see beyond that even: that he had always been Dat Man to the women in his life, his adultery against Alicia (he intended to do it, no difference whatsoever), seducing and then murdering Linda in his front yard (so what if she had driven away in her car, in his mind he had killed her, no difference), and in general practicing manipulation and guile in all his relationships, be they with women or men, according to the self-serving agenda and selfish motive *du jour*. He had been Dat Man all his life all right, and it was by no means a secret any longer. His life of crime had finally been exposed.

Stepping out to his porch with his coffee, Travis took in the weirdly summery day, and pondered at just what it was that was going on in nature. *Nature*. Was this ever-constant presence which we term Nature, the one Great Unchangeable, really in fact changing? Throughout human history, before these most recent generations, no one seriously considered it possible, but in recent years, with building evidence far more exhaustive than this one warm December day, all the signs seemed to confirm natural change as a fact. Heading back indoors, his musings turned from the external world back to the internal, as he thought about human nature in similar terms of mutability; but unlike greater Nature, Travis had come to conclude that human nature showed no signs of changing in the least. Human nature, as his Tuesday morning epiphany had made clear to him, was unshakably constant; while external alterations made to the environment were rewriting nature's standard operating procedure, no internal permutations, be they philosophical, psychological, spiritual or metaphysical, had any lasting effect on fundamentally changing the basic nature of the human animal. And to his shock and dismay, he'd been forced to admit that his conclusion agreed with his old enemy, the Bible. It was a funny thing what Beulah the church lady had done to him thought Travis, as he headed upstairs to get dressed for the day, this woman he had always laughed at, had mocked even; for her pedantic preachifying, which he'd always dismissed as ridiculous and backwards-minded, had nevertheless set its subliminal hooks in his psyche (*no Travis, don't deny it, call it what you know it really is- in your SOUL*), and as a result, despite his life-long disavowals of a biblical god he had come to a reconsideration of the Bible which his parents had tried so hard to raise him by but which he'd rejected at an early age. "For all have sinned, and come short of the glory of God"- this verse was the troublemaker which had popped his eyes awake earlier this morning; before then he had never given much thought to this short sentence of scripture, since his disbelief in the God of the second half of the sentence had always rendered the sentence's first half meaningless. But that first half had come to show itself this morning as not so easily dismissible, for with or without a god, it stood as truth on its own. Everyone, at some point, to some degree, in some public or private way, has acted badly. But why? Was it in fact man's nature? Why else, Travis wondered, would the smartest and most highly evolved animal, the only one who knows right and wrong and the consequences of each, the one animal who can imagine the goodness and perfection of a god, be at the same time the worst of animals, the only bad animal in fact, engaging in behaviors leading not only to the destruction of his species-mates but, incredibly, to that animal's self-destruction, to the point that the misguided species would seem to be pursuing its own extinction? Should not this human animal, blessed with an intellect unmatched in the animal kingdom, follow the better leadings of that superior intellect? And if that animal is unable to do so, how could it be otherwise than his very nature not allowing him to, superseding his intellectual resolve? Why else, he continued, as he pulled on his socks, would the human animal knowingly do what is wrong, unless its very nature was fundamentally broken? And where had the break occurred? As the now-dressed Travis took up his coffee and headed back downstairs, his thoughts returned to his parents' Bible, for it was in its pages where he'd reluctantly come to realize the answer resided. And the fundamentally broken human who most personified that answer was the very one who had caused the newly-converted

Travis all his trouble the past three days. Well, at least that same broken human had been good enough earlier this morning to have showed him the way out of those troubles.

Heading toward the shed for the tools he needed (he was resigned to working in the yard today, a little early-season digging and rubbish-burning, having repented of his childish refusal to perform any work for the next owner but now determined instead to atone for his childishness by paying it forward to 1418's next resident), Travis brooded over this noteworthy personage who provided both the explanation and cause of the human animal's defective moral nature, this Cain of old, and laughed to himself at how recklessly and stupidly he'd launched his spiritual relationship days earlier with this long-dead patriarch of the race. How innocuously had Beulah that Sunday afternoon reminded him of Cain, by her retelling of the oft-heard story of Cain's slaying of his brother Abel, her intention then being only to shame her neighbors into guilt concerning Sheila's demise. But beyond her intentions, her words had found a deeper target in his inner places, and like a virus those words had spread through his subconsciousness undetected until, when the perfect-storm conditions of his ill-advised moonlit visit to Sheila's burnt home allowed the virus to run unchecked, it had exploded into manic fullness, as when the manipulator of a Ouija planchette, for an innocent lark, scratches about from this letter to that until, having unknowingly provided the dark forces the entrance code, opens the dark portal, allowing those forces to swarm in and seize the Ouija player's psyche. Yet it was no psychic or occultish power which Travis saw behind his recent experience, but a wholly spiritual one, a power based firmly in his parents' Bible and the dusty stories from the book of Genesis. And he had Sister Beulah to thank for dusting them off.

As Travis sank the shovel blade into the thawed earth, he marveled at how his vulnerable emotional state had facilitated his warping of the Cain story so grotesquely, warping not only the story but its message; as he continued to dig, he reflected upon the true lesson of Cain which today's restoration of his right mind had provided him. Who was this Cain, he he had asked himself, who was this first murderer, and what was behind his great crime? For Travis, the circumstances leading up to the event were fairly pedestrian; two brothers had each presented the Lord with a sacrifice, with Abel the herder giving God something he killed from his flock and Cain the planter (Travis hadn't missed the parallel that Cain, like himself, was a gardener) giving God something he had grown, at which point the Lord approved Abel's sacrifice but didn't care for Cain's; Cain brooded jealously, then confronted his brother and killed him in the field. These basic facts of the case were of passing interest to Travis; what provoked his fascination as he dug in his yard was the deeper analysis of what constituted the essence of this initial crime of murder, and thus the essence of all murders to come. Murder, as Travis now saw it, represented the ultimate expression of one's belief that his own value was greater than someone else's, thus the ultimate act of selfishness. No act could be performed which placed one's own life before another's that was purer in theory and more conclusive in practice than bringing that other life to an end. To willfully end a life required the taker to consider that other life as less valuable than his own, as expendable- therefore the concept of value, and how value was assessed, lay at murder's core. Here once again was that word which had so often been the theme of Travis' professional and private life and continued to be the bugbear of his existence. This Cain had been the first man to make a value judgement against his brother; he was the first to ever put himself before his brother, and with this choosing of self before brother, i.e., valuing self above brother, therein lay the spirit of murder. The violent act which resulted was merely the physical manifestation of that spirit. The weapon Cain employed, therefore, had not so much been the one he held in his hand, but the one he wielded in his heart.

Thus was the path which Travis' garden musings had followed on this calmer, more contemplative Tuesday; and had his meditations carried him to this point and deposited him there, the journey would have amounted to a fairly mundane theological take on human behavior and little more. But so comprehensive had been the recovery of his sensibilities upon awakening that Travis' thoughts had travelled to points beyond these, and as he continued with his digging, he recalled each whistlestop along the line which had brought him to this afternoon's ultimate spiritual destination. Fresh from his new understanding of the nature of murder, Travis had returned again to the "all have sinned" scripture from before. Holding that truth as self-evident, he recalled once again the book of Genesis, from which it was explained (*how had I been an atheist for so long, when the Bible is so obviously true?)* that Adam, the first man ever and father of Cain, had been the first-ever sinner, and so had begotten from his loins all subsequent generations of natural-born sinners. Adam's first sin had caused the mutation of the perfectly-created, healthy genome, a mutation which passed to all his progeny the disease of a sinful nature, and to Travis' mind provided him the strongest proof of God's existence, in that nothing but the dissemination of Adam's fallen nature could explain the phenomenon of man's distinction as Worst Animal. Then Travis had made the next logical connection: since Adam passed the deformed sin genome to all his progeny, this included his first son Cain; and if Cain was the first to murder his brother, thus mutating the genome yet again, didn't that mean that the murder genome had been passed down by him as well, making all subsequent men murderers? When that notion had come to Travis while still lying in bed it seemed too incredible, too wide-sweeping a conclusion, this epiphany of "all have murdered," but as he tested it in his mind throughout the morning it had become truer and truer. Having murdered Abel, Cain was questioned about it by God; Cain brushed it off, saying he wasn't his "brother's keeper" (again, God bless Sister Beulah!) What is it to be one's brother's keeper? "Keeping" your brother, caring for, looking after, *valuing* your brother's life, is to keep his life; not keeping your brother is to not value his life. Therefore, if one declares that he's not his brother's keeper, he is allowing his brother's less-valuable life to drift away toward whatever Fate may do with it. To release yourself from the responsibility of "keeping" his life," you have left him to his own devices- in essence, allowing for, giving permission to, his death. And so, the man who has distanced himself from the responsibility of "keeping" his brother's life has already murdered him, in his heart. Now since Beulah had pointed out that we're all guilty, to some degree, of not being our brother's keeper, it only follows that all men are murderers. Travis' wide-sweeping conclusion therefore that all men are murderers was, frighteningly enough, a true one.

Having finished with his digging, Travis walked the shovel back to the shed, and recalled how, at that point in his morning epiphany, his focus had turned from general observations to more personal ones. Who, then, was Travis, but a man as all other men, born of Adam via Cain? And as a son of Cain, was he also not a murderer, the recipient of Cain's murder genome? Yes. And since it was so, then what manner of murderer was Travis? Once again he recalled his shameful life of self-serving, self valuing behaviors, the uncountable instances when he'd kept his own life and not kept his brother's (and more tellingly, not kept his sister's), and saw it all as a horrifying parade of murders, one slaying after another, placing his life before theirs and absolving himself of their blood by declaring to the god he formerly didn't believe in that he was "not his brother's keeper." Sheila had only been the most dramatic and tangible of his murders, the only killing which featured the actual burying of his victim's body *Yes I did murder her I murdered her in my heart no difference whatsoever.* So what if Sheila was the only one he wished might go to sleep and never wake up? That wish merely represented the most literal of his un-brotherly non-keepings; all the non-keeping he'd committed before Sheila had been no less murderous than the non-keeping which resulted in her body ending up beside the koi pond. Yes, the only corporeal body he had buried was Sheila's- but buried deep within the secret places of his blood-stained soul he had buried so many, many other victims, buried them away and carried them with him, hidden in there, never to be found out (he thought again of Devon, who he hadn't kept, who he turned away from and forgotten as if the boy was dead to him-

and if he was as good as dead, then who killed him?) And it was Sister Beulah, pedantic, Bible-quoting, spirit-led instrument of the all-knowing Almighty Sister Beulah, who had unknowingly found him out. And the all-knowing Almighty had found him out not long afterward.

Returning from the shed carrying his newspapers, gas can and matches needed for his rubbish burning (it was astounding and embarrassing to him now at how warped and demented his state of mind must have been when he'd laid hands on these things those other times), Travis ruminated on the conclusions which his deliberations from earlier in the morning had produced. That he was a murderer was now confirmed; that he'd always gotten away with his criminal activity was also established, as was the truth about the irreversibly sinful tendencies of his nature. As he distributed the crumpled newspapers around his burn pile, Travis reflected on how these three facts had all dovetailed into a neatly unified and crystal-clear revelation of himself, his real and fully exposed self, and he was most grateful for the morning's epiphany which had brought him to this point; pouring the gasoline on the newspaper, he thanked both Sister Beulah and the Lord above that both his sanity and his faith had been restored, and that he'd been shown the direction which his new life must take on the road to atonement and the better things he must do with the time remaining to him. Upon lighting the gas-soaked papers, the fire was well-established in an instant, and Travis felt the rising wall of its heat press itself against him and through him, so warm that the fire seemed to take as much of its source from somewhere within as it did from the mountain of gasoline-soaked scrap which lay in flames before his feet. It was a handsome fire alright; and while burning on private property in Cobb County was legal this time of year, Travis was sure its impressive size would draw a lot of attention. He hoped so at any rate. And sure enough, there now appeared first one nosy neighbor, then another and another, lining up out on the sidewalk, pointing and shouting. He better step back a few feet, Travis said to himself. It was getting warm.

By the time the first fire engine had arrived on the scene (the homeowner had considerately opened his iron gates minutes before to welcome his expected visitors) and the firemen had jumped out to set their hoses, the entire house was already fully involved by flames. One of the firemen noticed a man out in the yard, sitting on the ground, dressed all in black with a black beanie atop his head despite the warm weather and the heat from the house fire. The fireman approached him, and asked the man if he was the homeowner, to which the man had answered no, he didn't rightly own the home, he had stolen it from all the people he'd murdered, and so neither it nor he had any value anymore. At this point the police units arrived; among them was the unmarked car of Detectives McGill and Larson, who, upon seeing Travis sitting on the ground, walked up to him, as the sirens wailed and the skylight of the newly-renovated second floor crashed down through the center of the flame-filled structure.

"Mr. Riggins?"

"I was hoping you'd be coming back."

The detectives stood close enough now to take in the entire scene. "Who's your friend, Riggins?"

Travis held tightly to her hand. "My neighbor."

Black ash fluttered onto the ground next to where Travis sat, some of the ash falling atop the newly-dug pile of earth and some into the empty grave. "Which... neighbor?"

"The neighbor I killed."

As Larson held his handkerchief against his nose, McGill pressed on. "You killed her?"

"Yes," Travis nodded, as he gently stroked the shriveled gray hand, "and I killed many others. I'm ready to confess to it all. But they're all still buried."

McGill glanced about his feet in horror. "Buried... where?"

Travis stared up at him sadly. "You never came looking for her. Why is that? Was she of no value to you?" More fire units had arrived on the scene now, and the street was crowded with onlookers. Travis brushed away a fallen cinder from the decaying forehead. "Well, you can't ignore her anymore."

"Is there anyone else in the house?" It was one of the fireman, calling out to Travis from across the yard. "Sir*, is there anyone else in the house*?"

Travis shook his head. "No sir. I already killed them all."

As Larson stayed a few steps behind with his revolver readied at his side, McGill approached Travis warily. "Mr. Riggins, you're gonna need to come with us."

Travis gazed down at the X-shaped scar which the flames had not erased. "I was supposed to be her keeper." Travis glanced at the burned tricycle which had been pushed aside, then back up to McGill. "You were supposed to be someone's keeper once too, weren't you? But you didn't do a very good job." Looking back down at the sunken face, Travis slowly shook his head. "Well, I didn't do a very good job of keeping either. And so I'm giving her back."

By late afternoon, the fire had been contained and the scene in general had been stabilized, though by no means understood; the house was a total loss, thanks to Travis' efforts, and the coroner's team had removed Sheila's body (it had been obvious to them at a glance that she'd been severely burned, and while no one could explain at this point in the investigation how she'd ended up across the street, it was a foregone conclusion that Travis would be charged with the arson of her home as well as his own). For his own part, Travis was at peace, well satisfied with how the day's events had unfolded, as he sat handcuffed in the police car and reviewed what had transpired. Never again would his murderous nature impel him to kill and keep on killing, for he would never again be free to kill- he'd made sure to make his freedom a thing of the past; not another day would he bear the guilt of living a secret life of crime, escaping justice, for he had unearthed everything, the full confession of himself, or as much as the police were willing to hear about at the moment. He had answered the officers' questions as honestly and forthrightly as he could, but his answers only seemed to confuse and irritate them. Now they'd left him undisturbed in the back seat behind the wire screen, alone with his thoughts, marveling at how clearly everything had been revealed to him yet how little of it the police seemed able to comprehend. It was vision they lacked, God said to Travis, the kind of vision which can only be imparted by the eye of the camera, which is the eye of God, for what is God but that which bringeth vision? It was through the perspective of this more sublime vision that Travis stared out the window, gazing not with his mortal eyes at the objects surrounding him but well beyond that mundane scenery, gazing past the coroner's van, past the smoldering shell of his worthless home, gazing instead into the more valuable realm of the spirit, with his new powers of spiritual sight. What could his physical eyes see, after all, which mattered in the least, compared to what the eye of the camera had shown him? How could such an inferior level of understanding possibly hold for him any value? What value would it have been to Travis in that moment, for instance, if he were to finally understand why Corey had called him that night to thank him, after the fire? Would it be of any value to him to learn that Corey didn't see Travis light the fire, didn't see anyone light the fire in fact, but had only seen the house mysteriously explode into orange, then saw Sheila run across the street in flames, and that he'd called Travis simply to thank him for burying his enemy in the ground? No value whatsoever. Nor would it be of any value to him to learn that neither Cain, nor the spirit of Cain, nor anything spiritual whatsoever, was the hand behind the setting of the fire, but rather, an all-too human hand belonging to an all-too human person who had experienced no visions or epiphanies, who had not felt the hereditary urgings of Adam's fallen nature nor his mystical curse, but had instead been troubled by the purely carnal curse of one troublesome neighbor who had bloodstained her world and so received the blame for her ruined marriage, a hand which was moved not by an inherited sin genome but by simple human hatred; her stealth that night had eluded even Travis' eyes, for they'd been staring inward, transfixed on his imagined self burning down Sheila's house while Alicia was burning it for real, thereby giving form unknowingly to her husband's fantasy (so the husband, so the wife- were the two not one flesh?) No, this Travis of the Garden found no value in merely mortal vision of this kind. His camera, the camera of God, saw so much more than mortal vision could afford him; saw so much in fact that it saw even those things which were not there. For from the grave beside the koi pond he thought it was Sheila he'd unearthed, but he had not, for it was Sheila no longer; Sheila was gone, leaving behind only burnt flesh and bone. Sheila no longer continued in the bones she'd left behind. There was nothing of her to keep now; the opportunity for keeping her had come and gone. Nor had he found Monique in that same grave weeks before; he had only found dried bones, for Monique too was long departed from them, with poor Devon thinking he'd lost her again; but no, there was no one left for him to lose, nothing and no one to keep, no one who continued, just as the sins of Cain and of Adam did not continue, for they too had become dry bones, never to live again in flesh or spirit, no power in them which could murder anymore, no continuing essence of them which could pass their murderous ways down to others. Any murders to follow would belong only to the murderers, who would choose entirely on their own whether to murder or not. All which remained beneath the earth were dry bones, nothing which retained life nor power over life; and had Travis only known (but what value could he have gleaned from the garden of mere mortal knowing?) that below the bones of what had once held the life of Monique there had rested still other bones which once held the life of yet another murdered little girl, murdered thirteen thousand years before and buried on that same hill, bones which had long since returned to dust, but although the little girl had been dead for centuries she was no more dead forever than was Sheila, or Monique, or Cain, or Adam, or every superstitious myth which mankind stubbornly keeps alive despite the evidence of its passing, a most terrible animal clinging to a corpse of dead beliefs and the imagined power of curses but dead to the knowledge of what is real and living, the power of the here and now, the power of this very moment, when we are free to be as good or as evil as we choose, the only living bones being those which walk above the earth, not those which have turned to dust beneath it, the truly living bones which are not held by curses of the past but are powered solely by the uncursed human mind to take a forward step.

The car had come to a red light on its way back to the 6th precinct jail; looking into the rear view mirror, McGill took in the sight of his strange passenger who was staring out the window and was, of all things, smiling, smiling and nodding, as if thinking of a joke that only he had heard. "Hey. Riggins."

The face in the mirror suddenly stopped smiling; now it was glaring defiantly at McGill, a face the detectives had not seen their prisoner ever wear before. "You all right back there?"

"None a yo' gott damm bidness if ahm aright back heah."

McGill exchanged a curious look with Larson. "You want a water maybe?"

"Shee-it, ah don' want none a yo' po-leece watah, that shit prob'ly jus' nasty-ass hose watah."

"Riggins, why are you talking like that?"

"NONE A YO' GOTT DAMM BIDNESS!"

The two detectives left him alone; Travis smiled again as he stared out the window, happy to have put them in their places. Dey had dey chance t' listen to him befo', but dey weren't happy wit what he tole 'em. Oh well den. None a dey bidness why I talk to 'em dis way now. Dey don' wanna heah why inny damn way. Dey wooden unnuhstan how I'm tryin' t' keep her aftah all. I'll keep her inny damn way ah like. No, I ain' talkin' t' nobody no mo'. 'Cept Pernell. Fin'ly gonna see him in jail an' talk to 'im like I said I was gonna do. I got plenny t' say to him that he need t' know. Be like a Dat Man reunion, me and dat man."

The End

CPSIA information can be obtained
at www.ICGtesting.com
Printed in the USA
LVHW051643280423
745516LV00021B/395

9 781958 889046